Praise for the Ca

Matters of Doubt
The First Cal Claxton Mystery

"Warren Easley has created a character you can root for—a man who has experienced loss but still believes in a better future, a lawyer who vigorously pursues justice for the most vulnerable clients. *Matters of Doubt* proves that legal thrillers can indeed be thrilling."

—Alafair Burke, *New York Times* bestselling author

"A fast, fun read with a fascinating defendant and our hero, Cal Claxton, a small-town lawyer who risks his life to solve a big time cold case."

—Phillip Margolin, *New York Times* bestselling author

"Easley brings alive the world of street kids and the alternative social groups they form."

—*Publishers Weekly*

Dead Float
The Second Cal Claxton Mystery

"A fast-paced, tightly woven whodunit that kept me guessing to the end. Easley's vivid landscapes and well-drawn characters evoke comparisons to James Lee Burke, and Cal Claxton is as determined and resourceful as Burke's Dave Robicheaux."

—Robert Dugoni, *New York Times* bestselling author

"*Dead Float* starts with a man's throat cut ear to ear and Claxton's fishing knife found nearby, and gathers momentum like the midnight freight trains nearby. As a Deschutes [River] aficionado myself, I'll never listen to those lonesome whistles again without thinking of this story, and thanking the stars it was only fiction."
—Keith McCafferty, bestselling author
of the Sean Stranahan thrillers

"When someone tries to drown Cal, he uses his fishing skills to good advantage. What a showdown finish! Easley's folksy style belies an intense drama revolving around corporate greed and espionage. The second outing for this action-packed Oregon-based series succeeds in quickly bringing readers up to speed."
—*Library Journal*

Never Look Down
The Third Cal Claxton Mystery

"Easley exquisitely captures Portland's flavor, and his portrayal of street life is spot-on. Readers of John Hart and Kate Wilhelm will delight in trying a new author."
—*Library Journal*

"The Portland cityscape is as much a character as are the colorful graffiti artist and the lawyer who walks Portland's streets with his dog, Archie."
—*Ellery Queen Mystery Magazine*

Not Dead Enough
The Fourth Cal Claxton Mystery

"Masterfully crafted, this tale of greed, deception, and revenge has an added benefit—the stunningly beautiful descriptions of the lush landscapes of Oregon's Columbia River country. Easley's characters bring enough complex complications to keep you reading long after regular bedtime."
> —Anne Hillerman, *New York Times* bestselling author

"The narrative spends much time absorbing sights and smells of the glorious outdoors and detailing the political fights they engender... Fans of Tony Hillerman and C. J. Box won't mind... Advise readers not to jump to that last page. Easley deserves his surprises."
> —*Booklist*

"With a very likable sleuth, *Not Dead Enough* is sure to appeal not only to mystery lovers, but also to those interested in Native American history, Oregonian culture, and environmental issues like salmon migration. Although *Not Dead Enough* is the fourth in the series, it can easily read as a standalone, allowing fans of Tony Hillerman or Dana Stabenow to dive right into Cal Claxton's life."
> —*Shelf Awareness*

Blood for Wine
The Fifth Cal Claxton Mystery

A Nero Wolfe Award Finalist for 2018

"If you enjoy wine and a really good mystery, *Blood for Wine* is a must read."
—Phillip Margolin, *New York Times* bestselling author

"Warren C. Easley blends my favorite subjects—wine, food, a really cool dog, and of course, murder—into a tasty thriller set in Oregon wine country. With more twists and turns than a rain-swept coastal road, *Blood for Wine* is the fifth in this series with a tantalizing backlist just waiting for me to get my hands on. It promises to be a mystery maven's haven."
—Bookreporter.com

"Senseless acts of violence that hit too close to home upend Cal's personal life—but only serve to strengthen his resolve. Oenophiles and aspiring vintners will enjoy the wine lore in this well-wrought tale of love and betrayal."
—*Publishers Weekly*

Moving Targets
The Sixth Cal Claxton Mystery

"Intelligent dialogue, evocative descriptions of the Oregon land-scape, and sly pokes at the current cultural climate make this a winner."
—*Publishers Weekly*

"Easley continues in every installment of this series to get a better handle on his characters and the vital balance between principal and supporting plots."

—*Kirkus Reviews*

Also by Warren C. Easley

The Cal Claxton Mysteries
Matters of Doubt
Dead Float
Never Look Down
Not Dead Enough
Blood for Wine
Moving Targets
No Way to Die

NO
WITNESS

NO WITNESS

A Cal Claxton Mystery

WARREN C. EASLEY

Published by Poisoned Pen Press, an imprint of Sourcebooks
P.O. Box 4410, Naperville, Illinois 60567-4410
(630) 961-3900
sourcebooks.com

Library of Congress Cataloging-in-Publication Data

Names: Easley, Warren C, author.
Title: No witness / Warren C Easley.
Description: Naperville, Illinois : Poisoned Pen Press, [2021] | Series: A
   Cal Claxton mysteries ; book 8
Identifiers: LCCN 2020048788 | (trade paperback) | (epub)
Subjects: GSAFD: Mystery fiction.
Classification: LCC PS3605.A777 N613 2021 | DDC 813/.6--dc23
LC record available at https://lccn.loc.gov/2020048788

Printed and bound in the United States of America.
SB 10 9 8 7 6 5 4 3 2 1

This is for Barbara Peters and Robert Rosenwald,
with deepest gratitude and admiration.

"I have always found that mercy bears richer fruits than strict justice."
— ABRAHAM LINCOLN

"We asked for workers. We got people instead."
— MAX FRISCH

Chapter One

Dawn arrived as a gray streak in the dark pool of the eastern sky. I sat up in bed to watch the soft light fill the room, thinking about what happened the night before. I felt that old familiar feeling, a sense of loss, a sense that I'd screwed up a relationship one more time.

Tracy Thomas—a woman with warmth, intelligence, and drive—and I had called it quits after a year. A Portland city councilor, she'd been tapped by the governor to head up the Oregon Department of Human Services and decided to take the job. This didn't cause the breakup, mind you, but in that swirl of reexamination, it dawned on Tracy that our relationship was lacking. I had to agree. In truth, the lack of growth was more my fault than hers, so I was beginning to wonder whether the relationship I had with my deceased wife, Nancy, was a high-water mark. After a decade of starts and stops, it was beginning to look like it.

Archie, my dog, stayed in the corner on his pad, respecting my silence. Finally, I sighed, swept off the duvet, and swung my feet over the edge of my bed. Arch was there immediately, whimpering softly and thrusting his muzzle beneath my folded hands, his customary morning greeting. I stroked his broad back before putting on a sweatshirt and pants. When I fetched my jogging shoes from the floor of the closet, he gave a couple of sharp yelps and wagged his entire backside. He was obviously much more enthused about the upcoming run than I was. Then, again, Australian shepherds need a job, and Archie's job was to keep me in shape. He took his work seriously.

He led me down the back staircase of our old farmhouse, through the kitchen into the hall, and out the front door. I walked our long driveway and began jogging once we reached Eagles Nest Road, a stretch of worn pavement dimpled with potholes that teed into Worden Hill Road a quarter of a mile later. We headed north at the junction and up a steep incline to a pioneer cemetery at the crest of the hill.

Breathing hard at the summit, I pulled up for a moment, both hands on my hips, and turned to take in a view I never took for granted. The sun was up, and the Willamette Valley, framed by the Coast Range and the Cascades, stretched to the southern horizon, the muted patchwork reminding me of a Paul Klee painting. In the foreground, recently harvested vineyards fell away in undulating, vermillion-dappled profusion. It was fall in the Oregon wine country, and despite my failed relationship, the center seemed to be holding.

I gulped in a lungful of sweet air and clapped Archie on the back. "Okay, Big Boy, let's kick it home."

———

An hour and a half later I sat in my law office in Dundee, a small town twenty-five miles southwest of Portland. Perched adjacent to the Willamette River and named after the Scottish city by early settlers, Dundee was first a port and then a railway stop in the early decades of the last century. Now its fortunes were tied to the burgeoning wine industry, which had gravitated to the gently rolling hills west of town, where reddish, iron-rich soil favored viticulture, especially for the pinot noir grape.

I was expecting a client at ten o'clock, and in the meantime was busy slogging through paperwork, including more than a month's worth of filing that teetered in disorganized stacks on a corner of my desk and atop a filing cabinet. Not my favorite task by a long shot. Meanwhile, Archie lay in his favorite corner, patiently waiting for a walk, which usually amounted to a dash across the busy Pacific Highway to get a snack or lunch. It was nearly ten when a tentative knock sounded on my office front door, even though a sign on it read *We're open. Come on in.*

"It's not locked," I called out over the low hum of traffic out on the highway.

A young man entered wearing a white shirt with a pen in the pocket, a solid blue tie, and a nervous look. He wasn't the client I was scheduled to meet with. Arch stood up, cocked his head, and eyed our visitor.

"Are you Calvin Claxton?"

"I am. And you're either a salesman or a Mormon missionary," I said, showing a grin.

"No, neither one." He flashed a tentative smile to let me know he got the joke. "I'm Timoteo Fuentes." He offered his hand, and I stood and shook it. "I was, um, wondering if there's any chance you need some help around here?"

"What kind of help?"

"An office manager or something like that? I'd be glad to fill out an application."

"An application?" I had to chuckle. "This is a one-man operation." I motioned toward a chair facing my desk. "Have a seat." A few inches shorter than me, he had a crop of wavy black hair, neatly faded on the sides, dark eyebrows arched over luminous brown eyes, and a squared-off, slightly dimpled chin. He sat down as a look of disappointment spread across his face.

"What made you think of this particular law office?"

His face became animated, and he squared his shoulders. "I read about the case you handled for that kid from Coos Bay, Kenny Sanders. I admire what you did, Mr. Claxton."

He was referring to an effort that resulted in the exoneration of a young man serving a life term for a murder he didn't commit. "It's Cal. Thanks. We caught a couple of breaks on that case, for sure, and I had a lot of help."

Timoteo leaned forward in his chair, his hands planted firmly on his knees. "I want to be a lawyer, Mr. Claxton. I want to do work like that, to defend people and help change the criminal justice system for the better." The words may have had a ring of naivete, but his jaw was set, his voice firm.

I smiled again, out of surprise this time. "Change the system from the inside, huh?"

"Yes, that's where I want to start." He allowed a modest smile. "Maybe politics down the road."

I chuckled. "Well, that's a well-worn path. Are you going to school?"

"I'm trying to finish up at Chemeketa in McMinnville. I want to get my associate degree and transfer to the University of Oregon next year. Poli-sci, then law school."

"How are your grades?"

"Mostly A's so far, high school, too."

"Good work. Sounds like an excellent plan."

"I need to save for tuition." He leveled his eyes at me. "I'm tired of flipping burgers. I want to get some experience in the field I plan to work in."

I leaned back in my chair and glanced at the ugly stacks of unfiled papers, but thoughts of off-loading such tasks were quickly intercepted by the practical voice residing in the corner of my brain. Help around the office would be nice, it said, but this kid has *zero* experience. And besides, the voice went on, after paying your bills, there usually isn't much money left over.

The truth was, however, I hardly ever listened to that voice, and, damnit, I liked the kid's chutzpah. "If I had any work—and I'm not saying I do—it wouldn't be glamorous, like what you see on TV. Most lawyering is tedious, detailed work. The law's a thing of beauty, but she's also a complex bitch." I stopped there to gauge his reaction.

His eyes lit up. "I don't care. I want to learn the job from the bottom up, Mr. Clax, er, Cal."

It was then that my ten o'clock arrived. I asked my client to take a seat and turned back to Timoteo. "Tell you what. Let me look at my caseload and see if there's anything you could help me with." As if to confirm my judgment, Archie sidled over to the young man, who scratched my dog's head absently, his eyes locked on mine. "No promises, okay? And it won't be a full-time job."

Failing to suppress an excited smile, he said, "I'll take whatever I can get."

"Okay, then. Give me your contact information."

He pulled a wallet from his back pocket, extracted a business card, and handed it to me. "Um, when do you think you might let me know?"

"I'll need a couple of days."

As he left, I glanced at the card, which was made of thick stock and sported embossed lettering. It read—

TIMOTEO FUENTES

DREAMER AND DACA RECIPIENT

COLLEGE STUDENT AND FUTURE LAWYER

503-555-4785

Chapter Two

The weather held that afternoon, so I closed up early and headed back to the Aerie, the name my daughter gave to my five-acre refuge up in the Red Hills. I was anxious to continue building a rock wall on the east side of my farmhouse using chunks and slabs of blue basalt I spotted at a landscape supply yard. The rocks had just been delivered. On an impulse—which was the way I did a lot of my buying—I purchased the whole damn pile on the spot, thinking of the dry-stack stone walls I'd seen on a trip Nancy and I had taken to New England before Claire was born. I was drawn to the aesthetic of those walls, and I'd always wanted an enclosed herb garden but had never gotten around to it. Why not do it with a cool-looking rock wall built with my own hands? The project had been on my to-do list for years, and a distraction was just what I needed.

After tapping a keyboard most of the day, the heft and rough-hewn texture of the rocks felt good in my leather-gloved hands, and the challenge of selecting and arranging them stimulated a less-used region of my brain. I'd previously finished the trenching and leveling and was halfway through laying the base course. As sweat poured off me, the gloom stemming from another failure in my love life slowly bled off, leaving my mind as calm as a pond on a windless evening.

It must have been two hours later when a piercing *caw* from a crow overhead stirred Arch from a doze and brought me back. I realized I'd been softly humming a Beatles tune. As the light began to fade, my dog and I headed for the house.

"Hey, Cal," I heard a voice call out. I turned to see my neighbor to the north, Gertrude Johnson, a retired forensic accountant, and my faithful bookkeeper, who repeatedly claimed she was the reason I wasn't living on the street. I waved and walked across an acre of field to the fence line separating our properties.

"How's the dry-stack coming?" she asked with a wry smile as I approached. Wearing a faded flannel shirt, jeans, and boots, she stood with one hand on a hip and the other on the shaft of a rake. She'd made it clear when I started the project that low rock walls were, well, more a New England than a Northwest thing. She should know, I suppose, as a fifth-generation Oregonian. Gertie's family had come across on the Oregon Trail just after the Civil War and settled right here in the Red Hills. It was the only home she'd ever known, 'My pine box estate,' she called it once. When I looked puzzled, she explained, "Someday they'll carry me out of here in one."

I glanced back in the direction of my afternoon's handiwork. "I'm getting the hang of it." I had to smile. "Not as easy as it looks."

She laughed, crinkling the corners of her robin's-egg-blue eyes and pushing back a lock of silver-streaked hair. "You mind splitting a few logs for me? The nights are getting cold, and I'm about out of firewood."

I agreed, of course. There wasn't much I wouldn't do for this woman—my friend, my financial advisor, and my go-to for advice on virtually anything. I led Archie through the gate, and we followed her around the barn to where she stored her firewood.

Cedric, Gertie's big, ornery barn cat, took one look at Arch and bolted. My dog ignored him, having realized long ago that a chase was exactly what the cat wanted. Normally a fast walker who covered a lot of ground with her gait, Gertie moved a bit slowly. When I teed up the first log—one I'd cut for her the year before from a fallen cedar—I noticed her face had an uncharacteristic pallor.

"You okay?" I said as I brought the ax down, sending the two halves careening in opposite directions.

"I'm fine," she snapped back. "Just a little tired. Old age isn't for wimps, you know."

I laughed at that, and, as I worked the stack of rounds, I told her about Timoteo Fuentes. When I finished describing his visit, she said, "The good news is you're starting to recover from that stint in Coos Bay, and your cash flow's improving. The bad news is you still owe Mendoza over three thousand dollars for his work down there." She was referring to my Portland private investigator, Hernando Mendoza, better known as Nando. He'd worked with me in the Coos Bay case and taken a bullet in the process. He hadn't pressed me for the money or complained about getting shot, come to think of it. That's the kind of man and the kind of friend he was.

"If you keep the kid's hours below, say, twenty a week, you should be okay." She laughed. "If you can train him to keep better track of your billable hours, he'll pay for himself."

"Creative minds like mine balk at scut work, Gertie," I said, suppressing a smile as I put my back into a swing that halved another round.

She rolled her eyes dramatically. "Right. Trouble is, scut work puts cash in the till."

I teed up another chunk of cedar. "Okay. Point taken. He seems to be a smart kid. He's a Dreamer."

Gertie looked at me. "They all are at that age."

"No, I mean he's undocumented, but he grew up here in the States."

"Oh, of course. Those kids, my God. How could you deport people who've spent their whole lives here? No matter how they got here, that's just flat-out wrong."

"He gave me a card with his cell phone number on it. It said he was a DACA recipient, too." *Whack.* I split another cedar round.

Gertie furrowed her brow. "I don't know what DACA stands for, but I do know it was something that Obama did to protect those kids, right?"

"That's right. It stands for Deferred Action on Childhood Arrivals. In other words, we'll defer decisions on deporting Dreamers until we can get a final resolution in Congress."

Gertie made a sour face. "I thought our current president killed that program. No mercy for the unwitting lawbreakers."

"He tried, about two years ago, and it's being fought in the courts now. It'll wind up at the Supreme Court."

"Well, this whole damn immigration mess needs fixing." She swept a hand toward the rolling landscape falling away to the south of us and shook her head. "Without immigrant labor, the wine industry wouldn't exist here, or it'd be just a rich man's hobby producing a trickle of wine. And you can bet a high percentage of those workers are undocumented."

I agreed, and at the same time felt an unexpected twinge of guilt. She was right. The explosive growth of vineyards in the Red Hills had been driven by this immigrant workforce—men and women willing to do backbreaking labor, work that most Americans shun. They worked in the vineyards surrounding me and then retreated into a world I knew very little about and had very little appreciation for. That seemed wrong, somehow, even shameful.

After finishing up the log-splitting and stacking, I left with half a homemade blackberry pie, my reward from a grateful neighbor who was also a dynamite cook. Back at the Aerie, I began rummaging around in my kitchen for something to eat. I'd put off my shopping, as usual, but I did manage to root out an onion, a bell pepper, and a clove of garlic, which brought to mind penne arrabbiata, one of my favorite pasta dishes. The thought of it caused me to salivate.

After confirming I had a can of diced tomatoes, a jar of olives, red pepper flakes, and enough penne pasta, I poured myself a glass of local pinot, put some Wynton Marsalis on the sound system, and set to work at the chopping block.

Water was boiling, ingredients were sautéing, and Marsalis's quartet was halfway through "Angel Eyes" when my cell phone rang.

"Cal, it's Gertie. Can you come? I don't feel so well." Her voice was faint, labored.

"What's the matter?"

"I've got a goddamn elephant sitting on my chest. I can hardly breathe."

"Did you call 911?" I took her hesitation for a no. "I'll be right there after I call them. And if you can get to an aspirin bottle, chew one right now."

"The aspirin's upstairs," she said in a near whisper. "Bring some."

I made the call, turned the burners off, and flew out the front door with a bottle of aspirin in my hand. Alert for gopher holes, I sprinted across my upper acreage with Archie at my side, yelping excitedly. The lights were blazing on the first floor of Gertie's old, shiplap-clad four square. I burst through the kitchen door and found her lying on an antique daybed in the dining room.

She looked up at me, her eyes fluttering and unfocused, her face chalky white. "Thanks for coming, Cal. Christ almighty, this hurts," she said, managing to smile defiantly through the pain.

I took her hand. "I know it hurts, Gertie. Stay with me. An ambulance is on the way." I gave her an aspirin before taking her pulse, which was ragged and weak. She stayed conscious, and sixteen minutes later Archie alerted us that help had arrived. I watched as two paramedics loaded her into the ambulance and connected her to a portable EKG unit before taking off. I took Archie back to the Aerie, told him to guard the castle, and headed for the Newberg Medical Center.

———

"She's had a serious myocardial infarction," a young emergency doc told me an hour later. "We've stabilized her, and we're about to transfer her to the St. Vincent thoracic surgery unit in Portland. They'll decide next steps."

"Which would be?"

"Bypass surgery, almost certainly."

My gut tightened. "What's the prognosis?"

"Good. She appears strong." He allowed a thin smile. "And she strikes me as a fighter."

I returned the smile. "Oh, she's that, for sure."

"She mentioned a sister in Seattle but didn't have a number, said you might have it."

"Yes, I'll take care of contacting her."

"The procedure will probably be in the morning, early. There's a narrow window of opportunity for these cases," he explained. "The sooner the better."

"When can I see her?"

"Don't come the first day. She'll hate you for it, if she remembers anything. Day after tomorrow, earliest."

I nodded. "She's a worrier, too. If you can, tell her I'll keep an eye on her place and feed her worthless cat."

The doc kept a straight face. "I'll be sure to tell her that."

On my way back to Dundee, I called Gertie's sister and brother-in-law and reached their daughter instead. I'd heard about Gertie's niece over the years but never met her. "They're on a monthlong cruise," she said after she recovered from the shock of the news. "I just happened to be here checking the place and watering the plants." She promised to get in touch with the couple, and I told her I'd keep her in the loop.

Next I called Nando, who loved Gertie dearly, and left a message with his office manager.

When Arch and I got back to the Aerie, he reared up and placed his paws on my chest, something he rarely did. I scratched his head. "She's strong and she's a fighter, Big Boy," I told him. "She's going to be okay." He lowered his paws and wagged his stump of a tail. I took the gesture to mean he understood me, or maybe it was just that he figured I was finally going to feed him.

Chapter Three

"Um, Cal, this is my sister, Olivia," Timoteo said with a look of obvious pride. It was two days later, he'd accepted my job offer, and was reporting for his first day of work after a morning of classes. "She's dropping me off, and I wanted you to meet her." Trim, with lustrous ebony hair draped over one shoulder and restless dark eyes, Olivia Fuentes had a modest smile with the same radiant quality as her brother's.

I invited her to sit down, but she hesitated, glancing at her brother and then back at me. "I have some more stops to make, and I'm running late."

Timoteo shrugged and opened his hands. "We have four drivers in the family and only two cars."

As Olivia was leaving, she turned to me and showed the full brilliance of her smile. "Timoteo is very excited about working for you, Mr. Claxton. Thank you for hiring him. You won't regret it."

I gave my new hire a brief overview of my practice and took him through some of the tasks I had in mind for him—filing, keeping track of billable hours, answering the phone. "I've also got a pro bono practice," I said at one point, "which takes me to Portland most Fridays. I was thinking you could cover the office here."

He beamed a smile. "That works for me. I don't have any classes at all on Fridays."

By way of summary, I said, "The key thing about this work is confidentiality. Everything having to do with the business is confidential—names of clients, the nature of any litigation, exchanges you might overhear between me and a client, the content of letters you file, *everything*—understood?"

"Got it."

I smiled. "And lose the tie. Every day's Friday casual around here."

After we finished the orientation, I handed him a stack of unfiled papers just as a client arrived to join a conference call with her soon-to-be ex-husband and his lawyer. We began discussing how to divide up the assets and got stuck on who was going to get the family dog, a ten-year-old Chihuahua.

"Cha Cha never liked you, Byron, and you didn't give a damn about her," my client shot back at her husband, "And now you want her? Are you kidding me?"

The discussion went south from there, and, although we eventually came to an agreement, I felt a twinge of embarrassment. This was probably not what my new employee imagined I did with my time. But he'd learn soon enough that work like this kept the ship afloat and allowed me to do my pro bono work and tackle cases that interested me.

It was close to four when I got off the call and saw my client out. Timoteo had already put a nice dent in the stack of unfiled papers. "Come on," I said, "let's get a coffee." I clipped on Archie's leash before we dashed across the Pacific Highway and over a block to the Red Hills Market, where I tethered my dog to an outside table. We took our drinks outside, and I unclipped Arch, who wolfed down a treat the waiter had given him and chose a spot next to Timoteo to lie down. It was a sign he liked the young man. Archie's reaction to people was something I always paid attention to. He was an excellent judge of character.

"How's it going as a DACA recipient these days?" I asked.

Timoteo drew a breath and exhaled. "We're in legal limbo." He pursed his lips, shaking his head. "Maybe I should've listened to my father. He told me not to sign up. He didn't trust the government, even Obama's government."

"What did the Feds ask for when you signed up?"

He rolled his eyes. "*Everything*. Current and past addresses, fingerprints, phone numbers, height and weight, and a lot more. Oh, and five hundred dollars every other year. Look, I think Congress started with good intentions. The DREAM Act provided a pathway to citizenship, you know, but then it went nowhere in the Senate for years." He locked onto my eyes. "Did you know that in 2010 it failed to pass the Senate by just *five* votes?"

I shook my head. "I had no idea the issue's been around that long."

Timoteo curled a lip. "Now the current administration has the DACA database, a handy guide to the people they'd love to deport."

"Weren't assurances given when you signed up that your information would be protected?"

"Sure, we were told we fall under the federal Privacy Act, so no worries. What we weren't told is that Homeland Security could easily exempt themselves from the act. Federal agencies do shit like that all the time."

"How are you coping?"

He brought his chin up and smiled. "I'm not going to cower in the shadows. I crossed that bridge. I don't care who knows I'm a Dreamer."

"Is your sister a Dreamer, too?"

"No. She was born on *this* side of the border." The proud look again. "She'll start at Oregon next year on an academic scholarship. She delayed her start a year to save up some money."

"What's she doing?"

"She works for Prosperar—a nonprofit that provides health care services for migrant workers. She wants to be a doctor."

I sipped my cappuccino. "I've heard Prosperar does good work,"

"They're awesome. And they're lucky to have her." He laughed. "She practically runs the place."

"What's your father doing?"

Another look of pride. "He started as a laborer here in the Red Hills and worked his way up to become vineyard manager at Angel Vineyard."

I raised my eyebrows. Angel Vineyard was one of the largest wineries in the area. "Good for him."

"There's nobody better at growing grapes, and he knows winemaking, too. His dream is to become a winemaker someday."

"Where's he from?"

"A small town in the state of Jalisco. He came here to work in the fields over twenty years ago. After he got established, he sent for my mother and my brother and me. I was four when we came across. My brother was close to two."

"How did you get here?"

He shrugged. "My parents don't talk about it much. I know we were brought across by some *coyotes* my father trusted. I don't remember much about it, except for a long, hot ride in the back of a truck, and listening to Luis cry. I do know it cost every cent my father had managed to save."

I could only imagine the enormity of that decision. "It must have been a harrowing time for your mother."

Timoteo nodded thoughtfully. "Yeah, it was, but she was as determined as my father to make a better life for the family. It wasn't a hard decision for them, I think." He studied his coffee for a few moments, looked up, and smiled. "I heard she guarded Luis and me on that trip like a mother bear."

"I'll bet she did. What's she doing now?"

His brow furrowed. "She's sorting grapes at Angel. In the off-season, she cleans rich people's houses." He smiled. "But her main job is running our house and everyone in it. She's the real boss of the family, but don't tell my father."

"What's your brother doing?"

I thought I saw tension enter Timoteo's eyes. "Luis is, um, still trying to figure out what he wants to do with his life."

"Did he sign up for DACA?"

"No, he couldn't be bothered." Timoteo smiled ruefully and shook his head. "That's probably the only time Luis took our father's advice."

"What does he do?"

"Nothing right now. He was working in the kitchen of a restaurant in Newberg, but the place closed down."

We crossed the highway back to the office. While Timoteo resumed the filing, I wrote up the property settlement I'd just negotiated and then called St. Vincent's the second time that day to check on Gertie's condition. The bypass surgery had gone well, and she continued to be in satisfactory condition, I was told. A short visit the following day might be possible. I was to call first.

By the time Olivia arrived to pick up Timoteo, a squall had blown in from the south. She parked in the lot behind my building, and before her brother had his coat on, she rapped at the back door. I opened it, and she entered with wet hair and laughter, producing a bag from under her coat. "This is from our mother," she said, handing the bag to me. "They're homemade tamales, Guadalajara-style." She swung her eyes to Timoteo, then back to me. "She heard you're a bachelor and thought you could make a dinner from them." Her smile lit the room.

Timoteo watched to gauge my reaction. I opened the bag and smelled the contents. "Umm, smells *delicious*. This is too kind, Olivia. Please thank your mother for me."

Timoteo pointed to the bag, looking relieved. "Those go well with salsa verde. Mamá loves to cook for people."

The brother and sister hurried off, but not before Olivia fawned over Archie, who, of course, loved every moment of her attention. That dog of mine had a way with women. I opened the bag of tamales, which were still warm, and inhaled the aroma again, picking up notes of coriander, cumin, and another spice I couldn't quite place. I turned to Arch, whose eyes were fixed longingly on the bag, his nostrils quivering slightly. "Nothin' doing, Big Boy, this is *people* food." He wagged his stump of a tail, pretending not to understand me. I laughed. "Should have hired that young man a long time ago."

Chapter Four

Although Gertie's eyes looked particularly blue against her pale skin, they lacked their typical sparkle and playfulness. It was the next day, and I'd come to the ICU at St. Vincent's to check in on her. The room smelled of antiseptic, and a thicket of tubes, corrugated hoses, and wires ran from her body in all directions, while a monitor displayed a half dozen vital signs in living color, pulsing and beeping in a rhythmic, reassuring way.

I set down a vase with a large spray of fall flowers.

"Jesus, Cal, are those for me?"

"No. I brought them for the nurses. How are you feeling?"

She managed a wisp of a smile. "Terrible, but a lot better. I think they shot the goddamn elephant. How's Cedric?"

"As ornery as ever. Didn't thank me for his dinner last night. No purring. Nothing."

She held the smile. "Well, he never did like you."

"I'm told the procedure went well, and the prognosis is good. Anything I can do around your place?"

She exhaled a weak breath. "Aside from Cedric, nothing that can't wait until Zoe gets here."

"Got it. Your niece in Seattle. I talked to her on the phone. When's she arriving?"

"As soon as she can find someone to watch her parents' place. Just talked to her by phone an hour ago. I told her I'd hire a nurse, but she'd have none of it." The faint smile. "She's as stubborn as I am."

———

By the time I left the hospital, the traffic heading south on the 5 was crawling. It was Friday afternoon, after all, in a city that was becoming more crowded with every passing day, it seemed. We were heading back to Dundee to see how things had gone for Timoteo. It was his first day holding down the fort while I manned my pro bono office in Portland.

He was on the phone when Arch and I let ourselves in the back door. "Not a problem," he was saying as he looked up at us. He paused. "Would you mind if I put you on hold for a moment?" He pointed at the phone. "It's Ned Gillian, the attorney of the guy who wants the dog. Do you want to talk to him?"

I shook my head wearily. "No. Tell him I'll call him back."

Timoteo relayed the message and disconnected.

"Thanks for that. It's been a long day. That lawyer's going to be a pain in the ass, mark my words." I paused while Timoteo and Archie greeted each other. "How did it go today?"

He flashed a smile. "Great. You had three walk-ins, and I put them on the calendar for next week."

"Nice. That's three customers who might've gotten away. Well done."

"You saw my texts. You got a half dozen calls, including the one from the lady in Carlton who's involved in a lawsuit and needs representation."

"Right. I called her back. We'll meet next week."

"And I'm almost caught up on the filing."

I clapped him on the back good-naturedly. "Okay, then, I'd say you earned your keep today." Silently, I thought, wouldn't Gertie be pleased?

Timoteo broke out in the broad smile I was beginning to associate with the Fuentes family. He retrieved his phone from a shirt pocket and glanced at the time. "Olivia should be here any time now." Ten minutes later a text pinged in. He read it, looked up, and shook his head. "She's late to a fundraiser in Newberg. Luis is going to pick me up, but it'll be another half hour." He smiled and shook his head. "Why am I not surprised? Olivia always runs late."

"I can give you a lift home."

Timoteo looked embarrassed. "Um, thanks, but I'll just wait for Luis outside."

I laughed. Another front was passing through. "In the rain? Where do you live?"

"Off of Valleyview at Angel Vineyard. They provide a house for the vineyard manager."

"We're practically neighbors. Come on, let's go."

The cloud cover had extinguished most of the remaining light, and the rain intensified, coming straight down in big, pelting drops. We dashed to the car, and Timoteo texted his brother that he had a ride home. It was nearly dark as we arrived at the turnoff into the winery, a narrow road that bisected the planted acreage.

"Our driveway's down on the right," he said, pointing to a break in the rows of grapevines extending in either direction. I turned in, and after rounding a gentle curve a weathered pickup came into view, tendrils of smoke exiting the tailpipe. The truck was canted at an odd angle to the driveway, which was lined with big rhododendron bushes. Further on, I could just make out a small, ranch-style house with an attached carport.

"Huh, that must be Olivia," Timoteo said. "She's using my father's truck."

I let Timoteo out and made a U-turn. As I pulled away, I glanced in the rearview mirror and saw him waving frantically and shouting at me. I stopped, told Arch to stay, and got out of the car.

"Olivia's hurt. Oh, my God, she's bleeding," he cried out, his face twisted in anguish. "Oh, my God. We need to get her to a hospital."

"Where is she?"

"In the truck."

I rushed past him to the idling truck. Olivia was slumped against the steering wheel, her head covered by the hood of the camo sweatshirt she wore. It was stained with blood. I eased off the hood as small shards of glass from the driver's-side window slid off it and scattered on the seat and floorboard.

I sucked a sharp breath, pulling back in stunned disbelief. Her hair was wet and matted with blood, and she didn't appear to be breathing. I put two fingers on her wrist and thought I caught a weak pulse. I unclipped her seat belt, gathered her up, and lifted her out of the car.

"What happened to her?" Timoteo said. "Is she okay? Oh, God, Olivia."

"Call 911 and tell them we need an ambulance and the police," I answered as I carried her into the carport and gently laid her down next to another car. I searched for a pulse again, and this time I knew she wasn't breathing. I began administering chest compressions. After Timoteo made the call, I said, "Find a cloth you can press to her head. We need to stop any bleeding. Hurry."

He produced a handkerchief and dropped to one knee next to her. "There's glass in her hair. What the hell?"

I shook my head. "Looked like the passenger window was

blown out." I was sure of the cause, but I couldn't bring myself to say it. I kept administering the chest compressions to avoid having to tell the young man his sister was most certainly dead.

"Jesus, Timoteo. What's wrong with Olivia?" a voice rang out behind me. I turned my head enough to see a young man staring at us, his mouth agape. Luis.

"We don't know," Timoteo answered, he voice quavering. "Get Papi and Mamá ." His brother ducked back into the house. Timoteo gently stroked his sister's forehead with his free hand. "Come on, Olivia, open your eyes. *Please*."

The next few minutes seemed an eternity. The rest of the family hovered around Timoteo and me, sobbing and wailing. Finally, with sirens in the distance, he looked at me with disbelieving, tear-soaked eyes. "She's gone, isn't she?"

I didn't answer, but I'm sure they could see it in my eyes. Olivia's mother screamed out in denial and tore at her hair as the father tried to restrain his wife. But their daughter was dead. Every fiber in my being wanted it not to be so, but there it was.

My heart shrank into a shriveled knot.

Chapter Five

The paramedics and the Dundee-Newberg police arrived almost simultaneously. The paramedics confirmed that Olivia was dead, and the police, after questioning each of us and examining the car's blown-out side window and the wound in Olivia's temple, immediately cordoned off the area with crime tape and called in two detectives from the Major Crimes Response Team.

"*What?* Who would shoot my sister?" Timoteo cried out as I struggled to restrain him. We'd just been given a preliminary assessment by a young detective named Darci Tate.

"No! Nobody would shoot Olivia."

Word got out somehow, and friends of the family began to gather at the entrance to the winery, cordoned off on orders from Tate and her partner. However, they did let a young priest through to be with the family. By this time, Mrs. Fuentes was slumped in a chair on the porch, having fallen into a stunned, almost catatonic, silence. Timoteo, Luis, and their father were huddled around her, speaking in low tones. When the priest arrived, they opened the circle, and he knelt in front of their mother, taking her hand.

Detective Darci Tate approached me, notebook in hand, with a follow-up question regarding Timoteo's and my arrival time.

Mid-forties, with sharp features and short blond hair, dark at the roots, Tate had a no-nonsense approach bordering on brusqueness. We'd known each other since I handled her divorce four years earlier. After I answered her question, she said, "Ms. Fuentes was alive when you found her?"

I winced. "I thought I felt a weak pulse, so I took her out of the truck to try and save her, but when I checked again in the carport, she was gone." I shook my head. "I'm really sorry if I mucked up your crime scene, Darci."

"No apology required. I understand."

"What do you think?" I asked.

She exhaled. "Looks like the shooter waited behind those rhodies along the drive. The truck was parked in the carport. Ms. Fuentes came out of the house, got in, and began backing out. The shooter came out of the bushes, walked up to the truck, and put a round in her temple. He shot through the glass, so the murder weapon was not a twenty-two. He picked up his brass, so we don't know the caliber. The round didn't exit, so there's a chance we'll get ballistics. The younger brother thought he heard a faint pop but didn't think anything of it. Nobody else in the house heard the report. It's possible the shooter used a suppressor, although the rain at the time could have masked the sound."

"A *hit*?" The inflection in my voice indicated a question, but there really didn't seem to be one.

"Yeah, looks like it, but a nineteen-year-old girl? Jesus Christ." Tate looked at me, her eyes etched with pain. She had yet to acquire true cop eyes, the kind that no longer flicker with emotion. I hoped she never would. She exhaled a weary sigh. "You can go now, Cal. Should have your statement ready to sign tomorrow. I'll send you a text. Call if you think of anything else."

The family remained huddled on the porch with the priest.

I went to them and offered my heartfelt condolences, keenly aware that my words were utterly and completely inadequate. They thanked me and so did the priest, who had brought some comfort to them, but obviously not to Mrs. Fuentes, who was sobbing yet standing upright, clutching a crucifix. Mr. Fuentes's eyes were damp, and his expression reflected a mixture of grief, anger, and disbelief. Luis's shoulders were slumped, his head down.

Timoteo stood apart from the group, his hands on his hips, watching as they loaded his sister's sheet-covered body into the ambulance. When they shut the doors, his mother emitted a primal scream that carried across the silent vineyard.

As I turned to leave, Timoteo pointed a finger at his brother and said in a low, threatening tone, "This is your fault, Luis, isn't it? Olivia was wearing *your* hoodie. Whoever did this wanted to kill *you*, not her."

Luis looked up, his face contorted like he'd been struck a blow. "No, that's crazy."

Timoteo took a step toward his brother. "No, it isn't. You—"

Mr. Fuentes stepped between his sons and put his arms out. "Stop it. You are both disrespecting your sister. I won't stand for it." His voice was low, like a hiss, but it commanded respect. Both brothers dropped their heads in shame.

I left at that point, shaken to my core, and although I knew I'd done everything I could for Olivia Fuentes, I felt a lingering, hollow feeling, a sense of failure. I also knew from my criminal justice background that what I felt was to be expected. Something akin to survivor guilt. But that insight didn't help a damn bit.

I skipped dinner that night, opting instead to drink Rémy Martin while listening to Yo-Yo Ma playing Chopin. The plaintive chords, so close to the human voice, were somehow soothing and, like the crucifix for Mrs. Fuentes, helped keep darker thoughts at bay. Not only thoughts of what I'd just witnessed, but the death of my wife, Nancy. A place I'd learned to stay away from.

Sleep, when it finally came, brought swirling dark images over-laid with Timoteo's voice, asking his sister over and over again, "Come on, Olivia, open your eyes. *Please.*"

Chapter Six

When I awoke the next morning, Archie was standing silently next to my bed as if trying to will me awake. His coppery eyes were doleful, his demeanor anxious. After all, it was past eight o'clock on a Saturday, and we weren't out running. I reached out and patted his head, and he unleashed a couple of high-pitched squeals of frustration. The sound reverberated in my head like a point-blank siren. I groaned and swung out of bed. "Don't do that again, Big Boy," I pleaded, holding my head with both hands. Stumbling down the back staircase to the kitchen, I let him out, then steamed some milk, made a double cappuccino, and downed three aspirins with the first swallow.

Two hours later I was loading chunks and slabs of blue basalt into a wheelbarrow. The air was crisp, the sky clear, and my hangover had eased off just enough to allow some wall-building. The events of the night before teetered on the brink of flooding back to me. Block them out, I told myself. Stay focused on the physical work at hand, no matter how much your damn head aches. Archie lay off to one side, obviously pouting about not getting a run, and up in a nearby Douglas fir, a pileated woodpecker had joined us, his bright red plume bobbing as he pecked around for his breakfast.

My goal was to complete the foundation course of the wall, which consisted of hefting the biggest slabs I could find into the shallow trench I'd dug around the herb garden. The slabs were heavy and awkward to carry, but the physical effort was satisfying. Just what the doctor ordered to keep my head clear. When I finally laid and leveled the last slab three hours later, I stood back to have a look.

"Damn," I said to my dog, "Whataya think of that?" Archie raised his head to acknowledge my comment but made it clear he wasn't that impressed. Meanwhile, the woodpecker didn't miss a beat.

I took a break to run errands, get the week's shopping done, and swing by the police department to sign my statement. Detective Tate wasn't there, so I learned nothing new about Olivia Fuentes's murder. The visit prompted me to call Timoteo to check in and see if there was anything I could do for him and the family.

"Thank you, Cal," he answered. "We're in a state of shock here. Olivia's body is with the medical examiner right now."

"An autopsy's mandatory." I said.

He puffed a breath in disgust. "I know, but tell that to my mother. In our tradition, the body rests in the home before burial." He paused, and I imagined him trying to rein in his anger and frustration. "We'll be opening our home later this week. I'll, um, let you know when it is, if you'd like to stop by. You don't have to, of course."

I told him I'd be there.

I finally got back to my dry-stack wall late that afternoon. The next step was to fill the gaps of the base course with smaller, stabilizing rocks. This required bashing larger rocks with a sledgehammer, a process that felt good, almost cleansing. But, despite the physical effort, my mind drifted back to the murder, with Timoteo's question echoing in my mind—*Who would shoot my sister?*

The thought of that cowardly act caused bile to rise in my throat again. Was Timoteo right about the intended target being Luis? What caused him to say that? I felt the gravitational pull of those questions on my curiosity, to say nothing of my heart. Darci Tate and her partner would dig into them. They were good detectives. Maybe they'd catch the shooter in short order. One could always hope.

In any case, I told myself, let it lie.

I continued the rock-bashing until the head of my old sledge-hammer flew off during a downstroke. I wedged it back on, but after a couple more strokes it was clear the head wasn't going to stay put. The sun was low, but I had a stack of rocks I was intent on breaking up before I knocked off.

"Come on, Big Boy," I said to Arch, "let's go see what Gertie has in her barn."

We walked across the north field, through the gate separating the properties, and up to the barn, which was padlocked shut. Using a key hanging from a nail on an adjacent window frame, I let myself in and turned on the overhead lights, which flickered a couple of times and promptly went out.

"Damn fluorescents," I said as I fumbled around with my phone before figuring out how to turn on the flashlight app. "Should have looked here in the first place," I said a few minutes later, after finding a sledgehammer-chisel combination with a short handle, a tool I imagined a geologist or archaeologist would use in the field. Finding the perfect tool didn't surprise me. After all, Gertie's husband—who died of cancer a year before I moved to the Red Hills—was known to have more tools in his barn than the local hardware store.

The hammer was on a shelf beneath the workbench, and just as I reached for it, a voice sounded behind me. "What are you doing in here?"

I whirled around to see who spoke and smacked my head on the underside of the bench. *"Ouch."* A figure stood in the doorway, a silhouette backlit by what was left of the sunlight. "Uh, who are you?"

"Who are *you*?" the voice parroted back.

Archie emitted a single bark and approached the stranger. I said, "I'm Cal Claxton," as I gingerly touched my sore head. "I live next door." I pointed at my dog. "That's Archie. He's friendly." I waited, noting that Archie wasn't reading the confrontation as threatening.

"I'm Zoe Bennett, Gertie's niece. We spoke on the phone the other day." Archie came up to her, and she offered her hand for him to sniff.

"Of course. You arrived early, I see. Sorry, I was looking for a tool. I'm building a wall over at my place. The lights in here burned out just as I switched them on."

She moved, and I saw a glint of light on metal at her side. "Is that a *gun*?"

"Yeah. Sorry about that. My Ruger. When I saw the door to the barn was suddenly open, I figured I might need it."

I laughed. "We come in peace, Zoe."

She returned the laughter as she tucked the gun in her waistband, then turned her attention to Archie. "You have beautiful markings, big fella."

"He's an Aussie tricolor."

"Well, nice to meet you, Archie." She turned back to me. "Actually, I'm glad you're here, Cal. Would you mind coming in for a few minutes? I haven't been here in years, and I have some questions about the place."

Archie and I followed Zoe through Gertie's raised-bed gardens and up the back stairs. By this time a walnut-sized knot was throbbing on the side of my head. Under the kitchen lights, Zoe saw the lump and gasped. "Oh, dear. Does that hurt?"

"Only when I breathe," I answered.

Suppressing a smile, she looked more closely, then made a face. "Ugh, it's bleeding a little." She stripped off a paper towel from a dispenser and handed it to me. "Here. I, ah, I'm not the nurse type. Don't like the sight of blood."

I pressed the towel against the wound and pointed at an opened wine bottle with a half-full glass sitting next to it. "You could at least offer me a drink to ease the pain." It was a bottle of 2012 Le Petit Truc pinot noir. "I see you've found the good stuff in your aunt's wine cellar. It was made just down the road."

She looked a little embarrassed. "Okay, you caught me. I know this mark. I'm a big Oregon pinot fan thanks to Aunt Gertie, but I've never tasted a Petit Truc with this much age. It's incredible." She poured a glass, handed it to me, and picked up hers. We raised our glasses. Her ash-blond hair hung straight, brushing her shoulders, and her eyes reminded me of Gertie's but with deeper-blue irises. Her smile came easily, but she held something back, a wariness, perhaps.

We drank our wine and chatted for a while. I knew from Gertie that Zoe taught at the University of Puget Sound, clinical psychology, if memory served, and she was on sabbatical to write a book. This allowed her the flexibility to care for her aunt, whom she adored.

"It was no problem finding someone to take care of my parents' place," she explained when I asked her how she managed to get here so soon. "They live on Bainbridge Island looking straight out on the Seattle skyline. One of my girlfriends jumped at the chance to housesit there."

"You seemed to know your way around that Ruger," I commented.

She shrugged. "Well, I live alone, so I got it for protection. Took a course to learn how to shoot the damn thing." She made a face. "Actually, I hate guns, but my apartment was broken into once while I was there."

"What did you do?"

"I locked my bedroom door and called 911. He tried the door as I was calling. I think he heard me and took off. I felt so *helpless*, you know? He could have easily broken the lock."

"Sure, I can understand that."

She smiled and rolled her eyes. "You know what they say—a conservative's a liberal who just got mugged."

I had to laugh, although I was sorry I'd broached the subject of guns, because the events of the previous night came crashing back. Stupid me! I managed to talk and act normally after that. At least, I think I did. We finished our wine, and before I left, I explained the routine for feeding Cedric the cat, where the spare key to the front door was, and how to work Gertie's ancient thermostat.

As Archie and I walked back across the field, a silvery half-moon had just cleared the jagged tree line to the east, and a great horned owl made his presence known, calling *hoot, hoot, hoot-a-hoot, hoot*. I stopped in the middle of the field just in time to see a band of clouds turn luminous as it passed in front of the moon. I took a deep breath of cool night air and felt a semblance of peace.

The horror of the night before receded again, but even then I sensed it wouldn't remain at bay for long.

Chapter Seven

The following Wednesday morning—five days after Olivia Fuentes's murder—I called Detective Darci Tate to get an update. "We're a bit stymied," she said, after we exchanged greetings and I asked her how it was going. "The migrant community abhors what happened, but we're not getting much cooperation." She exhaled in frustration. "Back in the day, we had a fairly good relationship with those folks, but the well's been poisoned by what's going on now. They're afraid to stick their heads up." Another exhale. "And for good reason, I suppose."

"Does it still look like a hit?" I asked.

"Oh, yeah. We're just not sure who the intended victim was." I waited, but she didn't elaborate. "The autopsy didn't show anything unexpected. The ME released the body last night. One positive—the bullet was in one piece. We'll should get decent ballistics. It's a thirty-eight."

"I heard you released the body. I'm going to the wake out at the vineyard this afternoon." I asked a few more questions, which she chose not to answer. Finally, I said, "You sound tired, Darci. I hope you can get some rest."

"This case has gotten in my head. Sleep isn't exactly my friend these days."

"I know the feeling."

———

I stayed busy—a good thing—and when Arch and I got back to the Aerie that afternoon, I changed into my court-appearance garb—chinos, oxford shirt, and a blazer. I'd gotten rid of all my suits long ago. They reminded me of the past and felt like uniforms. I told Archie to chill and drove farther up into the Red Hills to Angel Vineyard.

"Come in, Cal," Timoteo said after I rang the bell at the Fuentes's house, "Thanks for coming." Packed with people talking in hushed tones, the small front room of the house smelled of fresh flowers and spicy food. Olivia's body lay in a casket in the center of the room, surrounded by bouquets of white roses and lilies. The casket was closed. Candles in ornate, waist-high candelabras burned next to each corner of the simple, white box. A small table held a large picture of the young woman, probably her senior high school picture. She looked out at the room, smiling and confident. Next to the picture stood a statuette of the Virgin of Guadalupe—a brown-skinned Madonna encircled by rays of sunlight with the moon and an adoring angel at her feet.

I moved through the room with Timoteo, and when we stopped in front of the table, I began blinking rapidly as a lump the size of an egg formed in my throat and visions of that night rushed back. "She was beautiful, Timoteo," I managed to say in a husky voice. "I'm so sorry for you and your family."

He put his hand on my shoulder to steady me. "She didn't suffer. That is some comfort." He met my eyes. "You knew she was gone, Cal, even as you continued your efforts to save her. You were trying to shield us, weren't you?"

I managed to stay dry-eyed. "I couldn't bring myself to tell you. I'm sorry for that."

He squeezed my shoulder. "No, no, it's okay. I get it."

"How are you holding up?"

He closed his eyes for a moment. "Olivia was the light of this family, the one with the most promise. We're crushed, but that doesn't begin to describe it." He looked across the room, where the young priest and three women sat with Mrs. Fuentes. "It's Mamá. She is taking it the worst. Cooking is how she usually deals with bad news, but she can't even do that. It worries me."

He led me over to her, and I offered my condolences once again. She was shrouded in black, and a delicate lace mantilla covered her braided, ebony hair and framed her handsome face. She looked at me with vacant eyes and spoke in a monotone. "God bless you, Mr. Claxton. Thank you for trying to save my Olivia. There is food in the kitchen."

A knot of people stood near the entryway to the kitchen. Timoteo stopped and after introducing me as his boss said, "These people are from Prosperar, where Olivia worked." A slender woman with dark, silver-streaked hair stepped forward and extended her hand. "I'm Sofia Leon, director of Prosperar." She turned to Timoteo, her eyes heavy with grief. "Olivia wasn't just a mainstay of our organization, she was a beautiful person, passionate about her work, a fighter for social justice." Leon made an inclusive gesture and shook her head. "We all loved her and are saddened beyond words." A woman standing next to Leon sobbed and shielded her wet eyes with a hand. A young man standing next to her laid a hand on her shoulder.

Timoteo thanked them for coming, and we moved past the group into the kitchen, where his father and several men his age were huddled around a wooden table talking in low tones. A squat liquor bottle sat in the center of the table, and they each had a glass of whitish-colored liquid in front of them. He stood when he saw me and offered his hand. "Carlos. Thank you for coming, Mr. Claxton. Do you want a glass of pulque?"

I declined his offer, suppressing an urge to blurt out, *Stop thanking me, for Christ's sake. I did nothing for your daughter.* Instead, after shaking his hand and expressing my sympathy, I surprised myself by saying, "If there's anything I can do for you and your family, Carlos, don't hesitate to ask."

He swung his gaze to his son, then back to me, and his eyes narrowed down some. "You could find out who killed our Olivia. Timoteo says you are good at such things."

I winced inwardly, realizing I'd walked right into that one. Out of the corner of my eye, I saw Timoteo lean in slightly. "I know the detectives working on the crime," I responded. "They are very good. I'm a lawyer. It's unlikely I could add anything."

Carlos was shorter than me with a powerful-looking upper torso and dark eyes that could drill a hole in you. He held my eyes and showed a faintly sarcastic smile. "Maybe they are good, but they tell us nothing so far." He opened his hands. "We migrants have no quarrel with the local police, but our relationship with them is, ah"—he turned to his son—*"delicado?"*

"Delicate," Timoteo prompted.

"Sí, delicate. Some people may not wish to come forward and cooperate. It is a problem in our community, especially after what *La Migra* did in Woodburn."

I nodded to signal I knew about the recent raids by ICE agents that resulted in the deportation of over a dozen farm and vineyard workers, some of whom had arrived three and four decades earlier and had families and deep roots in the community.

Carlos dragged a calloused hand across his face and showed

the faint smile again. "It is no secret that many of us are without papers, but we work hard and pay our taxes."

I paused for a few moments. "I would have to know much more about the situation before I could make a judgment." I glanced from Timoteo to Carlos. "Maybe we could talk later this week. Your son can arrange it." I raised a cautionary finger to them both. "Please, know that I cannot promise anything."

Exiting the kitchen, we ran into the owners of the winery, the Angels. I'd met them a few times over the years, so there was no need for Timoteo to introduce us. Chad Angel was tall, with wire-rim glasses and an affable demeanor. His wife, Hillary, was petite and normally effervescent. They both looked numb and shattered. "Olivia was like a granddaughter to us," Hillary told me, dabbing her eyes with a handkerchief. "This is all so…so unbelievable."

With one hand on his wife's back, Chad studied me for a moment. "Are you involved in the investigation in any way, Cal?" he asked. After all, I did have a bit of a reputation in the Red Hills.

I shook my head. "No. I happened to be with Timoteo when he found Olivia. He's assisting me at my office."

"I see. I understand the police have no leads."

"That's what Carlos told me. It's early in the investigation."

I left it at that, and when we moved on, I asked Timoteo where Luis was. He scanned the crowded room. "I don't see him. He's probably outside smoking with his friends."

I wanted to ask Timoteo if he still blamed his brother for Olivia's death. And I was curious about whether the ugly exchange between the brothers had been called to Detective Tate's attention. But it was neither the time nor place for that. I said, "I'd like to pay my respects to him."

Timoteo nodded, and I followed him back through the kitchen into the backyard. Luis was standing with three other young men.

He was shorter than Timoteo, more the height of his father, and he had the ebony hair and fine, sculpted cheeks of his mother. His companions eyed me with curiosity, a gringo. Luis flicked a cigarette away and shook my extended hand. "I'm sorry for your loss," I said. "I wish I could have done more."

He raised his eyes, his expression hard to read. "You did what you could. Olivia was the best of us. Our family will never be the same."

An awkward silence followed. I finally turned to Timoteo. "I've got to go now." And I wasn't kidding. My stomach was clenched, my psyche battered by Olivia's ghost, which seemed to hover in the next room. Timoteo insisted on showing me out, and when we got to the front door I said, "Don't come back to work until you're ready. There's nothing pressing."

"The funeral's Friday. I can come in on Saturday to finish up the filing if that's okay with you." He eyed me anxiously. "If you're going to be around, I could bring my father so we can have that talk."

I agreed.

I left Olivia Fuentes's *velorio* with the intention of walking directly to my car, which was parked along the entrance road that bisected the vineyard. But when I came to the point in the driveway where the shooting had taken place, I paused just long enough for curiosity to get the better of me. How had the shooter managed to get close to the Fuentes's cottage without being noticed? Of course, Tate and her partner had undoubtedly asked themselves the same question, but it persisted in my mind, and I hated unanswered questions.

I glanced back at the Fuentes's house to make sure no one was watching, then ducked into the thick row of rhododendrons lining the south side of the driveway where the shooter must have lain in wait. The first thing I noticed was that the assassin could not have gotten a very good look at his victim from that spot. The vegetation was dense, and it was nearly dark and raining that evening. I was surprised to see a clearing on the other side of the rhodies leading up to a barn. A long row of used, sixty-gallon oak barrels stacked three high lined the east side of the clearing, which was littered with out-of-service equipment, including an old front-loader tractor. I stopped at the barn and looked back toward the Fuentes's cottage. The window at the kitchen sink gave the only view of this approach to the driveway, but the barrels would have provided good cover for anyone sneaking in. The barn was connected to Valleyview Road by a service road that cut through the vineyard for thirty yards or so. Moving low between rows of grapevines parallel to the road, someone could have easily made it from Valleyview Road to the barn without being seen.

I followed the service road up to the gate. It was shut and padlocked. The gate and the fencing on either side were high to keep the deer out. Not likely the shooter climbed over. I examined the lock. It looked brand new. Had the shooter used a bolt cutter to gain entry?

I backtracked from there and, once at my car, another question nagged at me—where did the killer park his vehicle and begin his approach? Valleyview Road was narrow, with ditches for shoulders, making it impossible to park anywhere near the service road gate. As I headed out of the winery, I turned right on Valleyview, left on Sylvan Drive, and then another left on Buena Vista, a country block later. This put me above the vineyard, with a thick stand of conifers separating me from Valleyview. And Buena Vista had shoulders wide enough to park on. I pulled over and got out.

Yes, the killer probably parked near here and used the cover of the trees to approach the service gate.

I followed a faint trail through the trees, realizing Darci

Tate and her partner had almost certainly done the same thing. Halfway in, I saw a spattering of grayish-white material in the path. I smiled. Sure enough, she'd already been in there lifting a shoe print from the soft earth, using what looked like dental stone casting. I came out of the trees on Valleyview, not far from the service gate, then retraced my steps without finding anything else. When I got back to my car, I looked farther up the hillside. An old Victorian house looked down on the scene.

I made a mental note to check it out...*if* I decided to get involved.

Chapter Eight

"For having had my breastbone sawed in half, I'm not feeling that bad," Gertie quipped to me the next morning on the phone at my office. "Zoe's picking me up this afternoon. It'll be great to get the hell out of here. Hospitals give me the creeps." I offered my help, but she assured me that her niece had everything covered. She chuckled. "I understand you two met the other night. Isn't she something?"

"It was memorable."

"My sister and I are very different," Gertie went on. "She's well, you know, I won't say a kept woman, but she never found it necessary to work. Married a great guy, but rich as Midas. Zoe's a lot like me. Independent, probably to a fault."

I had to laugh. "I did notice some similarities."

———

That day at the office was agonizingly slow. Okay, I could have done some of the filing Timoteo hadn't gotten to, but instead I closed up early. The afternoon was cool and crisp, perfect for wall-building, I figured, and wall-building was perfect for banishing the cloud of Olivia Fuentes's death that still hung over me like a foul smell.

Back at the Aerie, I changed into a sweatshirt, jeans, and boots, and with Archie looking on like a foreman, continued the work of breaking rock into rubble and fitting the small chunks between the large stones at the base of my dry stack. I focused hard on the task, and soon my mind was calmer than it had been in some time. A breeze sifted through the Doug firs overhead, and I could hear the pileated woodpecker foraging somewhere in the distance—*rat tat tat, rat tat tat.* When I finally finished, the sun was setting, and the firs on the property west of us formed black silhouettes against a flaming gold sky.

I looked over at Arch. "I'm hungry. You?" Never one to be asked twice to dinner, he popped up and started heading for the house.

After feeding my dog and making myself a quick spinach frittata, I poured myself another glass of Sancerre and began making soup. I'd picked up a precooked chicken on the way home, which I shredded and added to a pot with chicken broth, carrots, celery, shallots, mushrooms, and noodles, the whole mix seasoned with tarragon.

Forty-five minutes later, I had a pot of homemade chicken soup for Gertie.

"Well, hello, Archie and Cal," Zoe said when she opened the back door and eyed us standing there. I was holding the pot with a couple of potholders. "Come on in."

I told Archie to stay, followed her into the kitchen, and set the soup down. "I, uh, just put this together. Chicken noodle. Thought Gertie might like it."

Wearing yoga pants, a loose-fitting cotton sweater, and big hoop earrings, Zoe uncovered the pot and sniffed it. "Oh, it smells delicious. You made this from *scratch*?"

I shrugged. "Not exactly. I bought the chicken precooked to save time."

She rolled her eyes. "That's from scratch as far as I'm concerned. How sweet of you, and your timing's perfect. I was just facing up to the fact that I have to make dinner." She made a face. "Cooking's not exactly my forte."

She prepared a tray for Gertie, and I followed her to a small guest room on the first floor. Gertie was dozing when we entered. The lines around her eyes and mouth seemed more pronounced, but she'd regained some of the color in her face. Her eyes opened at the sound of us, then she smiled when she saw me, saying, "Hello, neighbor." Looking at Zoe, she added, "Something smells good, and it's not hospital food, thank God."

Zoe and I pulled up chairs, and we chatted while my neighbor ate. When the topic of my cooking came up, Gertie looked at Zoe. "He cooks pretty well for a bachelor."

Zoe turned to me. "What's your secret?"

"I stick to the basics. Nothing fancy."

Gertie laughed. "He makes a mean double-reduction cherry sauce for pork loin and a mango salsa for halibut that's amazing. I'd call that pretty fancy."

"Yeah, but I can't make a fresh fruit pie from scratch, like you," I countered. "*That's* fancy."

She looked at me, then Zoe, chuckling again. "I've offered to teach him, but he's always too busy."

The banter stayed in that light vein until Gertie gave me a piercing look, the one that says, 'I'm sensing something you're not telling me.' She said, "You seem a little off, Cal. What's the matter?" Not wishing to burden my friend with sad news, I shook my head. But she pressed me. "Go on. Spit it out."

Knowing Gertie wouldn't drop it, I exhaled. "There's been a murder at Angel Vineyard." As the words left me, my throat tightened up. I looked at Zoe. "That's a vineyard not far from here." To both I said, "A young woman was shot to death last Friday night."

Zoe flinched visibly. Gertie said, "Good God, not here in the Red Hills." I sketched in the situation, and when I finished Gertie shook her head. "My heart goes out to the Fuentes family."

"They're devastated, Mrs. Fuentes in particular," I responded. "I went to the *velorio* yesterday. It was, uh, difficult."

"What about the Angels? How are they taking it?" Gertie asked.

"Devastated as well. Hillary told me Olivia was like a grand-daughter to them."

Gertie gave me a serious look. "Are you going to get involved, Cal?"

I shrugged. "Olivia's father asked me to. He said people would be reluctant to cooperate with the police since the raids."

Gertie nodded. Zoe said, "*Raids*? What happened?"

"ICE conducted a series of sweeps and deported dozens of people in the Willamette Valley, all farm and vineyard workers. Most were men, some with families with kids that are American citizens, like the Fuentes family."

"The local police don't cooperate with ICE, do they?" Zoe asked. "Oregon's a sanctuary state like Washington and California, right?"

"That's right, but the Feds are putting a lot more pressure on local law enforcement, and the migrants know this. What trust there was has been compromised."

"What did you tell Mr. Fuentes about getting involved?" Gertie asked.

"I said I'd discuss it with him. I'm meeting with him and Timoteo on Saturday. Olivia's funeral is tomorrow."

Gertie shot Zoe a knowing look. "He'll probably take the case."

To me, she added, "I usually don't encourage these open-ended ventures. You always seem to lose money, and they're dangerous as hell. But this is close to home, Cal. I hope you can help this family find out who killed their daughter."

That was as close to an endorsement as I ever got from Gertrude Johnson. I smiled. "We'll see, Gertie."

Gertie tired soon after that, and Zoe showed me out, walking with Archie and me to the gate separating our two properties. Light from a gibbous moon reflected off one of her earrings, and a breeze riffled and tossed her hair. She took no notice.

I said, "I apologize for being the bearer of bad news. I wasn't going to say anything, but your aunt reads me like a book."

Zoe laughed at that. "Nothing gets by her." She wrapped her arms against the breeze and looked out at the twinkling lights in the valley before turning to me. "Are you okay?"

I kept my eyes on the valley. "Yeah, it's just…I, uh, I tried to revive Olivia and all." I exhaled and my throat tightened again. "It wasn't a pretty sight, and it's staying with me."

"That's understandable. You've suffered a trauma, and you're grieving, too."

"I'm angry. This never should have happened."

"Anger's part of the grieving process, Cal."

I considered that for a moment. "That's true. And the end-point's acceptance, right?"

"That's right."

"Well, I don't expect to get to acceptance any time soon. Somebody needs to pay for this first."

"Oh, an avenging angel."

"Avenging, maybe, but no angel." After we said our good-nights and I was walking back across the moonlit field, I reminded myself to not let my emotions carry the day. No decisions until you talk to Timoteo and his dad, I promised myself.

That night, to keep Olivia's ghost at bay, I resorted to my old friend Rémy Martin once again. Instead of Yo-Yo Ma playing Chopin, however, I opted for a slightly more upbeat "'Round About Midnight" with Miles Davis and John Coltrane. I took that as evidence of progress.

Chapter Nine

That Saturday morning, I stood at my kitchen window watching fast-moving clouds sweep in from the south, thankful I'd stopped drinking in time to avoid another bad hangover. Rain billowed down from the distant front, and the wind it sent up the valley swayed the firs along my fence line like graceful dancers. In the foreground, sunlight bathed the valley in yellow light, bringing the soft autumn colors to full bloom.

I waited as my espresso machine squeezed out two shots to which I added hot, foamy milk—my first double cap of the day, and without the aspirin this time. Sipping the heady brew, my mind drifted back to mornings I'd spent commuting to the Parker Center when I was a prosecutor for the city of Los Angeles. It all came back—the dirty air, the insane traffic, the looming stress of the day's work. That seemed two lifetimes ago, at least. I shook off the annoying flashback, reminding myself that things could be a lot worse.

Two sharp barks from Archie announced the arrival of Timoteo and his father at my office at ten that morning. "Have you heard from Detective Tate?" I asked after we exchanged greetings and they were seated.

Carlos Fuentes locked his deep-set eyes on mine. "I spoke with the detective this morning. They have no leads." He wore a long-sleeved shirt with pearl buttons, dark blue jeans with a wide leather belt, and finely tooled cowboy boots.

Timoteo glanced at his father before speaking, his jeans, crew-neck sweater, and cross-trainers in sharp contrast to his dad's attire. "Actually, the detective said the investigation was progressing, that they couldn't share what they'd found."

Carlos puffed a dismissive breath. "*Por dios*. If she had something, she would've have told us. *¿Verdad?*"

I waved a hand. "It's hard to judge. They're not going to be very open with you at this stage. In any case, I've got some questions I'd like to ask you, okay?" They both nodded. "Let me start with Olivia that night. She was set to pick you up, Timoteo, but she had a conflict. What happened?"

Timoteo leaned forward in his chair, his face darkening at the mention of his sister. "She was late to a fundraiser in Newberg for Prosperar, the nonprofit she's…ah…was working for. She asked Luis to come get me."

I looked at Carlos. "She took your truck. Was that normal?"

He shrugged. "It was parked behind our other car. She hates the truck. It's a stick shift, but she probably didn't want to take the time to move it." A wistful smile flickered and died on his weathered face. "Olivia was always in a hurry."

I turned to Timoteo. "She was wearing Luis's hoodie that night. Why was that?"

"It was probably hanging on the coatrack next to the door. She grabbed it to keep the rain off."

To both of them I said, "Do you know of anyone with a reason to hurt Olivia?"

They looked horrified, saying in unison, "No." Timoteo added, "Olivia was loved by *everyone*. No one wished her harm."

"You mentioned Prosperar, the nonprofit health organization. What did she do there?"

Timoteo smiled sadly. "What didn't she do? She was in charge of their office operations, scheduling, keeping medical records, writing press releases, you name it. She was a tech whiz, too. She had that organization humming, everything computerized."

"Did she work for the director, Sofia Leon?"

"Yeah. She started out working for the office manager, but Leon fired him and didn't replace him. So, Olivia got the job de facto."

"This fundraiser Olivia was hurrying to... I gather the people attending knew she was coming?"

"Um, yeah. She was on the agenda. I know because she showed me. She was proud of it."

"So, the approximate time she would have left your house was known to the Prosperar group and the attendees? Anyone else know when she was leaving that night?"

Timoteo's eyes told me he'd caught my drift. "Um, no one I know of."

"Why didn't Luis come with you today?" I asked next, changing the subject.

Carlos dropped his gaze to the floor in front of him. Timoteo said, "Luis left. We haven't seen him since the funeral."

"He *left*? Why?"

Timoteo flinched at my words. "We don't know. I think it was my fault."

"Was it about the confrontation you had the night of the murder?"

He gave a slight shrug. "Luis started hanging with some guys I didn't like. I jumped to conclusions, I guess. I was out of my head that night."

Carlos raised his eyes. "We worry about Luis. He hasn't found his way yet."

Timoteo said, "Luis hates school, but he's an amazing artist."

"Art?" Carlos scoffed. "Unless you are Diego Rivera, it is useless. You cannot support yourself this way."

Timoteo shot me a frustrated look before saying, "He'll find his way, Papi."

"He also has a temper," Carlos went on. "About a year ago he got into a fight with a white man who spit on him and told him to go back to Mexico. We have tried to teach our children to walk away from such ugliness, but Luis is a fighter."

Timoteo said, "The white guy wasn't charged with anything, but Luis got arrested. We were terrified he was going to be deported, but the guy never pressed charges, so Luis was released."

"Do you know this man's name?"

"I can get it for you," Timoteo said. "I have a copy of the police report."

"Do that. What about these guys he was hanging out with? Tell me about them."

Timoteo curled up one side of his mouth and shook his head. "I don't know much. The disaffected, I guess. They gather at a little cantina in Lafayette. You know, they hate whites, blame them for everything but do nothing to help the situation. Okay, Latinos don't always get a fair shake around here, but playing the victim doesn't help." He exhaled a breath in frustration. "I told Luis he'd be judged by the company he keeps, but he didn't listen, of course."

"You thought one of them might've had it in for Luis for some reason?"

Timoteo shook his head again. "I was wrong. Luis said there was no problem."

"But he took off. Do you think he's in danger?"

"He's left before. He was pissed at me, probably needed to

get away. He was very close to Olivia. Our house's a depressing place right now."

"Was Luis going out that night?"

"He was going to the cantina, I think." Timoteo said.

"Would they have known he was coming?"

He shrugged. "I guess so."

"Did Luis or either of you tell Detective Tate any of this?"

Carlos shook his head. Timoteo said, "I didn't. I don't know for sure what Luis told her."

"Unless he suspected someone of the shooting," Carlos added, "Luis would tell them nothing. He is the least trusting of us all."

I looked at Carlos. "What about you? Do you have any enemies? It was dark, it was your truck, and like Luis, Olivia's about your height." I nodded in Timoteo's direction. "He's the tall one in the family."

Carlos's shoulders sank as he let out a slow breath. He looked at Timoteo, then drilled his dark eyes into mine. "Timoteo says that you are a man we can trust. I hope this is so, because I am going to tell you something I do not wish you to share with anyone else."

"You have my word, Carlos."

Timoteo shifted in his seat, signaling interest in what his father was about to say.

"I grew up in a village near Guadalajara in the state of Jalisco. My father died when I was five—a simple infection that was never treated—and my mother struggled to raise me and my two older sisters. We, ah, had no money and often very little to eat. When I was seventeen, I was recruited by a cartel."

Timoteo sucked an audible breath. *"A cartel?* You never told us this, Papi."

Carlos turned to his son and opened his hands. "Why would I? I was young and desperate. I knew it was wrong, but when your grandmother had her stroke, I became the breadwinner."

Timoteo's mouth dropped open. "Which cartel?"

"The Guadalajara. When I was eighteen, I met your mother," Carlos continued, allowing a wistful smile. "She captured my heart that first day, but she would have nothing to do with me because I was a Guadalajara."

Timoteo laughed in spite of himself. "No surprise there."

Carlos smiled. "I was a good organizer, and I rose rapidly in the organization." He stopped abruptly and eyed his son. "I was in operations, not security. I never hurt anyone during that time, I swear, Timoteo."

"Of course, Papi."

"I saved some money, and six years later I moved my mother and sisters to a small village in San Luis Potosi in the dark of night. We had cousins there. I found a job in a vineyard. I was just a field laborer, but that's where I learned to love growing grapes and making wine."

Timoteo leaned toward his father. I felt like I was intruding on an intimate father-son conversation. He smiled. "What did Mamá think of that?"

Carlos returned the smile. "I snuck back to Guadalajara a month later, but she wouldn't see me. I came back again a year later, and she agreed to come back with me. A priest married us at the vineyard. But it was a hard life, and there was no chance of advancing. After you and Luis were born, the call of El Norte was too strong, so I slipped across the border with a *coyote*. I was ambitious, and your mother and I wanted a better life for you both. You know the rest."

Timoteo looked thunderstruck. "*Wow*, I had no idea. There was no way out of the cartel?"

Carlos smiled bitterly. "The penalty for deserting Guadalajara was death for you and your family. You learn that the first day of training and every day after. Even though the cartel has now splintered into several factions, they vow to hunt you down if you desert."

"Even after twenty-some years?" I said.

The bitter smile. "They might. *Fanáticos*, all of them. My disappearance was a big thing at the time." Carlos dropped his gaze. "And I took some of their money when I left. Finding and killing someone like me here in America after so long could send a strong message, I think."

"Do you think they may have found you?"

He shrugged. "It is possible. I made some inquiries in Guadalajara to someone I trust, but he no longer has a source in the cartel."

"Do you fear that you and the rest of your family are in danger?"

Carlos's face grew hard. "In Mexico, they would kill us all. Here in America, they might not risk it. Perhaps killing a man's daughter is enough. But we are being cautious."

"That's wise," I said, then moved to another question. "I looked around the vineyard after I left the *velorio*. I noticed what looked like a new lock on the gate behind your house. Is that where the killer entered the vineyard?"

Timoteo looked surprised at my revelation but answered without questioning me. "Yes, we were told the lock was found open, which meant the killer had a key or was able to pick it."

I looked at Carlos. "Who had access to the key?"

"Many people. It hung in the storage barn. Now I have the only key to the new lock."

"Do you suspect anyone of providing a key to the killer?"

Carlos shook his head. "No one. But some of the workers are new, and I don't know them well."

"Did you hire them?"

"Yes, all of them."

"Do you have a list of names, their contact information?"

"I have given such a list to the detective," Carlos answered. "I'm afraid some of the information may not be accurate." He smiled. "Not even I am trusted completely these days."

We fell into silence. Archie got up from his mat in the corner and stretched, sensing the meeting might be over. Finally I said, "Anything else you think I should know?"

They looked at each other and shook their heads.

I leaned back and ran a hand through my hair. "It would be best if you told Detective Tate about the cartel, but I understand why you feel you can't. If you and the rest of the migrant community fully cooperated with the police, it would make little sense for me to be involved, but since that's not going to happen, maybe I can find a way to help." I put an index finger up for emphasis and moved my eyes from father to son. "I'll need your assistance, especially in convincing people it's safe to talk to me."

Carlos nodded, and Timoteo said, "We can do that. No problem."

It was a huge commitment, something I had no business taking on, but the crime was so personal, so deeply affecting. Did I have a choice? "We can discuss fees later, but there's one item we can dispose of right now," I continued. "I'll need your permission to share details about the case that could be construed as confidential in the attorney-client setting. I've learned the hard way that I need that flexibility to be effective in a situation like this, where I'm straddling the line between investigator and attorney. You'll have to trust my judgment that I'll be careful. Is that agreeable?" They said it was, and I drew up an informed consent agreement. After a discussion, Carlos signed it.

He stood, looking relieved. "Thank—"

I put a hand up. "Don't thank me, please. I haven't done anything yet. How's Elena?"

Timoteo shook his head. "Not good. She stays in the bedroom

with the blinds closed. She doesn't speak, doesn't go to work, no cooking, and she's hardly eating. And she won't talk to Father Mallory."

Timoteo went ahead, and Carlos lingered at the doorway. In a low tone he said, "My wife thinks the cartel killed Olivia by mistake, that they were after me. She told me she would never, ever forgive me." He sighed deeply, his dark eyes laden with sadness. "If she's right, I will never forgive myself."

"I can't say what the investigation will reveal about that, Carlos. The only thing I can promise you is that I'll be focused on getting at the truth, no matter what it is."

"I know. And that is what I want you to do."

After the father and son left, I looked at Archie and shrugged. "Okay, that was impulsive, but how could I say no?" He raised his chin off his paws and looked at me with a knowing expression that in my agitated state seemed to say, *Here we go again.*

Chapter Ten

"Shit," I hissed, shaking my hand after pinching my thumb between two large chunks of basalt. I was laying the first above-ground course of my wall and thinking about what I'd heard from Timoteo and his father that morning. The cartel revelation was a shocker, and it introduced an unexpected layer of complexity, to say nothing of personal exposure. I knew very little about how the cartels operated, except that their tentacles reached over the border, they had a ton of firepower, and they were ruthless to the core.

That's just dandy, the cautious corner of my brain said—the corner that habitually resorted to sarcasm.

At that point, it also occurred to me that I hadn't broached the subject of compensation. The Fuentes family wasn't well off, but I sure as hell couldn't work for nothing. I shrugged and looked at Arch. "Easy come, easy go, right, Big Boy?"

After my thumb stopped throbbing, I put my glove back on and wrestled the last rock out of the wheelbarrow and into place. I went back to the rock pile and sorted through it for a while before selecting the next candidates and reloading. Did I think the cartel was behind Olivia Fuentes's murder? I hefted a nice block of basalt and struggled to put it in place. Despite the cartel's vow of unrelenting revenge, that seemed a stretch, given the time that had elapsed. Maybe it was about settling some personal score, something Carlos Fuentes had held back from me and his son? That would make more sense. Assuming the worst, would the cartel have used one of their own hit men from across the border or would they contract it out? Probably the latter, I decided, which meant the killer might still be around. Would he try again? I tended to agree with Carlos that that wasn't likely, but it was certainly a possibility.

I stacked two thinner slabs next to the last block I'd laid in and stepped back, admiring the look. There was the issue of the padlock—an inside job? Detective Tate would be all over that, but since the grape harvest was in, many of the workers at Angel Vineyard were off to other jobs. Good luck locating them without inside help.

What about Luis Fuentes? Something seemed off about that story. Why did he bolt? It seemed just as likely that *he* was the intended victim, not his father. Was that the reason? Perhaps he felt guilty, too, like his father. The company he was keeping—the men Timoteo disparaged—were of interest, along with the man he'd fought with. How to approach them? I would need help for that, too.

I was getting a little better at spotting the right piece of basalt, and the next dozen or so placements went somewhat faster. Sweat dripping from my brow, I stood back again to view my handiwork. Clearly, I'd underestimated the task. As I worked, my mind finally turned reluctantly to Olivia Fuentes. Was she really murdered by mistake?

As I turned that question over, I heard someone clear their throat behind me. "Nice wall. Is Mexico going to pay for it?"

I turned to a smiling Zoe Bennett. Archie woke from a snooze, sprang up, and went over to her. "I asked, but they said no."

She laughed and knelt down to greet my dog, who was

obviously pleased to see her. "What's going to hold it together, the wall, I mean?"

"Gravity and the ingenious placement of the rocks," I said. "I'm still working on the second part."

"What are you going to put inside the wall?"

"Herbs. You know, parsley, sage, rosemary, and thyme." That brought a smile. "Right now, I grow them out of pots on the porch. Not ideal."

"What will keep the deer away?"

"Deer don't like most herbs, and there's plenty of natural feed around here." I glanced at my dog. "And every time a deer sets foot on the property, Archie's on it. He just wants to herd them, but they don't know that."

"What's your favorite herb?"

I paused for a moment, a chunk of basalt in my hands. "Depends on the food. Basil for anything tomatoey. For savory foods, rosemary, I guess. Yours?"

She rubbed the back of her neck and smiled with a hint of sheepishness. "I'm not sure, come to think of it. I mean herbs are wonderful, but I can't pick them out in a dish. My palate's not refined enough."

I laughed. "You know a good pinot when you taste it. How's Gertie?"

"Good. Getting her attitude back."

"Lucky you." I waited, sensing something was on her mind.

"Do you happen to have a cedar plank I could borrow? I'm cooking some salmon on the barbeque, and Gertie insisted I use one. She said to ask you."

"Sure. A plank makes the best salmon ever." I swiped my brow with a forearm and tossed the chunk of basalt back into the wheelbarrow. It wasn't going to fit where I needed it, anyway. Archie led us into the house, and after I extracted a nice, fragrant red cedar plank from a cabinet above my refrigerator, I said, "Ever cook with one of these?"

She shook her head. "Above my pay grade."

"It's easy. Have a beer with me, and I'll explain it."

"Great. I've got some time. Gertie's napping."

I popped the caps off two Mirror Pond longnecks, and we went out on the side porch. A light breeze stirred the Doug firs, and the colors in the valley whispered autumn. "Okay," I began after brushing the maple leaves and fir needles off two chairs at my weathered, wrought-iron table, "soak the plank *at least* two hours, fully submerged. Then bring your barbeque to medium heat. Brush the plank with olive oil before you put the salmon on it. I usually just coat the fish with olive oil and then sprinkle on salt, pepper, lemon juice, and brown sugar."

Zoe waited, and when I didn't continue, looked incredulous. *"That's it?"*

I drank some beer and chuckled. "Cook it *slowly*. At medium heat the plank should begin to char about the time the fish is done. The fish is cooked when little white globules of fat begin percolating to the surface. The thin end of the fillet will cook faster, so cut through and take the salmon off a section at a time. That way, it'll be evenly cooked."

Zoe showed a look of almost childlike enthusiasm. "I think I can do that. What's the plank for, anyway?"

"Flavor and moisture. It adds both. The Columbia River tribes cook their salmon this way."

"They should know," she said, then sipped some beer as the breeze ruffled her hair. She studied me for a moment, and her look grew softer. "How are you coping?"

I took a long pull on my beer. "Better. I decided to get involved after talking to Timoteo and his father this morning. That seemed to help, you know?"

"Doing rather than stewing?"

"Yeah, something like that."

"I'm curious. What convinced you to get involved?"

"The local police are in a weak position. I won't say they're going to get stonewalled, but they're sure as hell not going to get the full cooperation of the migrant community here. I'm thinking I can use Carlos and Timoteo to run interference for me. Maybe I can fill in some blanks, help find the bastard who did this."

"That's noble," she said with no hint of sarcasm, "but it sounds tricky. I mean, you'll be working kind of a shadow case and with people who're in this country illegally."

"Yeah, I'll be walking a high wire between client confidentiality and the need to turn evidence over to the investigating team. The family isn't under any suspicion, so that makes it easier."

"Did you learn anything this morning?"

I took another drink of beer and regarded her for a moment. She sat erect, her slender neck thrust forward and her facial features drawn up in rapt attention. She had Gertie's forthright manner, and I sensed her curiosity sprang purely from a desire to help or at least to understand. "I did," I answered, "but there are confidentiality issues."

"Of course," she said. "I'm curious how you go about something like this. And maybe I can help in some way, you know, from a psychological standpoint." She showed a smile, but it was clear the offer was serious.

I turned the exchange over in my mind. Something about Zoe Bennet intrigued me. She seemed insightful, and in view of the impact of the murder on the Fuentes family as well as me, having a clinical psychologist in my corner might not be a bad idea.

I said, "Well, I do have a certain amount of flexibility to discuss the case with people I think can be of assistance." She pursed her lips and waited. "You'll have to agree to hold what I tell you in confidence."

Her eyes got big. "Of course. I'm a PhD psychologist. I'm fully aware of the need for confidentiality."

After a playful handshake on the deal, I began sketching in the basic facts of the case gleaned from my discussion with Timoteo and his father. I finessed the cartel revelation, saying simply that there was always a chance someone from Carlos's past was involved.

When I finished, she leaned back and did that thing with her eyes again, doubling their size. "My God, this is complex. Who was the intended victim—the father? The son?"

"Or the daughter?" I added.

Her blue eyes flashed at me. *"No."*

I shrugged. "I haven't ruled out anything yet."

"And the mother's poised to blame the father because of something in his past?"

"Potentially."

Her face clouded over. "That's so sad but not very surprising. Tragedies like this can destroy a family. That bullet wounded them all."

I exhaled a sigh. "Yeah. I guess I'm hoping the father wasn't the target. Things are bad enough as they are."

She studied me for a moment. "You can't control the outcome, Cal."

"I know."

Zoe said, "I'm worried about the mother. A shutdown like she's experiencing can be permanently disabling, even life-threatening. Her grief's magnified by the trauma associated with the violence of her daughter's death. The technical term's traumatic bereavement. It's insidious."

"She's apparently refusing to talk to the priest," I said.

Zoe nodded. "She's probably mad at God as well as Carlos."

"What would you advise him and Timoteo to do?"

"Get professional help, but failing that, keep the lines of communication open, get her moving by coaxing her out of her room, and above all, remind her that Olivia would not approve of her giving up. Her love for her daughter is her greatest enemy right now, but it can also save her."

"Thanks. I'll pass that on."

Zoe glanced at her smart watch. "It's late. I better get back." She brought her eyes up to mine. They were steady and clear. "I'm glad you took the case, Cal. I hope I can be of help."

Always the gentleman, Archie got up and escorted Zoe to the edge of our property. I watched as they moved across the field, my dog in a pony trot with his tail up, and Zoe moving with strong, purposeful strides, the cedar plank grasped in one hand. "Bon appétit," I called out. She turned and waved the plank in response.

I sat back and drained my beer, surprised as always, at what the universe serves up. I may have stretched the bounds of client confidentiality a bit, but I had a new colleague now, someone I felt I could trust.

Chapter Eleven

I skipped my cognac and music therapy that night, which was apparently a mistake. I slept restlessly, and not that long before dawn, dreamed I was back in L.A., having arrived home after a day at the Parker Center. I entered the house and a feeling of dread came over me, because I knew what I would find up in the bedroom. But instead of my wife Nancy's lifeless body, I found Olivia's. I woke up sputtering "No, no," over and over again. Archie came over to comfort me, and I finally fell back to sleep with him standing next to the bed with his head resting on the mattress.

That morning, a Sunday, I forced myself into a hard jog followed by a hearty breakfast. After I showered and dressed, I called Timoteo and asked him to meet me down at the office. "No, that's not necessary," I told him when he asked if he should bring his father. "He should stay with your mother. You're point man. We've got a lot of ground to cover, and I'd like to get started right away. Be sure to bring the worker information your father gave the police." I paused, adding, "And ask him to mark the names of the workers he said he didn't know well, the ones who had access to the key. We'll start there."

After I hung up, I felt a pang of impatience mixed with anxiety.

I wasn't kidding about having a lot of ground to cover, and I knew that murder cases tended to grow cold very quickly. I was getting in late and didn't like it.

———

"Thanks," Timoteo said twenty-five minutes later at the Red Hills Market as the waitress set our coffees down on the counter along with a doggie treat for Archie. I couldn't help noticing the lingering look the young waitress gave my new assistant. A handsome young man by any standard, his cheeks bore a day's growth, the whiskers shading the dimple on his chin. He was unaware of her obvious interest. It was cool but sunny, so we sat outside instead of walking back to the office.

He pushed an envelope across the table. "This is the worker information and a copy of the police report you asked for. My father said some of the addresses are bogus. He asked around and wrote in where he thinks we might actually find these people."

"Good," I said, pushing the envelope aside. "Let's talk business first. Cases like this can get expensive, and I don't want—"

"I've been thinking about that," Timoteo said, looking anxious. "Would it help if I worked on the investigation for free? I'll do all the follow-up and whatever else is needed."

I took a sip of coffee and chuckled. "That's where I was headed. Of course, I'll pay you as we agreed for your routine work in the office." He voiced his assent. I named a discounted hourly rate and told him I didn't need an answer at that moment. "Discuss it with your father and let me know."

"Thank you, Cal, that's a generous offer. The funeral was very expensive. He usually takes my financial advice. I'm, um, not going to mention the price is discounted. My father's a proud man."

"I understand. Don't get hung up on the money," I said as an image of Gertie rolling her eyes flashed in my head. "We'll manage it." I paused, grateful to have that out of the way. "Now, any word from your brother?"

He grimaced in frustration. "Not directly. He let his best friend know that he wanted to be left alone for a while."

I felt relieved. "Good. He's safe, then. But it's critical that I talk to him."

Timoteo shook his head and smiled bitterly. "Olivia would know where he is. Luis told her everything."

"Who did Olivia confide in?"

He shot me a look. "*Right.* Mariana. She might know something. I'll call her right now." A few moments later he had her on the line. When he finished the call, he looked up. "She told me Olivia mentioned an older woman in McMinnville that Luis was seeing." He opened his hands and flashed a questioning smile. "*An older woman?* I didn't know anything about this. Anyway, she thinks he could be there. She'll have to do some digging to get a name and address."

"Good. I'd like to talk to Mariana face-to-face, too. Can you set something up?"

"Both of us?"

"Yeah, but I'll take the lead on questioning her."

"Sure, I'll call her back."

"And the bar Luis started hanging out in—I want to go there, see if anyone will talk to me. Maybe something happened there that he didn't tell you about."

"It's the Tequila Cantina on the Pacific Highway in Lafayette."

"I know the place. Good takeout, especially the fish tacos."

"That's the one. There're pool tables in the back." Timoteo paused for a moment. "I should go with you."

"Of course."

We agreed to go the following night.

I opened the envelope next and scanned the worker information. "So, we've got fourteen workers your father doesn't know or particularly trust." I pointed to the bottom of the page. "What about these last three names? There are no addresses listed."

"They were hired late in the season and never gave my father their addresses."

"Okay, let's see how many of the eleven we can find this afternoon."

"Excellent," he said, then hesitated for a moment. "How do you plan to approach them?"

"Straightforwardly. I'll ask about their work, then the key. Maybe one of them noticed something unusual. If they don't speak English, you'll translate."

Timoteo wrinkled his brow. "One of them might be in on it."

"True. He'll lie, then. Maybe we'll pick up the lie." I shrugged. "It's a long shot, Timoteo, but we have to start somewhere."

He scratched his cheek and looked hesitant again. "You, um, you should let me talk to them."

"Alone?"

"Yes. They won't even open the door, even if I'm with you. These days, undocumented people are being told not to answer the door if they're unsure who's knocking." He looked at me. "No offense, but they'll suspect you of being ICE because you're white."

I feigned a forehead whack with my palm. "Of course, I should have thought of that." I smiled. "How good are you at poker?"

He looked me straight in the eye. "I know the tells for people who bluff and lie, especially Latinos. I can handle this, Cal."

I had little doubt that he could. There was clearly more to my well-mannered assistant than met the eye.

The addresses of the first four workers on the sheet were crossed out. In the margin, Carlos had written in a single address.

Google maps took us to a small apartment complex in Newberg, near the Highway 18 bypass. U-shaped with a flat roof, clean and unadorned, the Woodbridge Apartments had a nearly full parking lot and an equally crowded play area teeming with small, energetic kids. Most of the attending mothers had their heads bent over their small screens. I parked away from the play area, wished Timoteo good luck, and waited with Archie.

A short time later, he slipped into the seat next to me. "They don't know anything."

"Tell me how it went."

He laughed. "It was chaotic—four guys packed into a two-bedroom apartment watching Mexican soccer and answering my questions."

"You believed them?"

"Yes. They're from Michoacán, good guys, the kind who send money back to their families every month. They said they had great respect for my father, called him a good *patrón*. They didn't even know about the key or where it was. The gate was open fairly often, but they didn't notice who handled the key or opened the gate while they were working."

"Okay. Four down, seven to go."

The next address Carlos had written in was for two men with the same last name, Guerrero. Victor and Paolo were probably brothers but didn't answer the door at a shabby, side-by-side duplex on the other side of Newberg. Of the next four on the list, two were home but neither one provided anything of interest.

The address for the seventh worker took us to a mobile home park just off the Pacific Highway past Dundee. We parked out on the street, and Timoteo walked in. Ten minutes later, a text pinged on my phone: join us. 4th on the right, a single wide.

"Cándido, this is Cal Claxton," Timoteo said as I stepped into the trailer, a small, cramped space, but clean and neat. After we shook hands, Timoteo said, "Cándido worked mainly in maintenance during the harvest, so he spent a fair amount of time in the barn tinkering with stuff." A thin young man with a wisp of a moustache and hollow, acne-pocked cheeks, Cándido nodded, indicating he understood some English. "Two days before, um, the shooting, he needed the key to let in a delivery truck, but it wasn't on the hook." He eyed Cándido. "You sent the truck through the main entrance, right?"

"Yes. And I get in trouble. *El patrón* is not happy. I tell him the key is gone, but when I go to show him, it is there again." His mouth formed an inverted U. "He did not believe me."

Timoteo looked at me. "That probably explains why my father didn't mention it."

"Do you know who had the key?" I asked.

"No. I am sorry. Any worker could have taken it," he said, glancing from me to Timoteo and back again.

Timoteo closed the space between them and said something in Spanish I didn't catch.

The young man opened his hands and shook his head. "This is all I know. Please. I do not want any trouble."

"Do you know how long the key was gone?" I asked.

He shrugged. "It was gone that morning. This is all I know."

"Could it have been gone overnight?"

He shrugged. "It is possible."

We both thanked Cándido, and without any prompting from me, Timoteo gave him a stern warning not to breathe a word of our discussion to anyone. The young man nodded with an earnest expression, and as we were leaving said to Timoteo, "I am very sorry about your sister. I see her several times at the vineyard. She is a beautiful girl. I am very sad about this."

At the car we took Archie for a short walk. Timoteo said, his voice excited, "What do you think?"

"I think you did a nice job of getting him to open up, and I think he's telling the truth."

Timoteo lifted his chin and broke into a broad smile. "Thanks."

We discussed the next steps and came up with a plan. I was impressed with my new assistant and felt good that we had our first lead. At the same time, a vague yet familiar feeling nagged at me, that sense that we were venturing out on a slope. Had I known just how steep and just how slippery it would become, I would've felt considerably less sanguine.

Chapter Twelve

"Give me a couple of hours to photoshop it," Timoteo said as he got into the family car back at my office. "I'll include as many as I can, but not all the vineyard workers show up." He was referring to the celebration that Angel Vineyard held every year at the completion of its grape harvest. We were hoping to utilize the group photo taken at the event to provide decent mug shots for all the workers who attended. The photo was posted on the vineyard's website. Privacy, after all, was a thing of the past.

Timoteo left, and Archie and I drove back to the Aerie so I could grab a late lunch—some smoked salmon mixed with a little mayo, crushed red pepper, and lemon juice spread on toasted Dave's Killer Bread. Archie was off somewhere patrolling the property, and I was out on the porch, facing south toward the valley, so Zoe's voice surprised me.

"Ever get tired of this view?"

I turned to face her. "Nope. Never. It's constantly changing. The fall colors are my favorite."

Her hair was up, and she wore tie-dyed jogging shorts and a faded blue sweatshirt that accentuated the color of her eyes. "I was out jogging, and I saw your car pull in. I have to take Gertie to the hospital tomorrow. Wondering if you could give me a hand with getting her into the car? I had a heck of a time when I brought her from the hospital."

I told her I could, then asked, "How did the salmon turn out?"

I think she actually blushed. "Oh, God, it was a disaster. The plank started smoldering about halfway through, then burst into flames." Her eyes got huge and she giggled, giving me a glimpse of what she was like as little girl. "It turned out to be salmon flambé."

After I stopped laughing, I said, "The barbeque was too hot. You have to cook *slowly* on a plank."

She looked at me with a sheepish expression, then smiled. "You did tell me that, didn't you. Well, I'm a klutz in the kitchen, but Gertie was a good sport about it." She paused and changed the subject. "How are you feeling about the case?"

"Is this a therapy session?" I said, smiling.

"Yes, it is," she answered, holding the smile. "Frequent doctor-patient contact is beneficial."

I described the lead we'd uncovered and how Timoteo and I planned to follow up. We kicked it around for a while before she said, "How about you? Still on the mend?"

"A little each day. It's, uh, hard to reconcile, you know? The absolute horror of it. Sometimes the scene just rushes back, unbidden. It was something that never should have happened."

She leveled her eyes at me. "Don't underestimate the trauma you've suffered, Cal. When it rushes back, let it. Don't bottle it up." With that, she turned to go, saying over her shoulder, "See you tomorrow at eight thirty."

"There were nineteen workers at the harvest feast. I printed out a headshot for each of them," Timoteo said an hour later, as he handed me a stack of photographs. "The resolution's not great, but it was the best I could do."

"These might work," I said after leafing through the stack. "There are two twenty-four-hour locksmiths in the area, one in McMinnville and one in Wilsonville. It's a Sunday, but they do house calls." The McMinnville shop was closer. I called that number first, reached the technician on call, and explained what I needed.

"Nope, I didn't copy no keys the night of the twenty-second," he said when he came back on the line. "Didn't make one service call that night. Real quiet."

I called the Wilsonville locksmith next. "The twenty-second? Hang on," he said. After a short pause: "I did duplicate one, as a matter of fact."

"What kind?"

"A key to a Master padlock."

I had my phone on speaker mode. Timoteo thrust a fist up. "Do you remember the person you did this for?" The line went quiet again. "I understand your hesitation," I said, quickly filling the void. "I'm conducting an investigation, and this information is vital."

"I don't know, I—"

"I just need you to look at some pictures, see if you can pick him out. I'll come to you or pay you for a service call. There'll be a tip in it for you, too."

He agreed.

We met the locksmith at the Coffee Cottage in Newberg twenty-five minutes later. A young man wearing a Seahawks ball cap, extravagant tattoos on both forearms, and thick-lensed glasses. "Nah, I don't think so," he said after carefully going through the stack. "He was Mexican like these dudes, but I don't know, his face was kind of narrow, he had a long neck, and his eyebrows were real bushy."

I felt a sharp pang of disappointment. "You're sure? This is important."

He handed the photos back to me. "Yeah, I'm sure. I'm good with faces. What'd he do?"

"Nothing. We just want to talk to him," I said. "Where did you duplicate the key?"

"In the parking lot of the Dundee Hotel. I can make a duplicate in a couple of minutes in my van."

"Was he with anyone?"

"Nah, I don't think so, but as I was pulling out, another dude came in on a motorcycle. The Mexican went over to him."

"Did he give the key to that person?"

The locksmith shrugged. "It was dusk. He handed him something. I'm pretty sure it was the key."

"Did you get a look at the guy on the motorcycle?"

"Uh-uh. He had on a helmet with a tinted visor."

"Tall, short, fat?"

He looked me over. "Maybe your height or a little taller, but skinny."

"White, Latino?"

He shrugged.

"Age?"

He opened his hands. "I don't know. Thirty or forty, maybe."

"What kind of bike?"

"Kawasaki. Black. That I'm sure of."

I asked a few more questions, but that was the extent of the information. We got the locksmith's name and cell phone number, paid for a service call, and gave him fifty bucks cash. He looked a little disappointed but didn't say anything.

Timoteo got back into the car and slouched down in the seat, looking crushed.

"Hey," I said, "don't be disappointed. Chances are, whoever

had the key made was a go-between, so the guy on the Kawasaki might have been the shooter. We now know someone else was probably involved, someone who rides a black motorcycle. That's worth the effort and then some."

Looking straight ahead, he said, "Yeah, but whoever had the key made would know who this guy is."

"Maybe. You said not everyone attended the harvest feast. Could your father make a list of the missing persons?"

Timoteo sat up a little straighter. "Sure. I'll get that right away."

As I pulled in next to Timoteo's car in the lot behind my office, I said, "How's your mother?"

He turned to face me, his eyes suddenly bright with a film of moisture. "Horrible. She still won't come out of her room, won't talk, doesn't want to eat." He shook his head. "I don't think she's even bathed since the funeral."

I felt a stab of guilt for broaching the subject, but Zoe's comments were fresh in my mind. "I'm sorry to hear that. I talked briefly to a psychologist about your mother. She said it's vital that you try to draw her out of her room, engage her in conversation, and remind her that Olivia would not want her to react like this."

Timoteo swiped a tear with the palm of his hand. "Thanks. That's good advice." He sighed and blinked rapidly to stanch any further tears. "There's something going on between her and my father, too. Something weird. They're avoiding each other at the time they need each other the most."

I wanted to explain the situation, but, of course, I was sworn to secrecy by Carlos. "Give it some time, Timoteo," I said, finally. "Meanwhile, let's catch the bastard who did this."

Chapter Thirteen

"Intel on the cartels? A tricky subject," Nando Mendoza said in response to my question. It was Monday, midmorning, and my PI and I were in my Dundee office discussing the Olivia Fuentes case. Nando had stopped by on his way down to the Spirit Mountain Casino to meet with its security head about a potential contract. "The cartels have crossed the border and have strong, reliable ties here, the kind that big money can buy. It is hard to know who to trust these days."

"If they tried to assassinate a runaway member, wouldn't there be some chatter in their circles about it?"

He paused and stroked the dark stubble on his chin with thick fingers. The Rolex on his wrist glittered in the overhead lights. "Ordinarily, yes. However, in this case they may have killed the wrong person. Perhaps they would not wish to brag about that."

"Can you at least put your ear to the ground, see what's out there?"

"Of course. I have one contact in L.A. who might know something. Also, I know a private investigator in Mexico City I can trust. I will speak to them both."

"There's one other item," I said, explaining that a man named

Darrell Benedict had gotten into a fight with Luis Fuentes a year earlier. "Luis was arrested but not prosecuted." I handed Nando a copy of the police report and asked him to get a line on the guy.

He glanced at the report and furrowed his brow. "This is a lot of work, Calvin. Is your new client good for it?"

Despite an effort, my smile probably looked sheepish. "Well, I'm giving them a discount, and I was, uh, hoping you could do the same."

A mock offended look. "Why would I do that?"

I rolled my eyes. "Come on, Nando, don't forget where you came from. They're immigrants just like you were when you arrived from Cuba. The only difference is you had a lot of help from the Cuban community in Miami. They've had nothing but their bootstraps."

He held my gaze for a few moments. "Okay, I will bill any searches at my cost and charge one hundred dollars an hour for my time."

"Agreed. Thank you."

A thin smile. "I should have known. You are such a pushover, my friend." I started to respond, but he wisely cut me off. "How is Gertrude?"

"I saw her this morning, helped her niece load her in the car for a checkup. She looks good. She's getting her mojo back."

He smiled, an incandescent flash that lit the room. He was as fond of my accountant as I was. "That is good news. Please give her my best." His look turned mischievous. "I was as concerned about you, my friend, as I was about her. I am thinking you might go broke without her."

"Well, you've got Esperanza to keep you out of trouble, don't forget." I was referring to his highly competent office manager and one of Archie's favorite humans on the planet. Before my friend could counter, I nodded toward his left shoulder, where he'd taken a small-caliber round six months earlier. "How's the shoulder?"

He raised his left arm partway, grimacing slightly. "I am making progress. And I am back to salsa dancing. I have had to modify some of my best moves, but I'm out there."

"Good. I'm sure Portland's salsa scene wasn't the same without you," I said in jest, but it was undoubtedly true. My Cuban friend sported a personality as large as his passion for dancing.

———

Early that afternoon, Timoteo called between classes to tell me his father had already identified the vineyard workers missing from the photo. "There were three of them," he explained. "Two have left for Washington to catch the end of the apple harvest, and one's still around here. He, um, told me he was going to talk to the guy in Dundee—"

"*No,*" I said. "That's not a good idea. Call him right now. Tell him we'll handle it, that we just need the address."

"Okay, but it may be too late. He was pretty worked up. He said he was going to Washington, too, and talk to the other two."

I exhaled a breath in frustration. "Tell him to call me before he does anything, okay?"

"Will do." Timoteo paused. "Are we still on for the Tequila Cantina tonight?"

"Eight thirty," I replied.

———

I planned to sneak out early that afternoon, hoping to clock some time on my rock wall, but my phone rang just as I was locking up. I groaned internally when Ned Gillian announced himself, admonished me for not calling him back, and told me he wanted to talk about the Chihuahua.

"Although Nathan purchased the dog, he's willing to compromise," Gillian said. "He's willing to share custody of Cha Cha with Veronica."

"He gave her the dog as a birthday present."

"So Veronica says. I have the credit card receipt to prove who purchased the dog." He exhaled noisily. "All he's asking for is alternate weekends and holidays. Simple as that."

A tired sigh escaped my lips. "Look, Ned, Veronica wants a clean break. She thinks this dog thing is just Nathan trying to hang on. I feel for the guy, but she's not going to give on this."

The line went quiet for a long time. "Jesus Christ," he said finally, "I'm a defense lawyer. I took this case as a favor. He's an old friend. I love him, but he needs a shrink, not a lawyer."

I knew Ned Gillian only by reputation as a top-notch attorney for those who could afford him, but I felt an immediate kinship. An acrimonious divorce put the worst of human nature on display, and we lawyers were guaranteed a front row seat. "Look on the bright side, Ned. We could be fighting over a couple of kids."

He sighed heavily into the phone. I pictured a sardonic smile forming on his face. "A fucking Chihuahua."

"Okay, I'll take this back to Veronica," I said, "Stay tuned."

"Thanks, Cal. I appreciate that."

"Look at it this way, Veronica," I said after I reached my client on the phone a few minutes later, "If you don't want to lose Cha Cha, you're going to have to make them an offer."

"Like what?" she snapped in a tone laced with petulance.

"A weekend a month. I think they'll take it."

"God, I want this over with. Okay, a weekend a month, but I get to choose which one. And, Cal, tell them that's my first and final offer."

I told her I'd take this back to Gillian, but he didn't pick up when I called. I left him a message. By the time I locked up the office and Arch had hopped into the back seat of the car, the afternoon light was dying fast. Although bummed at having missed an opportunity to work on my wall, a blazing sunset out over the Coast Range buoyed me as we climbed into the Red Hills.

At the gate to the Aerie, I got a call. "Cal? It is Carlos Fuentes. Timoteo told me to call you." When I inquired about his whereabouts, he went on, sounding apologetic. "I have already visited the man missing from the feast who lives here. His name is Plácido Ballesteros."

"And?"

"He claims to know nothing about the key."

"Do you believe him?"

The line went silent for several moments. "Some men are good at lying, even if they swear by the cross."

"Is he one of them?"

I waited through another pause. "I am not sure, but he would have a good reason to lie to me."

"What is the reason?"

"If he was involved in my daughter's death, he knows I will crush his neck with my bare hands."

"I see. I don't blame you for feeling that way, Carlos, but such an action would only make things much, much worse for you and your family."

When he didn't respond, I said, "Can you locate the two workers who went to Washington?"

"Yes, I think so. I have a friend there who can help me find them."

"Good. When you find them, you must not contact them yourself. Let me know so we can decide how to proceed. Is that agreeable? I need your word on this."

"Yes. I will speak to you first. You have my word."

"One other thing, Carlos. I have an investigator who has good contacts in Mexico. Have Timoteo text me all the information you have on these three men, their full names, birth dates, where they came from, and anything else that is known about them. I will ask him to see what he can learn about their backgrounds."

After we disconnected, I sat in my car at the gate with the motor idling. Night had fallen, and a light mist flickered in the shafts of the headlights that shone out over the field. Archie, sensing my mood, stuck his head between the seats and nudged at my elbow. I sighed and absently scratched him behind his ears. My blood had risen at Carlos's comment about garroting someone involved in his daughter's death, a reaction that made me cringe, but at the same time I could feel his pent-up rage. The law says only the state can exact revenge, not the individual. Yet, I could well imagine how I would feel in this man's shoes.

How far would I go if it were my daughter?

Chapter Fourteen

"Not a black Kawasaki to be seen," Timoteo said as we pulled into a parking space at the Tequila Cantina after making a complete circuit of the lot. As we exited the car, a man about Timoteo's age cruised in on a motorcycle, parked next to a couple of other bikes, and walked into the cantina ahead of us. Timoteo shook his head. "Metallic blue might be mistaken for black, but that's a Honda, not a Kawasaki. No way you mix those two up."

"If you say so," I quipped. "Could've fooled me."

He laughed. "Maybe, but the locksmith was definite about the make."

The cantina was buzzing with a crowd at the bar and a few late diners sitting at a line of tables along an opposite wall. Travel posters for destinations in Mexico decorated the space above the diners, and a rich female voice sang in Spanish against an acoustic guitar on the sound system. As we approached an arched doorway leading to a back room, we could hear the clink of pool balls above laughter and animated Spanish. I entered the space first, and a hush fell as a dozen sets of eyes swiveled in my direction, including those of the man we'd just seen.

Timoteo stepped up next to me. "*Hola, amigos*," he said and began to explain in Spanish that we weren't with ICE, that we wanted to ask a few questions about someone who's been coming here. *"Se llama Luis Fuentes. Es mi hermano."*

"If he's your brother, why don't you ask *him*?" a man sitting at a round table in the corner with two others replied in English. A smattering of titters broke out in the room.

"He's away," Timoteo said flatly with a hard look I hadn't seen before.

I walked across the room, smiled cordially, and stuck my hand out to the man. "I'm Cal Claxton." Timoteo followed me.

"Diego," the man said, leaving off his last name. He casually closed a laptop on the table in front of him, and without getting up, shook our hands with an indifferent grip. The two men with him got up and moved to the side. Maybe a decade older than the twentysomethings around him, Diego was compact with sloped shoulders and thick forearms. He showed a thin smile below dark, hooded eyes. "We haven't seen Luis for a while. He's not a bad pool player."

"Are some of you friends with Luis?" I asked, scanning the room for a reaction.

"He liked to play pool, that's all," Diego answered in a tone that made it clear he spoke for the group. To a man, they dropped their eyes.

I persisted. "Did he have any trouble here? You know, fights or arguments with anyone at the cantina?"

"*Nada.* We're just one big happy family." Diego's smile remained, but his hooded eyes had gone unfriendly.

Timoteo stepped forward and cleared his throat, but I extended a restraining arm, took a card from my wallet, and tossed it on the table. "Okay, then. If you think of something, give us a call."

We turned to leave, but Timoteo stopped and glared at the

assembled group. *"¿Por que este hombre habla por tu? Eres ovejas,"* he said, then added as we walked away, *"Baa, baa."*

When we cleared the room, I said, *"Ovejas* means sheep, right?"

"That's right. I told those *pendejos* they were a bunch of sheep."

I had to chuckle. Timoteo may have been a Dreamer, but he had a tough side, too.

We spent another five minutes in the front end of the cantina talking to the bartender, who had wrist-to-armpit tattoos, and a waitress who had mastered the art of looking bored. When Timoteo showed them a picture of Luis, they both recognized him but could tell us nothing else, except that he drank a lot of beer. "What do they do in there besides play pool and drink?" he asked.

The bartenders face turned blank. The waitress shrugged. "I don't know. They come in a couple of times a week. It's sorta like a club or something. Shitty tippers, all of 'em."

"What's Diego's last name, the big guy?" I asked.

"Vargas," the waitress answered. That was all we got, so we left.

"Oh, shit," I said as we approached my car. The right rear tire was completely flat with something protruding from it. As Timoteo stood by, I knelt down, gripped a handle wrapped in duct tape, and extracted a flat piece of steel ground to a point and with a wicked edge. I held it up. "A shiv."

"Those bastards," Timoteo said. "That guy on the Honda knew this was our car. Let's go back in."

I shook my head. "Let's not. I like your moxie but not the odds. Give me a hand. Let's change this tire and get the hell out of here." We had the spare on in a couple of minutes, and as we pulled away, Timoteo said, "I'm sorry, Cal. That was my fault. I shouldn't have taunted those guys."

"That probably wasn't the wisest move, but we might've gotten that shiv regardless of what you said."

"You mean it was a warning not to come around asking questions?"

"Could've been. And a prison knife underscores the point."

Timoteo smiled with half his mouth. "I didn't see any prison tats in there. With the possible exception of Diego, those guys are wannabes."

Impressed with his insight, I said, "What else did you learn?"

"Besides not to pick a fight when I'm outnumbered?" He exhaled and crossed his arms. "Diego's the *jefe*, of course. He ordered that flat tire for whatever reason. It's weird—they're not a gang, and they're sure as hell not a club. But, there's something more there than just hanging out for a friendly game of pool."

"I agree. Did you notice that he closed his laptop when we approached?"

"Yeah. What's up with that? After he closed it and shook hands, he laid a forearm on it."

"Right. A subconscious protective move. What about Luis? Why do you think he started hanging out there in the first place?"

"It's hard to get my head around that. Luis is disaffected like those guys, so they have that in common. But Luis has always been a loner. I can't see him getting involved with whatever's going on there. It just doesn't compute."

We drove on in silence for a while. The mist had turned to rain, forcing me to switch on the windshield wipers. I had to agree. Things didn't compute, at least not yet. But, if Diego Vargas thought flattening my tire with a prison shiv would frighten me away, he had badly miscalculated. And now I knew that my new assistant was no shrinking violet, either, a thought that raised a smile in the dim light of the car. What the hell's going on in the back room of the Tequila Cantina, and does it have anything to with the murder of Olivia Fuentes?

Those were questions needing answers.

Chapter Fifteen

Carlos Fuentes sat at his kitchen table with a bottle of pulque in front of him. Timoteo and I had just arrived from the cantina, and I agreed to say hello to his father. When I saw him, I knew why his son insisted I come in. With a thick gray stubble and dark half-moons beneath his eyes, he seemed to have aged a decade. The transformation was unsettling. He raised his eyes and forced a smile. "*Hola*, Cal. Please, sit and have a drink." I took a seat and Timoteo got me a glass. Carlos poured me some of the white liquid, we clinked glasses, and I took a sip. The liquid was thick, sour, and yeasty, and I had an urge to spit it out. He looked from his son to me. "Did you learn anything tonight?"

I turned to Timoteo, who took the cue and described the events, putting the best face he could on them. "So, we didn't hear that Luis had had any trouble there, or made any enemies, but they didn't like us asking questions," he concluded and then described the flat tire incident.

Carlos sipped his pulque. He'd been drinking, but he wasn't drunk. "Luis has problems, but he wouldn't waste time on *cabróns* like that. He must have had a reason to go there." He grimaced as if holding back tears. "I wish he would come home to us."

Timoteo patted his father's shoulder with tenderness. "He will, Papi, he will."

I said, "Anything new on the men who went to Washington?"

Carlos shook his head. "My friend in the Wenatchee Valley is still looking for them." He took another sip. "I have learned that Plácido Ballesteros is from El Tecuan, a city south of Guadalajara. It is not that far from where I grew up."

I set my glass down, and Timoteo leaned forward in his chair. "Could he be cartel?"

Carlos shrugged. "Many workers come from the state of Jalisco, so it is proof of nothing. Now that I know what city he is from, I can ask more questions. He arrived just before the grape harvest with the two men who have gone to Washington to pick apples."

"He could be the killer," Timoteo said, his face lit with a mix of hope and rage.

Carlos sighed and turned to me with a look of resignation. "We shall see, won't we?"

I shot a warning look at Timoteo. "Let's not get ahead of ourselves. It's too early to make any judgments." He nodded and his chin dropped. There wasn't much else to say. I got up to leave.

Timoteo said, "Wait a moment, Cal. Let me see if Mamá wishes to say hello." He went down the hall, and I heard a muffled exchange in Spanish, but the word "no" is common to both languages. "She, um, is too tired right now," he said when he reappeared. As he walked me to my car, he said, "I knew she wouldn't come out, but I wanted to shame her, anything to get her out of that damn room. In our family, a visitor is *always* welcomed by Mamá, usually with food in hand." He heaved a sigh. "She's getting worse, Cal, not better."

"Have you thought about getting professional help?"

A bitter laugh. "That's not going to happen. You don't know my mother."

———

Archie was waiting on the front porch when I arrived at the Aerie. I felt agitated and decided to walk it off. It had stopped raining, and a lopsided moon appeared through a thin gauze of clouds. We hadn't gotten far before Archie stopped dead, his ears came up, and he dashed across the field, disappearing into the darkness. I heard a commotion, and he began to bark. I called after him. He was probably chasing either deer or coyotes, but I worried about a cougar, the one animal in the Red Hills capable of harming him. "Archie," I called out again, "come here, boy."

"He's right here," a voice called back. It was the voice of Zoe Bennett. I walked across the field and joined them. "He just scared the hell out of two deer. I was taking the garbage to the compost bin when I caught a glimpse of the encounter. Archie's quick, but the deer are quicker."

"He knows he can't catch them. It's pure sport for him."

She laughed and moved into the light of a solar lamp on the gatepost. She wore a blue scarf around her head, and the soft light lit one side of her face, illuminating a pearl earring.

"You'd make a good model for Vermeer," I said.

She looked puzzled for a moment, then laughed again as she touched one of the earrings. "Oh, these. They are pearl, you know. I opened another 2012 Le Petit Truc tonight. Want some?"

"Does Gertie know about this?" I said with mock seriousness.

"No. And if you tell, you won't get any." Her eyes got big, and she covered a big smile with her hand. "Oh, God, that came out wrong."

I gave her a teasing look. "Freud lives."

"Oh, shut up." We both laughed, and she regained her composure. "Actually, Gertie asked me to open it tonight and insisted on half a glass with her dinner."

"That's a good sign."

She exhaled in frustration. "The truth is she overdid it yesterday and had quite a bit of pain last night. Today was a lot better. She's sleeping now."

I left Archie on the porch with a firm command to stay and followed her into the kitchen. She poured our wine, and we sat across from each other at Gertie's kitchen table. After clinking glasses—me for the second time that night—she studied me for a few moments. "Something's up, Cal. I can see it in your eyes. Want to talk about it?"

"Are we on the clock?"

"Of course."

I drank some of my pinot. "This beats pulque all to hell," I began and then went on to unpack the recent events.

"You've made good progress," Zoe said when I finished. "The killer was the guy on the motorcycle, then?"

"Possibly."

Zoe sighed. "Sent by someone from Carlos's past? Is that still a possibility?"

I shrugged. "That hasn't been ruled out."

She shook her head and closed her eyes for a moment. "God, the guilt, if that's the case. I can't imagine."

I traced a scratch on the table with a finger and blew a breath out. "Yeah, it could be a ticking time bomb for the family, what's left of it."

Zoe sipped her wine and looked at me for a moment over the rim of her glass. "Truth will out, Cal."

"I know. That's more or less what I told Carlos."

"Maybe the mother will find it in her heart to forgive him, if it comes to that."

"Maybe."

"What about the police? When do you bring them in?"

"Good question. I think I'll wait until Carlos finds the two workers in Washington, then decide how to handle it."

"How's the mother doing?"

"Getting worse, according to Timoteo."

Zoe's brows lowered, and a couple of vertical creases formed on her forehead above her nose. "I was afraid of that. I, ah, did a little research. There's a Spanish-speaking grief counselor in Salem. I checked him out. I can give you his number."

"That was thoughtful. Thanks. I told Timoteo they should get help, but he doesn't think Elena would ever agree. I'll pass this on, though."

She paused and regarded me. "What about you, Cal?"

I blew out another breath. "I'm okay. Scenes from that night come back at odd times, and I dreamed about it last night." I stopped there, realizing I'd probably said too much.

She kept her eyes on me. "Want to talk about that?"

It was a reasonable request but complying would require admitting that the death of Olivia Fuentes had resurrected the ghost of my deceased wife. That wasn't a place I wanted to go. I forced a smile. "It's fine. I, uh, just need a little time."

She smiled, a tease tinged with a hint of sarcasm. "The strong, silent types have gone out of fashion, you know."

I smiled back in equal measure. "I guess I didn't get the memo."

———

I had another dream that night, more vivid than the last one. This time my wife was wearing the hooded sweatshirt. I must have screamed, because when I awakened, Archie stood whimpering next to the bed with deep concern showing in his eyes.

I thought of Zoe's borderline sarcastic remark and felt a surge of irritation. Talking's overrated, I told myself in full defensive mode. Some things you just have to live with.

Chapter Sixteen

"I don't suppose you've got anything yet?" I asked Nando the next morning as I sipped a coffee from the Red Hills Market.

His laugh boomed through the phone. "I am good, Calvin, but not that good."

"That's not the reason I called. I've got three more names I'd like your source in Mexico City to check out, if possible. I need to know if any of them have cartel connections."

Nando paused before answering. "This source is touchy, especially when it comes to cartel business. Is there one of these three you are most interested in? I think it is wise to ask for only one additional favor."

I exhaled a breath and gave him Plácido Ballesteros's information, adding, "El Tecuan is near Guadalajara, where Carlos Fuentes grew up."

"Interesting."

I explained what Timoteo and I had learned about the key to the locked gate at Angel Vineyard, and how Carlos had already approached Ballesteros. "I don't like him as the hit man, but I can't rule him out as an accomplice."

"I see your point," Nando responded. "Why would Ballesteros

have the key copied if he was the shooter? He would have just used it and put it back."

"Exactly. But I still want everything your source can find on him."

———

Timoteo arrived at the office shortly after one that afternoon and promptly started in on what remained of the filing. I was on the phone with Ned Gillian about the fate of Cha Cha the Chihuahua. "That's my client's final offer," I told him, "I'm afraid it's take it or leave it."

Gillian's response was immediate, his tone grateful. "I think I can sell this. It's not about the damn dog, of course." He paused. "Ah, this is off topic, but do you mind if I ask you something, Cal?"

"Shoot."

"I know your sleuthing reputation, but I also understand you have a pro bono practice in Portland. How does that work, and is it satisfying to you?"

I gave him a helicopter view of my practice at Caffeine Central and finished by saying, "It's frustrating as hell at times. Some of my clients don't show up for court dates, or they get busted or start using again, that kind of thing, but I wouldn't trade the practice for anything."

"Yeah, I can see why you'd say that. I, ah, I've been too busy trying to make money in my practice, but when I look around these days, I feel like I need to give something back. There's so much inequity in the fucking system."

We discussed the status of the criminal justice system for a while and came up with a couple of pro bono possibilities for him, of which there were many, of course. "If I can help you get started in any way, just pick up the phone," I told him in closing.

I had no sooner disconnected when Timoteo's cell phone chirped. He looked up at me after a brief exchange. "It's Mariana Suarez, Olivia's friend. She just got out of class and can meet us for a coffee. She's at a Starbucks on 99W south of McMinnville."

Archie took the back seat, and Timoteo rode shotgun. On the way there, Timoteo said, "Mariana's a Dreamer like me. She's studying to be a journalist." He smiled. "I think she'll make a good one."

"How so?"

"She doesn't put up with bullshit, and she's fearless, like Olivia." I glanced over and saw his face darken. "Her family's been through a rough patch."

"What happened?"

"A family friend saw her uncle's car abandoned on the side of 99E during that big ICE raid in Woodburn. Agents had pulled him over and arrested him on the spot, handcuffs, the whole bit. The next time the family heard from him, he was in the Northwest Detention Center in Tacoma. It turned out ICE was looking for another Jesús Hernandez, who had an outstanding warrant, but once they had her uncle, it didn't matter. He's awaiting a deportation hearing. They call it collateral deportation."

"How's he holding up?"

"Terrible. He's hardly eating and doesn't sleep. It's tearing the family to pieces. He's an expert in hazelnut cultivation, and the grower he works for is desperate to get him back." Timoteo shook his head in disgust. "It really sucks. Migrants were encouraged to come here over the years, and now we're under attack. *For what?* Working hard and seeking a better life? Sure, laws were broken, but the laws were *ignored* for the sake of profits. It's unjust, and it doesn't make any sense."

Timoteo was right. It made no sense.

We arrived at the Starbucks in fifteen minutes. Archie

dutifully stayed in the car with the windows cracked. The place was filled with a youngish crowd—mostly students from the nearby Chemeketa Community College, I assumed. Tim waved to Mariana, who was seated near the back frowning at her laptop. We got our coffees, joined her, and after introducing me, Timoteo said, "Like I mentioned on the phone, our family has hired Cal to, um, look into the murder. I'm assisting him. Thanks for taking the time to answer some questions, Mariana."

Her eyes grew wet, and her chin trembled slightly. "Oh, damn it," she said, dabbing her eyes with a napkin. "I can't think about what happened without losing it." Even in sadness her face was lovely, her big, almond eyes expressive and golden brown in color. "I called because I finally found the name of Luis's new girlfriend, Marlene Mathews. She works at the same restaurant Luis did, the Wine Cellar. She's, like, thirty or thirty-five." Mariana shot Timoteo a sly smile. "An older woman. Who knew?"

I suppressed a laugh. "That's helpful. We should be able to locate her." I paused for a moment, shifting the focus from Luis to Olivia. "I know you've probably spoken to the police at length, but I have a few questions, if you wouldn't mind."

She grimaced. "Okay."

"What was going on with Olivia before the shooting? Anything out of the ordinary?"

"The detectives asked me the same question. Only two things I could think of. First, there was a guy at Prosperar she was interested in, but it was early, you know. They were just circling each other."

"His name?"

"Robert Harris."

"What's he do there?"

"He's their finance guy, I think. Keeps track of the money, donations, that kind of thing."

"Why was this unusual?"

Mariana shrugged. "I don't know, she just didn't seem into the guy, no enthusiasm. I tried to get her to tell me about him, but she was kind of evasive." She paused, and her gaze moved outside our table as if reeling in a memory. "The other thing was kind of weird. She was excited and secretive about something. I asked her what it was, and she said she wasn't sure yet, that she was working on it and would tell me when she knew more. I said, 'Girl, since when do you keep secrets from me?' She laughed and said, 'If I told you now I'd have to kill you.' I pressed her some more, but that's as much as she would tell me."

"When did she disclose this?"

"Oh, it was maybe three or four weeks before…" Her voice trailed off.

"What were you talking about when this came up?"

She brought a finger to her lips for a moment, then showed a faint smile. "I was blowing off steam about my job at the newspaper. I want my boss to give me more responsibility."

"Was she doing the same, talking about something at Prosperar?"

"Maybe. That's what I told the cops, anyway." She pursed her lips, hesitating again. "I felt bad about that. Prosperar's not going to be happy about a bunch of cops showing up, even if they're friendlies from Dundee." She looked at Timoteo. "You were smart to hire Mr. Claxton. Those detectives aren't going to get far in this screwed-up atmosphere. Nobody's going to tell them shit."

Timoteo nodded with a smirk.

I took Mariana through some more questions, but that was the gist of what we learned that day. Before we left, I said, "Timoteo tells me you want to be a journalist."

A smile bloomed on her face. "Yeah. I know it's like taking a vow of poverty, but that's what I want to do. I work part-time at the *News-Register* reporting dumb stuff like car thefts and lost dogs." The muscles along her jawline flexed. "But, when I get my degree, I want to become an investigative reporter, uncover bad shit, tell people the truth about what's going on."

"Good," I said. "We need journalists with the courage to do that."

When we got to the car, Timoteo was immediately on his phone. "Damn," he said a few moments later, "there's a Marlene Mathews in Ashland, but no one's listed by that name in this area. The White Pages suck."

I put a call through to Nando Mendoza. Esperanza answered, and I explained what we were looking for. She promised to get back to me ASAP.

As I pulled into the entrance to Angel Vineyard to drop off Timoteo, we saw Carlos Fuentes with a group of workers who were exiting the field to our left. He moved slowly and was slightly stooped, as if carrying some invisible load.

I slowed down and lowered the window. "The grapes are in, but your work doesn't end, I see."

He showed a thin smile. "A vineyard waits for no man." He looked at Timoteo and back at me. "Did my son earn his salary today?"

"Always," I said.

Timoteo asked, "Who's with Mamá?"

"Mrs. Angel." To me, Carlos added, "Such good people. They have been a blessing." He leveled his eyes at me. "It looks like the two men who left did not go to Wenatchee." He frowned. "It will take more time to find them, I am afraid."

"Let me know the moment you hear."

When I pulled into the Fuentes's driveway, I fished a card from my wallet and handed it to Timoteo. "This is the contact info for a grief counselor in Salem. A friend who's a clinical psychologist checked him out. He's Latino, good reputation, fluent in Spanish. You should give him a call."

He thanked me and took the card. "Yesterday, Mamá told Father Mallory she didn't want him to come anymore. I don't think a male counselor would get anywhere, but I'll try." He looked at me, his eyes suddenly etched in pain and anxiety. "If she abandons her faith, I'm afraid she might try to harm herself, Cal."

"Call the guy, talk to him. He might have some suggestions."

———

Instead of heading to the Aerie, I drove back to the spot above the vineyard on Buena Vista Drive where I thought the shooter parked the night of the murder. A mailbox marked the driveway of the old Victorian mansion I'd noticed earlier. With faded paint and overgrown foundation plantings, the house had obviously been there long before anyone thought of planting grapes on these rolling hills. A gravel drive led up to a rusted, gated fence. I stopped near the gate, and when I got out, a sixty-pound pit bull bounded off the porch to challenge me. His barking set Archie off, and I was treated to an earsplitting dog duet.

The front door swung open, and an elderly woman with snow-white hair came out, aided by a cane. "Sugar, hush," she growled. The dog obeyed her, and Archie followed suit. She glared at me for a moment. "You don't look like a real estate man, but if you are, I don't want to sell this property."

I smiled and showed my palms. "I'm not in real estate. How many acres you got here?"

"Twenty-five. Been in the family since the 1880s. What do you want then?"

"I assume you heard what happened at Angel Vineyard."

She recoiled at my words. "I already talked to a lady detective about that. Horrible thing. Just horrible. You with the police?"

"No. I'm an attorney working for the Fuentes family. I—"

"Well, I already told that detective I didn't see or hear anything that night."

"No cars or anyone on foot?"

"On foot? It was raining hard that night." She cocked her head. "Well, there was that damn fool on a motorbike."

"A motorbike?"

"Yep. Buzzed by here twice."

"What time was that?"

"Around six, I'd say."

"Did you tell the detective about that?"

"Nope. Thought of it just now. Should've, I guess."

"Did you get a look at the driver?"

"No. Just heard him and caught a glimpse as he went by the second time. It wasn't real loud, you know? That's why I forgot, I guess."

I thanked the woman and backed down the drive while Sugar the pit bull looked on. I thought about calling Darci Tate but decided to wait. I wasn't anxious to admit I was investigating a case she was working on. We were friends and all, but I didn't know how she would take the news.

As I pulled back out on Buena Vista, I had that feeling of satisfaction when two bits of information come together to form a solid lead. I now knew it was highly probable that the man I was looking for—the man who murdered Olivia Fuentes in cold blood—was skinny, about my height, and drove a black Kawasaki motorcycle.

It wasn't much, but it boosted my spirits.

Chapter Seventeen

The specters of my wife and Olivia Fuentes stayed in the shadows of my subconscious that night, and as a result, I woke up feeling pretty good. Archie and I were nearly to the cemetery on a jog when my phone sounded. I stopped, and when my dog pulled up, he looked back and gave me the stink eye. I opened my hands in a pleading gesture. "Come on, you know I have to take this." I caught my breath and glanced at the screen. "Top of the morning, Esperanza."

"Hello, Cal. I found an address for Marlene Mathews in McMinnville."

I recorded it on my phone and thanked her. "I hear Nando's back salsa dancing."

Her voice brightened, and I pictured a smile forming on her face. She was fond of her boss and watched over him like a mother hen. "Would you believe his new partner is his physical therapist?" Esperanza chuckled. "She was a complete novice but very coordinated and *very* beautiful. I watched them the other night. Nando's an excellent teacher."

Timoteo was in class that day, and I was looking at an unscheduled morning. A drive by Marlene Mathews's place wouldn't hurt, I decided. Maybe I could confirm she lived there, and if I got lucky, see some sign that Luis Fuentes was there as well. The sun broke through after a light drizzle just before I got to the Route 18 turnoff on the Pacific Highway. Ten minutes later I passed her house, a turquoise bungalow at the south end of McMinnville with an attached double garage and a sagging, moss-laden roof. A weathered Prius sat in the driveway.

I parked a half block down and watched in the rearview mirror for some sign of life. I didn't have long to wait—not more than ten minutes later, a thin blond woman came out the front door, followed by a small dog and a man I recognized immediately as Luis.

Bingo.

They started down the street, the dog in tow. I got out, hesitated for a moment before leashing up Archie. Having my dog along might soften the encounter, I figured. I followed them to Thompson Park, a small green space edged with deciduous trees. Arch and I kept our distance as they made a lap around the park and when they stopped at a water fountain, I made my move.

"Hello, Luis. Remember me?"

They both turned to face me as the two dogs met between us in a tense encounter. Luis's eyes flared slightly before recognition kicked in. "At the *velorio*. You're the attorney Timoteo works for."

"Yes. Cal Claxton. Can we talk?"

His sculpted cheeks bore a dark stubble, and his exposed forearms were thoroughly inked. He glanced at Marlene then back at me. "How the hell did you find me?"

"It wasn't hard. Your family's worried about you."

He cast his eyes down. "It's not about them." Marlene reached over and took his hand. "I have my reasons."

"I'm sure you do, Luis. I'm investigating your sister's murder, and I think you can help." I pointed toward a bench. "I have some questions to ask you. Can we sit and talk?"

Despite Archie's attempts at friendship, Marlene's dog—a mixed breed that looked like a little fox—growled and bared small, sharp teeth every time my dog got near him. Luis glanced at Marlene again. Clearly his senior and almost too thin, she had straight blond hair on the dishwatery side and an angular face pinched with concern. "Go ahead, baby. Talk to him," she said.

Luis shrugged and marched over to the bench and sat down. Archie and I followed him. "You said you had your reasons for taking off after the funeral," I began. "What were they?"

He pulled a pack of cigarettes from a shirt pocket, extracted one, lit it with a lighter, and inhaled deeply. After exhaling he said, "I couldn't stand being in the house. I mean, it was like that coffin was still sitting in the living room. I had to get away, man."

"Is that the only reason?"

He took another drag and studied me for a few moments before exhaling. "I, ah... I guess I was worried. Olivia was wearing my hoodie. Was she killed because of me?"

"Do you think she was?"

He met my eyes for the first time. "Timoteo thought so."

I waved a dismissive hand. "He was distraught. He doesn't feel that way now, Luis."

"Yeah, well, maybe he was right. I needed to get away from there, figure things out." His chin trembled ever so slightly. "If I caused this somehow, I could never forgive my—"

"Don't do that to yourself. It wasn't your fault, no matter what."

He lowered his eyes again and nodded.

"Do you suspect Darrell Benedict?"

He laughed with derision. "That *hijo de puta*? He doesn't have the *cojones* to pull a trigger."

"Are you sure? It was a cowardly ambush."

Luis took another drag, exhaled, and absently stroked his chin.

"I tried to look him up, but I found out he moved to Idaho six months ago to join some white supremacist militia."

"What were you going to do if you found him?"

"Just check him out, look him in the eye. I wanted to make sure."

"And if you decided he did it?"

"I would kill the bastard."

I swiveled my body around to face him fully. "That won't bring Olivia back, and it would put you smack on death row."

He shrugged defiantly. "So what?"

"Did you tell the detectives about him?"

"Yeah, I mentioned me and him had a fight."

"Okay. What about the Tequila Cantina? Why did you start hanging out there?"

He took another drag, exhaled, and eyed me more carefully. "Olivia asked me to."

I leaned in closer as my pulse ticked up a couple of notches. "She *did*? Why?"

He shrugged with a puzzled look. "She wouldn't tell me. She said the less I knew going in, the better."

"Back up. When did this happen, and what else did she say?"

"It must have been a month ago. She said something like, 'You like to play pool, right?' I said sure, and she asked me if I'd go to the cantina in Lafayette and start playing there. When I asked her why, she said that a group of Latinos hung out there, in the back where the pool tables are, and she wanted me to go there and try to find out what they were up to. I tried to get more information, but she said, 'Please, just go, play pool, be friendly, watch and listen. It's important.' I told her I would." He smiled bitterly. "I'd do anything for Olivia."

"What did you find out?"

He dropped the cigarette and ground it out under the heel

of his boot. "It was like a recruitment center of some kind. But I never found out what it was they were doing. You had to be selected by the *jefe*. One of the guys told me to be patient, that I'd probably get in. He made it seem like it was a good deal, kind of an honor. The *jefe* finally talked to me."

"What did he say?"

Luis paused and stroked his chin again. "He told me I looked like a man in search of a future, or some shit like that. When I said, 'I'm undocumented. I have no future,' he said, 'Sure you do. This is *America*.' I told him, 'That's the problem.' Then he just laughed and gave me this fake fucking smile. Said he might be able to help me, and we should talk later. He took my number and said he'd be in touch. Olivia got shot three days later, and not one word from him."

"The *jefe*'s name is Diego Vargas, right?"

Luis shot me a look. "How do you know that?"

"Timoteo and I went to the cantina to talk to the guys in the pool room. We wanted to know if you had any trouble there."

"*¡Mierda!* I didn't use my last name. Now they can connect me to Olivia."

"We didn't know you'd been sent there by your sister. You were thinking about going back to the cantina?"

Deep furrows appeared on his forehead. "I *was*, if Vargas called." He paused, and his young face grew taut. "Now I'm not sure what the fuck to do. I need to know if this somehow led to Olivia's death."

I met his eyes. "We all do, Luis. What did you tell the detectives about this?"

"*Nada*. At the time they questioned me, it didn't seem important. I was in shock, man. I don't trust them, anyway."

"Can you trust me? We can work together on this. Timoteo's helping me."

He didn't reply, and his expression was difficult to read.

"Does Vargas know where you're staying?"

He smirked. "Not unless you told him."

I ignored the barb. "It's a good idea to continue to stay out of sight. If he contacts you, would you call me? We can decide what to do. It could be dangerous if you do this alone." I went on to describe the shiv that got left in my tire in the parking lot of the cantina.

He held his inscrutable expression for so long I thought he wasn't going to respond. Finally, he nodded once. "Okay."

I handed him a card. He dropped it in his shirt pocket. "I know you're not answering Timoteo's calls. Will you answer mine?"

Another nod. "How's my mother?"

I exhaled a sigh. "Not good at all. She's staying in her room, doesn't want to cook, doesn't want to eat. She sent the priest away. Your father needs you, too. So does Timoteo."

He grimaced, and the pain returned to his eyes. "Ay, chingo… Tell them I'm okay, that I'll come by soon, that I, ah…love them."

Luis got up and joined Marlene. I watched them as they headed across the freshly mowed grass, the little fox prancing next to them. Luis's stout body next to Marlene's spare frame had a touching asymmetry, and when they joined hands, I felt a lump in my throat.

A hopeless romantic. That was me.

Chapter Eighteen

I called Timoteo on my way back to Dundee. When I finished filling him in, a long pause ensued. "Oh, man, I was such a dick that night. I blamed Luis for hanging out at the cantina. Hell, I blamed him for Olivia's death." An audible exhale. "It turns out she asked him to go there. No wonder he took off."

"Don't beat yourself up. You had no way of knowing what Olivia asked him to do. I think he understands. He told me to tell you all he loves you."

Another long pause. "I knew he was okay, but I'm still relieved. My father will be glad to hear this, too."

"Maybe this will help your mother's recovery," I offered.

"Maybe, but to be honest, I'm not sure she's missed him at all. If I left, she wouldn't miss me, either."

"Have you called the grief counselor?"

He exhaled another sigh. "Not yet. I have to get my father on board. He keeps hoping Mamá will snap out of it."

"Don't wait too long," I cautioned. "She needs help now."

"I won't," he said a little defensively before changing the subject. "Luis has no idea why Olivia sent him to the cantina?"

"That's right."

"What's going on there, anyway?"

"Good question. I've been turning that over. Diego Vargas is definitely recruiting young Latino men for something, but I'll be damned if I know what it is."

"What do we do if Vargas calls and wants to recruit Luis?"

I paused for a couple of beats. "If that happens, we need to be very careful. We have to assume Vargas is involved in the murder and is trying to lure Luis into the open. If Olivia was the intended victim and Vargas has made the connection between them, then he'll want to know what Luis knows, at the very least. If Luis was the target, then Vargas will want to finish the job. Either way, he's at risk."

Timoteo laughed, a single, bitter note. "Or Vargas is just recruiting Amazon drivers. In which case, my father was the intended victim, and we're back to the cartel theory."

"That's right, although it begs the question why Olivia sent your brother to the cantina in the first place."

The line went quiet. "Luis said he'd let you know if Vargas makes a move, huh?"

I didn't like the tone of that question. "He will, won't he?"

Another bitter laugh. "Luis? No telling what he'll do."

———

When I got back to the office, I had a wave of anxiety about sitting on the fact that the shooter may have been driving a Kawasaki but decided to let it ride a little longer. Things were in flux. The fewer cops the better at this juncture.

It was a quiet afternoon. I closed up early, loaded Archie in the car, and headed for the Aerie with the intention of getting in some work on my rock wall. The afternoon sky was cerulean blue, thanks to a fast-moving squall that had washed the air clean.

I changed, and when I came out on the porch, Archie stood there
with a tennis ball in his mouth and a determined gleam in his eye.

I laughed. "Okay, Big Boy, I get the hint."

Twenty minutes later, with my rotator cuff rapidly fraying, I
held up the slobbery ball. "Last one!" I heaved it as far as I could.
He tore after it, snatching it in midair on the first bounce.

"Nice catch, Archie!"

I turned around to see Zoe, standing at the gate and clapping
for my dog.

"Yep, he's still got it," I said as I walked over to her. "How did
Gertie's checkup go?"

"Pretty good, but she's been warned not to have a false sense
of security. She still has a lot of healing to do."

I laughed. "Keeping her quiet's going to be a challenge."

Zoe rolled her eyes. "You're telling me?" Archie trotted up
and dropped the ball at her feet, his tail wagging at full clip. She
picked it up and gave it an impressive heave. "What's the latest
on the case?" she asked as my dog bounded across the field.

I told her about finding Luis and what he had to say. She
scrunched up her brows. "Good grief, that scene at the cantina
sounds pretty sketchy. That thickens the plot considerably."

She was right. My stomach clenched a little at the thought.

We kicked the case around while Zoe kept Archie busy chasing
the tennis ball. "Does he ever get tired?" she finally asked after a
half-dozen tosses.

I shook my head. "It's not in his DNA." I laid the ball on the
ground and wagged a finger at him. "That's it, Big Boy." His ears
dropped, and he lay down between us with his chin on his paws.

Zoe said, "Luis sounds like an angry, mixed-up young man."

"Yeah. There's quite a contrast between him and his older
brother."

She leaned against the gatepost, crossed her arms, and looked pensive. "I don't blame him for being angry. I mean, he didn't ask to be brought here, to a country that's now telling him he's not welcome. I think his parents acted selfishly, bringing their kids here illegally."

"Really?" I said, a bit taken aback.

She looked at me straight on. "After the fact, they expect sympathy." She shrugged. "I don't know, maybe I'm not that willing to give it to them. They broke the law, after all."

"True, but it would look different if you were in their shoes, Zoe. They wanted a better future for their kids and themselves. Carlos was a laborer in a vineyard in Mexico with no prospects of ever becoming anything else."

"A better future? They live in fear now."

"It wasn't always like that. It was understood that if you had the guts and took the initiative to come here, there would be good employment, that the laws would be winked at. This country welcomed the cheap labor, even if the laws didn't reflect that. We've been schizophrenic on the issue."

Her blue eyes narrowed slightly. "We're supposed to be a nation that honors the rule of law. They broke the law, and now they're being called on it. Isn't that the only way to look at it? I mean, you took an oath as a lawyer, didn't you?"

I felt some heat rise in my neck. "Of course I did. But there should have been better laws, more clarity. It's hard for me to hold the parents responsible for having basic human aspirations."

She forced a smile. "Ask Luis how he feels about it."

"Ask Timoteo how *he* feels about it," I shot back.

An awkward silence ensued during which we stood there almost glaring at each other.

"I've got a dinner to cook," Zoe said quickly, and I silently thanked her for deescalating the situation. She knelt down and hugged Archie's neck, then turned and headed toward Gertie's house without saying another word.

Well, shit, I said to myself as she walked away. Like aunt, like niece.

———

My progress on the aboveground course of the wall looked pathetically insignificant as I parked the empty wheelbarrow next to the rock pile and slipped on my leather gloves. I tried to picture the completed structure, a low circular wall with the two ends offset to create an entrance, but the effort only discouraged me. "Whose idea was this, anyway?" I said to Arch, who'd taken up his position as foreman. He lifted his head and looked at me as if to say "It's not going to build itself."

With an hour and half of daylight left, I began working with a goal of laying at least another twenty feet of the first course, which would run a circular path of one hundred and fifty feet or so when completed. I had the look I wanted now—stacks of narrow slabs alternating with blocks of roughly the same height—and had become more adept at spotting the right chunks of basalt to pull it off. But the sense of tranquility I usually got from the work was absent that evening. The meeting with Luis was still churning in my head, and the encounter with Zoe had me flummoxed, for lack of a better word.

Damn it, she'd raised a sensitive issue—should compassion ever bear on the rule of law? Carlos and Elena Fuentes chose to break the law to provide their family the possibility of a better future. Did their admirable motives mitigate in any way their culpability? Or was there no room for compassion in judging what they'd done?

Zoe seemed to take the latter position. That surprised me,

although I suspected her comments reflected a bit of a contrarian nature, not unlike Gertie's. I pondered that as I picked through the rock pile. By the time I had the wheelbarrow loaded again, I was on to thinking about my own position. Sure, I'd taken an oath, but was a law valid if it was winked at or ignored? And should people who broke the so-called law for good reasons suddenly be judged and held strictly accountable? The questions were complex, and I reckoned that good people could come down on either side of them.

But my moral compass said no to both.

As the afternoon progressed, I became less philosophical and more focused on the task at hand. In fact, I was so absorbed that it came as a shock when the solar lights along my driveway lit up. I stood up, massaged my lower back with both hands, and surveyed my progress. I'd beaten my goal, having completed maybe a third of the first course. I should have felt good, but something weighed on me. Was it the silly spat with Zoe?

I hoped not, because that would suggest I was becoming emotionally entangled. And that was the last thing I needed.

Chapter Nineteen

Around three a.m. the next morning I surfaced from a deep sleep, suddenly fully alert but not knowing why. I lay there listening, and the only thing I heard was Archie's steady breathing until my friend the great horned owl came in with his four-note song. Realizing it was the owl's call that woke me, I got up and opened the bedroom window and sat next to it. The air was cool and still and the intermittent hoots carried from the shadowy line of firs along the east side of my property. The plaintive sounds stirred something deep inside me, a longing whose origin lay just outside my consciousness. Archie came over and placed his muzzle on my knee. I scratched him between the ears, and after we listened to several more choruses, I said, "We're kindred souls, that owl and us."

Timoteo was in his family's car in the parking lot of my office when Arch and I arrived that morning. We were late. "We took advantage of the weather to get a jog in," I explained as Archie trotted over to greet him. "We need to get you an office key."

He flashed a grin that told me he'd taken the comment as a compliment. "I'll take care of it today," he said. "I know a good locksmith."

The phone rang just as I sat down behind my desk. It was Nando informing me that he had obtained crucial video evidence in a lawsuit that had been on my back burner. While driving a motorized scooter in Portland, my client struck and injured a pedestrian who was suing for half a million dollars. Nando had obtained a video from a nearby hotel that proved the injured party, a tourist from Ohio, had crossed the intersection against the traffic light.

"Excellent work," I said. "Any news on the cartel front?"

"I have not heard from my source in L.A., but my man in Mexico City just got back to me. If the cartels that sprang from the Guadalajara breakup are involved in the hit, they are not bragging about it. He also told me Plácido Francisco Ballesteros grew up on a small farm outside El Tecuan and has no known cartel involvement. Nothing on the other two."

"Noted. What about Darrell Benedict?"

"He is in jail in Idaho. Manslaughter. He has been there for four months."

"Good. At least we can rule him out."

After Nando signed off and I brought Timoteo up to date on the conversation, he said, "Wow, Nando gets a lot done."

I laughed. "He's the best PI in Portland and probably on the West Coast. And I'm lucky to call him my friend." I extracted a folder from my filing cabinet and handed it to my new assistant. "Here's the file on the lawsuit. I want you to read this over, do some research, and write me a memo on what you think the next steps should be."

Without a trace of intimidation he said, "Sure, I'd love to do that. You, um, really want my—"

"Your opinion? Sure," I said with the twinkle of a smile. "Doesn't mean I'll agree. I'll look at it when I get back."

He flashed the Fuentes family smile. "Well, sure, okay, I'll do that. Where are you going?"

"To Prosperar."

"To talk to Sofia Leon?"

"Yeah, and also Robert Harris, the boyfriend. I'm taking a chance they're in. I like to pop in on people so they don't have time to rehearse."

Timoteo glanced over at Archie, who was snoozing in the corner. "Leave him if you want. I'll make sure he gets his walk."

———

Prosperar was located in a modest, one-story, brick building on NE 5th in McMinnville. An unobtrusive sign above the entry read PROSPERAR MEDICAL SERVICES, and a sign in the window promised *Aqui Se Habla Español*. As I entered, the receptionist looked up from her computer and smiled, and the eyes of at least a dozen people sitting in a waiting area turned in my direction. A couple of young kids in a play area paid me no mind. I was surprised at how busy it was and instantly regretted not calling ahead.

The young receptionist glanced at my card after I introduced myself. "Is Dr. Leon expecting you?"

"Uh, no, but this is important. It concerns Olivia Fuentes." Her smile crashed, and I felt a twinge of guilt. "If she could make some time, I'd appreciate it," I added with my best smile. The young woman disappeared behind a windowless double door.

By the time she reappeared, a young couple with an infant had queued up behind me. "Ms. Leon can see you now," she said to me. "Come with me, please."

I followed her down a hallway with treatment rooms on either side. The place had that antiseptic, hospital smell, and a couple of women hurried by in nurse's garb. Leon's office was at the end of the hall. The door was open, and she sat gazing at a large monitor. Leather and chrome seating, a standard-issue metal desk, and a photo-filled wall defined the space. The receptionist cleared her throat, and Leon looked up from the screen. Her thick, dark hair was pulled back unceremoniously, her smile was guarded, and her eyes, magnified by wire-rim glasses, looked tired.

"Mr. Claxton," she said as she stood and extended her hand, "you look familiar, but I can't place you."

"We met briefly at Olivia Fuentes's *velorio*."

The smile deepened. "Of course." She motioned toward a chair in front of her desk. "Please. Have a seat. What can I do for you?"

"I'm working informally with the Fuentes family to aid in the investigation of Olivia's murder. I—"

"Really?" She pushed her glasses up the bridge of her nose, and her eyes came alive. "Isn't that a matter for the police?"

I gave her my standard pitch about being a bridge between a distrustful migrant community and the police, in the hopes of improving the chances of catching the murderer. I made a sweeping gesture when I finished. "I'm sure you're confronted with similar issues here at Prosperar."

She tucked a lock of errant hair behind her ear and nodded. "I take your point. Serving the undocumented does present complications. I've already spoken to the police, but since you're here, I take it the crime's still unsolved."

"It is."

"No suspects?"

"None I'm aware of."

"The word in the migrant community is that Olivia's father was the target. Is that true?"

"We don't know. Who told you that?"

"My staff has been picking it up here and there."

"I understand you worked closely with Olivia. Did you notice anything about her behavior that seemed unusual before the murder?"

"No. Nothing at all." She paused, let a breath out, and adjusted her glasses.

I edged forward in my chair. "Small details can be crucial."

"Well, I did notice one thing, but I hesitate to bring it up."

I waited for her to continue.

"She was showing some interest in our finance manager, Robert Harris."

"Was that unusual?"

"I'm told he's seeing someone, so it seemed a little out of character for Olivia. She was such a principled young woman."

"Did Robert reciprocate?"

"I don't really know, but he's taken Olivia's death really hard. He hasn't been himself since the funeral." She paused for a moment and met my eyes. "Of course, we're all shaken to the core by what happened."

"When did Olivia's interest in him start?"

She looked to the side for a moment before answering. "Maybe a month or so before she died."

"Did you tell the detectives about this?"

"No, it just occurred to me, you know, with the way Robert's been acting and all. Should I?"

"I'd give Detective Tate a call. She'll appreciate it." Not wishing to have Tate learn of my involvement in this way, I added, "It would, uh, be better not to mention my name at this juncture. I haven't informed her of my involvement yet."

She eyed me for a moment as if considering my request. "Okay. I'll contact the detective and leave you out of it."

I followed up with more questions about Olivia and Robert but didn't learn anything of significance. I was curious about Prosperar and asked her about the organization.

"We're a nonprofit focused on the medical needs of farm, nursery, and vineyard workers and their families in the north valley. Virtually none of these workers have health insurance. They don't seek medical care until their problems become acute. Then it's often too late. It's a huge problem."

"I live in the Red Hills, yet I know so little about your clinic. I'm embarrassed to say that."

She flashed a smile. "That's by design. Most of our clients are undocumented, so there's always the potential for controversy." She rolled her eyes. "The last thing we want is to have some white supremacist group harassing us. We tend to fly under the radar."

"How are you funded?"

"Privately, through the growers—*some* of the growers, the generous ones—and we have a cadre of medical staff who volunteer their time—wonderful, committed people. We have the clinic here, and we also go to some of the larger work sites to give flu shots, vaccinations, and the like. We make house calls, too, when transportation's an issue."

"Impressive. I'm sure you're having a big impact out there."

A hint of pride in her smile. "We are. And we're planning to expand into California and Washington."

We exchanged cards, and as I was leaving I asked where I could find Robert Harris. "Second office past the exit to the lobby." She looked at her watch. "Better hurry. He'll be off to lunch soon."

Harris's office was locked, and when I asked the receptionist about him, she said, "He just went out. You might catch him in the parking lot. He drives a silver BMW."

Robert Harris was just getting into his car when I called out to him. He turned around and eyed me through dark glasses until I caught up with him. He was narrow in the shoulders with sandy hair, a slight paunch, and a decided lack of chin. Not exactly what I expected. I introduced myself and handed him a card.

"I'm hoping you could spare a few minutes to talk about Olivia Fuentes. Maybe we could—"

"I've already talked to the police," he said, cutting me off. His face grew taut. "I'm, ah, running late. If you want to know what I said, maybe you can talk to them."

"It won't take long."

He turned and got into his BMW, a Z4 sports car, and rolled down the window. "Sorry, gotta run." I started to argue, but his cell phone chirped, and he took the call. I walked back and got into my car just as the Z4 purred out of the parking lot and accelerated down NE 5th.

Hmm. That was odd.

Chapter Twenty

When I got back to the office, Timoteo was bent over his laptop, his fingers a blur on the keyboard. He looked up when I came in the back door. "How'd it go?"

I plopped down behind my desk, and Archie came over to greet me. "Interesting. Sofia Leon didn't seem to know much, but she did confirm what Mariana told us—Olivia and Robert Harris seemed to be at least in the flirting stages of an affair, but with a couple of twists. First, Leon was a little taken aback because, according to her, Harris has a girlfriend. She thought it was out of character that Olivia would pursue him." I paused, giving Timoteo an inquiring look.

"She was right about that. Olivia wouldn't hit on a guy who was taken." He looked away with a wistful smile. "She had guys lining up to date her."

"Not under any circumstances?"

He shrugged. "I don't know, maybe the guy was breaking up with his girlfriend, or he lied to her about it, or…maybe she wanted something from him. She'd have to want whatever it was really bad to violate her code of ethics." The wistful look again. "She was the most honest person I've ever known."

"This guy was no catch, believe me, so I tend to discount a romantic motive on her part. The other interesting thing was that Leon said Harris was upset since the funeral, 'Not himself' is the way she put it." I described my encounter with him in the Prosperar parking lot. "He was hard to read," I summed up. "Maybe he's shut down by the shock of Olivia's death, but I got a whiff of something else—fear, maybe."

"What would he be afraid of?"

"That's what we need to find out."

"How?"

"We keep digging, that's how. Olivia sent Luis to the cantina to find out what was going on there. At roughly the same time, she started cozying up to Harris at Prosperar."

"So, there's a link between Diego Vargas and Robert Harris?"

"Perhaps."

His face became animated. "Let me follow Harris, see what he's up to."

I had to chuckle at his eagerness. "Let's see what Nando Mendoza can find out about both of them first."

Timoteo's look grew concerned. "This will show up on our bill, right? How much does he charge us for a search like this?"

"For a straightforward background check, he'll use a cloud-based system, Experian or TransUnion, probably. So, maybe seventy-five bucks each. He's agreed to run your work at his cost."

Timoteo looked surprised. "Why did he agree to do that?"

I smiled. "Because he arrived here from Cuba in a homemade boat without a dime."

"*He did*? When?"

"Oh, fifteen years ago, now. He understands what immigrants go through."

Timoteo shook his head. "*Wow.* That's so cool. I had no idea. Tell him the Fuentes family appreciates this very much."

While I talked to Esperanza about the searches, Timoteo slipped across the highway and returned with sandwiches and coffee. As we sat down to eat, he handed me a couple of printed pages. "I recommend you go for a summary judgment on the lawsuit."

I think I did a double take. "You've finished the memo *already*?" He nodded, and I read through it while we ate and drank. "Not bad," I said, looking up when I finished. "You found the key point—there're no outstanding issues of material fact on the table now. When that's the case, the suit becomes a question of pure law, and a judge can rule on it without a trial."

"Thanks. That was fun. I think the case's a slam dunk."

I smiled. "It would be in any other state, but in Oregon, it turns out, it's hard to convince a judge to consider summary judgment. If there's any factual dispute *whatsoever*, the policy of the court of appeals is to allow the party to have their say in front of the jury or a court."

That led us to a discussion on the details of summary judgments, and when we finished, Timoteo said, "Can I see the motion when you finish writing it?"

"Sure." God forgive me, the cynical corner of my brain whispered, *another lawyer is born*.

———

Later that afternoon I was on the phone with a client when Timoteo's cell chirped. He took the call and then looked over at me, his forehead scored with worry lines. "What's up?" I said, after disconnecting a few moments later.

"That was Hillary Angel. She's sitting with Mamá this afternoon. She said two ICE agents came to the door asking for Luis."

"What did she tell them?"

"She said he wasn't living there anymore and that our family had no idea where he was."

I got up and alerted Archie with a flick of my head. "Let's go. I want to talk to her."

We closed the office, and ten minutes later, I pulled in behind Timoteo's car at the Fuentes's house. Small in stature with bright, inquisitive eyes, Hillary met us at the front door wearing a worried face. After she described the encounter, I said, "Are you sure they were ICE agents? Did they show you their badges?"

"No, they didn't. I should've demanded ID, but I was shocked, to tell you the truth. They wore black vests that said 'Police' on them. Big, burly men, both of them. Their car was black, unmarked."

We heard footsteps in the hall and turned to see Elena Fuentes staring at us, her body clothed in a tattered terry cloth robe, her face horror-stricken. She looked thin and emaciated. "What is it? Has something happened to Luis?"

Timoteo rushed over to her. "Nothing's happened to Luis, Mamá. He's safe and sound. Some people wanted to talk to him, that's all."

She pulled away from him, glaring at all of us, her eyes lit with fear. "I heard you say *ICE*. They want only one thing—to deport us, to destroy our lives here."

"No, Mamá. They don't know where Luis is. It's okay. They've gone."

Her eyes clouded over with grief, but no tears flowed. She put her hands on either side of her head as if she were going to scream. Hillary went over to her. "Come on, Elena, let's go back to your room. I'll make you a cup of hot tea. It's okay. Luis is fine. He's safe."

Hillary guided Elena back down the hall. I glanced at my watch. "Do you know where the nearest ICE field office is?"

Timoteo said, "On the highway, just south of Newberg. Brand-new concrete building, no sign out front, just the street address. Looks like a Gestapo headquarters."

"I'm going there now to see if I can learn anything. Alert your father about this and stay here with your mother. Don't go to the door if they come back. They can't enter without a search warrant. I'll be in touch."

Timoteo was right. The ICE facility was unmarked, although in front a large U.S. flag waved atop a flagpole. I'd driven by it numerous times when it was under construction. I suspected I wasn't the only one who didn't realize the building was part of the federal immigration control system. With two stories of buff-colored concrete and narrow windows, the structure had a wide, fenced-off driveway leading to an underground parking area on the left and a double-door entryway on the right.

Relieved that the lobby at least was open to the public, I presented myself to a young male receptionist as a uniformed security guard looked on. An anxious-looking Latino woman with two toddlers sat in an adjacent waiting area, where a smattering of potted plants and bad art failed to soften the bleak institutional atmosphere of the place.

I showed the receptionist my Oregon Bar Association card. "Earlier this afternoon, two of your agents showed up at the house of a client of mine and asked for him. I'd like to know what this is all about."

"What's his name?"

"That's confidential."

He looked up at me for the first time, his brows scrunched down in disbelief. "Then I can't help you."

"Of course you can," I snapped back. "Who would know whether you dispatched agents to arrest someone in this area earlier today?"

"That would be Field Supervisor Drake, on the ICE side of the house." I must have looked confused because he added, "I work for NEO. We're a contract agency."

"What does NEO do here?"

"Everything except make arrests—that's ICE's job. We're a holding center. We handle security, processing, and transportation of detainees to our regional detention center in Tacoma, Washington."

Noting the name on his badge, I said, "Look, Ron, I need an answer here. This is part of a murder inquiry I'm involved in."

He reappraised me for a moment. "Okay, Drake's kind of pissy, but he might be willing to talk to you. Take a seat and I'll see if I can get you in to see him."

I sat down in the waiting room, and the two toddlers came over to me like a couple of curious kittens. The mother called them back in Spanish. I smiled at her. "They're beautiful. Twins?"

She nodded and tried to smile but failed. Her eyes were the color of dark chocolate and laced with fear.

"Are you having problems with *La Migra*?"

She studied me warily for a few moments before answering. "*Sí*. My husband, he went to the court to pay a traffic ticket yesterday. He was picked up there. I have come to see him before they take him to the detention."

"I'm sorry to—"

"Mr. Claxton?" a voice interrupted. "Would you please come with me?" I got up, took a card from my wallet, and handed it to the young mother. "I'm a lawyer. If you need help, you can call me at this number." No way I was looking for any immigrant business, but what could I say to her?

I followed a middle-aged woman through a set of double doors and up a flight of stairs to an office at the end of an echoey hallway. "We prohibit the solicitation of business on the premises, Mr. Claxton," she said along the way, her tone just short of haughty.

"I'm not an immigration lawyer, but I can put the young mother in touch with one," I replied. "Looked to me like she could use some help."

Field Supervisor Curtis Drake had a weight lifter's build, a chiseled face with a meticulously cropped Vandyke beard, and small, narrow-set eyes. I entered his office, and he stood with a definite military bearing. "Mr. Claxton. What can I do for you?"

I handed him a card and sat down in front of his desk, arrayed with neat stacks of paper, a retro penholder, and a coffee cup that had "Go ahead, make my day" written on it. "I represent a family from Dundee. This morning two men identifying themselves as ICE agents came to their home and asked for one of their sons. They didn't show any identification, and there's no reason for ICE to be asking for him." The last part wasn't necessarily true, but I didn't want Drake to know that.

"Are you suggesting they might have been impostors?"

"I'd just like to confirm that they were on some sort of official business. The incident occurred around ten a.m. in the Red Hills. They asked for him by name. I'm concerned about the safety of the son and the rest of the family. And I would think you'd want to know if there are, in fact, people posing as ICE agents."

Drake showed a thin smile. "And the son shall go nameless?" When I didn't respond, he continued, "Immigration Control and Enforcement reports to Homeland Security. I'm sure you can appreciate we're bound by strict confidentiality guidelines. It's a matter of national security."

"National security? Come on. All I'm asking is for you to confirm the two agents were sent by ICE. Lives are at stake here."

He steepled his fingers and tapped them against his lips for a few moments before logging into his computer, whose screen was blocked from my view. After a few more strokes, he squinted at the screen. "I can confirm that two agents were dispatched this morning to an address in the Red Hills. That's more than I should tell you."

"Okay, thanks. I appreciate that."

We both stood, and his face tightened. "You know, I don't get you immigration lawyers. Always looking to cut corners for these people, finding ways around our laws."

"*These people?*" I said, holding his gaze.

He puffed a dismissive breath. "They aren't worth your time, Claxton. They enter this country illegally and then expect to be coddled." He raised his chin, his expression morphing into a look of smug self-righteousness. "It's a new day in this country. We're going to solve this problem once and for all."

I shook my head. "A final solution, huh?"

His small eyes grew hard and seemed to retract into his head. "We're done here." He got up and escorted me back down the hall without saying another word.

I left Curtis Drake's office feeling angry and, if not stupid, then certainly blithely uninformed. An ICE holding center had gone up right in my own neighborhood, and I knew nothing about it. Sure, there were those in the migrant community who deserved deportation—the scofflaws and outright criminals who're present in *all* populations—but Drake's condemnation was sweeping and all-inclusive.

There had to be a better way.

Chapter Twenty-One

My call to Luis Fuentes went to voicemail, but he called me back five minutes later. After I filled him in, he said, "Part of me wishes I'd been there, get the damned deportation over with. I'm a Mexican, not an American. No changing that. I—"

"Look, Luis," I said, cutting him off, "I know this is frustrating, but until we know more, you need to keep your head down, continue to stay away from places you might otherwise frequent." As a stark, unwelcome image of Olivia's limp body entered my head, I added, "This is no time to get careless. Keep your eye out for anything unusual."

"Got it," he snapped. "By the way, I've driven by the cantina in Lafayette twice. I didn't spot any familiar cars or bikes either time. Looks like they're not meeting there anymore."

"No word from Vargas?"

"*Nada.*"

"You'll call if he contacts you, right?"

"I said I would."

I called Timoteo next. "No, it's been quiet here," he told me. "Mamá has settled down, but she's going downhill so fast, Cal." He paused, and I pictured the worried look on his face. When he spoke next, a note of desperation crept into his voice. "My father has no clue. What should I do?"

"Let me talk to my psychologist friend again, see if she has any other ideas." Of course, that was going to be problematic after the disagreement Zoe and I had. "You're not leaving your mother alone, are you?"

He sighed heavily into the phone. "We're doing the best we can. She stays in her room with the door shut. Only Hillary is allowed in, and then not always."

"I'll see what I can do, but in the meantime keep a close eye on her, Timoteo."

———

At home that evening, I showered and had Blossom Dearie on the sound system and a glass of pinot at my elbow when I heard a knock at the front door.

"Hello, Cal," Zoe said when I opened the door, "I brought you a peace offering." She wore jeans, a cotton sweater, and the pearl earrings I'd commented on. Her smile had an edge of shyness I hadn't seen before. She handed me a warm pot with a lid on it. "It's lamb stew. Gertie said it's a favorite of yours. She, ah, coached me on the preparation." The shy smile again. "I think it's okay."

I smiled back. "Peace offering? You didn't have to do that." I smelled the stew and my stomach did a backflip. "It smells way better than okay. I was about to call you. Can you come in?"

She hesitated for a moment. "I suppose. I've already fed Gertie, and she's watching TV." After making a big fuss over Archie, she followed me into the kitchen. I set the pot on the stove, poured her a glass of wine, and sat down across from her at my old, nicked-up oak table. Blossom Dearie sang "I'll Take Manhattan" in the background. Zoe took a sip of her pinot and fixed her eyes on me. "I'm embarrassed about the other night, and I apologize, Cal. I know you're trying to help the Fuentes family. I respect that."

I put a hand up. "No, don't apologize. I'm embarrassed, too. You know, the issue you brought up goes back at least to the Old Testament. Abraham had a choice—obey God's law or break the law by sparing his innocent son. Same movie, just a different time."

Zoe's eyes widened in a way I'd to come to expect when something surprised her. "You're right." She shook her head. "God was dead wrong in that situation. I would have told him to go to hell."

I laughed. "So you don't believe in absolute adherence to the law?"

She shrugged. "Not in that situation, but it still bothers me when people—immigrants or citizens, it really doesn't matter— aren't held accountable when they break the law."

I took a sip of wine to gather my thoughts, which were far from settled on the subject. "I believe in the rule of law, too, but laws need to be just. Otherwise, they become tools for the power structure to rationalize their position. I had enough of that as a prosecutor down in L.A."

She shifted her gaze past me and chewed on her lower lip for a few moments. "Yeah, I guess our immigration laws are pretty screwed up, right?"

"Totally. We've needed reforms for decades. Meanwhile, millions of undocumented workers have made their homes here, started families, sent their kids to school. They're good citizens."

She brought her eyes back to me. There was a hint of tease in them. "Now they're as American as apple pie and tacos, huh?"

I smiled. "Something like that."

We both laughed and then sat in silence for a while. There was more to be said on the topic, but I sensed that she was as reluctant as I was to go any deeper at this juncture. Zoe drank some wine and finally said, "Who's that singing? She's great."

"Blossom Dearie." Without thinking, I added, "She was a favorite of my wife's," then instantly regretted it. Don't get maudlin, I said to myself.

Zoe held her gaze on me. "I'm sorry for your loss, Cal. Gertie told me what happened."

I forced a smile. "That was a long time ago, but this case has churned up the past, for some reason."

"That's not surprising, given what's happened. You must have been—"

"I'm starved," I said, looking over at the pot of stew. "Stay for dinner so I can run some new information by you."

She smiled in that knowing way of hers. "Okay."

I turned the heat on under the stew and started slicing some tomatoes and a chunk of mozzarella for a quick caprese salad. "I've got one solid lead," I said, then described what the locksmith and the woman on Buena Vista Drive told me.

Zoe curled a lip in disgust. "Now every time I see someone on a motorcycle, my blood's going to run cold. What about the person who supplied the key?"

"Nothing new on that front," I said as I arranged the tomatoes on a platter and began topping each one with a slice of mozzarella, "but I've uncovered something interesting at Prosperar, the medical nonprofit where Olivia worked. She sent Luis to the Tequila Cantina to find out what was going on there. At the same time, she started flirting with a staff member at the nonprofit." I described my meeting with Sofia Leon and my encounter with Robert Harris.

"Young women are easily infatuated with older men, you know," Zoe said when I finished.

"I know, but Timoteo told me there was no way his sister would do that unless she had a damn good reason."

Zoe leaned forward on her elbows. "What could it be?"

"I don't know yet."

Her face clouded over. "And it got her killed?"

"Possibly. I'm interested in whether there's a connection between whatever the hell's going on at the cantina and Robert Harris at Prosperar." I made a quick dressing with olive oil and balsamic vinegar and drizzled it over the tomatoes and mozzarella.

Zoe made a moaning sound. "Is that going to taste even better than it looks?"

"Guaranteed," I said as I stepped out the kitchen door. I returned with the last few leaves from a potted basil plant on the porch and sprinkled them on the salad. "Luis told me the meetings at the cantina have ceased, and the head guy there, Diego Vargas, hasn't contacted him, which doesn't help matters."

Zoe's eyes flared. "Do you think they stopped meeting because you're investigating them?"

"It's possible. I've asked my private investigator to dig into both Vargas and Harris."

"How's Luis doing?"

"I was coming to that," I said as I set the caprese platter down, dished out two plates of hot stew, and topped up our wines. "Two agents showed up at the Fuentes's home today looking for him."

Zoe's mouth dropped open. *"No."* I gave her an account of my visit to the holding center, and when I finished, she said, "You were worried they were *impostors*?"

"Yeah, the thought crossed my mind, but I guess they weren't."

"That means ICE is looking to arrest Luis?"

I shrugged. "We don't know that, and it doesn't seem very likely. Something seems off here. We'll keep him out of sight until we understand what's going on."

Over dinner the talk finally drifted away from the investigation, and I asked her about the book she was writing. She paused, dabbing her mouth with a napkin. "It's fiction with a psychological perspective, I guess you could say."

"Will you use the book in your teaching?"

She laughed. "Oh, definitely not. To be honest, I'm writing the book to take a break from teaching. I'm burned out." Her look turned mischievous. "Just don't tell my department head. He thinks I'm writing a scholarly treatise on new OCD therapies."

I laughed at that. "Testing the bounds of academic freedom, huh?"

She laughed and held her glass up in a toast. "Yep. Here's to academic freedom or a possible dead end on the tenure track." We clinked glasses and drank to that.

I asked her a few leading questions about the book, but she was about as forthcoming on that topic as I was on my wife. She did tell me she was bothered by writer's block and that long runs in the Red Hills seemed to help. "The running quiets my mind," she explained, "but it usually takes three or four miles for that to happen. Once it does, the ideas start to flow again."

We finished half the lamb stew, and she insisted I keep the rest. I'd like to say the stew was superb, but the truth was the meat was overcooked and the broth was way too salty. I never dreamed I'd find poor cooking endearing, but there it was.

After dinner, Arch and I walked Zoe back across the field. She turned to face me at the gate as a cool breeze fluttered her hair and moonlight glinted softly off her earrings, her Vermeers, as I'd come to think of them. For an instant, I caught myself wondering if she'd worn them on my account.

She said, "You haven't mentioned the mother. How's she doing?"

My expression must've turned sheepish. "I was, uh, coming to that, too."

When I finished describing Elena Fuentes's deteriorating

situation, Zoe sighed. "I was hoping no news was good news for that poor woman. Elena's in real danger, Cal." She paused for a moment. "I'm an academician. Direct counseling's not my strong suit, but let me try talking to her. Can you set something up?"

I told her I'd try and heaved an inward sigh of relief.

Back at the house, I cleaned up the kitchen, watched the late news, and started reading *Killshot*, an Elmore Leonard novel I hadn't gotten around to. I must have dozed off, because when my cell phone rang, my reaction pitched the book off my lap and onto the floor.

"Cal?" Luis Fuentes said, "Vargas wants to meet with me."

I came awake instantly. "When?"

"Right now. I'm on my way."

Chapter Twenty-Two

"You're on your way?" I said, keeping my voice calm. "Did he call you?"

"No, a text."

"Can you pull over and wait for me? We need to talk about this."

He actually laughed. "Hey, man, I'm just gonna talk to the dude, find out what the hell he wants. I'll let you know what he says."

A wave of frustration drenched me. "You're not getting the picture, Luis. This could be dangerous. Where are you going to meet him?"

"At the Road House. He said he would buy me a beer and tell me about a good business opportunity for a *migrante* like me."

I'd never been in the Road House, a small bar and grill on the Pacific Highway, but had driven by it plenty of times. I pictured the place, a low building that sat close to the road with a retro neon sign tracing the name of the place in cursive. What parking there was had to be behind the structure. I liked that he was meeting Vargas in a public space but was leery of the parking lot. What was the layout and the lighting?

"I'd like to be there, but I'll stay out of sight. Can you please pull over and wait for me?"

He exhaled audibly. "I don't need a fucking babysitter."

This time I struggled to keep my voice calm. "I know that, but this could be a trap. Two sets of eyes are better than one." I waited, mentally crossing my fingers.

After what seemed an interminable pause, he said, "I'll pull off where the highway divides just past Lafayette and wait for you there. I'm in Marlene's Prius, dark gray. Hurry, man. I don't want to keep him waiting."

I dashed upstairs, took my Glock down from the closet, slapped a full magazine into the handle, and tucked the gun in my belt. Don't be dramatic. You won't need that, the judgmental corner of my brain told me. Besides, you're a crappy shot. I took it anyway.

"Guard the castle," I told Archie as I stepped out the front door. I got a disgusted look in return.

Ten minutes later I pulled in behind the Prius. "Thanks for waiting, Luis," I said as I slid into the passenger seat. "Did the text say anything else?"

"No. That was it."

"Okay. Let me go to the Road House first and check out the parking lot. If it's clear I'll text you, and you can go ahead and meet him."

His look grew anxious as the bravado began bleeding off. "What's he want with me?"

"Hard to say. If Vargas had something to do with your sister's murder, your brother's and my visit to the cantina probably tipped him. Maybe he wants to find out what you know, why you showed up at the cantina in the first place. But he probably won't be direct. Whatever he says, just go along with it. If he offers you a job, tell him you need money, that you're all in. And Luis, don't use the restroom or go anywhere in the bar where you might be alone with Vargas, got it?"

His Adam's apple bobbed as he swallowed. "Okay. Then what?"

"We'll see what he says and go from there."

The Road House parking lot had an entrance on the north end and an exit that teed into a tree-lined side street on the south end. A single, low-wattage lamp on a flimsy pole cast a pool of light in the center of the lot, and a half dozen cars were clustered below it like moths. None of the cars appeared to be occupied. I parked at the south end and watched for a while. Nothing moved, but then I saw a pinpoint glow in the shadows of the building. The glow intensified for an instant—a cigarette in the act of inhalation. In the dim light I could just make out the smoker, a man in a white apron leaning against the wall between a row of garbage cans and the back door of the bar. I tensed up, but a moment later the glowing tip swept out an arc and hit the pavement with a shower of sparks, and the man went inside.

Nothing else moved. I texted Luis the all clear and told him to park in the illuminated section of the lot. He pulled in a couple of minutes later, and I watched as he got out, crossed the lot, and followed a path marked by solar lights to the entrance on the side of the building. I checked the time. Eight thirty-two. A light mist began to swirl and sparkle in the glow of the parking lot light.

At eight forty, Luis texted me: He's not here. I texted back for him to wait. Meanwhile, a couple came out of the bar and left, and another car parked in their space and discharged two young men who sauntered into the building.

From Luis at nine fifteen: Where is he?

Me: Wait another 45 mins. If he doesn't show, leave without approaching me in case we are being watched.

At 10:06, Luis came out of the Road House, followed the lighted path to the parking lot, and headed toward the Prius. He was halfway to the car when I saw it—a single headlight came on from the shadows of the tree-lined side street. I got out of my car and heard the low whine of a motorcycle engine as it lurched forward in Luis's direction.

"LUIS!" I shouted and began sprinting toward him with the Glock drawn. "LOOK OUT!"

He turned to face me as the motorcycle closed in on his back, a puzzled expression on his face. I was closer, but the motorcycle was much faster. "GET DOWN!" I shouted, but he stood there looking at me, frozen like a statue.

I kept sprinting and hit him like an NFL linebacker. At nearly the same instant, I heard *pop pop, pop pop,* four shots, over the whine of the bike. I went down on top of him and, expecting the assailant to take another run at us, twisted around and leveled the Glock in the shooter's direction. But instead, the motorcycle pulled out onto the highway and headed north at a high rate of speed. I listened until the muffled whine receded, then rolled off Luis, who lay facedown. Gently, I eased him onto his back.

His body was limp. I looked down at his face, which was covered with blood, and shuddered.

"No. God, no. Not again."

Chapter Twenty-Three

Luis groaned, and my heart nearly leapt out of my chest. "Luis, Luis, are you okay?"

He opened an eye, the one that wasn't bathed in blood and rapidly swelling shut. *"Mierda,"* he rasped, "What the fuck just happened?"

"Are you hit?"

He raised his head a fraction of an inch before giving up. "I don't think so. Was that dude on the bike *shooting* at me?"

"He was." I took out my handkerchief and dabbed at the blood on his face, revealing a nasty horizontal gash in the center of his forehead matched by a vertical wound below his left eye. He managed a weak smile. "I think he missed, but you sure as hell didn't."

"Me?"

He pointed his index finger up. "Yeah, when you took me down, I think I hit the mirror on the Prius."

I looked up. The driver's-side mirror was shattered and blood-stained and the housing bent forward. "Oh, shit. You're right." A sheepish smile. "Sorry about that."

"Hey, it beats a bullet in the head. You saved my life." He smiled again and gave me a weak fist bump. "But Marlene's gonna hate you, man. That Prius is her pride and joy."

I glanced at the bullet holes in the car door, eased the door open, and noted that two of the rounds had gone through it and penetrated the passenger-side door. There was a good chance at least one bullet had lodged inside the car. Marlene's pride and joy was about to be impounded as evidence in a crime scene.

I called 911 first and then Timoteo, telling him what happened and to meet his brother at the medical center. "You sure he's okay?" he asked, his voice quavering.

"He'll need some stitches, but I think he's okay."

By the time an ambulance arrived, Luis was propped against the back tire of the Prius holding a towel to his face that one of the waiters had brought him. Another waiter held an umbrella over him to keep the mist off. An officer from the first patrol car to arrive accompanied him to the hospital. "Keep an eye on him," I warned the officer. "The shooter's still out there."

I told his partner that the shooter was heading north on the Pacific Highway, was about my height, and drove a black motorcycle, probably a Kawasaki. After he called that in, I suggested he contact Detective Darci Tate. "This shooting's related to the Olivia Fuentes murder," I explained. The officer called Tate immediately, and she told him she and her partner were on their way.

Darci Tate wore a pair of faded jeans, cowboy boots, and a long-sleeved shirt with snap buttons. "Caught me at home," she said by way of an explanation I didn't require. "I snuck in a horse-back ride this evening." As her partner scoured the scene for spent shell casings and other physical evidence, she took notes on my version of what had gone down. When I finished, she said, circling back, "So the shooter waited on a motorcycle in those trees across the street?"

"Yeah. Looks like the text Luis got was a setup intended to lure him into the bar."

"And the guy who texted Luis, Diego Vargas, said he wanted to talk to Luis about a job."

I nodded. "I don't think Vargas was ever going to show. Someone in the bar probably tipped the shooter when Luis finally left."

"Why do you say that?"

"Not much light back here. It would have been difficult to know Luis was the target from across the street. And the shooter timed the attack perfectly." That triggered a memory. "The shooter's a lefty, at least that's the hand he held his gun in."

Tate added that to her notes. "What about the make of the bike?"

I shrugged. "Couldn't tell you. The locksmith said the guy he saw rode a Kawasaki, black. One thing I noticed, the bike seemed to be pretty heavily muffled."

"Makes sense, I suppose." Tate's not-yet cop eyes fixed on me. "Present at the scene again, Cal. Why this time?"

I knew what was coming and wasn't sure how it would go. Cops are never fond of civilians being involved in their investigations. "I'm working informally with the Fuentes family to take a look at their daughter's murder."

Her jaw clenched. "You're kidding. And you took the job?" After I gave her my reasons, she said, "Goddamn it, that's crazy. We don't hassle the migrants around here. This is wine country. We know how valuable they are. It's ICE that's stirring up all the fear."

"They're not making that distinction anymore, Darci. They feel like the whole country's turned on them."

She blew a breath out and kicked at some gravel on the pavement. "The truth is we don't have shit on the Olivia Fuentes case.

You're right, nobody knows anything, and nobody wants to talk to us." She half smiled. "You got anything I can use?"

"The shooter tonight is the same guy who killed Olivia." I went on to describe the key transfer and what the woman up on Buena Vista told me.

Tate shook her head. "I talked to that woman myself. She didn't say anything about a motorcycle."

I chuckled. "She mentioned it in passing, but after what the locksmith told me, it caught my attention."

"And Ballesteros and the two up in Washington?"

I shrugged. "Carlos Fuentes doesn't think Ballesteros is the key supplier, and he's trying to find the other two."

Tate eyed me again for emphasis. "We'll look for them, too, and you'll let me know if Carlos succeeds, right?"

"Of course. Something else you should know—two ICE agents showed up at the Fuentes's home yesterday looking for Luis. He wasn't there, and they didn't show any ID. I went to the field office in Newberg to check if they were legit. The ICE supervisor implied they were. I'm not so sure."

"You talked to Curtis Drake?"

"Yeah, that's his name. He's, uh, not a big fan of the immigrant community."

Tate laughed with derision. "He's rumored to have white supremacist ties. He *implied* they were legit?"

"Yeah, nothing definite. You know, can't compromise national security and all. But the thought lingers—it could've been a planned abduction. Take Luis alive and find out what he knows. When it failed, maybe they decided to take him out with the drive-by."

"Hmm. I've got a reliable source at ICE. I'll cross-check that and let you know what he says."

"Thanks."

She paused, as if to choose her next words with care. "Look, Cal, I appreciate the information, and I'm sure you're going to continue to investigate. This is a weird situation. Why don't we stay close?" She glanced at her partner, who was at the other end of the parking lot. "Keep it between you and me for a while?"

I smiled. "Yeah, I can do that. Maybe between the two of us, we can crack this thing." I was relieved and gratified she'd made the offer. It wasn't a typical cop thing to do, but then, Darci Tate wasn't a typical cop.

"Where does this guy Vargas fit in?" she asked next.

"Other than him setting Luis up, I have no idea. He's apparently connecting young Latinos with job opportunities of some kind." I described the scene at the Tequila Cantina that Timoteo and I witnessed.

"Know where we can find him?"

"No, but finding him shouldn't be difficult."

At this juncture, I held back the fact that Olivia had sent Luis to the cantina, because I didn't have any idea how that fit in. Let it ride for now, I told myself. You've given Tate plenty to go on.

———

"My father stayed with Mamá," Timoteo told me as we stood in the waiting area of the hospital. "I played it down, said the Luis had an accident but was okay. I didn't want to worry him until I knew more."

"That was wise."

Shortly after that, a nurse escorted us to Luis's room. The officer who arrived with him nodded as we entered the room, and Marlene, who sat next to the bed holding his hand, got up and flashed a nervous smile. Timoteo sucked in a breath when he saw his brother. Luis raised his other hand reassuringly. "Hey,

I'm gonna live, bro." Maybe a dozen stitches closed the gash on his forehead, and a butterfly bandage did the same for the lesser wound beneath his left eye, which was swollen completely shut.

Timoteo showed the Fuentes smile. "Next time Cal says duck, I bet you do it."

Luis looked at me and managed a groggy chuckle. "You hit like a truck, man."

I rubbed my right shoulder, which was stiffening up. "You felt like a brick wall."

We all laughed.

Luis introduced Timoteo to Marlene, and after they exchanged a couple of introductory comments, he turned to me. "The cops impounded her Prius. She had to Uber over here."

I looked at Marlene. "The police are going to dig the bullets out of your car before they give it back. It might take a week or more before they return it."

"A *week*?" She looked from Luis to me. "Will they fix it when they're done? I need that car."

"No, they won't. But your insurance might cover it."

She exhaled, rolling her eyes. "I just finished paying it off."

"It was my fault, Marlene," Luis said. "Don't worry, we'll figure it out."

She squeezed his hand and looked down at him adoringly. "I know, baby, I'm just thankful you're alive." To me, she said, "If you hadn't been there..." her voice trailed off and tears welled up in her eyes. "Thank you."

I nodded and said to Luis, "Did you notice anyone in the bar watching you?"

His right eye flared for an instant, and he paused. "Almost forgot. I'm out of it, man. As I was leaving I saw one of the guys from the cantina."

"Know his name?"

"Nope. Only saw him a couple of times."

"Did he have his cell phone out?"

"How did you know that?"

"Just a hunch. Did he realize you recognized him?"

"No, I'm sure he didn't. He was talking to the bartender when I saw him. I figured it was best that he didn't know, so I didn't look at him or anything."

"That was smart, Luis."

At that moment, Detective Tate came in and immediately asked us to leave. I leaned in close to Luis. "Be honest with her. You can trust her." The look he returned was laced with skepticism. Luis Fuentes was not a man who trusted easily.

Chapter Twenty-Four

"Sounds like you have the tiger by the tail, my friend," Nando said as we were having lunch at Pambiche, our favorite Cuban restaurant. It was Friday, my pro bono day in Portland, and I'd just finished bringing him up to date. "The stakes must be high for these bags of scum to react so violently. The Fuentes family has much to fear and so do you."

"I hear you. You would have been proud. I had my Glock out and was ready to use it if the shooter had turned around."

Nando's thick, arching eyebrows raised, and he flashed a brilliant smile. "¡Bravo! Calvin!" The basso profundo outburst turned several heads. "I am proud of you."

After the onlookers turned their attention away from us, I said, "What have you got for me?"

"Several things. First, and further to my point about danger, my contact just informed me that a cartel hit man who is believed to operate out of L.A. is on assignment, perhaps in the Northwest. He is an independent contractor and goes by the name El Solitario." Nando raised a forkful of braised oxtail halfway to his mouth. "And he is reported to have used a motorcycle in some of his hits. Drive by, bang, bang, and then he seems to disappear."

The scene at the Road House rushed back to me in excruciating clarity. "The guy I saw shot with his left hand."

Nando nodded grimly. "A witness to one of the motorcycle attacks said the same thing. El Solitario is a leftie, about six foot tall. He wears leather and a tinted face visor."

"Sounds like our man." I cut a bite of red snapper but left it on my plate. "Why do these guys always have dumb nicknames?"

Nando shrugged. "Nicknames that stick come from the cartels, from men with small brains, much testosterone, and no consciences. In some twisted way, the hit man is a hero to them." Nando's look grew grave. "His presence raises the stakes, my friend."

"Of course. What else is known about him?"

"Other than the fact that he has killed at least a dozen people, very little. He has left no DNA behind, but LAPD thinks they have one good fingerprint. He prefers a thirty-eight-caliber handgun, but he has resorted to a knife and even a lead pipe on one occasion."

"An opportunist."

"Yes. He operates on both sides of the border and is believed to have an American passport. His nationality is unknown."

"What else you got?" I asked before taking a bite of fish. It tasted flat and unappetizing.

"The mysterious Diego Vargas has a day job. He is the driver for a man named Gavin Whittaker, a man of considerable means, apparently. Vargas has a green card, but it is probably bogus."

"A driver? Who the hell uses a driver these days?"

"Status, my friend, status. Whittaker has an estate on the Willamette River with horse stables, tennis courts, and a polo field."

"Anything else on Vargas?"

"He lives in Woodburn with his wife and ten-year-old son. No prior arrests."

"What about Robert Harris?"

"A native Oregonian, grew up in Portland, educated at Portland State. Lives in a nice apartment in McMinnville with a woman named Patricia Stiles. No priors, but one interesting thing—his FICO is 485."

I groaned. "That's a horrible credit score. Any clues as to why?"

"No. Do you wish me to dig into that?"

I took a long pull on my beer while considering the escalating cost of the investigation. "No, hold off for now."

Nando swallowed a bite of oxtail. "Detective Tate has probably picked up Vargas by now. Any word?" I shook my head, and he continued, "Surely the man would not be stupid enough to link himself to the murder attempt by using his cell phone to text Luis."

I pushed my plate away and drank some more beer. "Yeah, that is weird. A text from a burner phone could be from anyone, of course. And if Vargas is implicated, he would make sure he has a good alibi for the time of the attack."

Nando nodded slowly, his face grim again. "There is much that we do not know and every reason to proceed with great caution."

I had to agree.

———

Back at Caffeine Central, I checked in with Darci Tate between clients and a quick walk with Archie. "You sound tired," I said when she answered.

"Yeah, we took Diego Vargas in for questioning around three a.m. Didn't cut him loose until seven. He's got a solid alibi. Drove Whittaker and his wife into Portland and was waiting outside the Schnitzer for them at the time of the attack. Some kind of concert. Drove them home before going to bed at his place. Judge

McMaster signed off on a search warrant, but we didn't find diddly shit at his place."

"His phone?"

"No record of a text to Fuentes on it, of course. And the phone used to contact Fuentes can't be traced." She sighed wearily. "A big, fucking nothing burger."

"Did Luis remember anything else of interest?"

"No. I had to drag everything out of him. He's not real forthcoming to law enforcement, even after somebody tried to blow his head off." I suppressed a smile, and she went on, "I'm concerned about his safety when he leaves the hospital, too. Getting the chief to authorize protection for his girlfriend's place won't be easy. Any thoughts?"

"You read my mind. Let me look into it and get back to you." I then went on to tell her about El Solitario.

"A hit man with a moniker, huh?" she said after thanking me. "This case is getting hairy." Her voice had acquired a sharp edge, as if she were energized by the challenge of the new information. "Why in hell would a Mexican cartel have it in for the Fuentes family?" The question hung there for a moment, suggesting Tate suspected I knew more than I was telling her.

She was right, of course. I did know about Carlos Fuentes's cartel connection, which I was obligated to keep confidential. However, it didn't particularly bother me to withhold this information from Tate, because I didn't see the relevance. After all, it appeared that Luis, not his father, was the target of the cartel hit man.

All I answered was, "Good question."

——

Timoteo was covering my Dundee office. I called him at my next break. "How's Luis?"

"My brother has a hard head," he answered with a slight chuckle. "He'll be released this afternoon."

"We need to talk about security," I said. "Going back to Marlene's house might—"

"I've got that covered," Timoteo interjected. "Marlene's cousin has a basement apartment in Carlton they can stay in until we catch the shooter. The insurance company's authorized a rental car. I told them to make sure they're not followed out there."

"Excellent," I said, marveling again at the initiative of my young assistant. "I'll let Detective Tate know. How did your father take the news?"

Timoteo sighed heavily into the phone, his voice suddenly unsteady. "He's like a crazy man, Cal. Olivia's gone, and last night we almost lost Luis." He paused, and I imagined him trying to find the words. "He's furious, but at the same time I think he blames himself for everything. We haven't told Mamá about Luis. God only knows how she would react."

At this juncture, I decided not to tell Timoteo about the shooter's possible cartel ties. I said, "*No*. Your father shouldn't blame himself. We don't know what's going on yet. Whatever it is, it's not his fault." Zoe's warning that Olivia's murder had wounded the entire family reverberated in my head. "Listen, Timoteo," I went on, "I have a friend who's offered to help. She's a psychologist. What if I brought her around tomorrow? Do you think your father would listen to her?"

He puffed a dismissive breath. "Probably not, but what the hell? It can't hurt."

Archie picked up something in my voice and after I disconnected came over to me with concern showing in his big coppery eyes. I scratched him behind the ears. "We could use a couple of breaks, Big Boy," I said. "There's a lot riding on this investigation."

He whimpered sympathetically, and I swear his look said, "What else is new?"

———

I got back to the Aerie that afternoon in time for an hour and a half of labor on my wall, which was urgently needed to blow off steam and quell anxiety. I was just finishing up in the twilight when my cell phone sounded. "Hi, Cal, what's up?" Zoe said, returning my call.

I gave her an update and explained the situation with the Fuentes family. "I could take you over to their place in the morning, introduce you, then come back to hang out with Gertie while you talk to them."

She paused before responding. "Yeah, that might work. It would just be a get-acquainted session." A nervous laugh. "This isn't ideal. I don't know the Latino culture very well."

"Of course. For what it's worth, Timoteo said it couldn't hurt."

"Okay, I'll give it a try."

An awkward pause ensued. It was a Friday night, and I had no plans for the evening, and she probably didn't, either. Perhaps she was waiting for me to suggest something, just like I was waiting for her. In any case, we disconnected without either one of us making an overture. I felt a sense of relief. I told myself I wasn't looking for a relationship. Hell, the truth was I was incapable of sustaining one.

Chapter Twenty-Five

Against all odds I slept soundly that night, and when I awoke, the house had a chill to it. My clunking, antique radiator system had underachieved, as usual. I pulled on jeans and a thick sweater and followed Archie down the back staircase to the kitchen, let him out, and flipped on my espresso machine. A thick, utterly still blanket of fog had transformed the valley below into the Sargasso Sea, or at least what I imagined such a body of water might look like. A couple of hillside summits poked through the gray mass like islands, and the newly risen sun cast the whole scene in a soft, golden glow. By the time I drank my first cappuccino, Archie had announced himself at the kitchen door with a single, sharp bark—the one that said "let me in, I'm ready for breakfast."

I was in my study reading the headlines on my computer when Detective Tate called. "It's Saturday morning. You should be out riding your horse," I greeted her.

"Don't I wish. My ICE contact finally got back to me last night. No ICE agents were dispatched that morning to arrest Luis Fuentes."

I snapped to attention. "You're sure of that?"

"Yes. I trust my source implicitly."

"Why would Drake lie to me?"

"I don't know, but it suggests Luis was the target of the first hit, *not* Olivia."

"Agreed. Any progress on the shooter?"

"Not much. Vargas fizzled, but we extracted two slugs from the door of the Prius. Thirty-eights, like the one that killed Olivia. They're at the state lab to see if we can get a match. We've canvassed all the motorcycle rental agencies in the state. The shooter didn't rent that Kawasaki in Oregon, that's for sure."

"What did Vargas say about what he was doing at the Tequila Cantina?"

"He said he was just trying to help some young men out. Counseling is the term he uses. Nothing formal or official. Said he used to do work like that at his church but found a pool hall was a better draw. We checked his story. It was true. Apparently, he has a lot of cred with young Latinos."

"Did he admit knowing Luis?"

"He told us, yeah, he'd been there a few times, but he didn't have any direct contact with him. He said Luis was kind of standoffish."

"Did you buy it?"

She showed a thin smile. "I'm a cop, I don't buy anything. We asked for a few names to check that out, but he refused to give us any."

"Of course he'd refuse. They're undocumented."

"Exactly. Vargas may be dirty, but we've got nothing we can hold him on."

"Do you happen to know anything about Vargas's boss, Gavin Whittaker? That name rings a bell."

"Not much. Comes from money. His grandfather was a major player in the timber industry in the Northwest. His dad was a state senator back in the day." She paused. "Why do you ask?"

"No reason except curiosity."

———

Timoteo came to the door when Zoe and I arrived at the Fuentes residence that morning. I introduced Zoe, and we followed him into the kitchen, where Carlos was slouched at his usual spot at the table, a half-full cup of coffee in front of him. Dirty dishes stood in the sink and on the counters, and crusted pots with protruding utensils rested on the stove. Carlos had a two-day stubble, and his dark eyes, which could burn like lasers, were now dull, his face vacant. He stood, brushed some crumbs from his shirt, and managed a smile.

Timoteo saw me glance over at the sink and said with a sheepish look, "Yeah, I've been meaning to clean up around here."

I said, "This is my good friend, Dr. Bennett. She has skills to help families recover from tragedies like you and your family have suffered. She's come to see if there's anything she can do for you."

Zoe gave Timoteo an inclusive look before saying to Carlos, "I'm sorry for your loss. I can't imagine what your family has been going through. These are the hardest things we humans must endure. I studied psychology at a university, and I'm here to offer my help if you'll accept it."

Carlos shot his son a told-you-so look before turning his eyes back to Zoe. "People do not have to go to a university to understand sadness."

Zoe smiled with genuine warmth. "You are absolutely right, Mr. Fuentes. But sometimes people in great pain need help to turn understanding into healing."

Carlos's expression remained impassive. Timoteo said with an anxious edge to his voice, "She's an expert, Papi. She has come to help Mamá, but she must talk to us first. Please, let's hear what she has to say."

With the exception of the low growl of a tractor out in the

vineyards, the room fell silent. Finally, Carlos nodded and motioned toward a chair across from him. "Please sit, Dr. Bennett." To his son he added, "Make a fresh pot of coffee."

I made a quiet exit, drove back to the Aerie, and walked across the field to Gertie's place, Archie trotting beside me. Napping on the porch rail, Cedric the cat snapped awake and sauntered teasingly around the house as we approached. Archie gave a couple of obligatory barks but otherwise ignored the creature.

"You're looking great, Gertie," I said after she led me into the kitchen. Her silver hair was pulled into a tidy bun, her cheeks had some color, and a mischievous gleam had returned to her eyes.

A hint of a smile. "Well, I've felt better in my life, but then again I've felt a helluva lot worse, too." The smile intensified. "I'm getting spoiled, that's for sure. That niece of mine can't do enough for me."

I made us some coffee as we chatted, the conversation quickly coming around to the case. "Do you think she'll be able to help them?" Gertie said when we finally came to Zoe's involvement with the Fuentes family.

"I hope so. Carlos Fuentes was at least willing to listen to her."

Gertie sipped her coffee and eyed me over the cup. "Zoe's been through a lot herself, you know."

"No, I didn't know." I waited while she seemed to consider what to say next.

"She had a miscarriage, and then her first husband died in a climbing accident. Fell five hundred feet on Mt. Rainier. She married again, maybe a decade later, some professor at the University of Washington." Gertie set her coffee cup down and made a face. "She caught the bastard cheating on her with one of his graduate students."

I winced. "Sorry to hear that."

"Well, I get the sense she's at some kind of crossroads, you know, trying to figure out what's next in her life."

I nodded. "She told me she was burned out teaching, that the book she's writing isn't what her university's expecting."

Gertie rolled her eyes emphatically. "I *know*. I told her it'd be a shame if she blew her chance at tenure. Good academic jobs are hard to come by."

I shrugged to avoid taking a position. I knew all about being burned out and starting over, how personal it was, and I didn't want to be drawn into what was starting to feel like a gossip session.

Gertie read my reticence immediately. "She'll figure it out." Then, with a look of obvious pride, she added, "Zoe's something, isn't she?"

I smiled and nodded. "Yes, she is."

———

"How'd it go?" I asked Zoe when I picked her up at the Fuentes's house two hours later.

She shook her head with a wan smile. "Hard to say."

"What happened?"

She hesitated. "I'm bound by confidentiality, but I'll share what I can. I began with Timoteo and Carlos, figuring there was no way the mother would join us. Actually, it was better that way. I wanted to get a sense of where they are, and I decided to start with Timoteo. I kept it low-key, asking him to tell me about his sister." She exhaled a sigh. "Olivia was the heart of that family—the youngest, the smartest, the most loving. Timoteo literally glowed as he told me all about her. He's wounded, but he's young, and the fact that he's working with you is giving him a sense of purpose."

"I'm lucky to have him."

She nodded. "He apologized to me for not having his brother there. How's Luis seem after the attempt on his life?"

"He's a tough kid. He has a girlfriend, an older woman. I think she's helping him cope. We're keeping him out of sight for the time being."

"Carlos, on the other hand, is in a much different place," she went on. "He didn't have anything to add as Timoteo talked about Olivia. It was clear that sitting across from him and asking questions wasn't going to work. Too much like interrogation." She chuckled. "So, I got up and asked Timoteo to help me straighten up the kitchen. As we puttered around, I got Carlos to open up just a little."

"Brilliant. That kitchen looked like a bomb hit it."

"Yeah, well, Carlos is old school, you know. Showing emotion's a sign of weakness." She shot me a look that I ignored. "Anyway, he's consumed with anger and depression, and I sensed that overlaying everything is an almost crippling sense of guilt. I avoided asking him about the guilt, figuring it was too early, that it would shut him down completely." She paused for a moment. "You mentioned earlier that Carlos feared an old enemy might have reappeared to settle a score. Was Carlos connected with a cartel back in Mexico?"

"Why do you say that?" I said, keeping my eyes on the road. I should have known she'd figure it out. That's what you get when you're dealing with smart, perceptive people.

She laughed. "Just connecting the dots. So he was fleeing a criminal past?"

"That's, uh, confidential. It's complicated, Zoe, and I'd appreciate you not bringing it up with Carlos, or he'll think we discussed it. What I can tell you is that he came here to find a better life for his family. The fact that the hit man went after Luis suggests he's been the target all along, that this has nothing to do with Carlos's past."

"Unless it's the cruelest of retributions. Don't these cartel brutes always go after the family?"

I shrugged, biting my tongue.

She paused again, and I could feel her gaze on the side of my face as I kept my eyes on the road. "Okay, you can't talk about this," she said, finally. "Well, it's not unusual for a parent to feel guilty about the death of a child, even if they're blameless. That's another possibility."

I nodded. "Once Carlos gets to know you, maybe he'll open up."

"Well, he didn't exactly invite me back, but at least the kitchen's clean. Timoteo said he'd work on him and let me know. As I was leaving, I asked if I could introduce myself to Elena. Timoteo took my offer back to her, but she refused to come out. The situation in that household's tenuous at best, Cal."

"I know," was all I could say.

———

After dropping Zoe off, I returned to the Aerie feeling restless and agitated. Archie met me at the gate and trotted along next to the car as I coasted to a stop in front of the garage. A thatch of dark grayish clouds to the south warned of rain. Archie lobbied once again for a jog, but I figured the chances of getting caught in a downpour were too great. When I came back downstairs with my work boots on and picked up my leather gloves, he whimpered a couple of times. "We're staying close, Big Boy," I told him. "You know you hate getting caught in the rain even worse than I do."

I'd learned in my research that each successive course in a well-constructed dry-stack wall needs to be narrower than the last. The resulting inward taper on either side, albeit slight, assures stability as the wall height increases. It was becoming clear, however, that the taper requirement coupled with my decision to attempt a circular wall demanded a skill level I wasn't sure I possessed. After an hour of maddening starts and stops and a string of well-chosen expletives, I tore the entire course off and started over. I was complaining to my foreman when my cell phone rang.

"Cal," Timoteo said in a voice that instantly alarmed me, "we, um, we've got a problem. Can you meet my father and me in Lafayette?"

"What is it?"

"I'd rather not say on the phone. Please. It's urgent." He rattled off the address.

"I'll be right there."

Chapter Twenty-Six

Ten minutes later I pulled in behind the Fuentes's Honda and an old Ford pickup that had replaced the truck Olivia died in. They were parked on 14th Street, just off Monroe in Lafeyette. Carlos and Timoteo both sat in the Honda. Timoteo got out when he saw me, his face tight with tension.

"What's the problem?"

He pointed toward the Honda. "We can talk in the car."

After I got in, Carlos turned to me from the front seat. "Plácido Ballesteros is dead."

I sat forward. *"What?"*

His dark eyes registered a mixture of fear and apprehension. "I went to his house after Dr. Bennett left and found him dead in his living room. Murdered." He grimaced and made a quick sign of the cross. "It was an ugly sight."

I sucked a breath and exhaled. "You're sure he's dead?"

"Yes. There was no breath in him."

I looked at Timoteo, who'd gotten in the driver's seat. "Were you with your father when he found the body?"

"No. I met him here after he called me. When he told me what happened, I called you immediately."

"Good. Listen, Timoteo, I want you to take the truck, go home, and don't talk to *anyone* about this. Got it?"

He looked at me in disbelief. "But I want to hear what—"

"Go, Timoteo. You don't need to be involved, and talking to Carlos in front of you would waive his attorney-client privilege."

A chastised look. "Okay." He got out of the car and left in the truck. I turned back to Carlos. "You'd already talked to Plácido about the key. Why did you go back again?"

He took a piece of paper from his coat pocket, unfolded it, and handed it to me. "Luis sent me this by email."

A young Latino man stared back at me from what looked like a sketch done by a police artist. I looked up and snapped, "Who is this?"

"Plácido," Carlos said. "Luis drew it. It is the man he saw in the bar, the man who tipped off the killer as he left. I knew it was Plácido the moment I saw it."

I stared at the sketch for a few moments. It was deftly rendered in exquisite detail. I looked up. "So, you received this drawing and decided to go see him. Why?"

Carlos opened his big, gnarled hands and gave me an incredulous look. "To talk to him. To find out who the killer is."

"And you found him dead. Did you take a weapon with you?"

He opened his hands again. "Only these."

"How did you enter his house?"

"The front door was not locked. I knocked first and then opened the door to call to him. That's when I saw his body."

"Describe what you saw."

Carlos flinched, causing his eyes to close momentarily. A sheen of sweat coated his forehead. "He was on the sofa. Shears in his chest," he said, thumping his chest with his fist. "His eyes were open and like those of a bug. There was much blood."

"*Shears*? What kind of shears?"

"The shears we use to cut the grapes from the vines at harvesttime."

"You mentioned the blood. Did it seem fresh?"

He grimaced again, shaking his head. "It was not fresh. It looked thick and dark."

"How dark?"

"*Casi negra*, almost black. He had been dead, I think, many hours."

"Did you disturb or touch anything in the house?"

He shrugged. "I don't know. I had"—he seemed to struggle at not finding the English word—"*el pánico*."

"You were afraid. You panicked."

"*Sí*. I got out of there fast." He opened a hand and made a gesture. "But then I think, this is not right. I stopped here and called my son."

"Did anyone see you enter or leave the house?"

"I don't know."

I shook my head with a mix of frustration and anger. "You should have called me when you received the drawing, Carlos. Now we have a potential problem. The police will suspect you because you have a motive to kill this man."

His lined and weathered face remained impassive, the face of a man who'd encountered many existential threats in his life. "I am sorry, I—"

I waved him off. "Look, Carlos, you have two options here. You can leave now and let someone else find Plácido's body. The problem is, you'll be in a hell of spot when the cops come calling, and they almost certainly will. Lying to them would be inadvisable, to say the least, and I would have nothing to do with that. The second option is to call them right now and tell them *exactly* what you found and what you did. It's your choice."

"Do I need a lawyer?"

"You might. We'll see."

The car became silent except for the rasping sound of Carlos stroking his chin. "If I go to the police, *La Migra* will know I have no papers?"

I shook my head. "The police would have no reason to involve ICE in a homicide investigation. The same detective who's investigating your daughter's death would probably be involved. She and her partner have no interest in your immigration status."

He paused as three people on bicycles passed by. "We will call the police, then."

"A good choice." I paused for a moment. "Have you told me *everything*?"

Carlos nodded.

———

"Jesus, Cal, your timing's impeccable," Darci Tate said when I called her and explained what I'd just learned. "I'm at the Bistro Maison with a date, and we just ordered lunch. It's my first day off in couple of weeks."

"Sorry about that, Darci. We called 911, and we're waiting at the scene. I wanted to give you a heads-up."

She sighed heavily into the phone. "My mom told me to become a teacher. Should've listened to her."

While the ME examined Plácido Ballesteros's body and a forensic team worked the scene, Carlos gave a preliminary statement to Detective Tate. An awkward moment occurred when I offered to sit in on the interview. Tate looked at me with narrowed eyes. "Are you acting as his attorney on this?"

"He may need an interpreter," I said, a bit disingenuously. Tate shot me a yeah-right look but went along with it. The interview wasn't particularly adversarial, and I saw no need to warn

Carlos off any of Tate's questions. However, the formality of the detective's tone when she took a brief statement from me made it clear our cooperation agreement was, at best, suspended. It was a smart move, and I expected nothing less from a good cop like Darci Tate.

After Plácido's body was removed, I followed Carlos down to the police station in Newberg, where he answered a few more questions, signed a formal statement, and submitted to a physical examination. When he reappeared forty minutes later, his boots were gone, replaced by powder blue hospital booties.

He looked down at the booties when he saw me. "They took my boots," he said with an incredulous look. "They looked at my hands and face and my hair, too. Even my fingernails and inside my mouth."

"It's normal. They're just eliminating you as a suspect. They may have found some blood on your shoes. You could have easily stepped in some that wasn't completely dry."

I headed back to the Aerie after parting ways with Carlos and mulled the situation over. Plácido Ballesteros's murder dealt the case a severe blow. He was a man who could've identified or at least provided a description of the shooter. Was this the work of El Solitario? Nando's intelligence made it clear the cartel assassin didn't always use a gun. But a pair of shears used in the vineyards? That was odd, although that may have been the intent—a murder seemingly committed by another field hand, unrelated to the Olivia Fuentes case. And then Carlos blunders onto the scene. The timing was interesting as well, occurring at it did on the heels of the attempt to kill Luis.

Was someone meticulous about tying up loose ends?

Chapter Twenty-Seven

The rain let up by the next morning, although the mottled, unsettled sky promised more. While Archie conducted his morning sweep of the acreage, I downed a breakfast of granola and blueberries and two double cappuccinos. Archie reappeared at the kitchen door and dutifully lifted each mud-coated paw for me for me to clean with a towel. I went to my study and was absorbed in the morning news when I heard whimpering behind me. I turned to find him standing in the doorway with one of my jogging shoes in his mouth.

I chuckled. "Not now, Big Boy. I've got work to do."

He whimpered again and gave me his patented doleful look, but when I turned back to my computer screen, I heard the shoe drop and his nails clicking down the oak flooring in the hallway. I could just see the pouty look on his face.

Claims and counterclaims, tweets and retweets, the news offered little to rejoice about that morning. An item on the fate of the Dreamers caught my eye. The Supreme Court finally agreed to hear arguments on whether DACA would survive the current administration's attempt to terminate the program. We're coming into an election year, I mused. A ruling one way or the other might force Congress to do something. But what?

My thoughts eventually turned to the case, specifically Diego Vargas, who seemed in the middle of this thing, despite his alibis. That brought me to his boss, Gavin Whittaker. Would Whittaker know something important about Vargas, perhaps unwittingly? On a whim, I typed Whittaker's name into my browser and hit search.

A handful of articles came up.

A brief item in the *Seattle Post-Intelligencer* described a wedding reception held at the Chilean consulate four years earlier for Whittaker and a woman named Isabel Torres, daughter of a prominent family in Chile. The article mentioned that the financier and the former Miss Chile met on a cruise and that the wedding, held in Santiago, was a major social event. A photograph of the couple cutting their wedding cake showed a tall, heavyset man smiling next to a slim, dark-haired woman of exceptional beauty.

Another reference to Whittaker popped up in a three-year-old article about the rush to invest in the burgeoning cannabis industry in Oregon. The story featured Whittaker, who had redirected the focus of his private investment firm from high-tech startups to cannabis production and sales. "Oregon will be a leader in this industry, and I'm positioning Whittaker Investments to participate in that growth in a major way," he was quoted. The article went on to describe the six large farms and the string of retail outlets he bought for a sum rumored to be well north of two hundred million dollars. I whistled when I read the amount.

Two short articles attesting to Whittaker's civic mindedness popped up in the *News-Register*—one highlighting his sponsorship of a local rugby team playing for a state title, and a second announcing his joining the board of a local nonprofit. When I read the headline of the second article, I sloshed my coffee on the desk as I snapped to attention:

WHITTAKER TO JOIN PROSPERAR
BOARD OF DIRECTORS.

In a press release today, Dr. Sofia Leon, Director of Prosperar, a nonprofit medical organization headquartered in McMinnville, announced that Gavin Whittaker, president of Whittaker Investments, would join Prosperar's Board of Directors. "We're thrilled to have Gavin join us," Ms. Leon remarked. "His business expertise and his generous heart will bolster Prosperar's mission of providing medical services to workers and their families who lack adequate health insurance. When citizens like Gavin step up, it reminds us all of the need to show compassion for the less fortunate among us."

After mopping up the spilled coffee, I stood and turned to Archie, who had slunk back into the room and taken up his customary spot in the corner. "Well, how about that? A connection between Diego Vargas and Prosperar once removed. What do you think?" He looked at me but barely lifted his chin from his paws. Not much, apparently.

I immediately dug Sofia Leon's card out and called her, hoping she'd pick up, despite it being a Sunday morning. I reached her voicemail and left a message. Next, I went on Facebook and tapped in Diego Vargas's name, and up came his home page complete with a nice headshot, which I copied, pasted, and printed out. Vargas's page was spare, showing only a few photographs and postings revolving around family events. One photo caught my eye—a picture of him and a young boy, with the caption "So proud of my son on his 10th birthday." Dangerously thin looking, the boy smiled bravely into the camera from a wheelchair.

"Huh."

I was headed for the kitchen to make another cappuccino when Leon called back. Twenty minutes later I pulled into Prosperar's parking lot, cracked the windows, and told Archie to chill. A car ride was no substitute for a jog, but he took the trade-off in stride. As I traversed the parking lot, I noticed Robert Harris's BMW in the employee section of the lot. Inside, the waiting room was crowded and rang with a chorus of coughs. Flu season.

"Ms. Leon's expecting you," I was told when I announced myself. "Last office on the right." This time I was allowed to find my own way.

Wearing jeans, a faded denim shirt with rolled sleeves, and a multicolored scarf covering her hair, Sofia Leon looked up from a handful of papers when I knocked at her open door. "Caught me working on a Sunday," she said with the look of someone in the midst of pressing tasks. She pushed her glasses up the bridge of her nose, and her look grew serious. "How's the investigation going?"

"Slow but sure. Thanks for taking the time, Ms. Le—"

"Sofia, please. I talked to Detective Tate about Olivia's possible interest in Robert like you suggested. She came back to talk to Robert a second time, but I don't know what came of it."

"Robert didn't say anything about the second interview?"

"No, nothing."

"How's he holding up?"

She absently laid the papers on the desk. "Not very well. And I think being questioned a second time only upset him more. We're all struggling with this, of course, but Robert seems to be a lot more sensitive than I realized." She paused for a moment and looked a little sheepish. "I did think of one other thing about Olivia and Robert." I waited. "Late one afternoon, maybe a month ago, I went to Robert's office to get a budget update he'd printed out for me. Olivia was sitting at his computer when I burst in. We were both startled, but she seemed, well, I don't know, pretty flustered, maybe a little guilty, like I'd caught her in the act of something."

"What did she say?"

"She said she was looking for a spreadsheet Robert had promised her." Leon smiled wistfully. "That was just like Olivia, such a go-getter. And Robert always promises more than he delivers."

"But you think she might have been looking for something else?"

Leon shrugged. "I don't know what it could have been. We don't have any secrets around here. It only seemed odd to me after all this mess happened." She shook her head. "It's probably nothing."

I thanked her for mentioning it and then fished the photograph of Diego Vargas from my shirt pocket and handed it to her. "I'm wondering if you know this man or have seen him around your facility."

She adjusted her glasses again and scrutinized the photo. "No. I've never seen him before. Who is he?"

"His name's Diego Vargas. He's the driver for one of your board members, Gavin Whittaker."

Her eyes flared slightly behind her glasses. "Oh, that's right. Gavin does have a driver." She made a face, indicating she didn't approve of such a show of wealth. "And why are you interested in this man?"

"Vargas is doing some great counseling work with young Latino men. I thought maybe Whittaker had mentioned it to you or members of your staff."

"No, but I could ask around, show the photo, but I don't understand—"

"That's not necessary at this juncture," I cut in, "but I'm wondering if you could help connect me with Whittaker. I'd like to ask him a few questions."

She handed the photo back to me, her expression remaining quizzical. "Sure, I could give him your cell number and ask him to call you. I'm not sure how he'll respond. The subject's this man, Vargas?"

I smiled hesitantly before deciding to disclose more information than I wished. "Yes. The police have already talked to Whittaker about him. One of the men Vargas counseled was Olivia's brother, Luis. There's been an attempt on his life." I was stretching the truth a bit on the counseling part, but I wanted to get her attention.

Leon sucked a breath. *"No. What happened?"*

I gave her a brief description, leaving out many of the details. "I'm just trying to fill in a few blanks. Whittaker can say no, of course."

"Of course," Leon said absently, her face twisted in anguish over my revelation. She looked at me. "Who in the world would want to harm the Fuentes family?" She removed her glasses and dabbed the corners of her eyes. "What's gotten into this world? I just don't understand."

A kindred soul. I nodded but then changed the subject. "Gavin Whittaker was quite an addition to your board."

"He's been a real asset." She paused for a moment as if deciding what to say next. "The truth is, we can thank his wife, Isabel, for pushing him into it. She's been a generous supporter for some time." A thin smile. "I asked Isabel to join the board first, but she demurred and suggested her husband might consider it. I doubt Gavin would've done it on his own."

"Did you get any blowback because of Whittaker's involvement in the cannabis industry?"

"I did, even from some of my own board members. But health care's expensive and our clinic has a high burn rate. Gavin wrote us a big check when he joined the board, and he has a lot of connections in the business world. And, besides, the cannabis business is legal now." She straightened in her seat. "My focus is on the families we serve, Cal. I'll take help from wherever I can get it."

"Makes sense," I said. "I, uh, noticed Robert Harris is here today. Do you think he'd mind if I popped in and asked him a few more questions?"

"Like me, he's working on next year's budget, so he's swamped. I'm sure you'll be respectful of his time."

I left Leon's office hoping Harris was still around. I was in luck. I saw him come down the hall from the opposite direction and go into his office. I don't think he recognized me. I followed him in and shut the door behind me with a sharp click.

He spun around, and I said, "Hello, Robert. It's me again, Cal Claxton. I'd like to ask you a few questions."

He froze with the look of a trapped animal on his face. "I've got a long day ahead of me. Why don't you—"

I didn't feel like dancing around with him again. "Cut the crap, Robert," I snapped. "If you care as much about Olivia Fuentes as everyone says you do, you'll make some time. Sit down, this won't take long."

He sat, folded his arms across his chest, and scowled back at me. "I've talked to the police twice. Why should I talk to you?"

"Because you want to help bring Olivia's killer to justice, right?" He nodded somewhat reluctantly. "You and Olivia were close, is that correct?"

"We were friends, that's all." His face clouded over. "Olivia was very outgoing."

"Did you notice anything unusual about her behavior in, say, the month leading up to her death? Was she upset about anything?"

"How many times do I have to answer that question?"

"One more time. Indulge me."

"No, I didn't notice anything. We were busy, adding patients right and left. She was her usual, energetic self."

"Did she ever mention a job-counseling activity being held at a bar on the Pacific Highway called the Tequila Cantina? Young Latino men? Her brother, Luis, attended a couple of times at her request."

His gaze dropped to the surface of the desk separating us, and when he swallowed, the Adam's apple below his missing chin did a little jig. "No, not that I recall." He looked up. "It doesn't surprise me, though. Olivia was plugged into a number of migrant causes in the valley."

I produced the picture of Diego Vargas. "Do you know this man?"

He leaned forward and rubbed a hand on his pant leg absently. "No. Why do you ask?"

"Just filling in background information."

His Adam's apple did another jig, and he glanced at his watch. "I got a budget to get out. Is there anything else I can help you with?"

I told him no and thanked him for his time. At the door I turned back and met his eyes. "I hope you haven't forgotten something important, Robert, something that could help the investigation. Last Thursday night, Olivia's brother was nearly killed, probably by the same man who killed Olivia. Think about it."

He recrossed his arms and leaned back, struggling to appear unconcerned. "That's all I got. Sorry."

As I exited the Prosperar building, I replayed the encounter in my head. I could understand a bit of defiance on Harris's part, even the nervous tells he exhibited, seeing as how this was his third interview on a subject that was painful to him.

But what I didn't get was what I saw in his eyes—*abject fear*. Robert Harris was afraid about something, and the fear was so strong I could almost smell it.

Chapter Twenty-Eight

"What's up?" Timoteo said, returning my call as I headed back to Dundee from Prosperar. "I was giving my father a hand and didn't have my phone on me. He's, um, upset about his boots, but he said you told him not to worry about it. He's not a suspect in the Ballesteros murder, is he?"

"The police know he's got a strong motive, but it's clear Plácido was dead when your father discovered his body. There shouldn't be anything to worry about, except that a cold-blooded killer's still out there. I haven't had a chance to ask, how's Luis?"

"He's on the mend, and they've settled in at the house in Carlton."

"That was quite a drawing he sent your father. He's got talent."

"I know. You should see his paintings. They're amazing." Timoteo went on to tell me the visit from Zoe had gone better than he'd anticipated. "She was great, Cal, and I think Papi might be okay with another visit." He chuckled. "Particularly if it means getting a clean kitchen thrown in."

I told him about the potential connection between Diego Vargas and Prosperar through Gavin Whittaker, and, after I finished describing my second encounter with Robert Harris, the line when quiet for a couple of beats.

"Is he still at Prosperar?" my assistant asked, his voice tinged with excitement.

"Probably. He said he had a lot of work today, budget issues."

Timoteo exhaled. "The more I think about Olivia cozying up to that guy, the more I think he's *got* to be involved, you know? I mean, she wouldn't waste her time. And what you just told me makes me think that even more. Let me follow him, Cal, find out what he's up to."

I paused. I'd gone back and forth with myself on that very idea because it had merit but could be dangerous. "I don't like the risks at all."

"Don't worry, I'll be careful."

"I don't think—"

"Olivia was my *sister*, Cal. Let me do this. I'll be careful."

I sighed. "Harris seemed rattled by my visit. He might do something careless. It's worth a try, but you—"

"I know, I know, I'll watch it. I can cover his lunch break and when he gets off work today and tomorrow. I've got classes the next day, but I should be able to get to Prosperar before they leave for the day."

"Let's see how it goes today, okay?" I described Harris's silver Z4. "If he sees you, he'll know we suspect something. Take the truck, it'll blend in. Stay at least four car-lengths back. Get the addresses of any stops he makes, and, if possible, make note of anyone you see him talking to. Use your cell phone camera if you can."

He laughed. "I can do better than that. Luis has a Nikon 3500 with a telephoto lens. I'll use that if I see anything interesting. Luis won't mind."

"Sounds like you're well prepared, not that it surprises me. Stay safe."

———

The rain didn't materialize, so I finally suited up for a jog, much to Archie's delight. Once we were outside, he tore down the driveway a hundred feet or so, then spun around and sat on his haunches to wait while I stretched. When I finally began jogging, he let out a high-pitched squeal, spun back around, and took off, barking with every stride.

Out on the road, we ran into Zoe, who was also taking advantage of the sunbreak. "I heard you coming," she said, smiling, "so I waited." She wore a ball cap with her hair threaded through the gap in the back and rain gear.

I laughed. "Everyone in the Red Hills heard us coming. Archie's squeals can damage your hearing." I pointed in the uphill direction. "We usually head up to the cemetery. Join us?"

She agreed, and we started off with Archie leading the way. I let Zoe set the pace and stayed abreast of her. However, I quickly found her pace was at the upper range of what I could sustain, particularly after we cleared the relatively flat portion of the run and began the steep, two-and-a-half-mile climb to the summit. It wasn't a race, but something close to it, and by the time we reached the Pioneer Cemetery, my lungs were burning, and we were both laughing.

"Oh, so we're stopping here?" she said, panting.

With a hand on each knee, I managed to say, "Only to take in the view. I'm not winded, are you?"

We both laughed, and she looked around. "I've been up here before. There're some old graves in this cemetery."

"Yeah. The first white settlers arrived here around 1850. Free government land, although it really belonged to the Native Americans. You know, manifest destiny and all that."

"But the Native Americans got their casinos," Zoe deadpanned.

I smirked. "Of course. Such an even trade." I looked out at the undulating hills that fell away to the south, their fall colors muted by a leaden sky. "Lots of farming was tried up here—sheep, prunes, hops, hazelnuts, you name it. But they didn't call it the Red Hills for nothing. Volcanic soil isn't all that fertile. Dundee never flourished until some vintners from California decided to try growing pinot noir in the early seventies."

"Why pinot noir grapes, anyway?"

"They're the grapes that made the Burgundy region's wines legendary. Turns out the climate and soil here produce wines that rival anything made in France. Oregon pinots have a wonderful complexity." I gave her a mock accusing look. "Like those 2012s you're pilfering from your aunt."

She pushed me hard and took off down the hill. "You lie," she shouted over her shoulder. Archie began to follow her but suddenly stopped and looked back, yelping frantically a couple of times. He was a herding dog, and his flock was becoming separated.

"Okay, Big Boy," I said, "I'm coming." I began jogging just in time. If I'd waited much longer, I would've never caught up to Zoe Bennett that afternoon.

———

I was in Gertie's kitchen, and the Yukon Golds, carrots, and onions were browning nicely in the skillet. I sprinkled on some flour and added a cup of sauvignon blanc. The wine hissed—a sound I never tired of—and began to simmer. At the end of our jog, Zoe had begun fretting about preparing dinner. "I have some chicken thighs," she'd said, "but I don't know what to do with them." I started riffing on the possibilities, which led her to finally ask, "Would you like to be our guest tonight…and do the cooking?" I told her I'd be right over as soon as I showered and fed Arch.

I put the pre-browned chicken thighs back in the skillet along with some chicken stock, thyme, and smoked paprika, covered the pan, and placed it in a hot oven. Meanwhile, Zoe worked on a salad. While the braised chicken and vegetables roasted, I sketched in the events of the last several days for her and Gertie.

When I finished, Gertie eyed me with the same look of despair I'd seen on Sofia Leon's face. "Another murder in the Red Hills? And what've you got at this point? A madman riding around on a motorcycle, a suspicious bean counter at Prosperar, and the chauffeur of one of their board members, who's the pied piper to some weird group of young Latinos? What the hell's going on? It makes no sense."

I ran a hand through my hair and exhaled. "I know the first murder was carefully planned, and Ballesteros paid the price for having supplied the vineyard key. The attempted kidnapping of Luis Fuentes and the subsequent attempt on his life suggests he was the intended target for the first murder."

"But you can't rule out Olivia," Zoe chimed in. "After all, she sent Luis to the cantina, suggesting she knew or suspected something."

I chewed my cheek for a moment. "That's right, I can't." I swung my gaze to Gertie. "That brings me back to Prosperar. I'm looking for something big enough to motivate this kind of violence and risk-taking. I just don't know what it is yet." The other possibility—that the whole mess had been triggered by Carlos Fuentes's previous cartel association—went unmentioned, of course.

The discussion of the case wound down over dinner, which turned out pretty damn good, if I do say so myself. It didn't hurt that I paired the chicken and vegetables with a young Carabella pinot I'd brought from my cellar. After dinner, Gertie retreated to her bedroom to watch a British whodunit on PBS.

Zoe and I cleaned up, and then she accompanied me and Arch, who'd been dozing on the back porch, to the gate. The moon shone hazily behind a veil of clouds, and as if on cue a four-note call drifted from the Doug firs lining the east side of my property.

"Is that an owl?" Zoe asked.

"Yep, a great horned owl. It's got a wingspan like this," I said, spreading my arms as wide as they'd go. "It took up residence in those trees about the same time you showed up."

"A good omen," she quipped, craning her neck as if to see the bird. The pale moonlight managed to just play off one of her pearl earrings. She'd put the pair on after our run. But who's noticing? She turned back to me, and her demeanor became serious. "This attack on the Fuentes family is frightening, Cal. Whoever's behind this might turn on you. I mean, you seem to be making more headway than the police. That won't go unnoticed."

I shrugged in false indifference. I was worried about that, too, but the death of Olivia Fuentes touched me deeply. There would be no turning back. "Not much headway from where I sit," I responded. "I've uncovered some facts, but I can't see a pattern yet. It's frustrating."

She took my hand in both of hers and squeezed. "Be careful, okay?"

I nodded and started across the field with my dog, trying hard to ignore what had just happened. When her hands touched mine, I felt something unexpected, but this is no time for that, I told myself.

Chapter Twenty-Nine

"Harris likes to gamble," Timoteo said over the phone just as I reached my front steps. "I followed him to an apartment building over by the Michelbook Country Club. I assume that's where he lives. An hour later he came out with a woman, and they got in the Z4. The light was low, but I got a couple of decent shots."

"The woman was probably his girlfriend," I said.

"Right. Anyway, they drove off." Timoteo laughed. "He may own a Z4, but he doesn't drive it like a sports car. I had no trouble keeping up with him in the pickup. They drove down to the Spirit Mountain Casino."

"That's interesting. Nando reported that his credit score was in the crapper."

"Makes sense. I put on shades and a ball cap and followed them in. Mariana went in separately, so Harris—"

"Wait a minute, you followed him into the casino? With *Mariana*?"

"Yeah. We were going to hang out before this came up and, you know, when I mentioned what I was going to do, she wanted to come along. I, um, I figured it would be better cover, you know, a couple, and she's not going to tell anyone."

I paused for a moment. "Look, Timoteo, that was *not* a good idea. Taking someone with you? And I told you to stay in the car."

"Um, sorry," he said, his voice contrite. "So Harris bought a stack of chips and—"

"Don't leave your car again, okay?"

"Got it. Sorry," he repeated. "Anyway, Harris started in at a blackjack table, the high-stakes one. His girlfriend played the slots. They left two hours later, when he'd lost all his chips. He didn't look like a happy camper, believe me."

"Okay, duly noted."

"We'll pick up the trail tomorrow when he gets off work. We can study while we're waiting, so no worries."

After we disconnected, a shudder ran through me. Nothing can happen to those kids, I said to myself. Should I shut the surveillance down? I thought about that. No, I decided. That ship had sailed. On the bright side, I was glad Timoteo was seeing his sister's best friend. Perhaps they could help each other heal.

———

The next day, a Monday, began with a minor victory when Ned Gillian called at nine a.m. to tell me his client had taken the Chihuahua deal I'd offered. "He's not happy about it, but I finally got him to agree."

"Fine. I'll draw up the papers and send them over to you."

"Okay. Like I said, Cal, I owe you for this."

I laughed the comment off at the time, but it turned out that I would, indeed, need Ned Gillian's help.

The morning flew by, and at half past noon, I was having a quick sandwich over at the Red Hills Market when a call came in. "Cal Claxton? This is Gavin Whittaker. I had a message from

Sofia Leon to call. What can I do for you?" He had a deep, reso-
nant voice, and his tone was brusque.

I swallowed a bite hurriedly. To be honest, I hadn't expected
to hear from Whittaker. "Thanks for calling. I, uh, was wondering
if you could spare a few minutes. I'm working with the Fuentes
family, whose daughter was murdered recently. I—"

"Sofia said this was about my driver, Diego. I've already spoken to the police, but if speaking to you will further clarify the
situation, fine. Diego Vargas is a good man and had nothing to
do with that ghastly murder or the drive-by, I can assure you. I'm
working from home today. You're welcome to stop by. I'm free
between one thirty and two."

An hour later, after dropping Archie at the Aerie, I turned off
Riverwood Road at the Whittaker residence. The entrance
was marked by massive stone pillars and an equally imposing
wrought-iron gate that had *Whittaker Landing* scrolled across its
intricate latticework. The landing was one of two large estates
along that stretch of the Willamette River, both of which har-
kened back to the Gilded Age, if not in longevity then certainly in ostentatiousness. I announced myself at the intercom
attached to one of the pillars, and the gate parted in the middle
and silently swung open. Following a long drive lined with
overarching alders, I came to a fork in the road. I stopped and
glanced around, but there were no signs to guide me. The left
fork led toward the river, which seemed the more likely route to
the manor house, so I took it.

I realized my mistake when I rounded a tight turn and came
to a large, red barn with a half dozen stables and an adjacent
paddock, where three sleek chestnut horses looked up at me

with curiosity. Beyond the paddock, white fencing enclosed a wide field stretching to the trees along the river, where a small, brightly painted shed marked a path to the river. A set of black-and-white-striped poles, maybe twenty feet apart, sat at either end of the field—polo goals, I surmised. I pulled into a muddy parking area next to a red Tesla Model 3 and was halfway turned around when I head a woman's voice.

"Can I help you?" I recognized her immediately as Whittaker's wife, Miss Chile, although she was much more beautiful than the photographs I'd seen in the newspaper. Wearing a checkered shirt with sleeves rolled up and jodhpurs tucked into well-worn riding boots, she regarded me with an appraising yet friendly expression.

I stopped and got out smiling at her. "I, uh, think I turned the wrong way at the fork. I'm Cal Claxton. I've got an appointment with Gavin Whittaker."

Her radiant dark hair was pulled back, her soft brown eyes expressive, and the syringe she held in her latex-gloved right hand caught my attention. She returned the smile, which rivaled Nando's in candlepower, and after confirming she was indeed Isabel Whittaker, said, "Yes, the house is to the right at the fork." As I thanked her and started to get back in my car, she added, "Since you are here at the stables, could you spare me a few moments?" She brushed a lock of hair from her forehead and held up the syringe. "I am trying to vaccinate a very nervous young horse, and it is not working. I need another pair of hands. It won't take long, I promise."

I noticed a line of deep bruises on her left arm that seemed to attest to her plight. "Of course." I followed her into the barn and down to the last stall.

"This is Emilio," she said by way of introduction as she rolled her sleeves down and buttoned them. "He is a four-year-old quarter horse, but I am not training him to race." Emilio eyed me suspiciously with big liquid eyes and snorted loudly. Laying the syringe on a low bench, Isabel reached into a bag and extracted a big carrot. "All you must do is hold his halter firmly and allow him to nibble this carrot. Just allow him little bites. It will calm him."

"Okay," I said, and she showed me where to grip the halter before retrieving the syringe. She slapped Emilio's neck twice and on the third stroke inserted the needle. His head kicked up, but I caught it and offered the carrot, and when he began to nibble, Isabel depressed the syringe plunger.

"Bravo," she cried, her eyes flashing delight. "It is done. Thank you so much."

She walked me to my car and, after I got in, eyed me with curiosity. "Do you mind my asking what your business is with my husband?" The question was direct and somewhat unexpected.

I sensed an opportunity. "I'm working with the Fuentes family in connection with the murder of their daughter, Olivia. I—"

Isabel gasped, and her hand flew to her mouth involuntarily. "Oh, my God, that was so horrible. Who would do such a thing?"

I shook my head. "I'm working with the family to help the police in the investigation. A sort of bridge between them and the immigrant community, you might say. There's not a lot of trust these days."

Her eyes flashed again. "Yes, these people have every reason to be afraid." She paused and cocked her head. "Is this about Diego Vargas? I know the police talked to Gavin about him. He had nothing to do with the attack on the girl's brother. He was with Gavin and me in Portland that night."

"I know. The brother, Luis Fuentes, was in a group Diego was counseling. The investigation has stalled, so I'm following up every connection, no matter how obscure."

"I see. You should know Diego is doing good work. These young men need all the help they can get. He used to do that work at his church, but he moved it to a pool hall to attract a wider, more underserved group."

"Commendable. Is he still doing this work?"

"As far as I know, yes."

"At the same venue?"

"I don't know."

I started my car, and a horse whinnied in the field. "Your horses are beautiful, or should I say handsome?"

She beamed. "They're both. Thank you." Inexplicably, the smile drained from her face. "They are my refuge," she said so softly I barely heard it. I waited for her to continue, but she seemed to catch herself. The smile reappeared, although her eyes betrayed a hint of sadness. "Thanks again for the help, Mr. Claxton." She placed a hand on my arm. "And I hope you find the person who killed that young girl."

It was strange, but I felt a connection to this woman, as if a bond of trust had formed between us instantly. Although I had no reason to, I handed her a card and asked her to call me if she thought of anything else.

———

A slate-roofed behemoth with a turret rising out of one side, the Whittaker residence could have been used to film a British period piece. The English ivy clinging to the front of the structure added to the effect. I parked behind a dark-blue Land Rover SUV with tinted windows that sat on the edge of a semicircular cobblestone drive with a gurgling fountain in the center. I half expected a butler in tails to answer the bell, but it turned out a young Latina wearing a nervous smile did the honors. She led me down a central hallway and knocked softly on an ornately paneled door.

"What is it?" an irritated voice snapped from within. "I'm on the phone."

"Your visitor."

"Oh, Christ. Forgot. Have him wait."

She looked at me apologetically.

"No problem," I reassured her.

The maid and I tried to converse, me in tortured Spanish and her in equally flawed English. I did learn she lived on the grounds with her husband, and they were both from the state of Michoacán in Mexico.

A good five minutes later the door burst open. "Sorry," Whittaker said, extending his hand, "I thought that damn conference call would never end." He was a couple of inches taller than me with coiffed, wavy black hair, a florid complexion, and a waistline that had gotten away from him some time ago. He retreated behind his hulking mahogany desk, and after I explained my role in the investigation, said, "So how's it going? It's been, what, nearly three weeks since the murder?"

"It's progressing."

He smiled. "*Progressing*? Come on. Surely the police have some leads, a suspect maybe?"

"I'm not privy to everything the Major Crimes Response Team has uncovered."

He held the smile, which had acquired a tinge of sarcasm. "What about *your* investigation? I hear you're a capable crime-solver."

"Progress has been slow, and I'm hoping you'll be able to help me."

He leaned back in his chair. "Of course. The thought of that butcher running free out there makes my blood run cold. As I mentioned, I've told the detectives everything I know, but go ahead, tell me how I can help you."

"Diego Vargas isn't a suspect here, but I'm interested in his counseling work. Did he ever talk about it with you?"

"Occasionally. Fine work he's doing."

You have to give a little to get a little, I said to myself before asking the next question: "Do you know of any connection between his work and Prosperar, the medical group whose board you serve on?"

"No." He said it quickly, with finality.

"He didn't associate with anyone at Prosperar?"

"Not that I know of. I mean, he drives me over there occasionally, but generally waits in the car."

"Were any of his counselees connected with Prosperar?"

"You'd have to ask him."

I leaned in. "Would Vargas talk to me?"

Whittaker paused. "After the way the cops treated him, I'm not so sure. I mean, we're talking Gestapo tactics. They stormed in and searched his house, scared the hell out of his wife and his kid, embarrassed him. And the kid's not well. All because somebody sends a text from a burner phone with his name on it? Come on." Whittaker's face took on some color. "And then, they came back *again* after that worker got stabbed up in the hills."

"Plácido Ballesteros," I said.

"Whatever. Is Diego going to be a suspect in every crime around here? Well, we were down in southern Oregon when that happened." He paused. "Are the two crimes connected?"

I shrugged a nonanswer. "Look, I can see Diego's point, but I'd still like to talk to him. I'm not with the police. Maybe he'll feel more comfortable talking to me. The smallest detail could be important."

Whittaker nodded. "Okay. I'll ask him and get back to you, but don't hold your breath. And, if there's anything else I can do, just let me know."

A crunching handshake and an exchange of business cards sent me on my way, escorted by the maid. As I traversed the central hall, my eyes were drawn to a large portrait of the man, a complimentary depiction of Gavin Whittaker in a crossed-arm, captain-of-industry pose suitable for a *Time* magazine cover. There were photos and plaques along the walls, too, de rigueur for a man intent on documenting his status in the world—an award here, standing with a well-known politician there, and even a shot of him with what looked like the rugby team I'd read about in the *News-Register*.

As I pulled out onto the Pacific Highway, I wasn't optimistic that I'd accomplished much of anything. However, two observations caught my attention. First, something in that rugby photo rang a bell, although I couldn't quite put my finger on it. Second, those bruises on Isabel's arm—the ones she apparently didn't want me to see—consisted of four evenly spaced marks, about the distance between the fingers of a large hand. Inflated ego aside, Gavin Whittaker seemed a decent enough guy, but those bruises gave me pause.

Chapter Thirty

It was late afternoon, so I drove straight to the Aerie, changed clothes, and began to work on the wall with Archie looking on in bored acceptance. I resumed laying the course I'd torn down, choosing the rocks with slightly more experience, all the while revisiting the encounters at Whittaker Landing. I kept coming back to Isabel's comment about her horses being her *refuge*. Not the words so much but that look of sadness in her eyes. Someone with a large, strong hand had grabbed her by the arm. Was it her husband? I had no way of knowing, of course, but the thought of it bothered me. A lot.

I was hefting a large slab of blue basalt when some somnolent synapse awoke and fired in my brain—one of the players in that rugby photo had a Vandyke mustache and goatee. *That* was what had caught my eye. I dropped the slab, sat down on it, and pulled out my phone. "What was the name of that team?" I asked Archie, who had snapped to attention owing to my odd behavior. "The North Valley Rugby Club," I said, answering my own question.

I pulled up the team photo on my screen and enlarged it to the max. The Vandyke guy was standing next to Gavin Whittaker, proud sponsor of the club. I looked over at Arch. "I'll be damned, Big Boy. That dude with the beard is Curtis Drake from the ICE holding center."

I sat there mulling that over and then got up and went into the house. I pulled a cold Mirror Pond from the fridge, popped the cap off, and went into my study. Taking a sheet of blank paper, I drew three circles, labeling them:

PROSPERAR CANTINA CARTEL

Inside the first I wrote *Olivia Fuentes, Robert Harris, Gavin Whittaker,* and *Sofia Leon.* Inside the second I wrote *Diego Vargas, Luis Fuentes, Plácido Ballesteros,* and *Others,* and inside the third, El Solitario. And off to one side, I wrote *Curtis Drake.* I studied the sheet for a while, then linked all the known connections with dotted lines.

I leaned back, looked at the sheet, and laughed out loud. A map of sorts but with no discernable pattern, it looked like a web spun by a drunken spider. Undeterred, I taped it to the wall, took out a second sheet of paper, and jotted down the questions and observations that came to mind.

1. *Why did Olivia send Luis to the cantina? What was Vargas doing there?*
2. *Who was the intended first victim? Luis, most likely, motive unknown. Olivia can't be ruled out, motive unknown. Carlos unlikely, motive could be cartel revenge.*
3. *Who sent El Solitario and why?*
4. *Who texted Luis?*
5. *Where does Robert Harris fit in, and what is he afraid of?*

6.   *Is Drake, ICE supervisor and alleged white supremacist, a player?*
7.   *Why did he lie to me about Luis?*

I taped the questions next to the spiderweb and studied them as I sipped my Mirror Pond. There were more questions than answers, and I had no theory of the crimes that made sense of the puzzle.

There was, however, a possible through line: Olivia sent Luis to the cantina, setting events in motion and connecting him to Vargas. Plácido Ballesteros was also connected to Vargas through the cantina, and it was Plácido who gave the vineyard key to El Solitario and tipped the killer at the Road House. And, as Whittaker's driver, Vargas could have been acquainted with Harris through Prosperar, and with Drake through the rugby club, although I didn't know how either of them fit in, if at all.

I redrew the spiderweb on another sheet of paper, putting Diego Vargas at the center, then taped it up on the wall and sat looking at it.

Is Vargas the key? I asked myself.

———

I was chopping fresh ginger and mushrooms for a stir-fry a half hour later when a call came in. "Cal? It's Timoteo." The anxious voice again. "It's my father. The Newberg-Dundee police just came and took him away."

My chest tightened. "They arrested him?"

"I didn't hear what they told him, but when I came out of my room, he was handcuffed and being led to a patrol car."

I exhaled a breath. "If he was handcuffed, it was an arrest."

"I warned him not to talk to anyone except you. Can you go

to the police station? I can't leave. Mamá heard them and saw the patrol car." His voice began to tremble. "She's crying uncontrollably. I don't know what to do, how to comfort her. I'm scared, Cal."

"I'm on my way to the station. I'll sort this out. Stay calm and do what you can for your mother." I thought for a moment. "I'll call Dr. Bennett and see if she can come to your house. Give me a minute."

I left Archie at the Aerie and on my way down the hill, called Zoe and explained the situation. She didn't hesitate. "We've just finished dinner here. I can leave right away. Gertie will be fine." I called Timoteo back and then stepped on it.

"What the hell, Darci?" I said as I entered her cramped office after checking in at the front desk of the police station. "You don't even bother to call me? What's the charge, anyway?"

She looked up at me. Tinged with guilt, her eyes rode above grayish half-moons. "We think he killed Plácido Ballesteros. I meant to call, but—"

"That is such bullshit."

She shook her head, dropped the pen she was writing with, and scowled at me. "You know the drill, Cal. My job's to gather evidence. DA Thornberg made the call on the arrest." Her eyes flashed at me. "It's a righteous case. You know Carlos had one hell of a motive."

"What else you got?" She hesitated. Sharing information at this juncture was a gray area. "Come on, Darci. I'm going to get everything in discovery anyway."

She leaned forward and propped both elbows on the desk. "We have two witnesses who heard Fuentes threaten Ballesteros. We know he received the sketch of Ballesteros from his son Friday afternoon. We have another witness who saw him leaving Ballesteros's house in his pickup at around three a.m., which is within the time-of-death interval Friday night. Our forensic team says he couldn't have picked up blood on his shoes when he found the body the next day. The blood was too dry. So, where did it come from? We're checking the origin of the murder weapon, but your client certainly had access to and was familiar with that type of harvest shear."

Trying to hide my shock, I shrugged. "*Righteous*? I'm not all that impressed. But, thanks, Darci. I'd like to speak to him now."

She got up, and I saw a momentary glint of compassion in her eyes. "Of course. There's one other thing. We found the burner phone used to lure Luis to the Road House at Ballesteros's place. Looks like *he* sent the text, not Diego Vargas." Her eyes hardened. "With all due respect for the dead, the son of a bitch was neck-deep in both Fuentes cases."

I couldn't have agreed more with her characterization.

Bent as if the charge against him were an actual weight on his shoulders, Carlos Fuentes looked a decade older. When he sat down across from me, the first thing he said was, "How is my family?"

"Timoteo is with your wife, and Dr. Bennett is on her way to assist him. I think it will be okay."

"*Bueno*." He looked me straight in the eye. "I did not kill anyone."

"That's a good place to start, but I'm disappointed, Carlos. There's a lot you haven't told me."

He kept his eyes on me. "It is true. Some details, yes. I am sorry."

Anger boiled up in my chest, but I kept my temper in check. "Damn it, Carlos. Those *details* could get you convicted of murder. Now, let's start over. Tell me again what happened the first time you visited Plácido."

He took me back through it, adding, "Two of his cousins were there when we talked. They went into another room, but I suppose they heard me."

"You threatened Plácido? What did you say to him?"

He shrugged. "I was angry. I said that if I found out he was lying, I would come back and twist his head off."

"Anything else?"

"No. I left after that."

"Did you mean it? Would you have killed him?"

He shook his head, allowing a faint smile. "My wife says my talk is sometimes bigger than my actions. I would've hurt him, yes. But kill him? No, I could never do that."

"The two cousins told the police about your threat. They're cooperating with the police, despite the fact they're both undocumented."

Carlos shrugged again. "It is understandable. *Es familia.*"

"Okay, tell me about the Friday of the murder. Did you go to Plácido's?"

"Yes. Twice. I was in my office at the vineyard when I received the drawing late that afternoon. It came on my phone from Marlene. I knew at once it was Plácido. I thought he could still be somewhere on the vineyard, so I started asking around for him. He was nowhere to be found." Carlos's look turned sheepish. "I was shaking with anger. My crew had never seen me like that. I think someone might've warned him. It was stupid of me."

"What happened next?"

"I drove straight over to his house. Nobody was home, so I came home and drank a little pulque. I couldn't sleep. Sometime around three a.m. I went back."

"*At three a.m.*? Why would you go back then?"

He shrugged. "I told you. I could not sleep." He balled a fist for emphasis. "I didn't care about the time. I just wanted to talk to him."

"What did you find?"

"Lights were on in the front room of the house, but no one answered my knocking."

"You didn't go in?"

"No. I was thinking about it, but a light came on next door, so I decided to leave and come back in the daylight. That's when I found his body and my son called you."

"A neighbor told the police he saw you. It was right around the time the murder happened." I met his eyes and held them. "That's a very damning fact, Carlos."

He glared back at me without blinking. "I did not kill him."

"Was the porch light on?"

He hesitated and closed his eyes, wrinkling his nose. "I'm not sure. The curtains on the living room window were drawn, but a light was on inside."

"Did you hear anything unusual inside the house? Voices, music, anything?"

"No. It was quiet."

"Did you notice anything looking like blood on the porch or the walkway?"

"No."

"They found Plácido's blood on your shoe. They're saying the blood was too dry the next day to transfer to your sole."

He shook his head, and his eyes flashed. "*Puta madre*. It looked sticky to me, Cal."

"We'll have an opportunity to challenge that." I paused for a moment. "Is there anything else you noticed, anything unusual?"

He exhaled a breath and scraped the thick stubble on his chin between his thumb and fingers. "I thought I heard something as I pulled up to Plácido's that night."

I leaned in. *"What?"*

"The sound of a motorcycle heading the other way. *Muy tenue.* I barely heard it but thought I saw a taillight before it turned off."

"That could've been the killer. I suppose he'd chance riding his bike at three in the morning."

"You think so? If I came five minutes earlier, maybe I could have caught him."

"He would have shot you, Carlos."

He dropped his gaze. *"Es posible."* After a long pause he said, "What happens next?"

"You'll be arraigned within a day or two. That means you'll go in front of a judge, they'll state the charges against you, and you'll enter a plea."

He nodded his head vigorously. "Yes, a plea. Not guilty. That is my plea."

"Good." Bail would be steep for someone charged with murder. I decided to hold that bit of bad news for a future meeting. "Meanwhile, you'll be held in custody. It's important for you not to speak to *anyone* about this. Is that clear? And I hope to God you haven't left anything else out this time."

His expression grew contrite. "I have not." He fixed his eyes on me. "Do you believe me, that I didn't kill Plácido?"

I drew in and exhaled a long breath and paused for a moment. I could've told him that a lawyer doesn't need to believe his client, that his job is to provide the best possible defense against the charges regardless of guilt or innocence. But I knew Carlos wanted an honest answer, and, besides, my gut had already taken a position. "I shouldn't, because you lied to me or at least left things out of your story. But no, I don't think you killed him." I had to smile. "I think your wife is right about you."

Carlos nodded once in acknowledgment. "Thank you, Cal. That is important to me." He sighed and dragged a hand down his cheek. "How bad is this?"

"It's a pretty strong case, but it's early. I'll be in touch."

Timoteo was standing in the waiting room when I came out, his eyes wide and filled with fear and something close to panic at seeing another nightmare for his family unfold.

"Why did they arrest him?"

"They think he killed Plácido."

"No, that's crazy. Papi would never kill anyone." He teared up, and his knees buckled slightly.

I gave him a bear hug. "We'll beat this," I said, glancing at two young men slouched in the corner watching us. "Let's not discuss this here. I'll meet you back at your house. Stay strong and don't worry. Your father's going to be okay. I promise."

He swiped a tear and nodded with a look of profound relief and absolute trust in me.

I instantly regretted the promise made. It was sincere but ill-advised. The truth was, the investigation into Olivia's murder and the attempt on Luis already had me scrambling. Adding a murder defense? Out of the question, and besides, there were legal issues involved in my getting involved in Carlos's case. But the cases were obviously related. Solve one and you solve them all. My gut twisted at the maddening circularity of the problem.

I needed help. The sooner the better.

Chapter Thirty-One

Zoe met us at the Fuentes's front door, and we followed her into the kitchen where Luis and Marlene were waiting. "Elena has calmed down some, but I need to tell her something now that you've arrived. What should I say?"

"Tell her Carlos has been detained by the local police, *not* ICE, and that we're going to clear it up. Nothing to worry about." It was sugarcoated but the best I could come up with.

She left for the back bedroom, and the rest of us huddled at the kitchen table. I began describing the situation and answering their questions. At the first lull, Timoteo said, "Papi just happens to go find Plácido right around the time he's murdered. Was that just shitty luck, or what?"

"I think Carlos's anger scared Plácido, and he took off," I said. "My hunch is he made the mistake of telling someone his cover may have been blown, and that resulted in his death. After all, he handed the key to the vineyard directly to El Solitario. That alone put him at significant risk."

Timoteo grimaced. "So, it *was* shitty luck."

"It looks that way. But keep in mind that what I've just outlined is a strong alternate theory of the crime, and that's a good thing."

I paused for a moment. "There's one problem that's weighing on me." Three sets of inquiring eyes locked on to me. "I'm too deeply involved in Olivia's and Luis's cases to also act as Carlos's defense attorney. He needs someone who can focus solely on his case. In addition, I could be called as a fact witness, which would jeopardize attorney-client privilege between Carlos and me. We can't take that chance." I regarded the shocked faces around the table. "Look, this isn't about me, it's about ensuring Carlos gets the best possible defense."

Luis rocked back in his chair, and Timoteo said with an incredulous look, "You mean we need another lawyer to defend Papi?"

"Yes. And I think I have a solution," I said in a voice that sounded more confident than I felt. "I can't share the details at the moment. You need to trust me on this." Luis shot me a skeptical look, but Timoteo and Marlene voiced their assent.

Zoe came back in the kitchen at that point. "How's Elena?" I asked, relieved to change the subject.

Her face registered concern. "She's worried about Carlos now, but the fact that it wasn't ICE who arrested him was some consolation. At least she's talking a little. That's a good sign."

I said, "Let's focus on next steps." I looked at Luis. "We now know that Plácido was part of Diego Vargas's group. I'd like you to work behind the scenes to see if you can find more of their members. Don't approach his cousins, because they think Carlos killed him. Start with any friends he had. Keep it as quiet as you can." I looked him in the eye. "The shooter's still out there, so continue to watch your back."

Always the skeptic, Luis eyed me, his forehead and cheek bandaged and his left eye black but no longer swollen shut. "What are *you* going to do?"

I looked at Luis, acknowledging the fairness of the question. "First, I'm going to get us some help, and then I'm going to focus my attention on Diego Vargas." I briefly described the spiderweb I'd drawn and the list of questions arising from it. "There's a pattern here, I just don't see it yet," I told them.

"What about the surveillance of Harris?" Timoteo asked.

"Stay on it this week. We'll see if we learn anything."

As our discussion trailed off, Zoe said, "This has been a serious setback for Elena. As you care for her, you need to stress that we have a strong team in place to help Carlos, that he's going to be okay." She paused. "She let me hold her hand for a while and asked me to come back. I will, if that's all right with you."

Luis nodded, and Timoteo said, "Of course, Zoe. That's good news. Come whenever you can. Please."

———

That night, after I cooked and ate the stir-fry I'd started earlier, Archie gave a couple of sharp barks at the sound of a knock. "Am I disturbing anything?" Zoe said when I opened the front door. She wore the blue scarf but not the pearl earrings, her soft smile was half in shadow, reminding me of another painting, one I couldn't quite place. I found myself wondering why her face evoked works of art. Not a good sign.

I invited her in, glancing at the bottle of wine she carried.

She held the bottle up. "Not a 2012." The smile again. "My conscience is getting to me. I picked this up at the Red Hills Market the other day."

"All the Carabella vintages are excellent," I said. She followed me into the kitchen, where I put a corkscrew to the bottle, poured two glasses, and joined her at the kitchen table. I raised my glass. "Thanks again for the help today. Sounds like you made some progress with Elena."

She shook her head with a pained look. "Not much, really.

She's been traumatized and retraumatized, but she did talk to me for a while. She needs a woman to confide in. Mrs. Angel is wonderful but, you know, she's the boss's wife."

"What's the prognosis?"

"If I can keep her talking, she should come out of it, be functional, at least. But losing a child, her only daughter, so abruptly and violently—it's, ah, it's a steep climb." Zoe inhaled a breath and let it out slowly. "She told me the story of Carlos's cartel connection. She loves him but is in no mood to forgive his past actions if they caused her daughter's death. I hope you can prove that's not the case, for the sake of their relationship."

I winced. "One miracle at a time. I need to get Carlos out from under a murder charge first."

She put her lips to her glass and sipped some wine, her deep blues intent on me. "I get why you can't represent Carlos against the murder charge. What's the secret plan?"

"It's no secret, and it's not much of a plan, so I didn't want to get into it with them." I went on to tell her what I had in mind, and we discussed it while we drank the wine.

"And if that doesn't work?" she asked when I finished.

I shook my head. "There's no plan B at the moment."

A second glass of wine later, Archie and I walked Zoe back across the field. Our friend the owl was silent, but it was crystal clear, and the night sky was on full, awe-striking display. She looked up in a northerly direction and sighed softly. "It's beautiful tonight. I needed this. Which one's the North Star? I'm never sure."

"See the Big Dipper?" I pointed in the direction of the constellation. She nodded. "The two outer stars in the bowl point directly to it."

"Oh, yeah. There it is. Wow, nice and bright."

Archie brushed against her leg, and she dropped to one knee and hugged him. I said, "How's the book coming?"

"Oh, God, don't ask," she said, standing back up. "I'm writing about a woman who needs to overcome obstacles and setbacks to find meaning and purpose in her life." She paused, looked up at the Big Dipper again and laughed sardonically. "Then I became involved with Elena Fuentes and her family. Suddenly my story seems so, so trivial, you know?"

"Yeah, I can understand that," I said, kicking myself for asking a question that broke the mood. She eyed me expectantly and waited. "But a problem doesn't necessarily have to pose an existential threat to be significant," I offered. "We stumble on lesser things all the time, and they can be just as devastating."

She paused as if turning that over. "True enough. It's just... well, I think right now I'm too caught up in Elena's story to think straight about my book." She laughed. "I'll say one thing, Cal Claxton—life has certainly been interesting since I met you."

I smiled at that. "You know what they say—may you live in interesting times."

Her eyes got huge, and she laughed again. "That's a curse, you know." Then, smiling, she leaned forward and kissed me on the cheek. "But I'm glad I met you. Good night, Cal."

Arch and I walked back across the field under the starlight, the kiss lingering stubbornly on my cheek.

Chapter Thirty-Two

"Pro bono? You want me to take a murder case pro bono?" Ned Gillian said as he lowered his coffee cup and looked at me through startled eyes. It was Tuesday morning, and I'd driven to his office in McMinnville to meet with him. When I called to arrange the meeting, I'd been vague about the topic. The proposal I had in mind would require a face-to-face to have any chance at all.

"You told me you were interested in doing something different, Ned, and this is that, for sure."

Tall and lithe with short, gray-flecked hair and a quick smile below probing eyes, he barked a sarcastic laugh. "You can say that again."

I opened my hands in a reassuring gesture. "I admit it's a challenging case, but I'll back you to the hilt. I just can't sit at the defendant's table."

"This is a heavy lift, Cal. It could burn a lot of resources."

"I know that, but look, if I can crack who killed Olivia and shot at Luis, Carlos's case may never go to trial. That person killed Plácido Ballesteros, too. No doubt in my mind. You just need to tread water for a while, make sure Carlos has a good discovery process, and respond to whatever the DA's up to. The trial's at least nine months off."

He paused for a moment and regarded me more carefully. "Why are you going to the mat for this family? This has got to cut into your ability to take on paying clients."

I shrugged. "To be honest, I didn't know this case would mushroom the way it did, but no regrets. The Fuentes family... Well, if you join me, you'll see why I'm committed to helping them."

He exhaled and shook his head slowly. "I've always told myself my career's about providing excellent legal representation, and I've done that by and large, at least for those who can afford me."

"You've got a great rep—"

He waved off the flattery. "But the truth is, it's been about the money, always the money. 'Become a lawyer. You'll be well-off'—that was my father's mantra." Gillian focused on something across the room for a few moments before returning his gaze to me. "That's starting to ring hollow, you know? And I've got some personal reasons that play into this, too."

The last statement surprised me. "You do?"

"I'll let you in on a family secret. My grandfather came here from Mexico illegally, Vera Cruz, right after the Second World War. He was a *bracero*, you know, a so-called guest worker, although the *braceros* weren't treated like guests, more like slaves. Anyway, my grandmother, who grew up in Woodburn, volunteered to teach the local workers English at a makeshift school." He smiled more fully. "They met in her classroom, and nature took its course. Instead of going back to Mexico as the law at that time required, he went missing and married my grandmother."

I chuckled. "Love knows no borders."

He laughed. "Exactly. By the time my mother was born, Grandpa had completed pharmacy school and was working as a druggist." His face clouded over. "But, my dad's side of the family was leery of the Mexican heritage of my mother, so Grandpa's past wasn't talked about much, and I never got to know my Vera Cruz relatives." He shook his head. "Such utter bullshit."

"It happens," I responded. "Race is a complex subject."

He sipped some coffee, and his forehead became a plowed field. "The Fuentes family's been through hell, I'll give you that. And I'm no fan of our so-called immigration policy. But, a murder trial? That's a big fucking commitment."

I felt like I almost had him but was wary of pushing too hard. I got up and shook his hand. "Take some time to think it over. You know how to contact me."

I exited his office and was nearly to my car when Ned Gillian caught up to me. "Okay, goddamn it," he said, beaming a smile and pumping my arm with a firm handshake. "I'm in."

———

A night in jail hadn't done Carlos Fuentes any favors. His dark eyes seemed to hide in the shadows of their sockets, and his face was gray with a thick stubble and blank as a piece of slate. I introduced Ned Gillian, explained why he was taking over, and we both answered Carlos's questions. When we finished, Carlos said, "I do not understand the law very well, but I accept what you tell me." He drew a breath and exhaled. "How will I pay for this?"

Gillian started to speak, but I jumped in. He was unaware of Timoteo's warning to me—that Carlos was a proud man who would refuse charity, even if it meant financial ruin. "We'll work the fees out with Timoteo," I said. "It's not something we want you to worry about right now." Carlos started to respond but apparently thought better of it. Gillian caught on immediately and let the subject lie. At that point, I excused myself and left them alone, a lawyer and a client beginning a journey together where the stakes couldn't be any higher.

On my way back to the office, I called Timoteo and briefed him on Ned Gillian agreeing to represent his father. "Don't worry," I told him, "you and I will be backing Gillian up, and he's agreed to take the case pro bono."

"*Really*? Why did he agree to that?"

I laughed. "It's an interesting story. Ask him about it sometime."

After disconnecting from Timoteo, my thoughts turned to the briefing I'd given Gillian prior to our meeting with Carlos. The discussion was drawn out owing to the questions my new partner had, all of them insightful. I'd obviously chosen well. I was supplying the information, but when Supervisor Curtis Drake's name came up during the description of my visit to the ICE holding center, Gillian said, "A guy by that name's rumored to be a leader in a militant white nationalist group in the valley."

"I heard something similar," I said, recalling Detective Tate's remark about Drake. I explained my interest in him—his connection to Diego Vargas through Gavin Whittaker and the rugby club. "What can you tell me?"

"The group's called Citizens for Immigration Justice, or CIJ. They're against Oregon's sanctuary law. Anyway, I had a client who got roughed up by them at a demonstration in Portland. She wanted to sue but changed her mind after she received several death threats. I did some preliminary due diligence on the case, and Drake's name popped up."

"I see. Based on a couple of remarks he made to me that day, it sounds like he's that Drake. It makes sense that he's staying below the radar, considering the job he has at the holding center."

I mentally filed away Drake's CIJ involvement as an interesting tidbit but didn't see how it connected to the case at hand. If anything, Curtis Drake and Diego Vargas were at opposite ends of the immigration spectrum. I wondered what could bring them together?

———

I was nearly back to my office in Dundee when I had to brake hard as a small red car turned in front of me and darted onto SW 7th, in the direction of the Red Hills Market. I caught only a glimpse of the driver, who was wearing a pair of dark glasses. I was pretty sure I knew who it was. I parked behind my office and let myself in, to the delight of Archie, who was waiting patiently for my return. I gave him a couple of treats, which he gobbled down, and said, "I'm hungry, too. Let's give you a walk and get me some lunch."

At the Red Hills Market, I ordered an egg salad and avocado sandwich and a double cappuccino and, owing to the bright sunshine, looked for a seat outside, where Archie could join me. That's where I found her, sitting alone nibbling a salad and studying her little screen. Every once in a while, fate deals a wildcard. This was one of those times.

"Hello, Isabel, mind if my dog and I join you?"

Her outsized dark glasses—which she didn't remove—rested above a delicate nose and classic cheekbones framed by a perfectly oval face. She looked up at me and smiled. "Oh hello, Cal. Yes, of course. Please sit down." She looked at Archie and extended a hand for him to sniff. "And who is this handsome creature?"

I introduced her to Archie, and after learning that she loved dogs nearly as much as horses, said, "How's Emilio?"

A radiant smile broke out on her face, but it was gone in an instant. "He's just fine. Thank you again for the help." She lowered her left arm to her lap, but I could still make out some faint bruises. "How is the investigation going?" she asked in an intimate tone that seemed to reestablish the inexplicable link between us.

I shook my head and frowned. "Frustratingly slow, I'm afraid." She would hear about Carlos Fuentes's arrest soon enough, so I went ahead and described the situation.

"My heart goes out to the family," she said when I finished. She set her jaw and drew her lips into a straight line. "I believe what you say about the father, but I would not blame him if he did kill the man who betrayed him and his family." She paused for a moment, but I didn't respond. "Did you learn anything of interest from my husband?"

I shrugged. "Just that he thinks Diego Vargas is above reproach, although he did offer to encourage him to talk to me."

She took a small bite of salad and chewed as if thinking my comment over. Finally, she showed a wisp of a smile. "It's not my place to mention this, but your visit did cause a reaction." I lowered my sandwich and waited for her to continue. "Whatever you said to Gavin, it led to a shouting match between him and Diego."

I kept a calm demeanor. "Really? I can't imagine why. What were they shouting about?"

Her turn to shrug. "I don't know for sure, but I did hear your name a couple of times. Maybe Diego didn't want to talk to you." She smiled again, but it was bitter. "He will probably come to you, now. My husband doesn't lose arguments."

"I hope you're right," I said before shifting focus. "I understand your husband's quite the rugby fan."

A look of bewilderment. "It is popular in Chile, too, but like American football, it is such a strange game, grown men running around, smashing into each other. But, yes, Gavin is passionate about the sport."

"Ever see the coach of the team around, a man named Curtis Drake? He's tall with a dark mustache and goatee."

"Yes, frequently. Why do you ask?"

I ignored the question. "Does Drake ever interact with Diego Vargas?"

She paused. "Sometimes. The three of them go places in Gavin's

Land Rover. Diego drives, of course." She showed a faint smile. "I think Diego prefers soccer over rugby, but I don't know this."

"Where do they go?"

"I have no idea." At this point, she looked away, revealing more of her face. Did I see the trace of a bruise under her right eye?

She noticed the direction of my glance and adjusted her glasses. "Is Archie a Bernese mountain dog?" she asked.

Sensing it would be counterproductive to press her, I went along with the abrupt change in subject, explaining that people often mistook Arch for a Bernese, that he was a tricolor Australian shepherd and just plain big for his breed. We talked about dogs for a while—especially a pug she had growing up in Chile named Poquito. Once the subject of her home country came up, her demeanor grew somber, reminding me of when she spoke about her horses being her refuge.

"Do you miss Chile?" I asked, knowing I was probably picking at a scab.

Her face softened around the edges, and she showed a wistful smile. "Your country is very nice, but yes, I miss Chile and my family." I started to respond, but she continued, forcing the smile from wistful to cheerful. "But I have a wonderful life here." With that, she glanced at a jeweled watch and announced she had to leave.

I stood up. "Nice seeing you again, Isabel, and thanks for the information." I fixed my gaze on her dark glasses, imagining her expressive brown eyes behind the opaque lenses, and then glanced down at her left forearm. "And, uh, I'm glad to see the bruises on your arm are healing. Those looked pretty angry the other day."

She pulled her arm back reflexively and forced another smile to cover her surprise. "Oh, that. It was nothing. Mucking stables is hard work, you know."

"Sure," I answered, fixing her with a look that said I knew

better. "Well, if there's any more help I can give you, you know how to contact me."

She patted Archie's head and hurried off to her red Tesla, having left half her salad uneaten. I sat back down, took a bite of my sandwich, and looked down at my dog. "Well, like the song says, 'Every form of refuge has its price.'"

Chapter Thirty-Three

Timoteo called just as I got back to my office. "I've been over at the vineyard talking to the workers. They said that when Plácido heard Papi was looking for him, he took off like a rocket. He figured Papi knew something, no doubt about it."

"Good work," I said. "Of course, that cuts both ways. We're saying that Placido left the vineyard and told El Solitario he'd been discovered and that's what got him killed. The prosecution will say that he ran because he was afraid of your father, who caught up with him at three in the morning."

"Yeah, I know. We're gonna need a lot more, but it's a start."

I gave him Gillian's cell phone number and told him to relay the information. "Ask him if there's anything else you can do for him. You'll see, he's a good man."

Timoteo agreed and went on, his voice suddenly emotional. "I also talked to Chad Angel at the vineyard. He, um, he said no way my father killed Plácido, no matter what. He told me to tell you he wants to help out financially."

"That says a lot about your father. I think Gillian's committed to defending him pro bono, but give him Chad's phone number and tell him what he said."

An hour later, Nando called to say he would stop by on his way down to the Spirit Mountain Casino, where he continued to have business. "Your timing's perfect," I told him. "There've been some developments, and I've got a lot on my mind." A half hour later I glimpsed his gleaming black Lexus as it turned off the Pacific Highway into the driveway next to my office. Archie needed a stretch, so I took him out the back door.

Wearing a tangerine blazer, an open-neck floral shirt, tan slacks, and fedora with a black band, Nando bent his large frame for a hands-on greeting to my dog. "Wow," I said, "Cuban high fashion lives."

He looked up and smiled. "I am asking for a bigger contract at the casino. I don't want them to think I am some communist from Cuba who will settle for a small potato."

I laughed at that. "I'm sure your reputation as a staunch capitalist precedes you."

He followed me into my office, hung his fedora on my coatrack, and took a seat while I began bringing him up to speed. When I finished describing Carlos's situation, Nando studied me for a few moments. "You are sure this man did not avenge the murder of his daughter and the attempt on his son's life? You always talk about the razor of Occam, and this is the simplest explanation."

"I know it may seem like that, but I'm convinced he's innocent," I answered, trying not to sound defensive. "We've already got a theory of how it went down, and Carlos thought he heard a motorcycle in the distance when he arrived that night."

A knowing smile creased Nando's lips. "Of course. But no man could have a stronger motive."

A bubble of irritation formed in my gut. Nando was right, and that's what irritated me. "Look, Carlos has a good lawyer now, and I'm free to focus on the other two cases. Trust me on this, okay?" He nodded his assent, and I began to sketch in the bigger picture, saying at one point, "There's a web of connections, but no discernable pattern, let alone any sort of motive for two murders and one attempted murder. Diego Vargas is a central player. After all, he ran the cantina group, which caught Olivia's attention in the first place. Vargas is potentially connected to Robert Harris through his boss, Gavin Whittaker. But there's another player in this—Curtis Drake, field supervisor of the ICE holding facility in Newberg. Drake implied a legitimate ICE team had come after Luis, but that turned out to be untrue. Did he lie to me to hide a kidnap attempt? If so, he's got to be implicated in whatever the hell's going on."

Nando's thick eyebrows raised. "How do you know he lied?"

"Detective Tate told me. She has a reliable source in ICE. Anyway, *now* I find out that Drake coaches a rugby team that Gavin Whittaker sponsors, and that Drake is a regular at the Whittaker estate. In addition, he may be involved in a militant white nationalist group, although I don't have a clue how that could fit in." I stopped and eyed my friend.

Nando studied his Gucci loafers for a while, then looked up. "Perhaps the spider in your web is Drake or Whittaker, not the employee, Vargas."

"Yeah, maybe I've been thinking too small. And there's something else about Whittaker. Aside from a titanic ego, he's physically abusing his wife, a charming Chilean woman, I'm almost certain of it." My stomach turned a little just saying it.

Nando's eyes grew hard. "A man who does such a thing is capable of other atrocities. What do you want me to do?"

"Drill down on Whittaker and Drake and an organization called Citizens for Immigration Justice, which Drake may be involved in. Find out everything you can about them. I know it's costly, but do a complete job."

He shot me that look, the same one Gertie gives me. "You are not a charity organization, my friend, and neither am I."

I swallowed a caustic comeback. He had a point, after all, and I still owed him money from the Coos Bay case. "I know that. Don't worry. I'm good for it."

"Of course you are," he said before announcing he had to hurry off to his appointment at the casino. The last thing he said to me was, "If El Solitario killed Plácido, as you claim, he could still be in the vicinity. Error on the side of caution, my friend."

I couldn't help myself. "Oh, like you did when you caught that bullet down in Coos Bay?"

Nando tried but failed to hold an offended look. "That was different."

"Sure it was."

———

Lo and behold, two walk-ins appeared in my office that afternoon—a local wine merchant who was being sued by a customer who'd fallen in his parking lot and a young woman charged with her second DUI. I cheerfully booked them both at my full rate. I was interviewing the woman when a call came in from Timoteo that I let go to voicemail. When she left, I returned his call. "I'm tailing Robert Harris. He left Prosperar early and headed straight for the Acey Deucey Poker Club on 99W," he told me. "The guy's got a gambling problem, for sure."

"You're not going in there, right?"

"No way. The place's too small, and I don't know anything about Texas Hold 'em. We'll hang here for a while, see if he comes out and goes anywhere else." He laughed. "This surveillance thing isn't exactly what I imagined."

"Be patient and don't get careless," I warned.

Toward the end of the afternoon, a call from Darci Tate came in. "Dropped the charges yet?" I greeted her.

"Give me a reason."

"El Solitario did it, you'll see."

"I hear Ned Gillian is Fuentes's attorney. How did you manage that?"

"My silver tongue, how else? Seriously, Gillian stepped up. He's taking it on pro bono."

"Pro bono? I thought Gillian was all about clients with big bucks."

"Not this time."

Tate paused for a moment. "I wanted to give you a heads-up. Maybe we can, ah, trade a little info."

I figured that was what the call was about. "You go first."

"We found some hairs on Ballesteros's body that don't belong to him. One of the hairs has a follicle attached. It's at the state lab now."

My stomach dropped a little, but I wasn't about to admit it. "I'll advise Gillian this is coming down the pike. It won't be Fuentes's DNA."

"We'll see, won't we? It would be a nice-to-have for us, but we don't need it to make the case." Another pause. "What's new at your end?"

I grimaced. "Mostly nothing." I went on to describe the connection I'd found between Curtis Drake, Gavin Whittaker, and Diego Vargas. "Seems significant, but I don't have the slightest idea why," I summed up. "Also, we're quietly checking Plácido's friends, hoping to locate some more members of Vargas's boys' club. And I had a chat with Whittaker. He said he'd ask Vargas to speak to me. I'll keep you in the loop if that happens, but don't hold your breath." I didn't mention the fact that we had Robert Harris under surveillance.

The phone went quiet at both ends. Finally, Darci sighed heavily. "Jesus Christ, Cal, we've got all kinds of threads but no cloth."

"It's early days. This thing'll start to make sense. Keep the faith, Darci."

The words sounded hollow, even to me, the eternal optimist.

Chapter Thirty-Four

"Since when do detectives share information with defense attorneys?" Ned Gillian asked me. I'd called him immediately after disconnecting with Darci Tate.

I chuckled. "It's a bit of quid pro quo. She's also got the Olivia Fuentes investigation. We're trying to help each other without crossing any ethical boundaries."

"Okay, suppose those hairs do belong to Carlos. That doesn't prove squat. He discovered the damn body."

"Agreed, but they'll argue that the hairs prove close contact, which is inconsistent with his statement. He said he walked in, saw the body, and got the hell out. No way he could have dropped a couple of hairs on Ballesteros. At least that's what they'll claim."

"Well, if they're *not* Carlos's hairs, that will help our case."

"Not necessarily. They'll simply argue they were acquired randomly."

Gillian paused for a moment. "Does a DNA profile of El Solitario exist?"

"Nope. Only a single fingerprint. That and the fact that he's tall and thin. We don't even know his nationality."

Gillian sighed into the phone. "Any more good news?" I told

him no, and he said, "The arraignment's tomorrow. I don't have a date for the bail hearing, but that's not going to go well. Since Carlos is undocumented, he'll be considered a severe flight risk, no matter what I tell the judge about his close community ties. The bail's going to be high." He paused for a moment. "What in hell have you gotten me into, Cal?"

"Hey, I never promised you a rose garden."

He laughed at that. "The truth is, I haven't felt this good about what I do for a long time. And I gotta tell you, Carlos Fuentes is a good man. I believe he's innocent."

———

Zoe Bennett pointed to a large chunk of blue basalt resting beneath a couple of smaller stones in the pile I was working from. "That one, the one on your left," she said. "That one looks a lot better." It was late that same afternoon and she'd wandered over to join Archie in watching me build my rock wall. Well, "build" might be too strong a word. Finding the right stone for the right place in a dry stack was not as easy as the YouTube videos, of which there were many, would have you believe.

I picked up the suggested stone, worked it into place, and stood back with my head cocked. "Damn, you're right. That's a nice fit. How did you see that?"

"I'm not just a pretty face, you know." She laughed, a carefree sound like water splashing on rock. I needed that after having just looked in on a morose Carlos Fuentes in jail. "That big, flat one to the right should go next." Again, she was right on, and again and again.

At one point, I said, "Hey, can I interest you in a full-time job here?"

She laughed again. "You can't afford me."

We explored every aspect of the case that afternoon and were closing in on completion of the second course of the wall when she looked at her watch. "Darn, I've got to run. Gertie insisted on pizza tonight, which is being delivered, and I told Hillary Angel I'd relieve her at the Fuentes's house until Timoteo gets home." She raised her chin slightly. "And I'm preparing tacos and black beans for him and his mother tonight."

"Great. Do you need any—"

She raised a hand with a look of faux defiance. "I've got a good recipe and all the fixings. I can handle this."

"Right," I said, failing to suppress a smile. "What could go wrong?"

Her blue eyes grew large and flashed at me, but with a hint of a smile. "Thanks for the vote of confidence. This cooking thing can't be that hard."

———

After a quick dinner that night, an email from Timoteo pinged in, with Surveillance on the subject line. I had to chuckle at his typical thoroughness. After leaving the poker club at 4:18, he wrote, the subject drove to the Quiet Hour Bar and Grill on NW 8th, where he stayed for an hour and eighteen minutes.

Photos of Harris and other patrons coming and going during this time period are attached. He drove straight home after that.

The eight attached photos didn't reveal anything, although I strained to make out the last two, which were taken just after sunset. I was pretty sure the seventh photo was Harris leaving the bar, and the eighth image, another male, was essentially a silhouette. Something about the figure stopped me, however— the shape and posture... *Could it be?*

I forwarded Timoteo's email to Nando's office manager,

Esperanza, with this note: Hello dear, any way one of Nando's photo jocks can lighten the shadows on the figures in the last two photos? I'm interested in their facial features. Thx in advance, Cal.

I knew Esperanza would expedite my request, but the thought of waiting was still frustrating.

I called Timoteo next to fill him in and compliment him for the job he and Mariana had done. "Keep up the surveillance on Harris this week," I said to finish up. "I'll let you know if photo eight reveals anything. By the way," I added, "How was your dinner tonight?"

A long pause. "It was, um, okay after we put out the kitchen fire. Frying tortillas in hot oil is always a little tricky." He chuckled. "The kitchen's fine, and Zoe didn't get burned or anything. Please don't tell her I told you about this. I don't think she wanted me to say anything about it."

I smiled to myself. "Don't worry, I won't. She's a brilliant psychologist, but she's just learning how to cook."

"I know. She's with Mamá now," he said, suddenly struggling to control his voice. "She's got her talking, Cal. I'm so grateful for that."

——

That night, close to midnight, I took Archie out for a stretch before we turned in. A breeze carrying a hint of winter stirred the upper reaches of my Doug firs and drove shreds of clouds across the moon like gray ghosts. I zipped my coat and put the collar up as Archie dashed ahead into the darkness. The great horned owl was silent. As I approached the gate, I could just make out my dog up ahead. He stood motionless facing the stand of firs and understory of blackberries, sword ferns, and salal that lined the west side of my property. When I caught up to him, he was growling, a low, guttural warning.

"What is it, Big Boy?" He whimpered a couple of times and looked up at me for permission to chase whatever it was he'd heard. "No," I said firmly. It wasn't the first time he'd heard some creature in the night I was unaware of. It happened fairly often, but there was something visceral in the tone of his growl that made me wary. I started back, but he didn't move. I clicked my tongue sharply a couple of times, and he reluctantly followed me.

Back at the house, I locked up and poured myself a couple of fingers of Rémy Martin. It was probably nothing but a skunk or a deer out there, I reassured myself. But before I climbed into bed that night, I took my Glock 17 down from the shelf in the closet and set the weapon on my nightstand. I tossed and turned for a good half hour before finally drifting off.

Sleeping with a loaded gun was not my favorite thing. Like Yogi said, it was déjà vu all over again.

Chapter Thirty-Five

The wind intensified overnight, and owing to my ancient heating system and leaky, single-pane windows, Arch and I awoke to a cold, drafty house. I got dressed in a hurry and scampered down the back staircase to turn on the espresso machine. Scoured by the wind, the sky was bright cobalt blue, and every so often a detached branch from a Doug fir tumbled across the scene like a wounded duck. The wind was nature's way of pruning the big trees, and it meant a serious cleanup session lay ahead at the Aerie. Lucky me.

Carrying a cup of hot cappuccino into my study, I logged on for a quick check of the news. The local paper, the biweekly *News-Register* published the day before, made no mention of the Plácido Ballesteros murder, which was just as well. However, the lead headline jumped out at me: ICE ARRESTS 5 IN YAMHILL COUNTY. I skimmed the piece, which described how early the previous Friday ICE agents stopped a van on its way to a large wholesale nursery near Unionvale. According to an ICE spokesman, the van was targeted because agents were looking for an unnamed suspect, who turned out not to be in the van. "Because of state sanctuary policies," the article went on, "we have no choice but to continue to conduct targeted arrests with less-than-perfect intelligence, which inevitably results in collateral arrests." The spokesman was Field Supervisor Curtis Drake, I noted.

I sipped my coffee and brooded on that for a while, trying to imagine what it would feel like to be on my way to work and have my life suddenly ripped apart. I looked back at the headline and noticed the byline for the first time—Mariana Suarez. I smiled and immediately called Timoteo. "Yeah," he explained, "the *News-Register*'s lead reporter was down with the flu, so Mariana asked her boss if she could cover the story, and she let her."

"A front-page story. Tell her congratulations. It was well written."

"I will. She loved doing it, but it was painful, too, given what happened to her uncle. She said there was no way ICE had a specific target in mind. That was just an excuse to stop a van full of Latinos on their way to work. She went straight to the holding center and demanded an interview with Curtis Drake. A rude, arrogant asshole, I believe were the words she used, but she got the interview and stood up to him."

There was a ring of pride in Timoteo's voice that couldn't be missed. Small things can warm a cold morning.

On the way to the office, I pulled over after turning onto Worden Hill and let Archie out of the back seat. My property line lay another fifty yards to the east, and I chose that spot for a reason. The soft earth on the shoulder was churned up in a couple of spots. I dropped to one knee and looked closely. There may have been evidence of tire tracks from a two-wheeled vehicle, but my untrained eye couldn't tell for sure. A car pulling off with one set of wheels on the pavement would have left a similar track. Farther along the thick understory spanning the strip I noticed a faint trail leading toward my property, probably a path used by coyotes, skunks, and other night critters. With Archie trailing behind, I followed the narrow trail, keeping an eye out for evidence of fresh passage. I saw none, although I surmised that it would have been easy for someone to traverse the path without leaving any traces, at least none I could see. At my fence line, a sizeable, well-worn trench under the wire confirmed it was, indeed, on an active animal trail.

I turned to leave and noticed something—a single thread caught between two protruding pieces of wire at a fence post. Not the cleanest piece of fence work, it was done by yours truly nearly a decade earlier. I probably wouldn't have noticed had the thread not been fluttering in the breeze like a tiny flag. I plucked it off and examined it closely. It was black and didn't look particularly weathered, although I couldn't tell for sure.

Had someone snagged a coat or sweater the night before?

When I got back in my car, I called Darci Tate. "You think El Solitario is still around and might have been casing your place last night?" she said after I filled her in.

"It's a definite maybe."

She laughed softly. "Your dog growling, an indeterminate tire track, and a single black thread, yeah, I'd definitely put it in the maybe category. You know, this dude's risking a lot by staying local and cruising around on a Kawasaki, one that we're on full alert for."

"Maybe his contract's still open, and he's got a mortgage payment to make. If it was him last night, he came here around midnight. Carlos Fuentes thought he heard a motorcycle around three a.m. leaving Plácido's house. It appears El Solitario moves late at night when he feels safer."

"Maybe. About Fuentes's statement—we covered the houses in his neighborhood. Nobody heard a motorcycle at three a.m."

"Heavy sleepers?" She chuckled again, and I added, "No word on the DNA from the hair follicle?"

"Ha," she barked with derision. "It's the state lab. You know how fucking slow they are. But we do have the ballistics back on the Fuentes's shootings. The bullets match. Same shooter for Olivia and Luis, like we expected."

"That's good to know. It's not going to be Fuentes's DNA, Darci. Count on it."

"We'll see. Meanwhile, watch your back."

———

That morning at the office started slowly, but at half past ten I caught a glimpse of a dark-blue Land Rover as it turned off the Pacific Highway onto my driveway. A knock at the back door followed, and when I opened it, Diego Vargas stood there with a nervous grin. His boss, Gavin Whittaker, stood behind him.

"We're headed to Portland this morning. Saw your office and decided to stop by," Whittaker said with what I took to be his version of a friendly smile. "Should have called first, but I know you wanted to talk to Diego." Vargas dropped his gaze and studied his boots at the mention of his name.

"Great. Come on in." I shook both their hands, and after they were seated, looked directly at Vargas. "As I mentioned that night at the cantina, I'm working with the Fuentes family concerning the murder of their daughter, Olivia. I—"

"Yes, I explained all that to him," Whittaker interrupted with an impatient tone. "He's here to tell you what he told the police, that he knows nothing about the murder or the attempt on her brother's life."

I swallowed a comeback and kept my eyes on Vargas. "Let's start with the present and work backward, okay?" A tentative nod. "One of the young men you counseled at the Tequila Cantina, Plácido Ballesteros, has been murdered. I know you've been interviewed by the police about that, but is there anything you can tell me? Something you might have forgotten or didn't feel comfortable sharing with them?"

"What's to tell? I heard the police arrested the girl's father." Whittaker again.

Ignoring him, I stayed focused on Vargas. His hooded eyes flared ever so slightly. His face was taut. "No, nothing. I am very sad about Plácido. He seemed like a good young man."

"A good young man? He was an accomplice in a murder and an attempted murder."

Vargas lowered his eyes, and Whittaker chimed in again. "He's not responsible for the kid, for Christ's sake. He was just trying to help him out."

I held my gaze on Vargas. "Who did he associate with at the cantina?"

Vargas pushed out his lower lip and shook his head. "I didn't notice."

"*Really*? You were one big, happy family. Isn't that what you told me that night?" He hesitated. "And the shiv in my tire. Do you know who did that?"

"He can't give you any names," Whittaker broke in. "You know that. He gave his word."

I locked onto Vargas's eyes. "But you *have* names, right? You must have a list of names, addresses, a means of communicating with these young men?"

He shot a quick glance to Whittaker, then back to me, his face frozen. That's when I saw it—a look of fear that was eerily familiar. Deciding to back off, I smiled with as much warmth as I could muster. "I get it. I understand your reluctance, and your work is commendable, Diego. On another subject, do you know of any connections between the young men you counsel and Prosperar, the medical facility where Olivia Fuentes worked?"

"No connections other than Luis, the girl's brother. I just drive

Mr. Whittaker there sometimes, that is all." The answer sounded rehearsed.

I leaned back in my chair and smiled again. "Okay." When Vargas's face relaxed somewhat, I came back at him with decided emphasis. "What about Robert Harris? Do you know him?" It was a gamble to reveal my suspicion of Harris, but I decided to chance it.

Vargas looked at his boss, his face taut again, a vein pulsing in his neck. "I, ah, don't—"

"You know, Robert, the guy at Prosperar," Whittaker coaxed. "We've given him a ride a couple of times."

"Oh, *sí*," Vargas answered, forcing a thin, uncomfortable smile.

Whittaker looked at me. "Why are you asking about Harris?"

I shrugged while scrambling to come up with a suitable answer. "I'm posing that question to everyone involved. He and Olivia were rumored to be romantically linked."

Whittaker looked incredulous. "You've got to be kidding." Then, glancing at his watch, he stood up, and Vargas vaulted out of his seat. "I've got a meeting in Portland in twenty-five minutes."

I thanked them, showed them out, and afterward sat at my desk drumming my fingers. Puppet and puppet master. There was no other way to interpret what I just witnessed. Was Whittaker simply acting out of misplaced sympathy, trying to shield Vargas from what he saw as an invasive or unnecessary line of questioning? Perhaps, although that didn't square with the most salient fact coming out of the interview—Diego Vargas was as spit-dry frightened as Robert Harris.

Chapter Thirty-Six

"A million, about what I expected," Ned Gillian said over the phone an hour later. He was describing the bail that had been set for Carlos Fuentes. "Chad and Hillary Angel did a great job of vouching for Carlos's character and emphasizing his deep roots in the Red Hills, but Judge McMaster gave a lot of weight to his undocumented status."

"How'd Carlos take it?"

"Like everything else, stoically. But I don't think it's sunk in just how long it will be before we go to trial. A guy like him who's work-oriented and full of energy is going to have a tough time dealing with incarceration."

Maybe we can short-circuit that, I thought but didn't say. I described my interview with Diego Vargas, how he didn't give me anything useful and how Gavin Whittaker seemed to orchestrate the outcome.

"You think they're trying to hide something?" Gillian said.

"The thought crossed my mind, but if they are, I couldn't tell you what it is." I stopped short of relating my take on the state of fear that both Vargas and Harris seemed to share. Gillian had enough on his plate, and, besides, I was still processing it.

———

The wine merchant who was being sued arrived at his appointment that afternoon, and we spent an hour going through his case. I wrote up some notes and then called my other new client, the one facing her second DUI. She'd obviously been drinking, so the call didn't go well. I told her there were people who could help her and gave her an AA contact. I doubted she'd follow through, but it was as much as I could do at that point in time.

At midafternoon, Luis Fuentes called. "A weird thing happened," he said after we greeted each other. "A dude who said he hung out at the cantina called me. I didn't remember him. Anyway, he said he wanted to meet with me, that he heard I was looking for information. I think he wants to sell it, but we didn't get into that."

I became fully alert. "How did he know to call you?"

"I've been quietly nosing around, like you asked. I guess he heard about it. I'd left my cell number with some folks I trust who have connections."

"Did you arrange anything?"

"Not quite. He wanted to meet at his place tonight at seven." A nervous laugh. "I told him no fucking way. I suggested Lumpy's Tavern in Dundee, but he wasn't down for a public meeting. I told him I'd find a private place and get back to him. What do you think?"

"Smart not to trust him." I paused, mulling it over. "Tell him we'll meet at my office at seven. Tell him I'm your attorney. He'll figure I'm good for some money."

Luis agreed, and that's where we left it.

At close to four thirty, my email inbox pinged, a message from Esperanza:

This is the best we could do. Hope it helps. XXX.

I clicked on the attachment and downloaded the photo Timoteo had designated as number seven. I leaned in and squinted at it for few moments. The male figure exiting the bar was definitely Robert Harris. I downloaded photo eight. The legs and torso of the figure were well resolved, but the partially shadowed face was still sketchy. I leaned in further and could just make out the traces of a beard, a beard in the style of a Vandyke.

"I knew it!" I blurted out. "That's Curtis Drake, no question." My outburst caused Archie to jump up with a concerned look on his face.

I concentrated on the enhanced image again and noticed something else—Drake clutched a flat, rectangular object in his left hand that was partially shielded by his body. A newspaper? A file folder or sheaf of papers? I couldn't tell for sure.

My pulse ticked up as I went back to Timoteo's original email and downloaded the first photograph—taken in better light—that showed Robert Harris *entering* the bar earlier that evening. I looked closely and this time saw the corner of something in his left hand that was almost completely obscured by his body. A newspaper? A file folder or sheaf of papers? Again, I couldn't tell, but my hunch said the latter.

I looked over at Arch, who was now watching me intently from his spot in the corner. "Whataya know, Big Boy? The spiderweb has another thread." He showed his approval by wagging his backside and whimpering a couple of times.

I was lost in thought when my phone went off a few minutes later. "Just checking in," Timoteo said. "Mariana and I are in position at Prosperar, waiting for Harris to come out."

"Good." I described what I'd just uncovered.

"Wow," he said when I finished, his voice inflected with youthful enthusiasm. "It looks like Harris and the guy who runs the holding center, Drake, met in that bar."

"For sure. That was no coincidence."

"And they exchanged something," Timoteo continued.

"That's a little more speculative, but my hunch says yes, something was exchanged."

"*Shit*. Mariana and I missed that completely. What a couple of assholes!" I heard her moan in the background. Timoteo had the call on speaker.

I laughed. "Hey, don't beat yourselves up, guys. We wouldn't have any of this without your initiative."

A momentary pause, their modest way of accepting the compliment. "What do you think they exchanged?" Mariana asked.

"That's what we need to find out. I have a hunch it's what's driving this whole thing."

I went on to tell them about the meeting Luis was arranging for later that night. Of course, Timoteo wanted to be there, but I told him no, and before we disconnected said, "Look, it's absolutely essential that you keep this information to yourselves. Not a word to anyone. Understood?" They both said yes. I wasn't worried about Timoteo, but I didn't know Mariana all that well and, after all, she was a budding newspaper reporter, and this was the potential scoop of a lifetime.

———

"I've seen this movie," Luis said with a look of worry and disgust as he rolled an unlit cigarette between his fingertips. It was seven fifty that night in my office. He was leaning back in his chair with one foot resting on the corner of my desk. "You think another no-show means trouble?"

I shrugged and was glad I'd brought my Glock, which rested uncomfortably between my belt and the small of my back. "Let's give him ten more minutes."

Luis nodded once. The ring around his left eye had faded from deep purple to yellowish-gray, but the stitches in his forehead still looked red and angry after a week. "His name's Eduardo Duran. We could go to his place, the two of us. See if we can find the *pendejo*."

"You have his address?"

"Hang on." Luis pulled out his cell and made some calls, all in Spanish. Finally, he motioned for a pen and paper and jotted down a set of directions.

Twenty minutes later we turned off the Pacific Highway just past Newberg onto a narrow lane ending at a cul-de-sac. A hundred yards of driveway to the left led to an attractive, low, stone house. "Shit," Luis said, eyeing me incredulously. "Duran lives *here*?"

I pointed toward a large barn perched at the top of the property. "Those windows on the second floor look like they belong to an apartment. Maybe that's where." We left Archie in the car and, after trying the bell at the main house without receiving an answer, walked to the barn and took an open staircase on the left side that led up to an apartment door.

"*Hola amigo, soy Luis Fuentes.*" Luis said, when a young Latino man answered his knock. "*Tu eres Eduardo?*"

"*No. Soy Arlo.*"

After an exchange in Spanish, Luis turned to me. "Arlo here says Eduardo left this afternoon in a big hurry. He doesn't know where he went."

"Does he know *why* he left?"

More Spanish, then Luis said, "Eduardo got a call on his cell, said he kind of freaked out after that. Packed a few things in a backpack and left in his car without saying why."

On a whim, I said, "Ask him if we can see Eduardo's room. Tell him it's important that we find him, that he could be in danger."

After another exchange, Arlo folded his arms across his chest and shook his head with finality. The three of us stood in silence for a few moments, the man frowning, Luis scowling. Finally, I said, "Okay," and turned to leave. Luis put a hand on my arm and addressed Arlo again, with more feeling this time.

Arlo glanced from me to Luis and forced a smile. *"No quiero problema."* He gestured toward a hallway and stepped aside. *"A la derecha."*

Luis stepped past Arlo into the apartment and said over his shoulder, "Down the hall on the right." I followed him in as second thoughts clouded my mind. We had no right doing this, but, dammit, we were here, and I felt the stakes were high enough to warrant a quick look.

We entered the room and closed the door. Luis turned to me with a quizzical expression. "What the hell are we looking for?"

I shrugged and looked around. A narrow closet was stripped bare, drawers in a small chest were pulled out, and shoes and items of clothing littered the floor. "I don't really know. Anything that might tell us where he's gone, anything that looks unusual."

Luis nodded. "Dude left in a hurry, that's for sure."

While Luis rooted around in the closet, I looked through a small writing desk that contained a few receipts, an unpaid cell phone bill, and nothing more. A wall shelf above the desk held a half dozen books, all in Spanish with nothing hidden inside them. I opened a Bible sitting on a nightstand, and a photo of a young boy with a huge grin holding a soccer ball fell on the floor. I felt a twinge of guilt at the invasion of privacy.

I handed Luis the photo. "There's writing on the back. What's it say?"

He turned the photo over, scanned it, and looked up. "It's a note from his mother thanking him for the money he sends.

It pays the rent, and she bought the football his little brother's holding for his birthday."

A wicker wastebasket next to the desk held a couple of torn envelopes that had once contained bills. I looked closer and saw a smattering of paper fragments beneath the envelopes. The pieces were small. Someone had taken the time to methodically tear up a sheet or two of paper.

Why?

I took me a while, but I managed to pluck all the pieces off the bottom of the basket and put them in my coat pocket.

We finished up shortly after that, and on the way out I had Luis ask Arlo where Eduardo worked and what kind of car he drove. "He said he doesn't know where he works, that he doesn't talk about it," Luis said after an exchange. "And he drives a dark-blue Kia Forte with California plates."

Back at the car, I turned to Luis and laughed. "What the hell did you say that made him so cooperative?"

He gave me a sly look. "I told him you knew the ICE *jefe* in Newberg, and that if he didn't let us look around, it might go bad for him." He shrugged. "Too bad we didn't find anything."

Luis hadn't seen me fish the torn fragments out of the wastebasket. Just as well, I remember thinking. They're probably nothing important, and besides, I'm lousy at putting puzzles together.

Only the last half of that thought was half right, it turned out.

Chapter Thirty-Seven

We returned to my office, and after Luis left, I called Darci Tate. "I've got a lead for you on the Olivia Fuentes case."

"I'm listening."

I went on to describe how Eduardo Duran had contacted Luis and our visit to his apartment. "It's a shame he took off, and I doubt he'll contact Luis again. Something spooked him."

"Maybe we can pick him up."

"I hoped you'd say that, although he probably won't talk to you. He's driving a dark-blue Kia Forte with California plates. It's worth a shot."

"I'm on it, Cal. Thanks."

"You owe me one. What's new at your end?"

"Nothing, as in zero." A pause. "Well, you should know DA Thornberg's not backing off on prosecuting Carlos Fuentes to the full extent. I hope Gillian's up to the task."

"So you're seeing the light?" I said with a slight tease in my voice.

"I didn't say that." She sighed deeply. "It's just that, I don't know, I guess I don't blame him for what he did. His daughter was a jewel."

"She was a jewel, all right, but he didn't do it, Darci."

―――

I was hungry when I got home that evening, but I'd been too busy to shop, and the fixings for a serious meal were in short supply. I did have a block of Tillamook cheddar, and when I spied a can of diced tomatoes sitting next to a can of chicken broth in the cupboard, I knew what I had to have. I fed Arch then sautéed some chopped onions, garlic, and red pepper flakes in butter and olive oil before adding the tomatoes and chicken broth. After a forty-minute simmer, I puréed the concoction, stirred in some fresh basil, and ladled a steaming portion of the soup into a bowl. Two cheese sandwiches I'd just removed from the grill and a glass of pinot rounded out the meal.

"What is it about tomato soup and grilled cheese sandwiches, anyway?" I asked my dog when I finished eating. He yawned with a look of indifference. It wasn't a meal that sparked his interest.

After cleaning up the kitchen, I went into the study, sat down, and pondered the list of questions and the spiderweb I'd taped to the wall. Not much progress on the questions, except that I now knew it was Plácido who lured Luis to the Road House and that Curtis Drake was probably a player in this game. I got up and put check marks next to those two questions. I turned my attention to the spiderweb, which showed Diego Vargas at the center. I took a clean sheet of paper and redrew the web, putting Gavin Whittaker's name at the center with lines radiating out to Vargas, Drake, and Harris. I added El Solitario but didn't show a connecting thread. I had no proof there was one.

I taped my new web over the earlier one and sat back with some satisfaction. That makes more sense, I told myself.

But what the hell's the game?

I fetched my coat from the hall, went back into the kitchen, and emptied the torn pieces of paper I'd found in Eduardo Duran's apartment onto the kitchen table. After spreading them out, I counted 206 pieces, printed on one side only. Not that many pieces as puzzles go, but the task still looked daunting. I exhaled a long breath. Was this worth my time?

I didn't know the answer, but unless Duran had some kind of shredding compulsion, he'd probably torn up that paper as he was making his hasty exit. If that were the case, it was of interest to me.

I turned all the pieces faceup and began examining them. Fragments of names and what appeared to be addresses became immediately apparent. It looked like all the names were of Latino origin. I started playing with the pieces, looking initially for scraps that obviously fit together. Twenty minutes into the mind-numbing task, Archie gave a couple of sharp barks that told me he heard something outside.

I opened the front door just as Zoe was taking the steps. Archie met her halfway and got a warm hug. She looked up and smiled, the porch light casting her in a soft yellow glow. "I just got back from a session with Elena. Thought I'd stop by and get an update." She handed me a paper bag. "Here. Gertie made these for you."

I looked in the bag and smelled the contents. "Mmm. Oatmeal cookies. My favorite. How is she?"

"She's prowling around in the kitchen, which is a good sign. I'm about out of a job."

I winced inwardly at the thought of her leaving but didn't comment. "How's Elena doing?" I asked after she followed me past the staircase, down the hall, and into the kitchen.

An audible sigh. "There's no such thing as brief therapy when it comes to trauma recovery, and the news about Carlos has set us back even further. Her energy is still depleted, and she's terrified the overwhelming grief she feels will be permanent. But I've got her talking about Olivia, about when she was a baby and a little girl. That's a positive step." Zoe smiled. "And she showed a flicker of anger about Carlos's arrest. Deep down, she's a fighter, and anger's one way to beat the paralysis she feels from her sense of loss."

I felt some relief. "That's good news."

I poured us each a glass of pinot, and after we sat down at the table, I brought her up to date. She listened intently, at one point remarking, "The ICE supervisor, Drake, and Prosperar's finance man, Harris, appear to be trading information. Maybe Harris is simply feeding Drake the names and addresses of undocumented persons. After all, Prosperar must have a huge database. Maybe Harris is selling the information to Drake. He probably needs the money, given his gambling habit, and Drake gets an atta boy from Washington for busting more illegals. They found out Olivia knew about it and had her killed."

I nodded, impressed with her quickness. "Yeah, that's the simplest explanation. But it doesn't tie in Diego Vargas's boys' club or explain why Olivia sent Luis to spy on them. Believe me, Vargas is wrapped up in this, and all my instincts say Gavin Whittaker is, too. And Whittaker's probably pulling the strings. This feels like something bigger."

"Whittaker's poor wife—do you think she knows anything about this?"

I shrugged. "I don't think so, but I'm trying to keep a line of communication open to her."

Zoe eyed me with the trace of a smile. "Miss Chile. She must be very beautiful."

"She is. And very vulnerable."

Zoe sipped her wine and glanced at the pile of paper scraps in front of her. "You really think there's something in there, something significant?"

I smiled. "They appear to be names and addresses of Latino people... What do you think?"

"Well, I like a good puzzle. Give me half the stack and you take the other half."

That said, we started to work. The font of the print was small, and many of the scraps had similar shapes, so the going was exceedingly slow. It immediately became a team effort. "I've got a 'nandez' here," Zoe said at one point. "Do you have a 'Her'?"

"One 'Her' coming up," I said as I searched through my scrap heap. I found it and slid it over to her. "Here you go."

She thrust a thumb up. "Okay, I've got a Hernandez, first name Arturo, and a partial address, 'Dabney Apa.' She took out her cell phone, tapped on it, and looked up a few seconds later. Dabney Apartments in Lafayette. It's billed as affordable housing."

I sprang up, grabbed a tablet and pen from a drawer, and wrote the information down. Forty minutes, another glass of wine, and a half-dozen oatmeal cookies later, we had five names and addresses:

Arturo Hernandez, Dabney Apartments #301A, Lafayette

Felix Barajas, Deacon Commons Apartments #22, Newberg

Maria Vasquez, Sunflower Hill Apartments #3B, McMinnville

Ramon Ortega, Hapworth Terrace Apartments #38A, McMinnville

Roberto Morales, Hapworth Terrace #16, Lafayette

We both sat back and admired our handiwork. Zoe said, "Judging from what we've done so far, I'm guessing there were at least two sheets of paper with maybe twenty or thirty names and addresses on them. What do you think this guy was doing with them?"

I shrugged. "I have no idea, but the first thing I want to do is try to cross-check these names with the clients at Prosperar. Duran was a member of Diego Vargas's club."

"That should be revealing. Are you going to question them?"

"You bet, with Timoteo's help. These five are enough to start with." I saw her stifle a yawn and sprang up again. "Come on, I'll walk you to the gate." I excused myself and, while she waited on the porch, went upstairs and tucked my Glock into my belt, covering it with a windbreaker. It was only ten thirty, but I was taking no chances.

A front was blowing in, and a gust of wind caught my jacket while I was under the porch light. "Is that a *gun?*" Zoe said, her eyes huge again. "Why do you have a gun?"

"Just a precaution." I told her about Archie sensing a possible night visitor. "Could be just a Fig Newton of my imagination."

She frowned at my attempt at humor. "I don't believe that for a minute. You know your dog too well." She raised her chin and set her jaw in a look of determination. "These are interesting times, indeed."

The moon was low, and clouds were on the move. We crossed the field in silence, but at the gate we heard our friend, the great horned owl, call to us from the Doug firs. We stood there listening, and when the four-note chorus ended, Zoe laughed. "Our song."

I turned to her. "Thanks for your help, Zoe, I—"

"Shhh. I don't want your thanks. I'm glad to help." She met my eyes, and her soft smile caused my stomach to drop a little. "And I think we make a pretty good team." With that, she leaned forward and kissed me on the cheek. "Good night, Cal."

I turned and crossed the field with Archie, trying to put some guard rails on my feelings. I had a chat with myself. Careful. It's too early for anything like this. You're caught up in the emotion of the case. Stay focused.

It was a hard sell.

Chapter Thirty-Eight

"Thanks for seeing me on such short notice," I said to Sofia Leon at nine thirty the next morning. She looked up from her computer, and her face was etched with such despair that I blurted out, "Are you okay?"

She absently pushed her glasses up the bridge of her nose. "It's not me. It's this world we live in. These new ICE raids are taking their toll. Families are cowering in their apartments, too worried to answer their doors." She sighed. "We had a woman die of cardiac arrest in her bedroom, because her husband was afraid to seek help. We just took the body out." Her eyes flashed at me. "Why can't we admit these people belong here, that we need them?"

I shrugged and shook my head. "I—"

"I'm sorry," she said, catching herself. "You didn't come here to listen to a diatribe. Did Gavin Whittaker call you?"

"No, but he showed up in person with Diego Vargas in tow. Thank you."

She waited for me to elaborate. When I didn't, she said, "I heard that Carlos Fuentes was arrested for killing some vineyard worker he suspected was involved in Olivia's death. Is that true?"

"Yes. I'm afraid it is."

Her face clouded over. "Oh, my God, what next? I met Carlos a couple of times, a nice man, a good father. Do you think he did it?"

"No. He was just in the wrong place at the wrong time. He has a good lawyer."

Her face softened a bit in relief. "Good, but the strain on the family must be horrific. How's Elena coping?"

"It's hit her the hardest, but they're a strong family."

She sighed deeply and motioned toward a chair. "What about the investigation of Olivia's murder? What can you tell me?"

"I'm encouraged," I answered, sitting down. "That's why I'm here. I have another favor to ask."

She removed her glasses and rubbed her eyes before replacing them and showing the trace of a smile. "What is it this time?"

I took a sheet of paper from my shirt pocket and unfolded it. "I've got a short list of people here, including their addresses. I'm wondering if they are in any way associated with Prosperar."

Her head tilted back slightly. "Why on earth would you want to know that? As you can well imagine, our client list is highly confidential. Maintaining trust is *everything*, and there are HIPAA rules, as well."

"I fully understand that. All I'm asking for is a yes or no on association. I don't need to know whether they're patients or not. I'm trying to connect some dots here. It's crucial, Sofia."

She looked past me and pursed her lips for a few moments. "I don't know. I'd have to ask my staff."

Damn. I was afraid of that. I sat up a little straighter and leaned in. "No one must know about this except you."

Her eyes narrowed. "Is this about Robert? Is there some reason why you don't want him to know about this?"

I held a neutral expression as her eyes bored in on me. "I'm trying to keep this line of inquiry as confidential as possible."

She held her gaze on me for what seemed an age. Finally, she smiled faintly. "I'll see what I can do." She reached for the sheet of paper. "I have your card. I'll call you."

I thanked her and started back down the hall just as Robert Harris emerged from his office. The sight of me seemed to freeze him, but only for a moment. I waved cordially with my best smile, and he nodded before hurrying down the hallway. I could only imagine what was going through his head.

———

Early that afternoon, Ned Gillian stopped by the Dundee office on his way back from a meeting with Carlos Fuentes. He wore a shirt and tie, slacks, and a navy-blue blazer. I had on a pair of jeans, a no-iron shirt with the sleeves rolled, and a pair of well-worn Merrills. Timoteo was working that afternoon, and if he noticed the sartorial contrast, he didn't let on. Since he was always neatly dressed, I knew he'd opt for the stricter dress code when he became a lawyer, and so he should.

The three of us fell into a discussion of Carlos's case. When I told Gillian that the police had canvassed the neighborhood where Plácido lived without finding anyone who heard a motorcycle around the time of his murder, he said, "How thorough was the canvass? Carlos is sure he heard a bike." The tone of his last statement made it clear he believed his client.

"Good question," I said.

Timoteo said, "There are Spanish speakers in that neighborhood. Maybe the cops didn't take a translator. And I doubt they were anxious to talk to the police, anyway." He looked at me and frowned. "Same old trust problem."

Gillian turned to Timoteo. "Maybe you and I could go over to Lafayette and try our luck. You could put the neighbors at ease, that this has nothing to do with ICE."

"He's good at that," I said.

Timoteo readily agreed, and Gillian said he'd get back to him.

———

Mariana Suarez arrived later that afternoon, the other half of our ad hoc surveillance team. After she greeted us and made a fuss over Archie, I said, "How's your uncle?"

She managed a brave smile. It was still luminous. "Thank you for asking. His morale is better, although his hearing has been postponed for at least two months." She made a face. "So many arrests now, the system is flooded."

"What actions has his attorney taken?"

Her smile brightened. "He's filing an application for naturalization and will ask the judge to stop the deportation. Now we must show that he has demonstrated exceptionally good behavior and is a good citizen."

"That won't be hard," Timoteo said.

She smiled a thank you, then assumed a more serious demeanor as she turned to Timoteo. "Are we on tonight for following Harris?"

"Well, I think instead we should follow Curtis Drake for a few days, see what he's up to after hours." He looked at me. "What do you think?"

I shook my head. "I don't like it. He's ex-military. Probably way more aware of his surroundings than Robert Harris. It's a risk."

Two sets of young, eager eyes bored in on me. Mariana said, "With the telephoto lens, we can stay way back."

"She's right, Cal. We can pick Drake up when he leaves the holding center and stay in the car, of course."

"I don't like you using the same car again," I countered.

"We can take mine," Mariana said. "No problem."

I exhaled a breath and showed my palms in a gesture of surrender. "Okay. Let's see how it goes."

Timoteo and Mariana left that afternoon full of hope and determination. A couple of Dreamers, kids who wanted nothing more than to be allowed to create a future here. I sat back and felt a twinge of satisfaction.

I wasn't at all sure how this case was going to shake out, but I was damn glad I was in the fight.

Chapter Thirty-Nine

There's no better way to start a morning in the City of Roses than with breakfast at the Bijou, a small café in Southwest, a couple of blocks off the River. The omelets weren't made in the kitchen, they were dropped down from the cooking gods in the sky. I was sipping a coffee and perusing the menu the next morning when Nando joined me. "I could eat two horses," he said, sitting down with his trademark smile in full wattage. "I have been up since six this morning."

"That's early for you."

He placed a file folder on the table and rolled his eyes dramatically. "A burst pipe waits for no man. My tenant was struck by panic this morning, and Arnold, my plumber, did not respond to my calls. He is a good worker, but he drinks too much. I had to grab my tools and take care of it."

"One of your places in Southeast?" He nodded. I was referring to a series of rental properties he'd acquired in anticipation of the flight from inner-city Portland brought on by relentless gentrification. Nando had read the tea leaves well and to his credit provided decent housing at fair prices.

After we ordered—an oyster omelet for my friend and a

mushroom and cheddar for me—Nando opened the file. "I have taken the deep dive you wanted on both Curtis Drake and Gavin Whittaker." He cleared his throat. "I will start with Drake. He retired as a staff sergeant in the Army four years ago. Had postings at Fort Bliss and Fort Lewis. Nothing to brag about except being a star player for the Fort Lewis rugby team. He hired on with Immigration Control and Enforcement two and a half years ago." Nando frowned. "There was a need for people with military experience to strengthen their enforcement arm. He coaches the local rugby team and is deacon at an evangelical church near Salem."

"New Faith Bible," I chimed in. "Gillian mentioned that."

"Yes, very devout followers of Christ but not so welcoming to immigrants."

"That's very Christian of them," I said.

"Indeed." Nando paused for a moment. "Here is something I found interesting—New Faith Bible is affiliated with a group called Citizens for Immigration Justice, CIJ."

"Gillian mentioned CIJ," I responded. "He didn't know much about them, except that Drake was rumored to be involved, and that they were trying to get rid of Oregon's sanctuary status by ballot measure."

"Yes, that is their stated public goal, but they are into violence, too, like busting the heads at immigration rallies. The Southern Poverty Law Center has them on their short list of white nationalist hate groups."

"Right here in friendly Oregon," I said. "Is Drake part of CIJ?"

Nando nodded. "The identity of their leadership team is held in strict confidence, but I have confirmed Drake is a member. I had to dig for that."

I knew better than to ask him how. We kicked the Drake-CIJ connection around for a while without coming to any definite conclusions.

Our omelets arrived along with generous servings of fried Yukon Golds and fresh coffee. We ate a few bites in silence until Nando said, "You know, Calvin, in Cuba my father used to say 'The smell of a bad fish taints everybody at the table.'"

"Drake's a bad fish?"

Nando smiled with uncharacteristic bitterness. "White nationalists have black hearts. Drake is involved in this case, we just don't know how."

"Now tell me about Whittaker."

He sipped some coffee and showed the smile again. "A man who lacks decency. A man who wishes to play in the big leagues but lacks the skill."

"Big leagues?"

"Capitalism, money, power. His father left him a fortune, and he has been busy most of his life squandering it. A string of high-end steak restaurants, a collection of boutique hotels in destination hot spots, an investment company, two acrimonious divorces. All big losers. Now he is betting the ranch on the cannabis industry."

"Interesting. I read about the cannabis play. How does it look for him?"

Nando shook his head. "Not good. Oregon produces more than twice the weed that people use here, and more capacity is coming online. Right now, there is more than six years' worth of supply sitting on shelves and at farms. Only big players with deep pockets will survive."

"Is he leveraged?"

"Highly."

"How?"

Nando pointed at me with his fork. "That is a good question, my friend. All I can tell you is that he is not financed through conventional channels. It is private money, very private."

"Any way to identify the source?"

"That will be very difficult, even for me."

I sipped some coffee and leaned back. "Whittaker's stretched thin financially. Anything else?"

"He has no priors but has used nondisclosure agreements, along with generous amounts of cash, to settle at least three sexual assault cases. One involved a young intern working in his investment firm."

I grimaced. "What do you know about his current wife, Isabel?"

He smiled the smile of a man with an appreciation for female beauty. "Miss Chile?"

I nodded. "She is the daughter of Juan Francisco Torres, patriarch of one of the most prominent families in Chile, but the family has fallen on hard times. High-placed Chilean families tend to frown on marriages to outsiders. Perhaps Torres thought his daughter landed a very rich American."

"Or Whittaker thought he married into a wealthy Chilean family," I said.

"Or both," Nando added.

We laughed at the potential irony, although my heart went out to Isabel. I finished a last bite of omelet and sipped some coffee before saying, "Another bad fish?"

Nando dabbed his lips with a napkin and eyed me. "Most definitely. There is plenty of badness to go around...but to what end?"

"That's the question," I replied. "What does a wannabe billionaire, an ICE supervisor who's also a sub-rosa white nationalist, a Latino driver who's probably undocumented, and the financial manager of a nonprofit serving the immigrant community have in common?"

My friend and I sat in silence because we had no answers.

Chapter Forty

From the Bijou Café I headed across town to Caffeine Central to spend a day doing pro bono work. A queue of a half-dozen people had already formed on the sidewalk, a minute fraction of the sixteen thousand homeless in the city. I tried to stay clear of the divisive politics of the homeless situation over the years, focusing instead on something I knew was needed at ground level—legal advice for a vulnerable population. Sure, it was a finger in the dike, but it was something *I* could do, something hands-on, tangible. As I parked and let Arch out, Sofia Leon at Prosperar came to mind. Were there enough fingers for all the holes in the dike? I wasn't so sure.

Like most Fridays at Caffeine Central I stayed busy until noon, then hung a sign on the front door announcing I'd reopen at one p.m. With Archie leashed up, I'd just crossed Couch Street on my way to grab a bite when I got a call. "Hello, Cal, it's Sofia Leon."

I stopped dead and returned the greeting. I didn't mention that I was just thinking about her and Prosperar.

She cleared her throat. "I can confirm that all five names you gave me are in our database." She paused. "That's all I can say on the matter. Can you please tell me what this is all about?"

"All I know at this juncture is that a person of interest in the investigation had a list of names, all Latino, including the ones I gave you. Your information makes an important connection that I really can't go into. Please trust me on this, Sofia."

"Other names? Has our database been compromised?"

"I don't know for sure. The list was partially destroyed. I may be able to come up with a few more for you to check."

"Would you do that?"

"Of course. It'll take some time."

She paused. "There's one more thing, something I probably should have told you earlier."

"Go ahead."

"It came to my attention some time ago that Robert Harris had a severe gambling problem. It was a delicate situation since he handles our finances. I was reluctant to bring this to the attention of the entire board, but I did mention it to Gavin Whittaker since he's in finance. He suggested I let him handle it. He said he'd talk to Robert, suggest counseling, that sort of thing. I went along with it."

"What was the outcome?"

"It's fine, now. Robert stopped gambling."

"You're sure of that?"

"Gavin assured me that was the case."

"I see. Why are you telling me this, Sofia?"

A long exhale. "I don't know, I just thought you should know. Robert handles our client database. Could this be significant in some way?"

A Rubicon moment, for sure, but I was confident I could trust her. "I'm not sure how significant it is, but I can tell you that Robert has *not* stopped gambling."

She sucked a breath. "Oh, God. What should I do?"

"Nothing at this point, please. Just be my eyes and ears at

Prosperar and above all don't breathe a word of this to anyone, least of all Robert. Can you do that?"

"Yes, I can. I'm counting on you to be as judicious as you can with the information you're uncovering. Prosperar's a fragile enterprise. It wouldn't take much of a scandal to knock us down."

"Understood."

———

Portland's explosive growth meant Friday afternoon commutes had taken on L.A. dimensions. That Friday was no exception. In fact, the traffic was so jammed up that I got off the 5 in Wilsonville and snaked along the Willamette, joining 99W in Newberg before heading south again. The reveal from Sofia Leon was churning around in my brain. I now knew that one of Diego Vargas's young men—Eduardo Duran—was connected to Prosperar through the list Zoe and I partially reconstructed. Did Harris give him the list? I also knew that Gavin Whittaker and Robert Harris had a direct relationship. Who was lying about the gambling—Whittaker or Harris or both? Why? The answers weren't there yet, but the web connecting the players had just gotten tighter, and Whittaker was still in the center.

On the way through Newberg I stopped in at the police station and was lucky enough to catch Darci Tate behind her desk. "How's it going?" I greeted her.

She looked up from a stack of papers and managed half a smile. "Don't ask. What's up?"

With Sofia's plea still ringing in my ears, I decided to withhold what she told me. "Just checking in."

Darci leaned back and absently ran her fingers through her short blond hair, which was showing more dark roots. "We found the Kia Forte but no Duran."

"Where was it?"

"Parking lot at Rogers Landing in Newberg, right next to the river. No sign of him. The driver's-side door was ajar."

I winced. "That doesn't sound good. You think he's missing?"

Darci shrugged. "The river's cold. Hope he didn't decide to take a swim. If he doesn't turn up soon, we'll haul Diego Vargas's ass back in and see what he has to say." She knitted her brows together in frustration. "This investigation is on a fast track to nowhere."

"Nothing on the hair follicle DNA?" I asked, changing the subject to Carlos Fuentes's arrest.

"Nada." She leaned forward and looked at me full-on. "Look, Cal, the DA wants this one bad. He's getting pressure from the folks who worry about the 'brown menace.' You know, these vineyard workers killing each other in Yamhill County isn't a good look."

I felt a wave of anger tinged with something close to nausea. "The murder of a young Latina, who's a U.S. citizen, doesn't worry him as much, huh?"

She cringed a little and shrugged again. "Olivia's case is dragging on, but he sees Carlos as a quick hit, a way to throw these people a bone. He's up for election next year."

I got up to leave. "Thanks for the heads-up, Darci. I'll pass that on to Ned Gillian." If steam actually escaped from human ears, it would've happened right then and there.

———

Back at the Aerie I let Archie out of the car while I opened the gate. He bounded into the yard and went straight after two deer up by Gertie's fence line. The deer, wily veterans of my Aussie's penchant for herding, waited until the last moment before nonchalantly hopping over the fence. He trotted back like nothing had happened. I'd seen that movie a hundred times but still had to laugh. "When are you going to learn, Big Boy?" He lowered his ears as if I'd embarrassed him, which made me feel bad. After all, I reminded myself, herding's in his DNA.

There was a bit of sunlight left, so I got some work done on my wall. Even without Zoe's help, I was starting the third course and beginning to think I might actually finish the project in my lifetime. After putting my tools up, I went straight to the kitchen. Zoe was spending the evening with Elena Fuentes while Timoteo was on surveillance duty, and I'd promised to make Gertie's dinner.

"That smells good," she said as she let me in her back door an hour later. Her silver-streaked hair had its luster back, and her eyes—those robin eggs—were clear and alert.

"Health food," I said, holding a covered platter in one hand and a half-full bottle of Pascal Jolivet Sancerre in the other. "Washington cod sautéed in a bit of butter and white wine, rice pilaf, and a tomato and cucumber salad."

While we ate, we discussed the case. "Well," Gertie commented, "you've certainly identified an interesting cast of characters. And they're all connected in one way or another to Prosperar and our friends who work the vineyards and fields around here." She paused, smiling sardonically, when we came around to Gavin Whittaker. "Don't know much about him, but my grandfather knew his grandfather, the timber baron. Can't say I ever heard anything good about the Whittakers. How desperate do you think he is for money?"

I shrugged. "We're trying to get a fix on that. According to Nando, his cannabis business isn't the first he's flown into the ground."

She smiled approvingly. "You're smart to follow the money."

After we finished eating, Gertie changed the subject. "Zoe has become quite involved with the Fuentes family, hasn't she?"

"To her credit, yes. She's making real inroads with the mother, as you probably know." I eyed Gertie carefully to judge where she was going with this. Was she disapproving of my getting her niece so involved in the case?

She smiled. "I'm proud of her and not surprised in the least. Zoe's that kind of person." She met my eyes. "But she's vulnerable, too. She's been hurt too many times."

I held her gaze, now getting her drift. "I understand that, Gertie."

"She's very fond of you."

I nodded. "She's a wonderful person."

My friend's eyes narrowed, and I felt she was looking straight into my soul. "But she'll never measure up to your wife, the woman you've got on a pedestal. Don't hurt her, Cal."

A knot tightened in my gut, and I swallowed an urge to defend myself and my intentions. Who was I kidding? She was right, and I knew it. "It's not that kind of thing, Gertie. Don't worry, I won't hurt her."

We said our good-nights shortly after that. As Archie and I crossed the field, the moon slid behind a cloud, and the great horned owl was mute. I asked myself whether I would ever escape Nancy's ghost. The answer came back—probably not. And I was left with a feeling of emptiness.

Chapter Forty-One

With the help of my old friend Rémy Martin, I set about reconstructing more names and addresses from the scraps of paper I'd gathered at Eduardo Duran's apartment. I wasn't nearly as adept as Zoe, but I had two more to add to the list when she called. I let it go to voicemail, then listened to it: "Hey, it's me. Had a really good session with Elena. I'm encouraged, Cal. Thanks for covering dinner for me. Gertie said it was great. If you want some help with the puzzle tonight, give me a call. *Ciao.*"

I sat there in the kitchen for a while, staring at the wall with Gertie's words echoing in my head. Finally, I poured another glass of Rémy and went back to work. I'd pieced together three more names when Timoteo called. "Just checking in with a surveillance update. Sent you an email with photos. Got some interesting stuff, I think," he added, his voice tinged with excitement.

I carried my cell phone into the study and logged on to my computer.

"Drake left the holding center at four thirty-five, drove south on the Pacific Highway, and turned left on Fulquartz Landing," Timoteo went on. "We didn't follow him in. No traffic on Fulquartz. Too risky."

"Smart," I said. "He was probably on his way to see Whittaker. There's nothing else in there except crop fields and his estate."

"That's what we figured. Anyway, we waited near the intersection in the hopes he would come back out. Ten minutes later, guess what? Robert Harris tools up in his Z4 and turns onto Fulquartz, too."

"Hail, hail, the gang's all here," I said. "Nice work."

"It gets better. An hour and ten minutes later, Harris comes back out and heads north on the highway. After another ten minutes, Drake comes out and heads south. We followed him to the Half Moon Lounge in McMinnville. Only a handful of people came and went during the time he was in there. There was a light in the entryway, so I got some decent photos."

I examined the photos and saw nothing of interest until I came to a shot of Drake leaving. "Who's the blond kid?" I asked.

"Open up the next email." I did, and Timoteo continued, "After two boring hours, he came out with that guy, early twenties at the most. They got into Drake's car and drove to the Grant Motel further down the highway. He waited in the car while Drake rented a room. They both went in."

I looked at the attached set of photos. They showed the two of them entering the room and leaving it. The photos were clear, the facial features well-defined. "When did they leave?"

"Fifty-eight minutes later. A quickie. What do you think, Cal?"

I exhaled a breath. "I think it's significant there was an apparent powwow at Whittaker Landing. The fact that they would chance a meeting like that suggests they could be worried. That says we'd better be on guard. Harris saw me leaving Sofia Leon's office today, and they might know we tried to contact Eduardo Duran. He might be missing, by the way." I went on to explain that Darci Tate had found his car but not him.

"Holy shit, you think Duran's been killed, too?"

"It wouldn't surprise me."

"You think Drake was soliciting a prostitute? He looked like a minor, too."

"Could be just consensual sex between two adults. Who Drake sleeps with isn't relevant to this investigation. I'm going to delete the photos."

"Maybe it's consensual, but the *hypocrisy*, Cal. I read that report from Nando. Drake's the deacon at a church that denounces gays, that says they're all going to hell."

"It's not relevant, Timoteo. We don't need the distraction. Finding your sister's killer and getting your father out of jail— that's what we're focused on."

"Yeah, okay."

———

That Saturday morning broke cold and wet, although the drizzle was light enough that I decided to get a run in. No fan of rain, Archie was a good sport about it, staying out ahead of me as we slogged up the hill toward the cemetery. When we got back, I fed him and made myself a light breakfast before calling Sofia Leon. "I've got five more names and addresses for you," I told her.

I read off the names, and she jotted them down. "Hang on," she said, "I'll check these for you now. I'm embarrassed to say I didn't know how to navigate our patient database. That's Robert's domain. But I figured it out." She came back on a few minutes later. "Yes, all five are on our rolls."

I said, "It looks like the young Latino man I told you about had a couple of pages of names from Prosperar. Can you think of any reason why he would have something like that?"

"No, I can't think of any reason. It's very troublesome. I need to get to the bottom of—"

"I understand that, Sofia. Can you give me some time on this before you get involved?"

She paused. "Yes, I can do that. By the way, Robert stopped by my office after you left yesterday. He was obviously fishing around to learn what you wanted with me." She chuckled softly. "He's not a very subtle person."

"What did he say?"

"He asked about the investigation, how it was going."

"How did you answer?"

"I told him you didn't discuss the case, that you had some questions about Olivia, about her contacts in the community. Routine stuff."

"Good thinking, Sofia."

"Well, I wanted to ask him about his gambling, but I kept my mouth shut. He went on to warn me about you."

"He did?"

"Yes, he said I shouldn't talk to you. 'Let the police run the investigation, not some small-time lawyer from Dundee,' he told me. 'It could get out of control, wind up hurting our reputation.'"

"What did you say to that?"

I pictured a sly smile forming on her face. "I figured the best thing would be to go along with him. I told him that was a good point, that I hadn't thought it through." She paused. "Going forward, don't come to Prosperar, Cal. Call me when you need to talk."

I thanked her, and when we disconnected, I sat back and gave thanks for people with good judgment and a moral compass. Sofia Leon had both.

———

By midday, the Doug firs along my property line began to sway, and the light mist turned to a gentle downpour, the kind of rain that soaks in, rather than runs off. Out over the valley, a shaft of sunlight had broken through the cloud cover, igniting the slope on a section of the Coast Range in brilliant emerald green. I watched the light show from the kitchen window while eating a fried egg sandwich and drinking a glass of orange juice. It was this view that had sold me on the Aerie, a view that never got old.

Twenty minutes later, Archie and I were at my office in Dundee. I figured a quiet Saturday meant a chance to get some paperwork done. I just finished lighting the woodstove to get the chill off when I caught a glimpse of a red car turning into my driveway. I opened the back door and watched as Isabel Whittaker got out of her Tesla. Wearing dark glasses and a hooded raincoat, she moved with the fluid grace of a ballet dancer.

"Hello, Cal. Are you busy?"

"No, not at all, Isabel. Come in."

Archie met her at the door like an old friend, and I watched as they got reacquainted. When she stood back up, she removed her glasses and placed them in a pocket of the raincoat before hanging it up. "I fell in the barn," she said, gesturing at her face, which showed the faint remnants of a bruise under her left eye. She took my offered seat and glanced around the office at the photos and paintings I'd collected over the years. "This is lovely." She scrunched up her brow. "So…how do you say it…so rusty?"

I smiled. "Rustic. Thanks. They're just places in Oregon that I love." I paused for a moment, and she waited. "What can I do for you, Isabel?"

She exhaled a breath, and her face darkened. "It's Diego Vargas. Something is going on with him. I'm worried, and I don't know who to talk to about it."

Not your husband? I thought but didn't say. "What's the problem?"

She studied me for a moment before allowing the hint of a smile. "Why do I feel like I can trust you?"

I leaned forward. "Because you can."

She looked away before returning her eyes to me, nodding once. "Yesterday I was at the stables rearranging the tack room. I needed to move some heavy shelves. Gavin was busy in his office, so I asked Diego to help me. He came, and we worked for a while, but he looked so...so worried, you know? And sad, I think. It's not the first time I have noticed this. I asked him what was wrong." Her eyes flared. "He broke down right in front of me. Tears in his eyes. A grown man. I said, 'Is this about your son, Tito?' He said, 'No, no, it's nothing,' and apologized over and over again."

"What's wrong with his son?"

"He has a rare form of cancer and is undergoing an experimental treatment at OHSU. Diego learned of the study and convinced the doctors to take his son. The treatment is keeping him alive."

"What upset him then?"

She inhaled a breath, then expelled it. "His son is undocumented, too. He was brought here by Diego as an infant after his mother died. If they are deported, Tito will surely die in Mexico."

"Are they in danger of being deported?"

Isabel shook her head. "No. Not at this time, but I think he's mixed up in something, something that could cause him a bad problem. I think this is what worries him. " She paused and studied me for a few moments. "I know that you're interested in him for your investigation, and I know Gavin brought him here for you to question. Can you tell me if you have found anything?"

"The investigation's ongoing, and I can't discuss it." I felt I had to give her something, so I added, "I can tell you that Diego is still a person of interest."

"I see. I wanted you to know this. I don't think Diego is a

bad man. He would never have hurt Olivia Fuentes, but I think someone is putting pressure on him."

Is she reluctant to admit she suspects her husband? I asked myself. Or is she in complete denial? I said, "Have you discussed this with Gavin?"

An incredulous look bloomed on her face and faded just as quickly. "Gavin is a judgmental man. I don't want to cause Diego a problem. He needs the job." She met my eyes and held them. "This is why I'm speaking to you, Cal."

It's not denial, I realized. "Thank you for this information. Every little bit helps." I paused, holding her gaze. "Is there anything else you want to tell me?"

She stood. "No, and I have to go now. Thank you for listening."

I decided it was time to be direct. "Those bruises on your arms and your face, Isabel. Is your husband hurting you?"

Her mouth turned down, and she blanched. "*No.* It is what I told you." She turned and headed for the door.

"I think he is, and I can help you. Please stay and tell me about it." She hesitated for a moment at the door without looking back, then let herself out.

When the door clicked shut, I noticed she'd left a card on the arm of her chair. I walked over and picked it up. It read *Isabel Torres Whittaker* in raised gold script and listed a home number and a mobile number below her name. The home number had been crossed out with a pen, a not-so-subtle hint not to use it.

I stood there motionless for several moments, stunned. I suspected that Whittaker was squeezing Vargas, and this suggested how he might be doing it. What better leverage than to threaten the life of a man's child, particularly a man who can't fight back because he's illegal? And Curtis Drake was right there to make the threat palpable. This revelation was a gift from a woman who couldn't bring herself to directly implicate her husband. Why? Was it something in her upbringing? Was it simply stark fear? I didn't know.

But one thing I did know—Isabel Whittaker had too much compassion and courage to keep silent.

Chapter Forty-Two

"I have to admit I was a little skeptical about the existence of a hit man from L.A. who uses a motorcycle," Ned Gillian said, "but I'm a believer now." He'd dropped by my office later that afternoon after he and Timoteo canvassed the neighborhood where Plácido Ballesteros was murdered. Ned wore a golf shirt, khakis, and boat shoes, his version of dressing down. "Very few people were responding, and we were about to chuck it in, when this teenage kid comes to the door. Most of the conversation was in Spanish, but the gist of it was he was up playing a video game when he heard a bike come by the night of the murder." Gillian chuckled. "Turned out he was playing a game called *Road Rash*, which involves motorcycles, no less. That's why it caught his attention. A point of irony, he said the reason he noticed it was that the bike was heavily muffled, not that it was making a lot of racket. He said very few bikes sound like that."

"That's exactly what I thought about the sound of the bike at the Road House the night Luis was attacked."

"And the timing fits perfectly," Gillian continued. "He'll make a good witness, too. He was born here, so he won't be shy about coming to court. It's still surprising to me that a pro like this El

Solitario would keep moving around on a bike. I mean, talk about high risk."

"I agree. Maybe it's arrogance. You know, big-city hit man comes to Podunk Oregon and has no respect for the local constabulary."

Gillian showed a grim smile. "I hope that's it. The son of a bitch is in for a surprise." I then described my conversation with Darci Tate, relating how Eduardo Duran had gone missing and that the DA's political agenda was a key factor in the prosecution of Carlos. His smile turned bitter. "Why am I not surprised? It's always about fucking politics. If they find Duran facedown in the Willamette, it will only strengthen our theory of the case. I mean, like Plácido Ballesteros, Duran is another one of Vargas's boys who knows too much."

"That's right," I said. "And finding that witness is another piece of the puzzle, Ned. Damn fine work."

He smiled modestly and got up to leave, adding, "You've got quite an assistant, you know. Timoteo is one sharp young man. He told me he wants to be a lawyer. He'll make a damn good one."

"He's a DACA recipient," I said, "a Dreamer. He arrived here with his brother when he was four."

"I wondered about his status." Gillian pursed his lips and shook his head emphatically. "Is Congress ever going to get off their asses and protect those kids? Timoteo's a smart, motivated young man, an *asset*. Hell, his English's better than mine. Deport him? Are you kidding me? We need kids like him in this country."

"We do, indeed."

He paused at the door and turned back to me. "Oh, yeah. Almost forgot." He reached into his briefcase and pulled out a paper bag. "Chanterelles. A client of mine gave me these, freshly picked at the coast. I heard you like to cook. I wouldn't know what to do with them."

I took the mushrooms, opened the bag, and smiled. "That makes two reasons I'm forever in your debt."

———

It was still raining when Arch and I pulled into the Aerie late that afternoon, but the cloud cover was starting to break up, and the sky to the west looked like a bed of hot coals. I started fixing dinner to the accompaniment of some old Lucinda Williams albums. I had an impulse to check in with Zoe but immediately thought better of it. Gertie was right, I told myself for the umpteenth time.

I started warming up some chicken broth and then washed the chanterelles before gently sautéing them in butter along with some garlic and shallots. I stirred in the arborio rice and had just added white wine and thyme when I heard a soft knock at the door, one I'd come to recognize. I had an impulse not to answer. At the same time, I wanted to see her. *Shit.* I finally resolved the conflict by reminding myself to just stick to the business at hand. After all, Zoe had become an integral part of the investigation. That's as far as it will go, I told myself.

"Hi," Zoe said when I opened the door. Her smile had an uncertain quality. Had Gertie said something? "The rain let up, so I'm out for a stroll." She wore jeans, an oversized sweater, and the blue scarf I liked, but not the pearl earrings.

I invited her in. "I've got something on the stove. Come on back to the kitchen."

"It smells wonderful. What is it?"

"Just a simple risotto. Ned Gillian gave me some nice chanterelles today. Have you eaten?"

"Oh, yeah. I, ah, made spaghetti tonight for Gertie and me."

I poured her some wine and began to ladle small amounts of the now-simmering chicken broth into the rice mixture. Absorbing the broth, the rice plumped a little with each addition. Zoe eyed me with an eyebrow raised. "You didn't return my call last night."

I apologized, explaining that Timoteo had called, and I got distracted. It sounded lame. "I was glad to hear you're making progress with Elena," I added, just to prove I had, in fact, listened to the call. Lame again.

She let it pass, and while I coaxed the arborio into plumpness, we discussed the latest developments. I described the surprise visit from Isabel Whittaker. "I think you're right about her reticence, Cal. Chilean culture is laced with machismo, you know, men are deemed superior, and strict wifely obedience is the norm."

"Yeah," I said, "it's like she's caught between her conscience and her upbringing."

Zoe nodded with a bitter smile. "And her bastard of a husband is abusing her. What irony if she thought marrying Whittaker, an American, would be different. I feel for her."

"What do you make of Diego Vargas's breakdown?" I asked.

She shrugged. "I wouldn't call it a breakdown. He did regain his composure, but I think Isabel's right. He's in over his head in something, and whatever it is has him very frightened. "

As I ladled on more broth, I told her what Sofia Leon had said about Whittaker offering to deal with Robert Harris's gambling habit. "What do you make of that?"

She drank some wine and then exhaled. "Sociopaths have a sixth sense when it comes to spotting the right people to manipulate and are highly adept at exploiting them for personal gain. They're also really good at impression management, meaning they know how to fool people into thinking they're paragons of virtue. Whittaker could fall in that category."

"Hmm," I said. "Robert Harris has a gambling addiction, and Curtis Drake, deacon of an evangelical church, prefers sex with men. It wouldn't even take a sixth sense to recognize their vulnerabilities."

The bitter smile again. "The ties that bind in a big, happy family."

I chuckled at that. "I know who the players are but still have no hint of a motive." I blew out a breath. "It's frustrating as hell."

"Maybe so, but look how far you've come."

I tasted the rice. "Al dente. Perfect." I was adding some freshly grated Parmesan when I caught Zoe's longing glance and decided I'd tortured her enough. "You want to join me?"

She smiled sheepishly. "I thought you'd never ask. I didn't eat much tonight. I, ah, I don't really like my own cooking."

I laughed. "What about Gertie?"

"She said she liked it, but come to think of it, there was a lot left over." Another sheepish smile. "She said she's feeling good enough to start doing more of the cooking."

"I made plenty," I said. "You can take her some."

I made a quick salad and sliced up a baguette. I was as hungry as she was, and we ate in silence for a while. Finally, Zoe said, "Where're the puzzle pieces?"

"They're in the study. I got five more names last night and passed them on to Sofia Leon this morning. She confirmed they were also on Prosperar's roll." We kicked that around for a while and then, after dinner, retired to the study to see how many more names we could come up with. While we worked, I caught myself stealing glances at Zoe, noticing the fine curve of her cheek, the soft shine of her blue eyes under the lamplight, the swelling of her chest as she breathed.

Hey, I told myself, knock it off. Remember your promise to Gertie.

It was past midnight when we stopped. We'd deciphered another eight names, and the remaining scraps looked useless.

Archie was the first out the door as we headed toward Gertie's. I was packing the Glock as a precaution. We'd gotten maybe a quarter of the way across the field when Archie peeled off and headed toward the driveway. He stopped just within my range of vision near the gate and faced the west fence line. The hairs on the back of my neck prickled. Had he sensed something on the other side of the fence again?

I stopped and put an arm out to halt Zoe and then clicked my tongue. Archie looked back at us but didn't move. Zoe started to speak, and I put my hand over her mouth. I clicked my tongue again, louder. To my relief, Archie turned and trotted toward us, an obedient dog.

"Do you have your car keys on you?" I whispered to Zoe. She nodded, I took her hand, and we walked across the field at a normal pace. Her car was in Gertie's driveway. I said, "Give me your keys, and then go in the house and lock up. Take Archie with you."

Her eyes got huge. "What is it?"

"Archie was pointing at something on the other side of my fence. I need to check it out. It's probably nothing."

"I want to go with—"

"No. Stay here, please. Take Archie and go inside."

She did, and I backed her car out of the drive and headed down Worden Hill Road with the lights off. I pulled over across from my mailbox with the car idling and sat staring into the darkness.

Nothing moved up ahead, at the spot where I'd discovered the animal trail leading to my fence line. Thirty-five minutes later, I heard a motorcycle start up and saw a red taillight as the bike pulled onto the road at that very spot.

I waited until the bike was maybe a block down the hill before slipping Zoe's car into gear. While I followed the distant taillight toward Dundee, I called 911. There was no time for explanations. "This is Cal Claxton," I said. "Someone just stole my motorcycle and is heading down Worden Hill Road toward the Pacific Highway. I'm following him in a silver Toyota. He's on a black Kawasaki, and I think he's armed." The operator said she'd dispatch a patrol car and warned me to keep my distance.

As I rounded a curve just past Crabtree Park, the taillight was gone. I slowed down, and as the road straightened out, the light came back on less than a hundred feet ahead of me.

"*Damn it,* he's seen me," I said out loud as the bike roared off at a high rate of speed. I turned my lights on and stepped on the gas, but there was little hope of keeping up with the Kawasaki.

I passed the Scenic Overlook and hit the straightaway leading down to the highway. The taillight was no longer visible. In the distance I heard a screech of air brakes, and when I reached the intersection, I came to a stop. A jackknifed tractor trailer rested in the middle of the highway. The driver was standing outside his rig holding his head in his hands. The Kawasaki was nowhere to be seen.

Chapter Forty-Three

I got out and approached the truck driver. "Did you see a motor-cycle? Which way did it go?"

The man dropped his hands and looked at me, his face anguished, his eyes wide. "He pulled out right in front of me. I couldn't stop." He pointed toward the cab of the truck. "He's under there. Can you call the cops? No need for an ambulance." He clasped his head in his hands again. "Aw, man, what was he thinking? Aw, man..."

I approached the cab of the truck, dropped to one knee to have a look. El Solitario was facedown in a jumble of twisted metal with one leg pinned under the left front wheel of the rig and an arm entangled in the truck's undercarriage. Strong gas fumes wafted up from under the truck. The driver was right. He would not need an ambulance.

A moment later, the patrol car dispatched by the 911 operator arrived with flashing blue lights.

While one officer placed flares and began directing traffic, the other briefly interviewed the truck driver. When she turned to me, I said, "You should call Detective Darci Tate right away. She needs to be here." I went on to explain that the victim was a suspect in the murder of Olivia Fuentes, which raised the eyebrows of the young officer. She called Tate immediately, then began interviewing me. As we talked, my phone rang. It was Zoe. I called her back after the interview, but just as she picked up, Tate arrived. "I'm okay," I told Zoe. "I'll fill you in when I get free."

Tate conferred with the officers, looked the scene over, and then came over to me. "You think the vic's El Solitario, huh?"

"It's him."

She shook her head. "Well, one thing for sure, there won't be any facial recognition. He took a total faceplant on the asphalt."

"I noticed."

"He was lying in wait at your place?"

"Yeah. He was planning to take me out tonight." I went on to describe the chain of events leading up to the accident.

When I finished, Tate said, "So, he was waiting by the gate to pop you when you walked by, but instead you decided to cross the field with your friend. He waited around for a half hour and when you didn't show, he got back on his bike and buggered off."

"That's the way it went down."

"You didn't actually see him, right?"

"Nope. I went by Archie's reaction."

She furrowed her brows. "He must have known you had a dog. Wonder how he planned to deal with that?"

I shuddered at the thought of what could have happened. "I think it was simple—shoot my dog first, then me." I shrugged, "Whatever he had in mind, he underestimated Archie."

Tate smiled. "Apparently."

The exchange got my back up a little, but Darci's cynical mindset was what made her a good cop.

I stayed around until El Solitario's body was removed in a bag and the wreckage cleared. The last thing Tate said to me was, "Now, all I have to do is prove that this guy was a notorious cartel hitter who killed Olivia Fuentes and attempted to kill her brother." She leveled her eyes on me. "The alternate scenario is that he was some local dude out for a ride who stopped to take a leak and panicked when he realized you were following him with your lights off."

I smiled. "Don't worry, Darci, you got your man, and you're gonna get a medal for this. The question now is who sent him?"

I was so wired and caught up in the activities at the scene that when I left around two thirty, I realized I hadn't called Zoe back. Thinking she was probably asleep by then, I texted her that I was on my way and added: El Solitario is dead. She replied immediately: What?! OMG! I'm in the kitchen. Come around to the back door.

Archie came to the door first, whimpering softly, and then Zoe appeared. She threw her arms around me. It felt so natural I followed suit. We broke apart quickly, both looking a little embarrassed. I bent down to stroke my dog, and she put a hand to her mouth. "My God, that *was* him behind the fence?"

"Yeah. I'd bet my mortgage on it."

She looked down at my dog. "Archie, you're a hero."

I chuckled. "Careful, he'll get a swelled head."

Zoe and I sat in Gertie's kitchen and talked until the buzz wore off. By the time Archie and I headed back across the field, the sun was silhouetting the Doug firs along the east side of the Aerie. I slept soundly for four hours, showered, and then called Nando to give him the news.

"This is huge, Calvin," he said. "El Solitario is dead. A notorious cartel hit man. You killed him."

"I didn't kill him, damnit. He was a careless driver."

He laughed. "That is a good way to put a spin on it. We don't want the cartels to blame you."

"Hey, he was an independent contractor, doing high-risk work. Why would they blame me?"

Nando laughed. "Oh, of course, they are such reasonable people. But don't worry, my friend, your secret is safe with me."

"Secret?"

"Yes, that your dog is the real hero."

I had to laugh at that.

I called Timoteo next. After briefly recapping the events, I said, "Call Luis and have him come to your place. I'll be there with Zoe in an hour. We need to talk."

The front had blown through, leaving in its wake a cobalt-blue sky and air with a crispness that only occurs in late fall. Marlene came to the Fuentes's front door to let us in. Her smile was lovely, something I hadn't noticed before, and her eyes gleamed with expectation. We followed her into the kitchen where Luis and Timoteo were sitting on either side of Mariana, who looked up at me with equal expectation. I was surprised to see her, but it made sense. She was on this team, after all. Cups and saucers were set out along with a pot of coffee. The aroma was tantalizing.

While I poured myself a cup, Zoe said, "Excuse me. I'm going to see if Elena wants to join us." She returned a few minutes later, looking disappointed. "Maybe next time." She looked at the two brothers. "I didn't say anything. I'll let you two tell her."

They all sat in rapt attention while I described what happened. Luis spoke first, a grim smile on his face, which still bore the scars of the attempt on his life. His voice was husky, his eyes shiny in the overhead light. "Bam, he's crushed by an eighteen-wheeler. My only regret is that the *cábron* didn't suffer."

Timoteo said, "How will the cops prove he's the killer?"

"Good question," I said. "They'll be looking for a weapon and try to trace it back. We know the same gun was used in the murder and the attack on Luis. They'll run his prints and DNA in the national system and see what comes up. In addition, they'll be looking for his cell phone and anything else they can trace back to the person who hired him. It's on them to prove it, and believe me, they've got plenty of incentive."

Mariana said, "They'll be able to compare his DNA with the hairs they found on Plácido Ballesteros's body, too."

"That's right," I said. I wasn't going to mention that, because I didn't want to unduly raise their hopes about Carlos's situation. "Let's hope we catch a break on that, too."

Timoteo leaned in, his face taut. "On Friday night, Mariana and I watched Curtis Drake and Robert Harris turn off the Pacific Highway onto Fulquartz, which leads to only one place— Whittaker Landing. One night later, El Solitario shows up at Cal's place." He looked directly at me. "That's no coincidence. Those bastards sent him to kill you."

And my dog, I thought but didn't say. The attack on Archie and me made it even more personal, but this was no time to give in to blind anger. "It looks that way, but we've got no direct proof of anything yet."

That set off an impassioned discussion of what to do next. An hour later we had come up with the semblance of a plan. Luis would try to make contact with yet another one of Diego Vargas's boys. Surely, we could get one of them to talk. Timoteo and I would start interviewing the persons on Eduardo Duran's pieced-together list. What do they have in common? Meanwhile, the surveillance would go on, I would press Nando Mendoza for results on his probe of Gavin Whittaker's finances, and Zoe would bolster the home front by continuing to counsel Elena Fuentes.

After the meeting broke up, and Zoe and I were headed back to the Aerie, she laughed and said, "That's quite a group you've assembled. Cal's Army."

I shrugged and shook my head. "I sure didn't plan it that way. It just sort of happened. One thing's for sure—there's no doubting the commitment of my army."

We drove on in silence for a while. Zoe looked over at me. "You seem a little down. What is it?"

"Not down, pensive. El Solitario is off the board, and that's a great thing. But there's one nagging problem—I chased down and caused the death of the one man who could lead us directly back to the person or persons behind this. " I sighed. "We'll be hard-pressed to find a direct link now."

"Come on, Cal," Zoe said, "it's not your fault that you didn't take him alive. Cal's Army will find a way."

"We'd better," I said. "There won't be any closure unless we do."

Chapter Forty-Four

"Well, what do you think?" I asked Timoteo. It was the next evening, and we'd just finished questioning another person on Duran's list. Of the six doorbells we'd rung so far, only three people agreed to talk to us.

He shrugged. "I don't know. I wasn't too sure of that first guy at Abbey Heights in Dayton. Seemed like he might know something but didn't want to tell us. The other two? I don't think they know anything. It's weird. Why did Duran have that list, and why did he bother to rip it up?" He waved a dismissive hand and laughed. "Maybe it has nothing to do with the case."

By the end of the evening, we'd talked to six people and drawn an absolute blank. As we were heading back to Angel Vineyard to drop off Timoteo, he said, "It's like that was a customer list or something. Whatever the list was intended for, I don't think Duran had made any contact yet." He exhaled in frustration. "Mariana and I should have been out there tonight following either Harris or Drake. El Solitario's death probably stirred the pot."

"Could be, but it's more likely they'll be even more cautious now. He was the enforcer." I looked over at my young assistant. "You and Mariana make a good team."

He smiled. "Funny, she was always, you know, just my kid sister's friend, but then I got to know her. She's pretty amazing. She's got real substance, Cal."

I suppressed a smile at his characterization. It was such a mature thing for someone his age to say. "I have a feeling she feels the same way about you."

"Well, we both have serious goals we want to accomplish, so neither one of us is looking for a relationship right now." He paused for a moment. "She, um, wanted me to ask you again about her covering this investigation for the paper."

"You tell her to take good notes, and when we find out who hired El Solitario, she can have the exclusive. But not until then."

———

The following morning Detective Tate dropped by my office. She looked as tired as I felt. "I figure I owe you this," she said as she took a seat. "It turned out No Face was packing a thirty-eight and a suppressor. Got the ballistics back last night. It's the same gun that was used to kill Olivia and in Luis's drive-by."

"I'm not surprised."

"He had no ID on him, and no scars or tats. We've requested expedited fingerprint and DNA searches. We'll see if the LAPD is right in claiming they have the only print of him, won't we?" She paused, and her look told me a surprise was coming. "We also found an unmarked van tucked in off the road near the overlook. It—"

"That's how he did it!" I said, breaking in. "Of course!"

She laughed. "Yep. It was locked up, but we lifted a print off a door handle that matched the vic's, so we got a search warrant to open it. It's one of those vans with a low ramp. Quick and easy to take a bike off and back on."

I said, "He stashes the van in some unobtrusive spot, takes the bike to the hit, and then returns, puts it up, and drives off. Not bad. Registration?"

"A company in L.A. with a P.O. box. We're checking, but it's probably a front of some kind. We also found a burner phone in the van. Several calls to one unlisted number on it. We're trying to pinpoint the location of the cell corresponding to that number as we speak."

"That's good work, Darci," I said, then fixed my eyes on her. "He killed Plácido Ballesteros, too."

She shrugged. "It would be a lot cleaner if he would have used the thirty-eight."

I rolled my eyes. "What's it going to take for you to see the light? Gillian went back to the neighborhood where Plácido was living. He found a young man who heard a motorcycle at the time of the killing, a credible witness you missed."

She held my eyes for a moment before looking away. "Doesn't surprise me. We didn't get a lot of cooperation when we covered that neighborhood, you know." She got up. "It's not like the old days when the migrant community was more trusting." With that, she left.

I'd already briefed Ned Gillian on the accident the day before, but I called him back to relay what I'd just heard. "If they take this to court, we'll annihilate them," he said when I finished. "We have a rock-solid alternate theory of the case now. Reasonable doubt abounds, baby. They'd be wise to drop the charges." He sighed. "And I hope to hell they do. Carlos is in despair. I'm worried about him, Cal."

When we disconnected, I sat there for a while, feeling optimism but tempered by the news about Carlos. It was no surprise, of course. Timoteo had told me the same thing.

Hang in there, Carlos, I said to myself.

———

Nando showed up right on time for an afternoon meeting we'd arranged that morning. "I have sensitive information," he'd said on the phone, "and I prefer to give it to you firsthand. Besides, I must pay homage to the man who killed El Solitario."

"Very funny."

Archie announced Nando's arrival, and when I let him in the back door, he handed me a magnum of Dom Pérignon and removed a package wrapped in white butcher paper from his briefcase. "This is for Archie, a pound of filet mignon for the hero dog." Archie had picked up the scent of the meat and was watching the package with keen interest.

I held the champagne up. "Thanks. We'll drink this when we nail the bastard who hired El Solitario."

"We will come to that," Nando said, "but first a treat for my favorite dog." He took a pearl-handled switchblade from his pocket, opened the package, and cut off a chunk of the steak. Archie caught it on the fly and wolfed it down. Nando looked at me, his mouth agape. "I don't think he chewed that."

He took a seat, removed a folder from his briefcase, and crossed his legs. "I have consulted a forensic accountant down in Los Angeles who I use from time to time. He is a good man, very discreet. The finances of Whittaker Investments are, shall we say, interesting. As I told you last week, his forays into restaurants and hotels did not go well. He weathered the bankruptcies and a couple of divorces and then started Whittaker Investments. Nothing much happened for a year or two, and the question was, does Whittaker Investments have any financial clout? Suddenly, it shows up with a two-hundred-million-dollar stake in the Oregon cannabis industry."

"Not a bank loan, I take it."

He laughed. "Banks are unwilling to go there because of the conflicts between Oregon and federal laws. Too much risk. The cannabis industry operates primarily on a cash-only basis."

I felt a pang of disappointment. "Nothing on his backers?"

"A few have been disclosed—wealthy friends of Whittaker's—but the vast majority of the investment is unaccounted for. My source said that when it is this opaque, one immediately suspects the underworld."

"Cartel money?"

"It is a good possibility. They are constantly seeking ways to launder their profits. And whatever the source, you can be sure Mr. Whittaker is under enormous pressure to service the debt."

"Enter the motive," I said.

"Perhaps. The cash is not flowing, and a hit man is dispatched to remedy a perceived threat to the arrangement. But kill a young woman and a couple of field hands? *What* arrangement? It makes no sense, Calvin."

We sat in silence for a while. The workings of the human mind remain a mystery to me. That lurking synapse of mine must have fired again somewhere in the back reaches of my brain, because a hazy picture of the *what* came to me.

But I wasn't the least bit sure, so I kept my mouth shut.

Chapter Forty-Five

A lull descended on the investigation until the following Thursday, when Darci Tate called midmorning. "We got a hit on No Face's fingerprints. One's a match for the print LAPD uploaded five years ago. Looks like they were right about having El Solitario's only fingerprint."

"We have confirmation, Houston," I quipped. "Have you contacted them?"

"Oh, yeah. They're excited. They can close that case, and after they compare the ballistics on the thirty-eight, maybe some more. Trouble is, nobody knows who this dude is."

"I told you you were going to be a hero, Darci."

She laughed. "Cut it out. Your dog gets all the credit."

"Nothing on his DNA?"

"It isn't in the system, but the DNA from the hair follicle we found on Ballesteros finally came in." She paused for dramatic effect. "They're a match."

I sucked in a breath and let it out slowly. "Well, that's the best damn news I've heard in a long time. What's DA Thornberg's position on Carlos Fuentes now?"

"I gave him the news, but he hasn't said yea or nay. Gillian should get on it immediately. Thornberg hates to give up on a case."

———

You can tell a lot about a person by the orderliness of their workspace. Take me, for example—both my offices were characterized by a kind of organized chaos, where a flat surface, any flat surface, was a good thing, because papers, books, and files could be spread out on it for quick, easy access. I'd like to think this was less about a disorganized mind and more about a driving desire to get the next task done without wasting time and effort on trivial tasks like picking up after myself.

District Attorney Sheldon Thornberg was my polar opposite. His office was antiseptically clean and dust-free, his statute and court rules law books neatly arranged in a handsome mahogany bookcase, and his desktop held nothing but his folded hands. Appearances mattered to this man.

Since I was a key witness in the El Solitario accident, Ned Gillian asked me to sit in on a meeting he'd called with Thornberg to discuss the disposition of Carlos Fuentes. He wanted me there not to argue on his behalf but simply to underscore the cunning viciousness of the hit man. After all, I'd nearly walked into his trap. It was no stretch to believe that he stabbed Plácido Ballesteros with a pair of harvest shears.

Gillian had just taken us through his reasoning as to why Yamhill County should dismiss the charges against his client. Thornberg unfolded his hands and flicked a piece of lint off the sleeve of his coat. "An interesting argument, Ned," he said. "Let me remind you that your client had the strongest of motives to kill Mr. Ballesteros and was seen at the scene around the time of the murder. We're willing to concede that the victim had incidental contact with the hit man, but that—"

"*Incidental* contact," Gillian interjected. "How did three of his hairs wind up on the victim's dead body? That's more than incidental."

Thornberg stayed motionless, but his eyes blinked rapidly. "The victim was stabbed with an instrument familiar to Mr. Fuentes. The hit man's weapon of choice was a thirty-eight semiautomatic."

Gillian's face took on some color. "Not in every case. You need to talk to LAPD. Using harvest shears was the whole point— shift the blame to the angry father who works in the vineyards. El Solitario struck at three in the morning. Who's going to alibi Carlos Fuentes at that time—his family? It was a setup, Sheldon."

"Nevertheless, Carlos Fuentes was there at the time of the murder."

"His misfortune. That doesn't mean he killed Ballesteros."

Thornberg's face grew rigid and impassive. "We've heard these arguments, and we're not persuaded. We think this was a premeditated revenge killing, a heinous act."

"You're missing another fact," Gillian said, obviously trying to rein in his temper. "I've identified a credible witness who will testify that he heard a motorcycle pass by his house, which is a block and a half from Ballesteros's house. It was right around three a.m. Your investigators missed him."

Thornberg's eyelashes fluttered again. He would make a lousy poker player. The room grew quiet, except for the wail of a distant siren. Finally he said, "We might be willing to discuss a plea, manslaughter one."

"*A plea*? Are you kidding me?" Gillian shot to his feet and looked at me. "Come on, Cal, we're out of here." He turned to Thornberg. "This is a travesty. See you in court, Sheldon. You're gonna lose."

Timoteo was waiting in the lobby of the County Building when Gillian and I came out. "How did it go?" he asked, his face filled with a mix of hope and anxiety.

"Thornberg blinked," Gillian said. "He's offering a plea of manslaughter."

"*Manslaughter*? Papi didn't do anything. He'll *never* take a plea."

I said, "We know that. Ned hit him with the witness you found, and Thornberg immediately offered to negotiate. That's a good sign."

"That's right," Gillian said. He faced Timoteo and grasped him by the shoulders. "We'll let this marinate and see what Thornberg does. The guy's a prick, but he's not stupid. I think he'll come around. The worst that can happen is that we'll kick his ass in court."

Timoteo nodded and tried to smile but failed. He knew all too well how long the case could take to get to court, and the toll the jail time would take on his father was unthinkable.

———

Back in my office later that day, I found myself wondering once again about the Plácido Ballesteros murder. Where did El Solitario get the harvest shears? He certainly wouldn't have risked procuring them himself. I thought of the cast of characters I'd identified. One of them stood out as the potential go-between—Diego Vargas, the trusted counselor of vineyard workers, who spoke their language.

I filed that away.

That afternoon, a stiff breeze swept in and sent the cloud cover scudding northward. Archie and I headed home, and as I turned off the highway, I tried to push down the memories of the wreck and focus instead on the late-autumn beauty of the vineyards. The vines were shedding their rust-colored leaves and would soon become a vast army of stick soldiers marching in precise formation. The sight buoyed my spirits.

Back at the Aerie, I changed clothes and began working on the wall. The rocks felt like old friends, and I was soon blissfully lost in the process of finding where to put the next one. It wasn't easy—in fact, it was damn hard—without my spotter, Zoe. When I finally finished the third course, I went up on the deck and looked down at my handiwork. I was pleased with the shape of the wall, the offset ends providing an entry point and suggesting a spiral in the making. I imagined the herbs I would plant within its boundary and how I was going to arrange them.

"This might be worth the effort," I said to Archie.

I glanced across the field for a final time, hoping to see Zoe heading in this direction, but she didn't appear. Just as well, I thought.

Chapter Forty-Six

Things went sideways for the next week. District Attorney Sheldon Thornberg continued to dither on Carlos's murder charge, Luis's search for more of Vargas's boys was a bust, and the surveillance of Harris and Drake turned up nothing of importance. At least that's what Timoteo reported back to me. Even so, I should have felt better at that point. After all, El Solitario was now dead, and I even had an inkling of what Whittaker and his crew were up to. But there were still way too many missing pieces.

I'd just gotten off the phone with a client—the one charged with a second DUI—when Darci Tate called. "A friendly heads-up," she began. I waited. "I just got word that Thornberg is cutting Carlos Fuentes loose."

I pumped a fist. "When?"

"Early afternoon, if they can complete the paperwork. I'm sure Thornberg's office will contact Gillian. We're going to close the Ballesteros murder on the strength of the hair follicle DNA and the witness that heard the getaway motorcycle."

"That's great news, Darci. Carlos and his family will be thrilled to hear this." I paused before adding, "Any news on the burner phone?"

"Nope. Not yet. Our tech guys aren't the most brilliant, but they're working on it. Anyway, since El Solitario's dead, no trial's required." She chuckled. "Thornberg's not a happy camper. He still likes Fuentes for the murder, but he doesn't feel he can get a conviction."

"That figures." I thanked Darci and immediately called Gillian.

"Yep," he said, "I just got word. Thornberg's no hero. He just knew he was going to lose. I'll be at the jail at one o'clock sharp. You know the family better than I do, Cal. Why don't you contact them?" I agreed.

"Yes!" Timoteo shouted a few moments later. "I'll call Luis." I told Timoteo I'd meet them at the jail.

"I wouldn't miss it," Zoe said when I called her next. I told her I'd pick her up at twelve thirty.

———

Located a few blocks southeast of downtown McMinnville, the Yamhill County Jail was a nondescript building with very few windows. Marlene Mathews was working, but the rest of Cal's Army gathered in the waiting area after clearing the security checkpoint. It was a subdued, I'll-believe-it-when-I-see-it atmosphere with no smiles or high-fives exchanged. True to form, Luis seemed particularly anxious. At one twenty, he looked at Ned Gillian. "What if they change their mind?"

Gillian shook the question off. "They won't. The call I got was from the assistant district attorney. It's official."

Timoteo said, "The case against Papi was shit, even without the DNA evidence." He glanced at Zoe. "I'm not sure she's even missed him, but this will help Mamá's recovery, right?"

"Oh, she's aware that he's gone," Zoe responded, "but she's blocked it out because it's too much to deal with right now. Did you say anything to her about this?"

Timoteo showed his palms. "Oh, God, no. I wanted to make sure, first."

"Good," Zoe said. "It'll be good for her. Maybe it would be best if I broke the news. What do you think?" Timoteo voiced his agreement.

After a period of silence, Mariana looked at me. "Have the police learned anything from El Solitario's phone?"

"If they have, they haven't told me about it." That's a bitter pill, I thought. I was hoping the phone would lead them back to the perpetrator.

"Why can't they get search warrants for Whittaker, Vargas, Harris, and Drake? One of them had to be communicating with El Solitario."

"There's no probable cause," Timoteo answered.

"That's right," I said. "There's not enough evidence to convince a judge to sign search warrants."

The group fell silent again, and I was left with a vague feeling of guilt, like I'd let them down somehow.

At one forty, Carlos Fuentes appeared in the lobby, escorted by a single officer and wearing the clothes he was arrested in. He looked gaunt and tired, but when he saw his boys, his demeanor brightened. They went to their father and held him in a dual hug. It was Luis, the tough guy, who broke down crying. Carlos came to me next and shook my hand with both of his, then he turned to Ned Gillian and smiled. "Thank you for being there for me. I admit I had just about given up. You make me think there is some justice after all."

Gillian returned the smile. "You're welcome, Carlos. We would have beaten them in court."

Carlos turned back to me. "And you chased down the man who killed my Olivia. I will be forever grateful to you for that."

I nodded. "And we're not done yet."

The day was clear and bright, forcing Carlos to shade his eyes as we exited the building. Gillian hurried off to a meeting, and Zoe and I lingered for a few moments, watching Timoteo, Luis, and Mariana walk joyfully with Carlos toward their car, parked toward the end of the lot. They were halfway there when two black SUVs entered the lot, one from each end. A uniformed, armed agent got out of the SUV closest to Carlos and approached him.

"Carlos Fuentes," he said in a voice that carried across the lot, "you are under arrest for violating U.S. immigration laws."

Luis and Timoteo stepped in front of their father. Luis said, "Fuck off, you pieces of shit, you can't do this. He just got released from jail for something he didn't do."

"Sir," the agent said, "I'm going to need you to step aside." He looked at Timoteo. "You, too, sir."

Neither Luis nor Timoteo moved. A door clicked open, and a second agent got out of the nearer SUV. He was much bigger than his partner. No one moved in the other SUV, but I thought I recognized the person sitting in the passenger seat.

"Stay here," I said to Zoe and hurried off toward the confrontation.

"We're not moving," Timoteo said with defiance ringing in his voice. "You'll have to arrest us as well."

Mariana stepped in next to Timoteo and linked arms with him, tears streaming down her face. "And, me, too."

"Oh, shit," I said under my breath.

The bigger agent said, "This is your last warning. Step aside so we can arrest this man. We don't want any trouble here."

"You don't want any *trouble*?" Luis snarled. "What you're doing is trouble, you ass—"

"Luis, Timoteo, Mariana, do what he says." I said, catching up to the group. "This is *not* the place to fight this." Carlos looked stunned and confused, but both his sons eyed me like I was some sort of traitor. I held their anguished gazes. "Not here. You won't win this. Trust me, step aside, *please.*"

The tableau remained for what seemed an eternity. Finally, Timoteo took his younger brother by one arm and Mariana by the other. "Cal's right. This isn't the place."

He moved to one side with Luis and Mariana in tow. "Fuckers," Luis said under his breath.

I turned to the two agents. "I'm this man's attorney. Do you have an arrest warrant?"

"Yes," the bigger agent said. The smaller agent went to the SUV, returned with a clipboard, and showed me the warrant. It stated that Carlos was being arrested for being undocumented and was duly signed off. There was nothing I could do.

I turned to Carlos. "Go with them now, but don't worry, we'll get this straightened out." He didn't say a word. He knew the gravity of the situation only too well.

Zoe joined us, and we all stood by as Carlos was patted down and handcuffed. I said, "Carlos, you have the right to remain silent. Don't talk to anyone, no matter what they tell you. Ned and I will be in touch."

"Stay strong, Papi," Timoteo added as Carlos was escorted to the SUV. "We'll get you out, I promise." Carlos looked back at his son, his face blank, unbelieving.

I spun around and headed toward the second SUV, which was just pulling away. As I came alongside, the car stopped, and the passenger window slid down. ICE Field Supervisor Curtis Drake looked up at me. "You didn't have to do this," I said, my voice low and trembling with anger. "What a chickenshit move."

He showed a reptilian smile. "It was a righteous arrest, Claxton.

The man's an illegal alien. You just witnessed the rule of law in action."

I put a finger in his face. "This won't stand, you bastard."

He nodded to the driver, the window slid up, and the SUV pulled away.

I stood there seething with anger. Telling Drake the arrest wouldn't stand was pointless, because I had no clue how that could be accomplished. But it felt damn good saying it.

Chapter Forty-Seven

I've experienced some low points in my life, but the arrest of Carlos Fuentes by Immigration Control and Enforcement ranked right down there near the bottom. Of course, what I felt was nothing compared to what his sons were experiencing and Mariana, too, who'd suffered a similar trauma with the mistaken arrest of her uncle. We stood in a tight cluster in the parking lot of the Yamhill County Jail. I let them vent their immediate anger and heartbreak. At one point, Luis said, "Yeah, this is right out of ICE's playbook. They hang around the courthouse, too, and pick off working people who are paying parking tickets and shit like that. I should have been looking for this."

"It's not your fault, Luis," Zoe said. "No one expected this to happen."

Timoteo looked at me. "Who was in that other SUV, the person you spoke to?"

"Curtis Drake. He came to watch the show."

Timoteo's face hardened, and he suddenly looked much older. "I thought so. Why do this to Papi at this time?"

"Good question," I said. "I think Thornberg tipped ICE that Carlos was being released. He's a sore loser. But Drake didn't have to send his agents, of course. ICE has plenty of fish to fry. I think Drake wants to distract us." I blew a breath out. "If anyone's to blame, it's me for not expecting something like this."

"It's not your fault, either," Timoteo said. "Drake and Whittaker are afraid we're getting too close to them."

We grew silent for a while. Finally I said to the brothers, "Look, your father raised three outstanding kids, has an exemplary employment record, and no criminal record. An immigration judge is going to take all of that into account. I'm going to call Ned Gillian, and the two of us will go to the holding center immediately and demand to see Carlos." I paused for a moment and looked at each of them in turn, including Mariana. "Meanwhile, he needs you to stay strong, too."

By the time I dropped Zoe at Gertie's place, we had replayed and dissected the arrest of Carlos Fuentes a couple of times. The last thing she said to me was, "Well, one good thing—Timoteo didn't say anything to his mother. Raising her hopes and then dashing them again would have set her back immeasurably."

"Thanks for small favors," I said.

———

Needless to say, Ned Gillian was shocked and angry when I broke the news to him. "Don't worry, Cal," he told me, "I've got this, and I'm seeing it through. They'll deport Carlos Fuentes over my dead body."

Brave words, but we both knew the odds of prevailing were slim to none.

I sat in on the meeting with Carlos at the holding center. The shock had passed, and he had regained his composure—the composure of a man steeled by decades of hard work and worry, a man completely unaware that his dignity shone like a bright light. He regarded us both with a look of profound resignation. "What every immigrant fears, no? *La Migra* has caught me. What about my family? What's to become of them?"

Gillian said, "We don't know how ICE will react. They must have probable cause to question them."

"Is not my arrest probable cause?"

Gillian's face grew taut. "We'll fight that. Your hearing's at least two months off. We have time to prepare a strong case. Meanwhile, you need to have faith and stay healthy, my friend. Your family is counting on you to do that."

Carlos nodded with resignation. He knew the score. He was essentially a condemned man.

———

I was still in a funk after dinner that evening when Archie announced Zoe's arrival. I went to the door and saved her the need to knock. "Hey," she said, "I just came from a session with Elena, and something came up I thought could be important."

My heart did a little stutter step when I saw her, despite my vow to Gertie. I stepped aside and she entered, producing a dog biscuit for Archie, who was as pleased as me to see her. "I bought a whole box of these for the hero dog, but he only gets one at a time," she said as he gobbled it down with his butt wagging.

I laughed. "He's going to get spoiled. Nando brought him a piece of filet mignon."

She looked down at my dog with mock seriousness. "Don't let him buy your affection, Archie. These biscuits are better for your teeth."

At the kitchen table she said, "I had a good session with Elena this evening. The death of El Solitario has made a difference, somehow, almost a breakthrough. She was telling me more about

Olivia, how she kept scrapbooks and diaries over the years but always in secret. Typical girl stuff. But before the police arrived to search her room, Elena removed the items from her chest of drawers. 'They were too personal,' she said. 'I couldn't let strangers see them.'"

I scooted my chair closer to the table. Zoe had my attention.

"Anyway, Elena brought out this cloth bag filled with Olivia's secret treasures. She said she felt comfortable sharing them with me. She showed me the scrapbooks and read me some of her favorite diary entries. The last one was four months before her death."

"No entries just prior to her murder?"

"That's right." Zoe reached into her pocket and set a thumb drive on the table. "This was in the bag, and Elena didn't know anything about it." She met my eyes. "This is a digital diary, Cal. I think she might've gone digital at some point. I tried to open it on their laptop, but it's password-protected. I, ah, told Elena I would try to figure out how to open it, so she could read the contents. I told her it could also be important for the investigation and asked if she would mind if I consulted with you. She gave me permission."

I picked up the thumb drive. "Nando knows a guy who can open this for us. It may take a while, though. He's always in high demand."

Zoe looked at me. "I have another idea."

Chapter Forty-Eight

An hour later, Mariana, Timoteo, Zoe, and I were in my study, huddled around my computer. "Okay," Mariana said, "I've made a list of possible passwords. With this software, it has to be eight characters, at least one uppercase, and a number. I know her better than anyone. It's something to do with music or books, the two things she was most passionate about, aside from social justice and medicine. I don't think she'd use a serious password."

I slotted the thumb drive into my laptop, and the password prompt came up.

Mariana exhaled a noisy breath. "I'm going with music first. Try Caifanes18, her favorite Mexican rock group. We went to one of their concerts in 2018 in Seattle."

I typed it in. "Nope."

"Try SaulHernandez18, their lead singer. Use both names. She wouldn't split it up."

"Nope."

"Crap. I thought sure that would be it. Try Jaguares19. They toured the U.S. in 2019."

"Nope."

She scowled at her list. "Café Tacvba, another fave band of

hers. Just try CafeTacvba17." She spelled it for me. "That's when we really got into this band."

I typed it in, then shook my head.

She exhaled again. "Okay, it's got to be books, then. Her fave book of all time was *House on Mango Street*." Mariana paused for a moment and smiled, the one that could melt an iceberg. "I'm going with Mangostreet14. She always said that book changed her life, and we both read it our freshman year. Try that next."

I typed it in and waited. "*Bingo*. We're in."

The four of us jumped to our feet and high-fived all around. Zoe said, "I've got an ethical problem now. I told Elena only Cal and I would see what's on this thumb drive." Both Timoteo and Mariana looked crestfallen.

I said, "Under the circumstances, I don't think Elena would mind if her son and her daughter's best friend saw the contents as well. There may be nothing of value on it, but Timoteo and Mariana might be able to spot something we'd miss."

Zoe paused for a moment. "Let's take a look. I'll read it out loud. If it gets too personal, I'll skip over that content."

She read rapidly for maybe twenty-five or thirty minutes. It was engrossing, introspective, and heartbreaking, the story of a young woman with her whole life ahead of her. Zoe had to stop numerous times to regain her composure, and one entry in late September caused Mariana to begin sobbing.

The news about Mariana's uncle being arrested by ICE spread like wildfire today. I'm so worried about him and for her and her family. Papi came to me today and told me to make a copy of my passport and keep it in my purse. Me! A U.S. citizen! These raids are inhuman. I'm trying not to get depressed, but it's so hard. ☹

It was an entry dated October 5 that caused Zoe to slow down her rate of reading.

Something weird happened today. I burst into Robert Harris's office looking for a damn purchase order he'd promised me days ago. He was standing by his printer and jerked around like a kid with his hand caught in the cookie jar. I didn't say anything about what he was printing out, but I can read upside down really fast. It was our patient database! No question! That's highly confidential. Why in the world would he do that? I acted like I hadn't noticed anything.

And on October 8, Olivia wrote:

While Robert was out somewhere, I went into his office for his supply room key. I keep misplacing mine. There was a big envelope in his middle drawer where the key was. It wasn't sealed. Okay, I shouldn't have peeked, but I've always been nosy. Just ask my mother! Anyway, a printed copy of our patient list with names and addresses was in there, along with a note in his handwriting that said: 'Diego Vargas, Tequila Cantina, Lafayette, Thurs night before 7.' Was Robert delivering our database to some dude named Vargas at a bar? WTF? ☹

"There's the Vargas connection," I said, my pulse ramping up a couple of notches.

The entry on October 13 read:

Okay, I admit it, I snuck into Robert's office while he was at lunch. Nothing in his middle desk drawer this time, but there was a file in his briefcase that made me curious. On the file tab Robert had written "El Seguro." The file had some spreadsheets in it with names (all male Latino), dates, and what looked like dollar amounts, payments of some kind, in multiples of 100, none higher than 300. Totally weird! There was a handwritten note in the file (not his writing) that said, "Vargas needs more manpower. Latino males who need work, discreet, willing to buy in." This looks really suspicious to me. I'm not going to Sofia until I know what's going on. I may have to come on to Robert a little, but we do what we have to do. ☺

Timoteo said, "That's when she recruited Luis to go to the cantina."

I nodded. "And that's when she started flirting with Harris."

On October 15, Mariana wrote:

Whoops! Sofia caught me snooping in Robert's office! I almost told her what I suspected but caught myself. I need to be sure!

"Sofia told me about that encounter," I said. "I wish Olivia would have confided in her."

Timoteo sighed. "That's just like Olivia. She gave Harris every benefit of the doubt."

On October 18, she wrote:

Oh shit! Got caught today in Robert's office. I told him I was looking for the storeroom key. He gave me this look and said, "It's not in my briefcase, Olivia. Why are you in here, anyway?" I felt trapped, so I just point-blank asked him what the hell El Seguro meant and what was up with that guy at the cantina. That's when he gave me a look that almost made me pee my pants. "That's none of your business," he told me. "You need to leave now and stay out of my affairs." I got the hell out of there.

Timoteo looked at me, his eyes narrowing to slits. "She was killed five days later."

I nodded, and the room became quiet.

Finally, Mariana looked at me in bewilderment. "They're selling *insurance*? That's what *El Seguro* means."

It all clicked into place for me. "Not insurance, exactly. They're selling *protection*. This whole scheme is about protection for undocumented Latinos. It's perfect when you think about it. A vulnerable population, people who don't dare go to the police, who keep to themselves, and know how to keep secrets."

Timoteo's brow furrowed. "What *kind* of protection?"

"Curtis Drake's in on it, right? It must be protection from

getting deported. People are paying money to stay out of Drake's crosshairs. Imagine the peace of mind if you knew you were protected from deportation. You'd be willing to pay for that, and also willing to keep your mouth shut, right?"

"Yeah, but Drake's job is to deport people," Mariana said.

"First of all, maybe he *does* deport the ones who refuse to pay. And for the rest? There are around 110,000 undocumented people in Oregon. He's got plenty to choose from, even if he's protecting some."

"Would a scheme like that pay off?" Timoteo asked.

"I think it would. Let's say they get only five percent to buy in at, say, two hundred dollars a month." I paused, doing some quick math in my head. "That nets over a million dollars a month or close to thirteen million a year, tax free. Do it all in cash and launder it through Whittaker's cannabis business, and it can't be traced. And that leaves ninety-five percent of the migrant population as future customers."

Timoteo whistled. "Holy shit."

"Whittaker's at the center of this," Zoe chimed in.

"He's gotta be," I said, opening my hands for emphasis. "Necessity's the mother of invention. His cannabis business is hurting, and he needs money in a bad way. He probably borrowed cartel money to get started."

"And Diego Vargas is the recruiter and trainer for the protection sales force, right?" Zoe added.

"That's right, and they get paid based on how many people they can sign up and then collect from. This is right out of the Mafia playbook. And Robert Harris is the accountant for the operation, which was apparently just getting off the ground when Olivia got suspicious."

"Why did they use Prosperar patients?" Mariana asked.

"It was a place to get started. Harris provided a list of

undocumented people and their addresses, a ready customer list that would be difficult to come by any other way. They could branch out from there into the general undocumented population."

"So what they were doing was like a trial run?" Timoteo said.

"Exactly. Get it started, iron out the kinks, and then scale it up for really big money."

"That list Eduardo Duran tore up was his customer list, right?" Zoe chimed in.

"Right," I said. "It was top secret stuff in this operation. He was having second thoughts and was getting ready to talk to Luis. Someone warned him they were coming after him, and he didn't want to get caught with it on him."

Timoteo rocked back in his chair. "Awesome. It fits together like a jigsaw puzzle. Well done, Cal."

I waved off the compliment. "It's been a team effort all the way."

"Cal's Army," Zoe said, and we all laughed.

Timoteo said, "Now that we know what the bastards are up to, how do we catch them?"

Chapter Forty-Nine

"That's one fucking complicated theory," Darci Tate said to me after I sketched in the *El Seguro* scenario and showed her key parts of Olivia Fuentes's digital diary. It was the next morning in my office, and she'd stopped by at the beginning of her workday at my request. "Sure, it all fits into a neat little story, but you're gonna need a ton more evidence before I can do anything."

I was prepared for a cynical reaction, but I still had to swallow a comeback. "I understand that, Darci. That's why I asked you to stop by."

"I know. God knows we could use a break or two. You nailed El Solitario, but we still don't know who ordered the hits on Fuentes and Ballesteros."

"Gee, I'll try to do better next time."

She looked a little sheepish. "Sorry. I didn't mean it that way."

I said, "Like I explained, Whittaker has each one of his accomplices either compromised or scared shitless or both. It's a tight chain, and I don't see any weak links. However, his wife, Isabel, is a different story." I went on to describe my encounters with her, and my gut feeling that she suspected her husband of something nefarious but couldn't bring herself to turn on him. "But," I said when I finished, "I think that if I present her with this evidence, I might be able to convince her to cooperate with us. I think she has good instincts."

"Cooperate how?"

I blew out a breath. "That's the question, isn't it? Maybe she'd agree to wear a wire, get Whittaker to say something incriminating, at least enough that you could get a search warrant. There has to be something linking him with El Solitario."

Tate raised her eyebrows. "A wire? That's a heavy lift. I'd have to run it up the chain."

"You got a better idea?"

She looked at me with her almost-cop eyes. "You're good, Claxton, but do you really think you can talk this woman into going against her own husband?"

I shrugged. "What do you think?"

Tate shook her head with a knowing smile. "Not a snowball's chance."

I laughed. "Then I'm going for it for sure."

———

Tate got back to me at midmorning the next day. "Okay, it wasn't easy," she told me, "but I got a green light on the wire. My chief said if I get Isabel Whittaker hurt, he'll have my badge. You still think you can get her to agree?"

I said I'd give it my best shot, and after we disconnected took the card Isabel had left behind at our last meeting and called her cell. "Very well," she said a little hesitantly, "I can stop by your office this afternoon. What do you wish to talk about?"

"I have some information I think you should know. Shall we say around two p.m.?"

———

I busied myself around the office that morning, had lunch at the Red Hills Market, and at two twenty, Archie's single bark announced Isabel's arrival. I watched as she got out of her Tesla. Her dark hair was pulled into a tight ponytail and she wore no makeup, which only accentuated her beauty. She fawned over my dog, and after taking a seat, showed a cautious smile. "What is this information you have for me?"

"You were right about Diego Vargas," I began. "He is involved in something illegal."

Her smile died, and lines appeared on her smooth forehead. "Oh, no. What is it?"

"He's involved in a protection scheme to take money from people who can least afford it." I went on to explain how it worked and the role Vargas played. "Other people are involved in this scheme," I continued. "Robert Harris, the financial manager at Prosperar, is keeping the books on the operation, and Curtis Drake, the rugby coach and ICE field supervisor, is making sure people who pay don't get deported and those who refuse to pay become targets for ICE." I stopped there and looked at her.

A muscle in her face twitched, and she looked away.

I said, "Isabel, you and I know who is behind this scheme, don't we." It wasn't a question.

She took a breath, exhaled, and except for the drone of traffic out on the highway, my office went quiet. Finally, she looked back at me as her eyes filled with tears. "I have had my suspicions for some time. I have overheard conversations, seen some papers on Gavin's desk..." She raised her chin, and a single tear broke loose and traveled down her cheek. "I am not as stupid as he thinks."

I nodded in understanding. "It's important that you know the whole story, Isabel. I suspect your husband had something to do with the murder of Olivia Fuentes."

She sucked a breath, and her wet eyes got huge.

I went on, "Olivia had discovered their scheme. There were other crimes, too—the attempt on her brother's life, the killing of the vineyard worker, Plácido Ballesteros. The actual killer is dead now, but we want to know who hired him to commit these crimes." I stopped again.

She raised her gaze to meet mine. "Money, yes, it is always about money with Gavin, but the Fuentes girl, you believe Gavin had something to do with that?"

"He's physically abusing you, isn't he? And think of Diego, the way he's been acting. Could it be guilt and fear because your husband is manipulating him?"

Her face grew pale. "What is it you want from me?"

"We need to know if your husband is linked to the hired killer. The police can't search Whittaker Landing without a good reason. If you wear a hidden microphone and get Gavin to admit something about the protection scheme, we can use that to get a judge to sign a search warrant."

She recoiled in horror. "*A microphone?* You want me to wear a hidden microphone?"

I tried not to look sheepish. "I know it's a lot to ask, Isabel, but it's the only way to get justice for Olivia. If we find nothing, that could help clear your husband." I didn't believe that, but I said it to soften the ask.

It didn't work. Isabel shook her head emphatically. "I could *never* do that. I am a terrible liar. I would be bathed in sweat in two minutes. Gavin would see right through my attempt." She shuddered perceptibly. "And then what would happen to me?"

"I would coach you on how to handle it, and the police would be listening near—"

"No. I want justice for that young girl, but I lack the courage for something like that." She stood abruptly. "I'm sorry, Cal, but I have to go now."

As she turned to leave, I said, "Think about it, Isabel, that's all I ask. I have a feeling you have much more courage than you realize. You know how to contact me."

She was gone a moment later. I turned to Archie, and his ears came up. "That certainly went well, didn't it?"

Chapter Fifty

I went home that afternoon in another funk. Olivia's digital diary confirmed what I suspected but offered no solid proof beyond that, and I knew for certain the *El Seguro* operation was on hold until the heat came off. Darci Tate had been right about my ability to enlist Isabel Whittaker's help, too. That snowball melted. And just to top it off, Carlos Fuentes now sat in a detention cell with no prospect of ever living in the United States again. I could smell the approaching rain but changed to my running gear anyway and took a somewhat reluctant Archie out for a hard jog, the best therapy I knew. When we got back, I fed him and made scrambled eggs and toast for dinner.

That evening I put some oldies on the sound system and tried to read to get my mind off the case. Accompanied by John Coltrane, Johnny Hartman was halfway through "You Are Too Beautiful" when I got up and turned the system off. I should have seen that coming—it was a song that always brought Nancy to mind, and that was the last thing I needed. Her ghost was palpable that evening. Just to keep it complicated, Zoe called a couple of times. I let her calls go to voicemail. Gertie was right, I reminded myself.

I slept fitfully that night and woke up late feeling fuzzy-headed. A thick cloud cover had moved in overnight, promising more rain. It was a Sunday, the day I set aside to clean the house, and I began the task with a decided lack of enthusiasm. As usual at this point, I thought again about hiring a housecleaner. "Jesus Christ, Cal," Gertie had remarked once after swiping a finger on my desk and displaying the dust, "you need a maid around here." She was right, of course, but I'd never gotten around to it. The Aerie was and always would be my private space, dust or no dust.

The call came in that afternoon. "Cal, it's Isabel. Something terrible has happened. Can you come to the landing?"

"What is it?"

"Gavin has been stabbed."

"Is he alive?"

"Yes, but barely. I have called 911."

"I'll be right there."

The gate to Whittaker Landing was open when I arrived and so was the front door of the mansion. I called out to Isabel, and she answered that she was in Gavin's study. I found her kneeling next to her husband, holding a bloodstained towel against his neck. A bloody letter opener was lying next to his body. His eyes were slits, but when I stood over him he raised his arm slightly, pointed a finger at me, and tried to speak. It came out a gurgle, and his arm dropped across his bloody chest.

The paramedics arrived shortly after that, and in no time Whittaker was on his way to the hospital. I knew the police were on their way, so I sat Isabel down. "Tell me exactly what happened."

A nasty bruise was blooming on one cheek, and a smear of blood was drying on the other. She let out a breath and hung her head. "Diego and Gavin were here in the study, and I could hear they were arguing again. I came to the door and tried to listen.

I couldn't follow everything, but I heard the words *El Seguro* a couple of times." She looked up at me, her eyes burning with a resolve I suspected had been there all along. "I got very angry. I went into the study and told them I knew what *El Seguro* is and that they were taking money from the migrants.

"Diego kind of froze where he was standing, but Gavin came over and hit me, hard, in the face." She grimaced and gestured toward her cheek. "When I fell to the floor, he cursed and kicked me." She pulled up her skirt to show deep bruises already forming on her leg. "Diego screamed at Gavin to stop, and the next thing I knew they were fighting. Diego fell back on Gavin's desk and came up with the letter opener. He stabbed Gavin in the throat and then ran out."

"Where did he go? The Land Rover's out in the driveway."

She paused for a moment. "We have a dock on the river. He likes to go there and just sit. It's past the stables and the polo field. When I can't find him, that's where I always look first."

"Okay," I said. "Stay here, and when the police arrive tell them what happened. I'm going to look for Diego."

I called Detective Tate next, and when she didn't pick up, I left a voicemail: "Darci, Gavin Whittaker's been stabbed at the Landing. He's still breathing. You need to get here ASAP."

I went out the front door and broke into a jog. When I crossed the paddock in front of the stables, Isabel's horses lifted their heads up and watched me go by, unconcerned. I crossed the polo field next and took a path at the shed that led through the trees toward the river.

Isabel was right. Vargas was standing on the dock, staring at the slow-moving water.

"Diego," I said as I approached, "it's Cal Claxton." He spun around with a frightened look on his face. I raised my hands. "It's okay. I just want to talk. Maybe I can help you."

When I stepped onto the dock, he said, "Is he dead?"

"No. He's on his way to the hospital. Tell me what happened. I know all about *El Seguro*, so don't give me any bullshit."

He exhaled, and his dark eyes revealed the depth of his sorrow. "I told him I wanted out, that I couldn't take it anymore."

"What did he say to that?"

His eyes flashed anger. "Sure," he said, "you can go back to Mexico, and take Tito with you. That's my son. He's very sick."

"Yes," I said, "Isabel told me about Tito and his special care at OHSU. You wanted out. It's because of the murders of Olivia Fuentes and Plácido Ballesteros, right?"

He looked out on the water. "Robert warned us that the Fuentes girl knew about *El Seguro*, and then she was dead." He brought his eyes back to mine. "I didn't believe it for a while. I didn't think Gavin would go that far, but he was so proud of his little project, a model for the whole West Coast, he used to tell us." Vargas turned to look at me, his eyes filled with pain. "But he did it, he hired that killer immediately. No mercy for the young girl."

"Can you show me any proof of that?"

He shrugged. "I don't know. None of us ever talked about the killings. We were too scared and too ashamed." He smiled with bitterness. "That's the way Gavin wanted it."

A call on my phone interrupted us. "I'm here," Darci Tate said. "Where the fuck are you?"

I told her I'd be right there, and after disconnecting said to Vargas, "Come on, let's go back to the house. The police are there."

He tensed. "I just stabbed a man. I am screwed. My son is screwed." He looked out on the water. "I can't swim. I was thinking about jumping in when you arrived."

"No, Diego," I said. "You can't do that to Tito and your wife. What just happened sounded like self-defense to me. And if you cooperate with the investigation of Whittaker, the prosecution might offer you a deal. Don't give up."

He stood motionless for a long time, then nodded once and followed me back to the mansion without saying another word.

Darci Tate was standing next to Isabel on the front porch. She said, "Hello, Mr. Vargas. I understand you witnessed the fight and the stabbing."

He started to respond, but Isabel cut him off. "Yes, he was there when Gavin attacked me, and he saw me stab him with the letter opener. It was after Gavin hit me and kicked me."

Vargas looked confused and started to speak again, but I cut him off, saying to Tate, "That's right, Darci. He just told me about it. He said it was self-defense."

Tate said to Vargas, "I'll need a statement from you and Mr. Claxton, but not right now. I need you to hang around, okay?"

Vargas glanced at me, his look saying he understood what had just happened.

Tate pulled me aside. "Whoa, so the little woman took it to Whittaker."

"Yep. She finally decided she'd had enough." I paused for a moment, looked at Darci and smiled. "Are you thinking what I'm thinking?"

She smiled back. "Oh, yeah. In view of this potential crime, we're going to thoroughly search the premises. Who knows what we might find?"

Chapter Fifty-One

Darci had Isabel driven to the hospital to have her injuries treated and documented. Meanwhile, she and her partner were conducting a search of Whittaker's study, while Vargas waited in the Land Rover, and I paced back and forth on the porch. My thoughts kept coming back to Isabel, who had committed a selfless act. I was in awe. If she hadn't taken the blame, the future of Vargas and his son would have been destroyed.

I'd told her she had more courage than she knew, and she just proved it.

As for me, I was a witness obligated to tell the truth. But how did I know Vargas hadn't lied to me at the river to protect Isabel? No, the version Isabel told would stand, and I was confident she would not be prosecuted for defending herself.

An hour and ten minutes later, Tate and her partner emerged, carrying a couple of evidence bags. After her partner left with the bags, she pulled me aside. "We didn't find shit unless there's something on his laptop or cell phone." She huffed out a breath and frowned. "Whittaker's a wife beater, no doubt about that. And maybe with Vargas's cooperation, he'll get stuck with extortion and racketeering charges of some kind, but we still have nothing connecting him with El Solitario."

Accompanied by a patrolman and wearing a hospital gown, Isabel arrived back from the hospital just as Tate was preparing to leave. Isabel's normally flawless face was swollen and distorted, and she walked with a slight limp, but her eyes burned with new-found confidence. "Gavin is still alive," she said. "He is in surgery. I didn't stay. I never want to see him again." She looked at Tate. "Am I under arrest?"

"No, ma'am. But I'll need you to come down to the police station to make a formal statement, and we'll go from there."

"Very well." She gestured toward the patrolman. "He has my bloody clothes in a bag. Give me a few minutes to change."

While we waited, Vargas got out of the Land Rover and came over to Tate and me. "There is one more thing," he said. The words seemed to hover in the air between us for a moment. We looked at him and waited. "A week ago, Gavin came to me with a briefcase. It was locked, and it was very heavy. He said, 'Put this in the river. Not here, but off the St. Paul Bridge. Do it now.'"

I glanced at Tate. "He'd probably heard about El Solitario's accident."

She nodded and Vargas went on, "I took the briefcase, but I didn't throw it in the river."

"Where is it?" Tate said.

Vargas allowed himself a faint smile, seeming in no hurry to recount this. "When I came to the fork in the driveway, I pulled over. The briefcase was locked, but I quickly opened it with my knife." He paused, frustrating us both.

Tate said, her voice ringing with impatience, "What was in it?"

"Papers showing *El Seguro* payments and a barbell weight to make it heavy. I wasn't going to throw the case off the bridge, but I wasn't sure what to do with it. I took the driveway to the barn instead of the gate and put it in the polo equipment shed."

Tate shot me a quick glance. "Is it there now?"

"Yes. I can show it to you."

We got in Tate's unmarked and drove to the barn. The equipment shed was at the far end of the polo field. We crossed the field under the careful scrutiny of Isabel's horses, and when we reached the shed, Tate said, "Mr. Vargas, I want to confirm in front of Mr. Claxton that you freely offered to show me a briefcase given to you by Mr. Whittaker. This is not part of a search on my part, is that correct?"

"Yes, that is correct." He took a key hidden under the eaves, and when he opened the shed we were treated to a blast of musty air. The briefcase was at the bottom of a barrel filled with polo mallets, balls, and other equipment. Tate said to Vargas, "Did you touch anything inside the case?"

He shook his head. "No, I only opened it, saw the paper on top, and then closed it."

"Good." She donned a pair of latex gloves and examined the contents. As advertised, it held a tranche of papers held down with a ten-pound barbell weight. The papers showed names, dates, and dollar amounts for people being shaken down by the *El Seguro* operation. In addition, there was a record of several wire transfers of substantial sums of money and stashed in a compartment in the lid of the case, a nice, shiny TracFone.

Tate regarded me with a satisfied look. I said, "That burner phone didn't get burned, or in this case, I guess I should say drowned. Any way you could ask your partner to get El Solitario's phone out of evidence and try to call us? I'd like to know now, wouldn't you?"

She smiled. "I like the way you think. We tried triangulating the only number on that phone to get a location, but El Solitario's calls pinged off only one tower. That gave us such a broad swath of real estate it wasn't of any use."

"Did the swath include this location?"

"It did."

Tate called her partner, and we waited in the polo field for twenty minutes. A light breeze stirred the firs separating the field from the river and carried the occasional whinny from one of Isabel's horses. Finally, Tate's phone pinged. She looked down at her screen. "Okay, he's trying it now." She gave me that sardonic look of hers and said, "Hail Mary, full of grace." We waited, our eyes glued on the TracFone. Finally, it trembled once, made a faint buzzing sound against the papers, and then went silent like a dead insect.

A smile bloomed on Tate's face. "It was on vibrate and had just enough juice for one ring."

"Yep," I said, "You now have a direct link between Whittaker and El Solitario. Nice work, Detective."

Tate bagged the evidence, and we drove back to the mansion. She instructed both Vargas and me to meet her at the station. To Vargas she said, "I'm investigating two murders, Mr. Vargas. I have no interest whatsoever in your immigration status. Do you understand?" Vargas nodded and she paused before adding, "Tell me something. Why did Whittaker trust you to get rid of the briefcase?"

Vargas smiled bitterly. "The man never did anything for himself. And he knew I was his slave because of my Tito and the fact that he and I have no papers. He is an evil man, Detective."

As Vargas pulled out, she said to me, "That financial evidence looked pretty comprehensive."

"Yes, very thorough. The work product of Robert Harris, no doubt. Vargas told me Whittaker was proud of *El Seguro*, that he was going to scale it up on the entire West Coast. I guess he wanted complete documentation."

Darci nodded. "El Solitario's phone had outgoing calls after the hits on Olivia and Plácido and the attempt on Luis to only one number—this one. It's game over for Whittaker." She shook her head. "My God, If Vargas had been a loyal employee, we wouldn't have diddly shit on Whittaker right now."

I laughed with relief. "You know what they say, Darci—it's better to be lucky than good."

Chapter Fifty-Two

"We arrested Whittaker for aggravated murder this morning," Tate said to me over the phone on the following Wednesday. "We also picked up Harris and are considering charging him as an accomplice based on Vargas's testimony. Harris admits to being in on the scheme but not the hiring of El Solitario. Not sure how that one's going to swing."

"What about Curtis Drake?"

"He's in our crosshairs, but my boss wants to make sure we've got all our ducks in a row. He's a federal employee working for Homeland Security, after all." She went on, "Whittaker's in a wheelchair now, so we're going to arraign him at the courthouse this afternoon at two. He'll be coming out of the hospital around one thirty. You didn't hear this from me, but I thought maybe you and some of Olivia's family members might want to witness that. But, Cal, tell them not to do anything stupid, okay?"

I thanked her and immediately called Timoteo. "I'll get in touch with Mariana, Luis, and Marlene," he told me. He paused for a moment, his voice growing thick. "I wish Papi and Mamá could see this."

"Me, too."

I called Zoe next and then Ned Gillian, and they wanted to witness the event as well.

When I disconnected from Gillian, I looked over at Archie and laughed. "Looks like the whole army will be there, Big Boy." He lowered his eyes in a kind of plead. "Okay, you can go, too."

An hour before Whittaker's perp walk, another breath-stopping call came in. "Cal Claxton?" a familiar voice said. "This is Carlos Fuentes. I am at the ICE holding center in Newberg. Can you come, please?"

I tensed up. "What's the matter, Carlos?"

"They have just released me, and I am confused about why they did this."

"Released you?"

"Yes, they said I was free to go and nothing more. I am standing outside on the sidewalk."

When I arrived, he was still standing there. "Can you talk to them?" he said when I approached.

I thought about it. "They said you were free to go?" He nodded. "Then, let's take you home. I can talk to them later." I glanced at my watch. "No, I've got a better idea."

Carlos and I were nearly to the hospital when Zoe called. "Cal, I just did something a little crazy. I swung by the vineyard and asked Elena if she would come with me. She said yes. She's sitting right next to me."

I smiled. "Good. That will be quite a surprise."

I pulled into the parking lot shortly before Zoe and Elena arrived, got out, and leashed up Archie. Carlos emerged from the passenger side just as Zoe and Elena cruised by. The car jerked to a halt, and they both got out. Zoe looked at me, her eyes huge and questioning, but she didn't say anything. Neither did I as the couple slowly approached each other. Carlos reached out a big, gnarled hand, and Elena took it. They stood looking into each other's eyes for the longest time. Elena said, "I am sorry that I blamed you, Carlos. Can you forgive me?"

Carlos gently stroked her cheek. "There's nothing to forgive. It's okay. I understand."

They embraced, tentatively at first and then with feeling. Zoe and I turned away as we both blinked back tears. Up at the hospital entrance, I saw that the rest of the army had gathered. They were focused on the entrance doors and didn't see us until we were nearly upon them.

"Papi, Mamá!" Timoteo said when he saw them. Luis looked at his parents and spread his arms, speechless, his mouth open. We gave the Fuentes family some space as they stood together, hugging, talking softly, and smiling.

It was Marlene who said, "They're coming."

The hospital doors swung open and two uniformed officers came out first, followed by a wheelchair being pushed by a nurse. Gavin Whittaker sat slumped in the chair. He was unshaven with matted hair, and his eyes were fixed in a kind of manic glare.

He looked around, taking in the scene. We stared back. No one said a word, and as he neared the end of the gauntlet, I cleared my throat. "Mr. Whittaker, this is Olivia Fuentes's family and some of her good friends. We've come to wish you a happy arraignment."

He tried to speak, but it came out as an unintelligible squawk. We stood and watched as he was loaded into a van and whisked off. As the army began to break ranks, I peeled Timoteo off. "Okay," I said, "what do you know about your father's release?"

His face tensed. "Mariana and I followed Curtis Drake a couple more times. One night he picked up the blond kid and another kid, who was *definitely* underage. I, um, took some more pictures, and I also did some checking around. The blond kid's a prostitute." He lowered his eyes. "It turns out Drake didn't want anyone to know about this, you know, photos like that could get out. He is a deacon in his church and is probably facing a high-profile trial. So my father's ICE records went missing. It happens sometimes."

"I see."

Timoteo brought his eyes up and met mine. "I know it wasn't right, Cal. Are you angry?"

I put my hand on his shoulder and smiled. "No, Timoteo. I'm not angry. Sometimes in life, we do what we have to do."

Chapter Fifty-Three

SIX WEEKS LATER

It was a winter day with the sparkle of the finest crystal. Cal's Army was gathered at the Aerie, not to celebrate and not to mourn losses, but to enjoy each other's company and acknowledge, perhaps, what had gone right over a course of events that had rocked all our lives. It was Zoe's idea, and she and Elena were in charge of food preparation. Elena, who was still being counseled by Zoe, was somewhat withdrawn but had returned to the things that brought her joy, and her prognosis was good. When Zoe broached the plan for the gathering, she did so with a warning look. "No comments about my cooking," she told me. "I'm in good hands with Elena."

We were out on the deck around my firepit sharing the Dom Pérignon Nando had given me. Ned Gillian, who had taken on the defense of Diego Vargas, was holding forth. "One thing's for certain, Vargas is not going to be charged with Whittaker's stabbing. Whittaker tried to blame the attack on him out of spite, I think, but the DA didn't buy it for a minute."

I winced inwardly at the statement. What really happened

in Whittaker's study would remain a secret between me, Isabel, and Vargas.

"We're negotiating with the DA right now to allow Diego to come out of this clean," Gillian went on, "even though Gavin Whittaker's trial will not be going forward now." He shook his head. "That was our biggest bargaining chip. After all, Vargas provided the briefcase that led to Whittaker's arrest. He's no angel, but Whittaker had him in a vise over the status of his son."

"What are his chances?" Zoe asked. "I mean, his son's life is hanging in the balance, right? If he's convicted of a felony, he'll be deported along with his son."

Gillian nodded with a worried look. "We'll see. We're fully cooperating in the broader *El Seguro* investigation, and we're hoping that will be enough to get his charges dropped."

Luis was standing next to Marlene, who had been given credit by the family for softening his brooding anger. The touch of an older woman. "What happened to Whittaker, anyway?" Luis said, turning to me. "Pneumonia?"

I shrugged. "I don't know for sure. Apparently, he contracted some new virus going around called COVID-19, I think. Whatever it was, because of his neck wound, they couldn't intubate him, and he died alone in an ICU."

Feet shuffled on the deck. "Rest in peace," Timoteo said with a bitter smile. "Roberto Duran's body was found weeks ago. Anything new on that?"

I shook my head. "He was found floating off Sauvie Island, which meant his body passed through the city of Portland without being noticed. That's all I know. It's assumed El Solitario killed him, but we may never know."

"What about Whittaker's wife? What's happening with her?"

"Isabel? First off, she's not going to be charged for stabbing her husband. The DA agrees it was self-defense. I'm representing her in the settlement of Whittaker's estate. Her prenup guarantees a tidy sum, and she'll receive it before the vultures descend on the rest of Whittaker's assets. She's pledged every cent of her settlement to buy the building Prosperar's currently leasing and fund a full-time doctor." I looked around at the group. This was something I'd been saving. "She and Sofia Leon have decided to name the building the Olivia Fuentes Medical Center."

Timoteo said, his voice suddenly husky, "*Really?* That's, um, that's a really beautiful thing for them to do."

Marlene took Luis's hand. He said, "Olivia always wanted to be a doctor. This is a good thing. Something that will last, no matter what happens next."

Except for a couple of crows cawing up in the Doug firs, the deck fell silent for a while. Finally, Timoteo said, "What about Whittaker's financial backing? Anything new on that?"

"Detective Tate told me the Feds are interested in the question," I said. "The source of capital that put him in the pot business is a tangle of shell companies, probably cartel in origin. Whatever the source, he was under immense pressure to service the debt. That'll take time to sort out, I'm afraid."

"Did the source send El Solitario?" Timoteo asked.

"The evidence doesn't indicate that. The burner phone record shows Whittaker was the *only* contact to El Solitario. As for Vargas, Harris, and Drake, it's clear they weren't directly involved in the murders. It was all on Whittaker."

Always keen on the law, Timoteo said next, "Do you think the motion by Whittaker's legal team to suppress the burner phone evidence would have prevailed had it gone to trial?"

I paused for a moment. "I don't think so. Tate was very careful about how she handled the briefcase and the evidence in it." Ned Gillian nodded in agreement.

Marlene looked horrified. "You mean Whittaker could've gotten off on a technicality?"

I shrugged again. "It's moot, now. There won't be a trial."

Timoteo and Mariana were standing together. Eye protection was required when the two of them smiled at the same time. She said, "What's going to happen to Curtis Drake?"

"Detective Tate says they're still developing the case," I said. "Drake has lawyered up and shows no interest in cooperating, so they're not inclined to go easy on him." I smiled. "Your newspaper article was the talk of Yamhill County. Once it published, things have not gone well personally for Drake, that's for sure."

She cast her eyes down in modesty. "I just reported the facts and what Vargas and Harris said about *El Seguro*. It didn't take long for Homeland Security to fire Drake."

Timoteo put a hand on her shoulder with a look of genuine pride. "The *News-Register* gave her a raise and made her a full-fledged reporter."

Luis smiled with relish. "Drake got more than fired. His white nationalist buddies in the CIJ turned on him when they found out he'd been taking money from Whittaker to protect undocumented people from deportation. You can imagine how that pissed them off. He was supposed to be a true believer. They burned his house down and the garage with his truck in it."

We all knew that bit of irony, of course, but it was therapeutic to hear it repeated.

The subject of Robert Harris, the remaining *El Seguro* player, loomed large but went unmentioned. We all knew that after being interviewed by the police, Harris had gone home and hanged himself. It was a tragedy, no matter what he did. My mind drifted back to Sofia Leon's call after the news broke. She was in tears. "I'm sick about this," she told me. "Gavin sucked Robert in. Instead of helping his gambling habit, he must have found ways to encourage it. Robert was hopelessly in debt. And I know that when he went to Gavin about Olivia's suspicions, he had no idea it would result in her murder. I think that was more than his conscience could bear."

The chatter on the deck had moved to happier topics by the time Zoe and Elena called us in to eat. We gathered around my large dining room table. The food kept coming from the kitchen— made-from-scratch salsa and guacamole, chickpea and chorizo tostadas with lime slices, grilled pork tenderloin in charred chile adobo, salmon tacos, and a dessert of churros with a semisweet chocolate sauce.

After the food was served, and Carlos said grace at Elena's urging, he raised his glass and managed to show the full Fuentes smile, something I'd never seen him do. "To the memory of Olivia and to all of you who helped bring justice to her, thank you and God bless you." We all drank to that.

Sometimes bittersweet is just plain sweet, and that was one of those times.

———

After the feast was over, the kitchen was cleaned, and the guests departed, Zoe and I stood out on the deck as the sun sank in a blaze of gold, and the sky above it faded from blue to violet. Archie lay in the corner watching us, chin on paws. She sighed. "Timoteo's and Mariana's Dreamer status is being challenged at the Supreme Court, and the rest of the Fuentes family is still living in limbo. Will this country ever resolve this? I mean with legislation instead of mass deportations and endless conflicts between the rule of law and human compassion?"

I shook my head. "I hope so." I turned and looked at her. "They're made of steel, you know. They know how to live with uncertainty, and they do it with incredible dignity."

She acknowledged the comment with a nod. We stood side by side, leaning on the railing as the light faded. She gazed down at my dry-stack wall and smiled ruefully. "You think you'll ever finish it?"

I exhaled a breath. "Probably about the same time you finish your book."

She laughed. "Touché. I've gotten four chapters written in the last couple of weeks. So there."

"Actually," I said, "I still need help. I've already mapped out where to place all the herbs. It's going to look great." I met her eyes, dark blue in the low light that shone softly off one of her Vermeers. "I guess Gertie's about good as new, huh?"

She held my gaze, and her smile turned playful. "I don't know. She hasn't brought it up, and I haven't asked her."

I turned to face her. "Look, Zoe, I know I've had this hang-up about my wife, but I, uh, I think it's something I can put behind me. I don't want you to leave. I know it sounds selfish, but—"

She cut me off. "I've got my own issues, you know. I don't trust men all that much." Her smile deepened. "But for you, I might make an exception."

I chuckled. "A match made in heaven, but you might want to consult your aunt. She doesn't think I'm such a good prospect."

She laughed. "Gertie means well, but I know what I want." She moved closer, reached up and clasped her hands around my neck and pulled gently. No peck on the cheek this time, her kiss was long, soft, and deep.

Read on for an excerpt from

MATTERS
OF
DOUBT

the first exciting Cal Claxton Mystery!

Chapter One

Sometimes, when I'm working in my office, the sound of traffic out on Pacific Highway reminds me of a river. I close my eyes and there I am, hip-deep in the current, casting my fly rod as ravenous trout and steelhead rise around me. But there was no time for fly-fishing fantasies on this particular day. I was booked solid from nine until four. Not that being busy meant I was making much money in my one-man law practice. Money's tight in the small town of Dundee, Oregon, particularly since the downturn, and I found myself bartering for my fee more often than I'd like. Just the week before, I'd agreed to handle a man's divorce in exchange for his repairing the fence on the south side of my property. Thank God I have my early retirement from the city of Los Angeles to fall back on, meager as it is.

I was a chief prosecutor down there. You probably know the type—uptight, ambitious, nose to the grindstone. I called what I did for a living my *career*, like it was some precious thing one kept in a glass case to admire. That seems a lifetime ago, and now my needs are more modest up here in Oregon. Enough cash to cover the mortgage and underwrite my fishing habit does me fine.

It was noon, and I had just unwrapped a bagel with cream

cheese, red onion, capers, and a thick slice of Chinook salmon I'd smoked the week before. I groaned when I heard a tentative knocking on my back door. The parking lot's behind my office, so most people come in at the rear, although I have a front door that opens directly onto the street.

"Crap. Can't a guy even eat lunch around here?" I asked my Australian shepherd, Archie, who, at the sound of the knocking, had let out a short, irritated bark from his favorite spot in the corner. Vowing to make short work of my visitor, I opened the door and said, "Can I help you?"

"Are you Calvin Claxton, the lawyer?" Tall, pencil thin, maybe twenty, he sported black, spiky hair and a silver ring thrust through his eyebrow that matched a smaller one through his lower lip. Tattoos decorated both forearms and one crawled out of his scruffy black T-shirt, disappeared around his neck, and reappeared on the other side. It was a strikingly realistic depiction of a coral snake.

"Yeah. That's me. What can I do for you?" My tone wasn't particularly friendly. I felt ambivalent about pierced, tattooed, dressed-in-black types. I'm all for rebellious youth—how else are we going to change anything on this damn planet? But there was an odd uniformity to their look that put me off, and I had a sense they were passive and uninformed when it came to the real issues battering this world. On the other hand, I felt just as ambivalent about most politicos dressed in blue suits and red power ties.

"I want to, uh, talk to you about something." Lightly pocked with acne scars, his pale cheeks joined his chin at a sharp angle. He had dark, liquid eyes that were clear and alert. I caught something in them—urgency, for sure, and something deeper with an edge to it I couldn't quite read.

"I'm taking a lunch break right now. You want to make an appointment?"

He shook his head and sighed. "I came all the way out here from Portland, man. I need to talk to you now."

I hesitated for a moment, then stepped back from the doorway. "What's your name?"

"Picasso. That's what everyone calls me. My real name's Danny Baxter."

"Okay, Danny. Come on in. I hope you don't mind if I eat while we talk."

He took a seat facing me across the desk. His high-top combat boots gleamed shiny black like the cheap plastic briefcase he was opening. He pulled out a file stuffed with papers, and while I munched a bite of my bagel, he said, "I want you to help me find the person who murdered my mother."

I set the bagel down and came forward in my chair. Not exactly what I expected to hear. My guess was he'd been busted for selling or possession or both. "I'm sorry for your loss, but I'm afraid that's a job for the police."

He sneered at the word. "They don't give a shit. I've given up on them, man."

"So, why me?"

"I met a kid in Portland from around here. He told me you helped his mom out. His old man was threatening to kill her. He said you're smart, that you don't give up. I want someone like you, someone who's not a cop."

I had to smile. I remembered the case. "I might've done that, but it sounds like what you need is a private investigator. I'm just an attorney. I don't do investigative work for a living."

His face remained impassive, but his eyes registered pain, like I'd just slapped him. "I can pay you. I've got money."

I'm not good at saying no. In fact, I'm lousy at it. Just ask my accountant. Sure, there was something about the kid I liked, his pluck, I guess. But my getting involved in some cold case in Portland made absolutely no sense. And his idea of money probably wouldn't cover my first day. You've got bills to pay, I reminded myself.

I stood up and said, "Sorry, but I'm not your man. I'd be glad to suggest someone who might be able to help you."

I expected him to push back, but instead, he tossed the file in his briefcase and muttered, half to himself, "Should've known better." The abruptness caught me off-guard. It was like he was used to being turned down, and considering his appearance, I supposed it was a regular occurrence. This tugged at me, but I resisted the temptation to ask him to stay.

I showed him out the back way. When I returned to my desk, I glanced out the side window just in time to see him pedaling north on a beat-up street bike with his briefcase bungeed to a rack over the back wheel. A dark band of clouds hung on the horizon in front of him. It was probably twenty-five miles back to Portland, and I knew he'd get soaked, for sure. I shrugged and asked Archie, "Why the hell didn't he just phone me?" Then I turned back to my desk and opened the file of my next client.

I had work to do, but the thought of that kid slogging all the way back to Portland in the rain made it hard to concentrate.

Chapter Two

I didn't finish up at the office until late that day, and as I started climbing into the Dundee Hills toward my place, a hard rain let loose. It was early summer in Oregon, when sun and cloud vie for dominance with neither gaining the upper hand for very long.

A hand-carved sign outside the gate to my house says, *Claxton's Aerie. Welcome.* The sign was a gift from my daughter, Claire. The place is perched on a high ridge overlooking the north end of the Willamette Valley. I love it here, probably more than I should. Claire says it's not healthy to live alone in such an isolated place. But I have my dog, Archie. He's as fine a companion as any human could hope for. I have mornings when the fog burns off, and the colors in the valley come on like someone flipped a switch. I have nights when the stars glitter like big marbles, not the pinpricks you see—if you're lucky—in the city. I can hear owls and coyotes, too, and even the occasional cougar, whose calls during mating season sound like the wail of a grieving woman.

Okay, my leaky old farmhouse is a sitting duck for the storms that roar up the valley in winter. But I've gotten pretty good with a caulk gun, and every once in a while a storm leaves a perfect rainbow in its wake.

At my mailbox I jammed a ball cap on my head and hopped out to check the mail before climbing the long driveway, opening the gate, and popping open the back car door. Archie whimpered but didn't move. Oversized for an Aussie at seventy-five pounds and decidedly opinionated, he didn't care for rain, or water in general.

After dinner the rain subsided, but I could see more on the way. It hung like a gray veil below a line of fast-moving clouds out in the valley. I called Archie in, and five minutes later more rain drummed in from the south. My thoughts turned again to the young man who'd visited me that afternoon. Surely he was home by now, I told myself. I'd made the right call. After all, my accountant keeps harping that I've got to think more like a businessman.

The rain had brought a chill to the air. I poured myself a splash of Rémy Martin, padded into my study, and logged on to my computer. I pulled up *The Oregonian* newspaper search engine and typed in the three words—"Baxter," "murder," and "Portland." This is what came up:

DESCHUTES RIVER—REMAINS TRACED
TO WOMAN MISSING 8 YEARS

Skeletal remains found in a reservoir bed on the Deschutes River five weeks ago have been identified as belonging to Nicole Baxter of Portland, according to the Jefferson County Medical Examiner's Office. Chief Medical Examiner Dr. Ernest Givens stated the identification was based on the dental records of the deceased woman. He also stated that the preliminary findings suggest the cause of death was a single gunshot wound to the head. Ballistic tests on a single bullet found in the skull indicated a .22 caliber weapon was used.

Baxter, an investigative reporter for *The Oregonian*,

disappeared on May 18, 2005. An extensive investigation by Portland detectives at the time failed to identify any substantive leads. The missing person case became inactive in early 2006. Baxter is survived by her son, Daniel Baxter of Portland, and her sister, Amy Baxter Isles of Gainesville, Florida. A spokesman for the Jefferson County Sheriff's Department said the investigation of Baxter's death would be coordinated with the Portland Cold Case Unit.

The swivel chair creaked as I leaned back, my stomach tightening as I thought about what I'd just read. Eight years on the bottom of that reservoir. A young mother in the prime of her life, thrown away like so much trash. I thought about Danny Baxter's frustration with how the case was being handled. Out in sparsely populated central Oregon, Jefferson County didn't have a cold case unit to begin with, and they probably figured this was more Portland's case than theirs, anyway. And recent budget cuts had probably hit them as hard as the Portland PD.

As for Portland's Cold Case Unit, they—like all the others that had sprung up in the wake of the advances in forensic technology—were looking for cases with latent DNA evidence, a quick and easy way to score. There would be no DNA evidence in this case. So, although killing a reporter was close to killing a cop, I could see how this case might slip through the cracks like Danny claimed.

I remembered the thick file Baxter had brandished in my office and found myself wondering what information he had. I pictured him riding into that rainstorm, frowned, and shook my head. Maybe that glint in his eye—the one I couldn't read—was sheer determination. Tattoos and piercings aside, I liked that in a person.

I pulled up an earlier article describing the discovery of the remains of the then-unidentified Nicole Baxter. I learned that a caretaker named Homer Burton had found human bones in the bed of a reservoir that had been emptied after a dam gave way. The reservoir was on the property of a private fishing cabin owned by Hugo Weiman, who, it was noted, was the head of Weiman and Associates, a lobbying firm in Salem. I wasn't that attuned to Oregon politics, but I knew Weiman was a big-time power broker who'd amassed a small fortune by greasing the state's political skids.

As a regular on the Deschutes, I knew approximately where the cabin was located. I was also pretty sure the lodge was on the other side of a locked gate, meaning only owners and guests with keys could drive into the property. The article included the following quote from Hugo Weiman:

"I was shocked to learn that human remains were found on my property. I have no knowledge of how or why this horrible crime was committed, and I am fully cooperating with the police to help find the person or persons responsible."

My eyes began to droop. I drained the Rémy, logged off, and took the back stairs up to my bedroom with Archie in close pursuit. I opened the window and stood there in the wash of a cool breeze as a throng of frogs down by the pond belted out their mating songs. Then, having made a decision, I slipped quickly into a deep, restful sleep.

Three days later the phone rang at my office. It was my friend and sometime Portland business associate, Hernando Mendoza. My online search for the address of Daniel Baxter had proven futile, so I'd asked Nando for help. A Cuban exile with an intense appreciation of the U.S. capitalist system, he dabbled in real estate, had an office-cleaning business, and was the least-known, but in my opinion, the best private investigator in Portland.

"Calvin. I have something for you," he said in his basso profundo. "This young man you're looking for, Daniel Baxter. He has no address because he lives on the street. Somewhere in Old Town, I am told."

"You mean he's homeless?"

"Yes. Like many other young people in Portland. I do not approve of children living under bridges. It is shameful. In Cuba, people are poor, yes. But if their families cannot take care of them, the state will."

"So why did you leave your island paradise?" I teased. Nando had rowed a boat of his own making to Florida eight years earlier—a five-day trip with very little food and water. He regarded his homeland with equal measures of love and disdain, and although he would never admit it, I knew he missed Cuba very much.

He laughed heartily. "It was a non-brainer, my friend. I wanted to come to America and get rich. You know—"

"I'm sure what you're going to tell me is fascinating," I interrupted, "but I'm a little jammed here, Nando." I really did love his stories about Cuba, but it was a topic he could expound on for hours. "How do I find the kid?"

"He is working at a community health center on Davis. Old Town Urgent Care. I am told he can be found there most days."

"Good work, Nando."

"I had no luck until I forgot about asking for Daniel Baxter and started asking for Picasso, the name he uses on the street. And the name seems to fit."

"How's that?"

"I am told this young man is an artist of exceptional skill."

After talking to Nando, I made a few more phone calls and cleared my calendar for the following day. This was something I did on a regular basis, although usually for different reasons, such as a good steelhead run. I'd make a quick trip to Portland to see if I could start over with the young man known on the street as Picasso. I wasn't sure he'd talk to me, and I sure as hell didn't know how I could help him, but it seemed like the right thing to do.

ACKNOWLEDGMENTS

It's called writing a book, but the truth is, at least for me, it's more like living it. I certainly inhabited this story, which in the making had more than its share of emotional ups and downs and a lot of sideways motion as well. I'm indebted to my partner in crime and in-house editor in chief, Marge Easley, for first readership, inspiration, advice, and a ton of encouragement.

I'm also fortunate to have had a cadre of outstanding Portland writers critique early drafts of the manuscript. Immense thanks to LeeAnn McLennan, Janice Maxon Alison Jakel, Debby Dodds, and Lisa Alber. What a talented crew! Despite all this literary firepower, it still fell to my editor, Barbara Peters, to work her usual magic on the manuscript. Thank you, Barbara and the whole talented and responsive crew at Poisoned Pen Press/Sourcebooks.

Special thanks to Karen Bassett, MA, QMHPC, for invaluable insights into the psychology of trauma, loss, and healing. The discipline of psychology is lucky to have such a talented and dedicated professional! Finally, deepest gratitude and heartfelt thanks to Mariana Molina, who took the time from a busy academic schedule to speak to me openly and candidly about being a Dreamer and a DACA recipient. Your courage is an inspiration, Mariana. Keep the faith no matter what.

ABOUT THE AUTHOR

Formerly a research scientist and international business executive, Warren C. Easley lives in Oregon, where he writes fiction, tutors GED students, fly fishes, and skis. As the author of the Cal Claxton Mysteries, he received a Kay Snow national award for fiction and was named the Northwest's Up and Coming Author by Willamette Writers. His fifth book in the Claxton series, *Blood for Wine*, was short-listed for the coveted Nero Wolfe Award. For more information, visit: www.facebook.com/WarrenCEasley and www.warreneasley.com.